H. Frances Dav

South and South Central Africa

H. Frances Davidson

South and South Central Africa

1st Edition | ISBN: 978-3-75233-022-9

Place of Publication: Frankfurt am Main, Germany

Year of Publication: 2020

Outlook Verlag GmbH, Germany.

Reproduction of the original.

SOUTH AND SOUTH CENTRAL AFRICA

BY

H. FRANCES DAVIDSON

INTRODUCTION

With utmost confidence and pleasure, I give an introductory expression for this intelligible, authentic, and most valuable little volume, the product of great sacrifice and long experience, by one who was favored and honored with lucrative educational positions, being a classic.

I have been acquainted with the authoress for many years, and am a member of the Foreign Missionary Board under whose auspices she has most effectually labored during an unbroken period of one and one-half decades; therefore I speak with great assurance of the merits and hope of her book, destined to be prolific and incentive to active missionary operations in foreign lands.

The photo-engravings have special interest, having been taken from real life and nature as she found them in dark Africa—places, people, environments, customs, habits, and religion, which she saw with her own eyes and mind. Having thoroughly mastered various dialects of tribes among whom she has labored so many years, having gathered many historical facts relative to uncivilized races, and also having special tact, instinct and God-given ability through the gift of the Spirit, making her very efficient in her call to these dusky tribes, she is qualified in a very proficient sense to compile the story of this strange people.

On meeting Sister H. Frances Davidson, one is quickly impressed with her modest and unassuming disposition, the rare gift that characterizes all the truly noble and great.

Her heroism and unfaltering faith in Jehovah is most remarkably demonstrated in her adventure—accompanied by Sister Adda Engle (Taylor) and a native boy—into the wilds of Central Africa, unfrequented by the tread or touch of any Gospel missioner, among a class of raw natives that were very shy, rather hostile, and of another tongue, and a country infested with wild, vicious animals.

When the planning of this adventurous trip was heard by the Foreign Missionary Board, steps were taken to discourage it, on the ground that no white man was available to accompany them to the new prospective mission field; but before the Board's protest could be made effective, the dangerous journey was heroically and successfully executed and a new mission station planted north of the great Zambezi, which is the northern boundary of South Africa.

Such an adventure would almost challenge the courage of the bravest man. It must have been the leadings of the Lord—the inspiration of the Holy Spirit.

We all love to read the truthful words that drop from the pen of such fearless, devoted, and consecrated souls.

The book is written in a clear, graphic, and condensed manner, just the thing for this busy, rushing generation.

We bespeak for it a precious harvest of lasting fruitage.

Yours in the hope of the Gospel,

J. R. ZOOK,

Chairman of the Missionary Board
of the Brethren in Christ's Church.

PREFACE

Africa holds a unique place in the world today. In no other continent is there such a world-wide interest and such a variety of interests centered; the religious, the political, and the commercial world are alike concerned in its development and progress. It has been a sealed book for so many centuries that the majority of people have excused themselves on that score for their ignorance of its conditions and their indifference as to its welfare; but the day of pardonable ignorance is past.

While kings and emperors have been eagerly seeking to obtain as large a slice of its territory as possible, and moneyed men have been unearthing some of its vast wealth, missionaries, too, have been having a share in it. In the development of Africa they may, without boasting, claim to be making the most permanent contribution to its welfare, but even their work is only begun. The various interests, which for a long time were concerned with only the countries along the coast, have now penetrated and opened up that vast interior to civilization and missionary enterprise; and it remains for the Christians to say whether it shall be left to the influences of a corrupt civilization or whether they will shoulder their responsibilities and rise to their privileges in taking the country for God.

Many missionary bodies are already at work, and much is being accomplished; but the continent is so gigantic, the distances to be traversed so immense that it will require the united efforts of all God's children to pay the debt humanity owes to this long-neglected continent and those downtrodden pagans.

It has been my aim in these pages to give, without embellishment, some idea of the nature of the Africans, their character, customs, religion, and surroundings, as well as some of the difficulties, methods, encouragements, and discouragements of missionary work among them. Missionaries are often censured for being too optimistic, for giving only the bright side of their work, therefore I have studiously sought to avoid this attitude and to give an unvarnished account of missionary enterprise. Judging from my own convictions and beliefs in reference to the work, it seems to me that if I have erred in this respect, it has been by understating rather than overstating the value and encouraging results arising from such labors.

This book does not claim to be a complete history of the Brethren in Christ's Missions in Africa, but rather some of the experiences of one member of that mission body. Since, however, it has been my privilege to be with the work from its inception, the enclosed narrative will have the added value of giving at least something of the beginning and early history of the mission. My only apology for recounting so much of my personal experience and impressions in the work is that I am unable to give, properly, the experience and viewpoint of anyone else.

We desire to express our thanks to Mrs. Myron Taylor, formerly Miss Adda Engle, for the majority of the photographs with which this work is illustrated; also to Elder Steigerwald and the other missionaries who have furnished a number of them. We had hoped to have some later ones from Matopo and Mtshabezi Missions, but have failed in securing good ones.

If this little volume in some small degree arouses a greater interest among Christians in the evangelization of the Dark Continent, and is a means in God's hands of getting the light to a few more of the vast millions of pagan Africans, I shall feel more than repaid for sending it on its mission.

H. FRANCES DAVIDSON.

Auburn, Ind.

PART ONE

MATOPO MISSION

"Go ye therefore and teach all nations"
—Matt. 28: 19

CHAPTER ONE

The Beginning of Missionary Effort

It was at the General Conference held in May, 1894, that the Foreign Missionary Work of the Church of the Brethren in Christ originated.

Previous to that time the old fathers of the church had made many missionary journeys through the United States and Canada for the advancement of Christ's Kingdom and in the interests of the faith they so dearly loved. These journeys were made without remuneration and often with great discomfort and sacrifice of time and money. The precept that the Gospel was free, "without money and without price," seemed so instilled into their hearts that some of them, no doubt, would have felt pained for people to think that they expected money for their services. So while the laity were busy with their own temporal duties, these heralds of the Cross would often leave their little farms in care of their wives and of help, hired at their own expense, and devote weeks and months to evangelistic work, expecting what? Nothing but their food and sometimes sufficient to pay their car fare, if they went by train. But it often happened in those early days that the entire expense of whatever sort was borne by themselves. They looked for no reward on earth save the consciousness that they were about their Master's business and seeking to extend His Kingdom on earth.

Much honor is due those old soldiers for their self-sacrificing labors. In that Great Day when the books are opened, perhaps the record of their labors may astonish some of us who sometimes criticise them for their slowness in launching the foreign missionary work of the Church.

Among them were some who were greatly burdened for the heathen. Some felt this lack of Church activity so keenly that they almost severed their connections with it on this account. Others saw the need, but, realizing the smallness of membership and the limited resources, thought the Church was too weak to launch out into foreign missionary enterprise.

In the meantime individual members were agitating the question, and some were planning to go independently to India and to Central America, while others were contemplating going under other Mission Boards.

While this agitation was going on, the question of foreign mission work was brought forward at the General Conference in May, 1894, held in the Bethel Church, Kansas. On Friday, the last day of the Conference, a paper on the subject was read by Mrs. Rhoda Lee, but no active steps were taken and the question was tabled indefinitely, to the great disappointment of some present. Later, on the same day, Elder J. E. Stauffer arose, and, placing a five-dollar bill on the table, stated that it was for foreign mission work, then sat down. This action brought matters to a crisis. Here was missionary money and something must be done with it.

After consultation it was decided that the donor be appointed Foreign Missionary Treasurer, and any desiring to donate should give their offerings to him; and that, as soon as sufficient money was in the treasury to justify the measure, active steps would be taken toward sending out missionaries. By the close of the day thirty-five dollars had been placed in the hands of the Treasurer. The funds increased slowly but steadily.

At the Conference of 1895 held in Ontario, "A Foreign Mission Board, consisting of Brethren Peter Steckly, B. T. Hoover, and J. E. Stauffer, was appointed to hold office for five years, subject, however, to the advice and control of General Council." At the next meeting of Conference in 1896 in Pennsylvania, "The Treasurer of the Foreign Mission Fund, J. E. Stauffer, submitted his report, and he was congratulated for his successful effort. The amount in the treasury is $419.60." This amount had been donated in two years. These data have been given that it may be seen how the work has grown.

At this meeting it was decided that the funds had increased sufficiently to take an advanced step. The Board was increased to twelve members with an operating board of three. Of this Elder Samuel Zook was appointed treasurer, Elder Henry Davidson, chairman, and Elder Jesse Engle, secretary. The Board was empowered to secure volunteers for starting a work among the heathen in some foreign country, no particular country being designated.

Of the General Board of twelve members, Brethren Peter Steckley, J. R. Zook, and Peter Climenhage are still on the Board after a lapse of eighteen years.

Just what was done in the interim I cannot say, but on January 15, 1897, there appeared in the *Evangelical Visitor* the following:

AN APPEAL

We would call attention to the fact that the committee appointed at last Conference is ready to act on the foreign mission work, but up to this time they have received no applications. Why is it? Does the Lord not speak to some hearts? Or is it because the Church is not praying the Lord of the harvest to send laborers into His harvest?

The field is white. The harvest is ready. Who will go forth in the name of the Master, filled with the Holy Ghost, ready to lay his or her life down for the cause of Christ's salvation to the heathen? It means something to be a foreign missionary. It means a full sacrifice of home, friends and self—a perfect cutting loose. But, praise the Lord! when it is done for Christ's sake and the Gospel's, we shall receive an hundredfold in this life and eternal life in the world to come.

The Lord has provided money—somebody was willing to give it, but who will give himself? I believe the Lord has spoken to your heart. Just say, "Lord, speak, thy servant heareth." And if the Lord tells you to go, don't do as Jonah—try to get away from the Lord—for as Jonah did not fare well, neither will you. But if you obey God, He will go with you into the ship. We are ready and waiting to receive applications, but somebody must be willing to obey God or the work will be delayed while souls are perishing.

If the Lord lays it upon your heart to give because you can not go yourself, please send your donations to Elder Jesse Engle, Donegal, Kansas, as he is the committee's secretary and will keep a correct account of all money received and hand it over to the treasurer. The committee has not decided yet where the field shall be, but will decide when such workers present themselves as are believed to be called of God. South Africa has been spoken of; also South or Central America. No doubt God will direct when the time comes that somebody is willing to go. Who shall it be?

SAMUEL ZOOK.

At that time I was teaching in McPherson College, Kansas, and was greatly enjoying the work. It was my seventh year at that place, and just the day before the article had appeared I had entered into a verbal agreement with the other members of the faculty to remain for some years, the Lord willing. No thought of the foreign field had entered my mind previous to this, except a readiness for whatever the Lord had for me to do. Up to that time I verily thought I was doing His will by being in the classroom.

The day that "The Appeal" appeared in the *Visitor*, it was read like the other matter and nothing further was thought of it; but the day following the Lord came to me, as it were, in the midst of the class work, in the midst of other plans for the future, and swept away my books, reserving only the Bible. In reality He showed me Christ lifted up for a lost world. He filled me with an unutterable love for every soul who had not heard of Him, and with a passionate longing to go to worst parts of the earth, away from civilization, away from other mission bodies, and spend the rest of my life in telling the story of the Cross.

We prefer not to dwell too minutely on the feelings of that sacred hour. Sufficient to say that there and then He anointed me for service among the heathen. Not that I have measured up to all that He placed before me on that day. On the contrary I have fallen far short; but the consciousness of that call has ever been with me, and has strengthened and kept me, in the thickest of the fight in heathen lands. Even when the battle was sore and defeat stared me in the face, the conviction that it was His appointment and His work for me kept me fast.

My first step was to go to my colleagues and ask to be released from the agreement into which I had entered with them. They were as much surprised at the turn affairs had taken as I had been, but readily agreed not to stand in the way of the Lord's call. A letter was then sent to the Mission Board, informing them of the call to service and my readiness to go and at once if they deemed it advisable to send me.

Much had been said about missionary work and many had seemed eager to go, so that I somewhat tremblingly awaited the result, feeling that they might not consider me fitted. At the same time a private letter was dispatched to my father, who was Chairman of the Board, telling him of my convictions and call. A letter came first from dear father. He had been quite unprepared for the news contained in my letter, and his answer can best be summed up in two of his sentences: "How can I say yes? and how dare I say no?" He closed the letter by advising me to wait a year or two until others were ready to go. The official letter from the Board through the Secretary, Elder Jesse Engle, stated that I was the only applicant so far and had been accepted, but that there would be time to finish the year's teaching. It was quite a surprise and disappointment to me to learn that there were still no other applicants, but not long afterwards word came that Elder Jesse Engle and wife were likewise seriously considering the question.

He, as many of my readers know, had realized a call to give the Gospel to the heathen while he was still a young man, but probably from lack of encouragement and from other seemingly insurmountable obstacles had not obeyed. Now, at the advanced age of fifty-nine years, he still felt that his work was not done; and he was ready to enter the field, if his way opened, even though it might appear to be at the eleventh hour. And she, who had nobly stood by his side for so many years, could still say, "My place is beside my husband. Where he goes I too will follow."

In the meantime the question as to the location of this first missionary venture was beginning to agitate the minds of some of us. The Board felt that the missionaries should be consulted in the matter. The conditions then existing in South America were attracting the attention of the Christian world. Some countries, notably Equador, were for the first time being opened to missionaries. The sore need there appealed to me and led to correspondence with others in reference to that field; but no one was ready to go there. Later I learned from Brother Engle that he was led to Africa, the country of his early call. The location was immaterial to me, for my call was to the neediest field, and I soon realized that Africa, with its unexplored depths, its superstition and degradation, its midnight darkness, was surely in need of the Light of Life.

The cheering news soon came that Miss Alice Heise also had applied and been accepted as a foreign missionary. That increased the number to four.

At the General Conference in May, 1897, at Valley Chapel, Ohio, the following report was given and adopted:

> Report of the amount of money in the hands of the Treasurer of Foreign Mission to date, $693.46.
>
> Four candidates presented themselves for the foreign mission field and have been accepted as follows: Elder Jesse Engle and Sister Elizabeth Engle, his wife, of Donegal, Kansas; Sister H. Frances Davidson, Abilene, Kansas; and Sister Alice Heise, Hamlin, Kansas, and if approved by Conference, it is recommended that they should be ready to start for their field of labor as early as September or October, provided that sufficient means are at hand to pay their passage to their place of destination, which means are to be raised by voluntary contributions as the Lord may direct, and to be sent directly to the address of each of the missionaries.
>
> The Board recommends that to complete the number of workers there should be one more added to the number in the person of a brother as an assistant to Brother Jesse Engle.
>
> The Board further recommends that the Conference now in session select some well qualified brother to fill the vacancy occasioned by Brother Jesse Engle on the Foreign Mission Board. Brother W. O. Baker was appointed to fill the vacancy (provided Brother Engle should go); all of which is respectfully submitted.

HENRY DAVIDSON, Chairman.
SAMUEL ZOOK, Treasurer.

The summer of 1897 passed slowly for some of us who were eager to be on the way; but even the days of waiting and visiting were a part of our preparation. They were solemn and momentous days also to others besides those who were going. Some of the friends felt that we should not go; others with tears bade us Godspeed, feeling that we might probably never look one another in the face on earth again. In October a little farewell meeting was held at Dayton, Ohio, where God's blessing was invoked on the work, and here I said good-bye to dear old father, realizing that it would likely be for the last time. At Harrisburg, Pennsylvania, we were pleased to receive into our number Miss Barbara Hershey, of Kansas, who also was called to the work.

The actual moving out of the missionaries was also a great impetus to the financial part of the undertaking. During the few months previous to sailing $1,500 was given by voluntary contributions into the hands of the missionaries themselves, more than half of which was handed to Brother and Sister Engle in their extended tour of the Brotherhood. In addition to this, $639.70 was during the same time handed to the Treasurer, making $1,211.64 in his hands.

On November 21 a general farewell and ordination meeting for all was held in the Messiah Home Chapel, Harrisburg, Pennsylvania, where the five prospective missionaries were set apart for the work of the Lord. No brother had volunteered to go along as a helper to Elder Engle. This was a solemn time to those going, for a new and untried field was before them and a voyage and country of which they as yet knew nothing. And yet there was no fear, no anxiety. On the contrary, to some of us the joy of having the privilege of being His messengers to those sitting in darkness transcended all other emotions, and our journal of that time is full of expressions of longing to be in darkest Africa. At that meeting Elder Engle delivered a farewell address with power and unction from on High, and the rest told of their call. After the ordination of all had taken place, we commemorated the death and sufferings of our Savior.

If we may judge from expressions made at the time and since, there were others in that large audience that evening to whom the occasion was an important and impressive one. The Church was rising to a sense of her opportunity and privilege—yes, and duty of carrying out the Great Commission. As we went forth, we felt that the prayers of the entire Church were bearing us up, and that gave renewed strength and courage all along the way. Those prayers buoyed us up as we went forth even into the blackness of heathendom; they opened doors that otherwise would have been closed; yes, and best of all, they opened dark hearts that the light of the glorious Gospel of Christ might penetrate. Those prayers yet today are rising as sweet incense in behalf of the Dark Continent.

CHAPTER TWO

The Voyage and Landing

Now the Lord had said unto Abraham, Get thee out of thy country and from thy kindred and from thy father's house, unto a land that I will shew thee.—Gen. 12: 1.

Seventeen years ago a voyage to Africa was not the common occurrence to us plain country folk that it is today. The majority of us had never seen the sea, we knew no one who had made the trip, and we knew less about the continent of Africa.

It had been decided that we should sail November 24, 1897. While Elder and Mrs. Engle were making their tour of the churches, some of us had finished visiting and were waiting the time of sailing. So he suggested that we secure the tickets. We did so to England, and through an agent, Mr. Mills, of England, arranged in advance for tickets from England to Cape Town. The tickets were bought, the good-byes were over, and the date of sailing found us all at New York Harbor, a little anxious, it is true, but eager to launch.

Being inexperienced, we had a little difficulty in having some money matters attended to. Sister Hershey and myself had each a draft which we desired to have exchanged for one on an English bank, and were told by one of the men to take them to the bank on which they were drawn and have it attended to there. So we were obliged to go up into the city the morning of the date of sailing, when the steamer was to leave at 12 M. We were gone all morning, only to find on reaching the bank that there was no one to identify us, and nothing could be done. Hurrying back to the hotel, we secured our hand baggage and hastened to the wharf. The rest of the company had already embarked, and only a few minutes remained until time of sailing, but we appealed to our agent to exchange the drafts for some on an English bank. Although one of the other men objected on account of the shortness of time, he promptly attended to them, Elders Jacob Engle and John Niesly, who were brothers of Brother and Sister Engle and had come to see them off, going security. The gangway for passengers had already been removed from the steamer and we hurried along that on which baggage was carried. As soon as we were aboard, the steamer *Majestic* began to move; and ere we found the rest of our company on board, a narrow stretch of water lay between us and our native land.

This, our first voyage across the Atlantic, was a delightful one. The sea was unusually calm for that season of the year, so that none of our number became sick, except one, as we neared the coast of Ireland. The passengers on board were on the whole congenial. As we paced up and down the deck, many thoughts crowded in upon us too deep for utterance. What did the future have in store for us? What awaited us on the other side? The Lord alone, whose messengers we were, could foresee. The great, wide, boundless space of water was an ever-increasing source of interest and delight, and greatly enlarged our conception of the power and majesty of Him "who hath measured the waters in the hollow of His hand." We felt in truth that we had let go the shore lines and had launched out into the ocean of His love.

The second day out was Thanksgiving Day, and in company with another missionary on board we had a very enjoyable service which was attended by most of the second-class passengers. Sunday morning there were the regulation Church of England services, and later our genial table steward asked Elder Engle to preach in the evening. He did so to a large, intelligent, and interested congregation. As there had been much conjecture among the passengers as to who we were, and what our belief was, he embraced the opportunity, while speaking, of setting forth some of the tenets of our faith, much to the satisfaction of those present.

On November 31 the steamer reached Liverpool, England, and the first part of the voyage was at an end. As we stood on deck gazing at the strange scenes around us and at the sea of unfamiliar faces looking up into ours, and awaiting our turn to disembark, we realized in truth that we were strangers in a strange land. How was our agent to be found on that crowded wharf?—but this question was quickly settled. No sooner had we stepped off the gangway, than a gentleman approached, and, naming us, introduced himself as Mr. Mills, our agent. What a relief it was to all of us in our ignorance of foreign travel! We were thus forcibly reminded that He was going before and preparing the way so that we need have no anxious fear. This thought was further impressed upon our minds as we entered our room in the little hotel in Liverpool, for there, on the opposite wall, as we opened the door were the words, "The Lord shall be thy confidence." Mr. Mills then and there took charge of us and our baggage and did not relax his vigilance until we had safely embarked for South Africa.

Fortunate it was that our baggage was in such good hands, for part of it had been miscarried and reached the steamer at Southampton only about an hour before we left that port for South Africa. English travel has many things to recommend it, some of which Americans would do well to profit by; but one learns to appreciate the excellent system of handling baggage in America only after he has had a little experience of the slipshod manner in vogue abroad.

This fact was again brought to my attention on my first furlough to America nearly seven years later. When I disembarked at New York, an English lady from the same steamer bought a railroad ticket from New York to San Francisco and checked her baggage.

I said to her, "Now you need not trouble yourself about your baggage until you reach your destination."

"So they tell me," she replied. "It will seem so strange to travel without having to look after one's luggage."

One is pleased to note, however, that the increased amount of foreign travel of late years has brought about some improvement along this line, even in conservative England.

The ride from Liverpool to London was most enjoyable, and would have been still more so had there been some one to point out the places of interest. The fields, still green at that late date, were well kept; but the methods employed in farming seemed somewhat antiquated to people fresh from the farms of western America. As the train glided along we were favored with a glimpse of a hunting party in their brilliant colored costumes in pursuit of the poor little animals on one of the game reserves. The small private compartments on the train were a pleasing novelty, but there was no one to call off the names of the cities through which the train was passing, and the surroundings were too new for us to know where to look for the names. Once when the guard came to examine our tickets, I inquired the name of the place. Concluding from his silence that he had not understood, I ventured to repeat the question. The stare he gave made me realize that I had been guilty of a breach of something, but what it was is not exactly clear to me to this day. We also had a glimpse of London, that great metropolis, with its narrow, crowded streets, its rush of business, and its perfectly-controlled business traffic. Here our company was met by another agent, who conveyed us to Black Wall and placed us on the steamer *Pembroke Castle*, of the Union Castle Line, for a three weeks' voyage to Cape Town.

The associations on the *Majestic* had been pleasant and we expected a similar experience on this second steamer; but the long voyage to Cape Town leaves much to be desired. One may always find some congenial spirits, but even under the best circumstances the voyage finally becomes tiresome. Only too often the more turbulent element gains the upperhand, so that drinking, gambling, dancing, and even grosser evils prevail.

After sailing from Southampton one soon leaves behind the cold, chilly winds of the temperate climate and begins to enjoy the soft, balmy breezes of the subtropical climate. However, as the heat becomes more intense, this enjoyment gradually gives place to discomfort. The only stop on the way to Cape Town was at Las Palmas, on Canary Island. As we approached the place, the low-lying mountain peaks could have been mistaken for clouds, but soon the entire island lay before us in all its beauty. What appeared at first sight to be bare cliffs were soon seen to be clothed with verdure; and while we were feasting our eyes on the scene, on one side of the steamer, our attention was called to the opposite side where the city of Las Palmas lay. It was indeed a magnificent scene and beggars description. The city, which is almost entirely white, rises tier after tier up the mountain side, and the whole had a dark background of mountain peaks. We were in the bay with the island nearly surrounding us. In a short time our steamer was encompassed by a number of small boats full of natives, some of whom came to sell their wares of fruit or fancywork. Other boats were full of diving boys, ready to plunge into the sea for money thrown from the steamer into the water.

In a short time the steamer was again on its way; but where was it taking the little band of missionaries? and what was to be their final destination? Their tickets called for Cape Town, but beyond that the way seemed like a sealed book. Africa, with its barbarism, its unknown depths, its gross darkness, lay before them; and they were keenly conscious of their ignorance of the continent. They had implicit confidence, however, in their Great Leader, and believed that they were going to a place which the Lord said He would show them. Many prayers ascended that they might understand His voice when He spoke to them.

Personally their ideas about the location of the work differed. At first Elder Engle felt drawn for various reasons towards the Transvaal (not Johannesburg), because that was not so far inland. To one of the party the call had been distinctly into the interior and most needy regions where Christ had not been named. All, however, were ready to let the Lord lead.

A number of the passengers on the steamer were familiar with some parts of Africa and gave valuable information. One of the officers, the chief engineer, was especially helpful. He brought out his maps and went carefully over the ground, showing where missionaries were located and where there was need. Ere the party left the steamer, the consensus of opinion seemed to be that Rhodesia, or the part of it known as Matabeleland, was the Lord's place for them to begin aggressive missionary work. This was further confirmed when it was learned that the Cape to Cairo Railroad had just been completed as far as Bulawayo, the chief town of Matabeleland.

This having been decided upon, the next question was as to how long they were to remain at Cape Town before proceeding into the interior. The amount of money at their disposal was not large, and as it was the Lord's money it was necessary to know His will as to its disposal. They soon learned that He was continuing to go before and prepare the way. Those were precious days of waiting on Him; for never does His will and guidance seem so precious as when He is showing only one step at a time, and as one becomes willing to take that, lo! another is revealed just beyond. Why then do we so often halt, fearing to walk alone with Him, knowing that we cannot stumble as long as we keep hold of His dear hand?

On December 26 the steamer entered beautiful Table Bay, and the long voyage was over. Praises ascended to Him Who had given such a prosperous journey. It was Sunday when land was reached and the passengers were allowed to remain on board the steamer until Monday if they so desired. All of us attended divine services on land Sunday morning, and in the afternoon Brother and Sister Engle went to the Y. W. C. A. Building where the Secretary, Miss Reed, offered to help them look for rooms.

They accordingly went on Monday morning, the rest of us remaining with the boxes and in prayer. They at first were unsuccessful in securing rooms, but after again looking to the Lord for guidance, Miss Reed was impressed to take them to a Mrs. Lewis (nee Shriner), a prominent temperance and reform worker of Cape Town, and a most devoted Christian. This lady was a friend in need to many of God's children. She had lately rented a large building in connection with her work; but the venture had not been as successful as she had hoped, and she was in prayer about the matter, pleading that the place might be made a blessing to some one. Even as she prayed, three persons stood at her door desiring to speak with her. These were Miss Reed and Elder and Mrs. Engle, whom the Lord had directed thither. As soon as she heard their errand, she felt that here was an answer to her prayer. Arrangements were immediately made by which they were to receive three plainly-furnished rooms for a sum which was very moderate indeed for Cape Town. She said she would prefer to give the rooms gratis if she were in a position financially to do so. Together they fell on their knees and thanked the Lord for answered prayer which meant so much to all concerned. When Elder Engle returned to the waiting ones their hearts, too, leaped for joy at the good news. They thought it was almost too good to be true, that so soon rooms had been secured, and that they were to have a little home of their own without the expenses of a hotel. Truly, "He is able to do exceeding abundantly all that we ask or think." Boxes were soon transferred to the new home and our feet planted firmly on African soil

CHAPTER THREE

Preparation and Progress

We were here on the threshold of Africa, eager to move out. We realized, however, how meager was our knowledge of this vast continent and its needs, so it was necessary to go slow and gain all possible information from this vantage ground.

Cape Town is the oldest of South African cities and is the largest seaport town, having a population of about 80,000 inhabitants. The long, tiresome sea voyage being over, the sight of this picturesque city, nestling so cozily at the foot of Table Mountain, is one long to be remembered. The mountain rises abruptly 3,850 feet in the background of the city. Its majestic flat top is two miles long, and when the weather is clear, it stands sharply outlined against the blue sky. Frequently, however, a white cloud, known as the "Table Cloth," comes up from the sea from the back of the mountain and rolls down over the face, a sign that a change of weather is imminent. It has been said, "The glory of Table Bay is Table Mountain," and "The glory of Table Mountain is the Table Cloth." Bay, town, and mountain combine to make the picture beautiful and unique of its kind.

Cape Town was laid out by the Dutch, and the substantial, antiquated-looking houses in the older parts of the city bear ample testimony to this fact. There are also many fine, modernly-built houses. The place is supplied with all the latest improvements, which are a necessary part of a modern city. The population is most varied. Dutch, English, Hottentots, Malays, and Kafirs abound. The scenes on some of the streets at that time, especially in the evenings and on holidays, were most varied and picturesque. There were to be seen Europeans in civilian dress, others in soldier's uniform, Malays in their turbans and bright, flowing robes, well-dressed blacks, and the raw native African with only a gunny sack to cover him, for clothed he must be before he can enter the city.

Mr. and Mrs. Lewis, together with other Christian people whom we met at Cape Town, thought Matabeleland, the chosen field, was a good one, especially the Matopo Hills, as there were no missionaries in that locality. The late Cecil Rhodes, who was still powerful in Rhodesia, was at that time living on his estate, Groot Schuur, near Cape Town, and Bishop Engle was advised to go to him and endeavor to obtain from him a tract of land for a mission site. This was another special season of looking to the Lord on the part of the little company, that He might overrule it to His glory and to the advancement of His Kingdom. Brother Engle was received kindly by the gentleman, and his request was favorably considered, especially the suggestion of going to the Matopo Hills. He at once gave Brother Engle a letter to the British Charter Company, of Rhodesia, with the recommendation that we be given 3,000 acres of land in the Matopo Hills for a mission station. He added that "missionaries are better than policemen and cheaper."

Every forward step only served to confirm us in the decision on the steamer that Matabeleland, which is a part of Rhodesia, was the Lord's place for opening up His work in Africa. The fact that the railroad had just shortly before been completed that far, thus making it easier of access; the advice of those on the steamer who were familiar with the country; the advice of the spiritually-minded friends met at Cape Town, and the encouragement given by him, the "Empire Builder," who perhaps more than anyone else had the welfare of the country at heart and whose name, Rhodesia, the country bore, together with the conviction of the missionaries themselves, all served to set at rest any further question as to location that might arise.

Sister Hershey, it is true, was somewhat burdened as to whether Rhodesia was the Lord's place for her. While she was seeking to know His will in the matter, she received a letter from Mr. and Mrs. Worcester, of Johannesburg, inviting her to come and assist in the missionary work at the Compounds. She felt at once that this was the Lord's place for her, and accepted it as from Him. We were truly sorry to lose so valuable and consecrated a colaborer in the work, but felt to bow in submission to Him Who knoweth best.

While we were waiting at Cape Town, we learned that the Tebele language spoken by the natives in Matopo Hills and vicinity was a dialect of the Zulu language. The Bible had been translated into the Zulu, and there were grammars and dictionaries to be had, and we at once endeavored to procure these so that we might do some studying. Efforts were also made to secure a teacher, but the Zulu teacher recommended did not have sufficient English to be of any real service to us except in the pronunciation of Zulu words, so we were obliged to study on alone and consequently made very little progress.

We had arrived at Cape Town in the midst of the summer and dry season. Like California, Cape Town and vicinity have rains chiefly in the winter, and a most healthful climate the year round. Other parts of South Africa, however, have their rainy season in the summer, and in some localities, notably Rhodesia and farther inland, the deadly malarial fever is especially severe during the rainy season. So we were advised to remain at Cape Town until the rains were over in Rhodesia. Mr. Lewis was contemplating going north with us to assist Brother Engle in opening the work; but before this could be accomplished, both he and Mrs. Lewis were summoned north to Bulawayo by a telegram to minister to one of their friends there who was very sick.

After reaching Bulawayo they immediately sent a telegram south telling us to remain at Cape Town, and under no consideration to venture into the interior until the rains were over. As if to emphasize the message, both of them, while attending to the sick, were stricken with fever, and all were obliged to hasten south as soon as possible. We also came into contact with some of the Seventh Day Adventists in Cape Town, and through them learned that two of their missionaries in Rhodesia had just succumbed to the fever.

From the illness brought on at this time Mr. Lewis never fully recovered, and shortly after our departure from Cape Town, we learned, much to our sorrow, that he had been carried away by the disease. We were often made to feel, as Mrs. Lewis expressed it, that the Lord had sent them before us to preserve life. Otherwise we would undoubtedly have gone to Bulawayo at an earlier date than we did and would probably have had to suffer in consequence. We shall never forget the great kindness of these friends during the entire four months of our stay at Cape Town. The wise counsel, the spiritual and financial aid which they gave, will ever be a green spot in our memory. And not only then, but in later years, Mrs. Lewis' home, "The Highlands," and her large heart were ever open to our missionaries. As each recruit stepped foot on Africa's shores she was the first to welcome him. When any needed rest, her house was wide open for any who might choose to come and rest there. When a few years ago word came that she had gone to meet her Savior Whom she so much loved, we all felt that we had indeed lost a friend that could not be replaced.

At last the time came when it was considered safe to move out, Sister Hershey to Johannesburg and the rest to Bulawayo. Mrs. Lewis had given us a nice large tent, 16 x 16 feet, which could be used as a dwelling place while huts were being built, and she had also on her trip north met some of the white people of Bulawayo who were ready to assist us. Other friends at Cape Town also kindly helped us on the way.

On April 28, 1898, we took the train at Cape Town, bound for Bulawayo, 1,362 miles inland. We traveled four days and four nights in a comfortable coach and reached the place May 2. The same journey formerly required six months and longer with an ox team. We passed through only a few towns worthy the name; Kimberley, the center of the diamond mines, being the principal one. Some of the country through which we passed looked like a desert; not a blade of grass to be seen, but the red sand is covered with bushes. This is known as the Karroo, and, as rain seldom falls on much of this land, one is surprised to see flocks of sheep and here and there an ostrich farm. There are many flat-topped mountains and hills, at the foot of which one occasionally catches sight of a farmhouse with its accompanying sheep pen. A letter sent to America at the time adds:

> Parts greatly resemble Kansas prairies, while the last four or five hundred miles of the journey the country looks like old, deserted orchards. We were also introduced to African life in its primitive state, and during the latter part of the journey no white people were visible save the few connected with the railway service, but many native huts were to be seen. Some were made of mud, others formed of poles covered with various-colored cloth, forming a veritable patchwork, while the natives in semi-nude condition came crowding about the car windows, begging for money and food. How my heart bled for these poor souls! Although the railroad was built, ostensibly, for the purpose of developing the commercial and mining interests of the country; yet, as I looked upon those poor natives, I wondered whether the real purpose of it under the Providence of God was not to bring the Gospel to them. Other missionaries are here before us, but I believe we are the first to make use of the new railroad for this purpose.

CHAPTER FOUR

Matabeleland

Before proceeding with my story let me introduce to my readers the people and the country to which we had come. The Matabele are a branch of the Zulu tribe of Southeast Africa. During the reign of the great and despotic Zulu King, Tyaka, they revolted under the leadership of Mzilikazi, or Moselikatse, and started north through Africa, proving a terror to the various tribes along the way and meeting with numerous hardships and varying degrees of success. About the year 1836 found them in this country, to which they gave the name Matabeleland. This land, together with Mashonaland, constitutes what is now known as Southern Rhodesia.

Here they established themselves by ruthlessly slaughtering all who opposed them, and enslaving the natives already in the country. After the death of Mzilikazi, his son, Lobengula, became King. He was more or less tyrannical, like his father, and he lived with his sixty wives about two miles from what is now known as Bulawayo—the killing place—or, as the natives often say, "o Bulawayo," meaning murderer. A rock near this place is still pointed out as the place where a number of his wives met a violent death.

This King Lobengula ruled his people with a rod of iron. The young men were all enlisted in his army and the women and children left to carry on the work in the gardens and kraals. Rev. Helm, one of the first missionaries in the country, said it was impossible to get hold of the young men; and even if the boys did start to school, the King would take them for his own use as soon as they were old enough. He, however, never molested the missionaries themselves, and probably considered it an honor to have a white teacher in the country; but, as Mrs. Helm remarked, they were careful not to offend him.

The British Charter Company had obtained some concessions from the King in 1889, and, in the next year, Europeans entered the country to prospect and mine the gold. It was a foreseen conclusion that there would eventually be a conflict between a savage despot, to whom many of the white people were obliged to cringe, and a civilized people. The inevitable reached a climax in 1893, when war broke out between the King and the white people of the country. There were only a few white men in the country at that time, but assegais and other native weapons were no match for Maxim guns and European tactics. The King's house being burnt, he himself fled and eventually died in January, 1894, thus causing the war suddenly to come to an end, as there remained no one to keep the forces together. The British South

African Company took possession and began to occupy and build up the country.

The Matabele, however, did not consider themselves conquered, and many circumstances conspired to bring about a second conflict. Perhaps the chief among these was the fact that all the cattle were regarded as the property of the King, although being distributed among the people and used by them as their own. However, since the cattle belonged to the King, the British Company looked upon them as theirs by right of conquest, and proceeded to appropriate some of them. This greatly angered the natives, as also the rinderpest, which came later and swept off many of the remaining cattle. Then 400 of the subject tribes were armed and enlisted as native police; and this was most galling to the proud Matabele warriors, that they should be exulted over by their former slaves. The disease among their cattle, the locust, which devoured their crops, and numerous other troubles were all, by their witch doctors, laid at the door of the white man. Umlimo (their god) also affirmed that their King was still alive and was ready to assist them in gaining their liberty.

This second conflict, known as the Matabele Rebellion of 1896, came very suddenly upon the 4,000 white people, scattered in various parts of the country. No one seemed to expect danger, although there were several who had had a little warning, and many natives who were working in Bulawayo were called home by their parents. One boy in speaking of the time said:

"I was working in Bulawayo when my father sent word that I was to come home. I did not want to but I was afraid to disobey. I was afraid to look at my father, he looked like a mad man. He said, 'We cannot live and be oppressed like this. We would rather die than be treated as we are!'

"The rest of the people, too, looked just that way!"

The natives rose against the Europeans and suddenly murdered 200 in the outlying districts, including a number of women and children. Some of these were murdered by their own servants. The rest of the white people hastily gathered into the new town of Bulawayo, while soldiers scoured the country in search of native troops. A large number of the native police had gone over to the enemy, carrying their rifles with them, and a number of the natives, both in Matabeleland and Mashonaland, had in some way secured several thousand firearms; so that in this war the natives were much better prepared.

This rebellion lasted eight months, and the natives were finally driven into the Matopo Hills. In these, nature's vast strongholds and caves, all efforts of the European soldiers to dislodge them proved unavailing. Here finally came Mr. Rhodes, unarmed, into the midst of the enemy's camp and made peace with them. The tree under which this famous council was held is still pointed out not many miles from where Matopo Mission now is. We entered the country a little over a year after the close of the rebellion, while all the causes and events were still fresh in the minds of the natives. What is still more significant, we were located in the very heart of these hills where no missionary had yet penetrated, and being surrounded by many of the rebels themselves, we were able to glean much of the above history at first hand. When we went among them they were still seething with discontent from the same cause which led to the Rebellion.

Mr. Rhodes, who had made peace with these natives, was always respected and trusted by them, and while he was no religious man himself, he thoroughly believed in missionary work among the people. His desire that we come to these hills and his statement, that "missionaries are better than policemen, and cheaper," was actuated by no mercenary motive. It was his conviction, borne out by experience and by long years of contact with the Africans, that missionary work and the Christianization of the natives was the only solution of the native problems.

But to return to our story, we arrived at Bulawayo late in the evening and were taken to the Royal Hotel. This was a good, up-to-date hotel, with an up-to-date African price. In the morning, as we looked out of the window, the first sight which greeted our eyes was a large African wagon drawn by eighteen oxen. Except for this and similar sights we could easily have imagined that we were in an American town, for this place, with broad streets and thriving business, is said to have been patterned somewhat after American cities. My impressions of the town and vicinity written at the time were as follows:

> Bulawayo is a modern wonder, an oasis of civilization in the midst of a desert of barbarism and heathendom. It has nearly 3,000 inhabitants, and has been built since 1894. Before that time Lobengula, the great Matabele King, held sway about two miles from here at the place where the Government House now stands. This place reminds one of the booming Kansas towns of a few years ago, but it is hundreds of miles from any other civilized place, and is well built of brick and iron, has good stores of all kinds, five churches, public library, electric lights and telephone, not only in town, but also extending to various police forts in the surrounding country, but no public schools. There are comfortable riding cabs, or traps, drawn by horses or mules, but the traffic is carried on by heavy carts or still heavier wagons drawn by a large number of oxen or donkeys. The manual labor is done chiefly by the native boys, the white people considering it beneath their dignity to do anything a

native can do.

The surrounding country is very pretty and level, and one can see an abundance of the "golden sands" mentioned by the poet, and even gold sands are not wanting, but I am sorry to say that the "sunny fountains" rolling down them are very few, especially at this season of the year when there are seven months of drought!

This for Bulawayo in 1898 and first impressions.

We remained at the hotel only two days. Our tent and the other goods had not yet arrived, but a gentleman, to whom we had a letter of introduction through Mrs. Lewis, most kindly offered the use of his house and furniture for two weeks, which offer was gratefully accepted. Before the end of that time our tent had arrived, and this being placed on a vacant lot furnished ample protection for that season of the year.

Bulawayo, being of such recent growth and being surrounded by pagan tribes, would have afforded abundant opportunity for missionary work. Daily these raw natives would come to our tent door to sell wood or other articles; and we longed to tell them something of a Savior's love, had we been able to speak to them. One morning thirteen native women, each with a great load of wood on her head, arranged themselves, smiling and expectant, before the door of our tent. We could only smile in return, that one touch of nature's language which is akin the world over. We were thankful that we could do so much, but back of the smile was a heavy heart that we could do so little.

During the two months we remained at Bulawayo efforts were made to secure a suitable location among the Matopo Hills. Mr. Rhodes' letter had been delivered to the government officials, and they generously undertook to assist in locating the work. The first place to which they took Brother Engle—the one recommended by Mr. Rhodes—was found to have been surveyed by a private individual. They then made another selection, about thirty miles southeast of Bulawayo, the place now known as Matopo Mission, and they agreed to give us here a Mission Reservation of 3,000 acres. The officials, as well as other Europeans in Bulawayo, rendered us much assistance. In addition to these the Seventh Day Adventist missionaries also greatly helped us on the way. These had a mission station about thirty miles west of Bulawayo, and about fifty miles from the place selected for us; and while we were waiting in Bulawayo, they kindly took out, at different times, Brother and Sister Engle and Sister Heise, for a visit to their station.

The time came for us to move out to our location among the hills, and the question of how we should get ourselves and our goods to the place was becoming a serious one. Transportation, like everything else in the interior of

Africa, was exceedingly expensive. In this emergency Mr. Anderson, of the Seventh Day Adventist Mission, offered to come that long way with his donkey wagon and move us for half the sum required by a regular transport driver.

It is difficult for the reader to form any conception of what these various expressions of kindness along the way, coming so unexpectedly from entire strangers, meant to that little band of missionaries out in the heart of Africa. Even as I write these things, after a lapse of sixteen years, and live over the events of that time, tears of joy unbidden come and my heart wells up in gratitude as I again recall these evidences of the wonderful "faithfulness of a faithful God."

We had been ignorant of our destination when we left the American shore, and even more ignorant of the cost of living in the interior of Africa; so that, by the time supplies had been purchased to take along to the hills, the money on hand was about exhausted. We knew not how long a time would elapse before a fresh supply could reach us. Knowing, too, that the Church had very little experience in foreign missionary work, one could not fail at times to be a little anxious. Thanks, however, to the wisdom, ability, and promptness displayed by the old fathers who formed the Mission Board, and to their support, backed up by the Church; as soon as conditions were understood at home means were forthcoming and we were never allowed to be in want.

CHAPTER FIVE

The Opening of the Work

> We must remember that it was not by interceding for the world in glory that Jesus saved it. He gave Himself. Our prayers for the evangelization of the world are but a bitter irony so long as we only give of our superfluity and draw back before the sacrifice of ourselves.—M. Francois Coillard.

We heartily echo the words of this sainted missionary to the Barotse, but we believe that the thought uppermost in the heart of each of the four waiting ones at Bulawayo was not sacrifice but privilege, on that July morning, so long ago, when the command to go forward was given. We were soon to reach our destination, the place to which we had started from New York over seven months previously. An account of this trip written at the time reads somewhat as follows:

> We left Bulawayo on the evening of July 4 and traveled three nights and two days before the mission valley was reached. The nights were cool and a bright moon lighted up the way, so that traveling went better at night than during the heat of the day. The wagon was about eighteen feet long, very strong and heavy, and was drawn by eighteen donkeys. These were led by one native boy, while another with a long whip was doing the driving. The load of about three tons was very heavy—too heavy, in fact, for a part of the way. Donkeys can travel only two miles an hour on good roads and on poor roads it sometimes requires two hours to go one mile. Occasionally we stopped from two to four hours to let the donkeys rest and graze.

> During such times we would build fire on the veldt, and cook and eat our food; or, if it were night, we would wrap our blankets about us, take our pillows, and lie down in the shelter of some friendly bush and sleep. Mother Engle usually preferred the shelter of the tent on the back of the wagon, although the place was too much crowded for her to rest comfortably. Since the load was so heavy we spent a great deal of the time walking. We would walk ahead of the wagon for a distance, then sit down and rest until the wagon reached us. Only two of three settlers' houses were visible, and no native kraals, and we were informed that as soon as the white man makes a road, the natives move away from it.

After twenty miles of travel we came to Fort Usher. At this place there reside an English magistrate and a number of white police. Here we were kindly received and given a native guide for the rest of the journey. We now left the government road and plunged into the hills. The wagon went along another five miles with very little difficulty. Then it mired on going through a swampy place, one side sinking nearly to the hubs of the wheels, and further progress was impossible. All put forth every effort to extricate it but to no avail. What was to be done?

While we were in this dilemma, the Chief of the natives in this part of the country, Hluganisa by name, with some natives came to meet us and bid us welcome. They gave us a very friendly reception, and then joined in to assist in extricating the wagon, but without success. Mr. Anderson, who could speak the native language, explained to the chief who we were and our object in coming, and he promised to meet us at the mission site the next day, as it was now evening.

Mr. Anderson then took our party forward a little distance to a dry spot, where we rested during the night. He and his native boys returned to the wagon, and, removing the greater part of the load, carried it beyond the marshy place. The donkeys were then able to pull out the wagon. It is needless to add that Mr. Anderson and his boys were extremely tired after this laborious task and were glad to snatch a little rest. Even under such circumstances they did not indulge long in the much-needed rest, but at an early hour were again ready for the journey. Those of us who had enjoyed a good night's rest were also aroused, and we started on our last trek into the hills. We reached the valley, which is to be our home, on the morning of July 7.

This valley is surrounded by immense granite hills and boulders, some of which cover hundreds of acres, so that at first sight the rocks seem to constitute the chief part of the country, but a closer inspection showed us to what a beautiful place God had led us for His work. There, spread out before our eyes, was a beautiful rolling valley of rich, dark earth, well supplied with an abundance of fresh water. It was stated that the "sunny fountains" are rare in this part of Africa, and that is true. Here, however, in this beautiful valley, in the heart of Matopo Hills, are sparkling fountains of beautiful water, crystal clear, oozing from under the surface of the rocks, and flowing down the valley. Some contain delicate mosses and pretty water lilies, and surpass the Michigan lakes in transparency.

In the meantime the Chief had sent word to the headmen of the various kraals to meet us. So, in the morning, obedient to the call of their superior, they came and sat in a semi-circle while their chief addressed them (Mr. Anderson interpreting for our benefit):

"These are not like other white people."

The deep-toned voices of the headmen responded in unison, "Yes, my lord."

He continued, "They have come to teach you and your children and to do you good."

Again came the response, "Yes, my lord."

"Now do what you can for them and help them."

And again the same response was repeated.

> One may imagine how that impressed us. Here we are, far from other white people, among a class of natives who have never been subdued by the English soldiers. They are kept in subjection only by forts of police stationed among the hills, the nearest being ten miles distant. Yet these people recognized us at once as their friends and received us with kindness far above what we dared expect. Our hearts overflow with thankfulness to Him who rules the hearts of men.

The Chief and one or two other natives went with us to look up a location on which to pitch the tent and build huts. The tent was finally pitched under the shade of a large umkuni tree, Mr. Anderson returned to his station, and we were left without an interpreter, and with no practical knowledge of mission work. We had, however, a Great Teacher, and we were willing to be taught.

Both Matabele and their subject races, known as Amahole, live in the Matopo Hills. The majority of them are not black, but a chocolate brown, and some have features resembling white people. They are generally large, well-formed, and intelligent-looking. They are more or less rude in manner, uncouth in appearance, and wear little or no clothing except the loin cloth. This in the men usually consists of the skin of small animals, and among the women a short skirt of cloth or skins. Over the upper part of the body is sometimes thrown a larger piece of cloth.

Among those that gathered about us that first day were some who had been quite active in the late rebellion. As we gained their confidence, they often pointed out to us the caves where they stored their grain, and where they themselves hid during that terrible time. A year of famine had followed the war, and some had starved to death. At the time we entered upon the work there was a great deal of destitution all about us; for some had not yet been able to grow grain, and they had no flocks to fall back upon as they usually had in time of grain famine.

Many of the white people in the country and in Bulawayo were continually talking about and expecting another uprising. They looked for it to come from these Matopo Hill natives, and some sought to warn us not to venture into this, the enemy's stronghold. We, however, living among them from day to day, saw no cause for fear.

The natives came to see us in large numbers. Sometimes fifty would appear in one day and crowd around the door of our tent, desiring to have a good view of the newcomers and their belongings. Many of them, especially the women and children, had never seen a white person before, or at most a white woman. Some three or four families had heard a little of Jesus, but the great majority knew absolutely nothing of the Gospel.

Our ignorance, both of the language and the people, led to many blunders, both ludicrous and otherwise. The desire to help them and to show them that we were their friends caused them often to take advantage of our kindness. We soon learned that the African is not so much interested in the things that are for the good of his soul as in that which ministers to his body and appetite. It was so difficult to know just what to do at all times, for they were destitute of nearly everything which we considered necessary for comfort. They were confirmed beggars, and the more they received the more they wanted. The missionary opens his Bible, and reads, "He that hath two coats, let him impart to him that hath none; and he that hath meat let him do likewise"; he then gets down on his knees and prays that the Lord might help the poor souls about him, but he often feels that his prayers do not ascend very high. What he needs to do is to get up and answer his own prayers.

Hut Built by H. Frances Davidson and Alice Heise at Matopo.

When we made a contract with them for work, and told them what pay they would receive, they always wanted more than the contract called for when the time came to settle. This is characteristic of the native in dealing with the white man. He sees that the other has clothing and many comforts of which he is deprived, hence concludes that the pockets of the white man are full of money. Socialist that he naturally is, he thinks that the property should be equally distributed. It never occurs to him that his laziness and shiftlessness have much to do with his destitution. In fact, that thought does not generally occur to the missionary when he goes among the heathen for the first time, unless he is with some one who understands the situation.

It is necessary to make the natives understand at times that the kindness of even the missionary has a limit. One day I was in the little straw shed which served as a kitchen, and was endeavoring to bake bread. As usual a number of people were about the door, and one man, taking advantage of my kindness, came in and sat down by the stove in front of the bake-oven door. He made no effort in the least to move away when I tried to look into the oven door. I bore it for some time, not wishing to be rude to him, and not knowing how to ask him in a polite way to move. Suddenly it dawned upon me that the proper native word was *suka*. So I made use of the word and told him to *suka*. He looked up in surprise and repeated the word to know if he had correctly understood, but he moved. Afterwards, in looking for the word in my dictionary, I found that it was a word often in the mouth of the white man when addressing a native. It really meant a rough "Get out of this." So the look of mild reproach in the eyes of the native was accounted for. Some of the softness in the missionary, too, soon wears off as he is obliged to deal with the native from day to day. He finds that it is necessary to make the native understand their relation one to another as teacher and pupil.

Living in a tent during the dry and healthy season is not unpleasant in such a climate, except that one suffers from the heat by day and the cold by night.

Matopo Mission is located about 20½° south latitude and 29° east longitude. It is 5,000 feet above sea level, so that, although it is within the tropics, it has a delightful and salubrious climate the entire year. From the middle of November to the middle of April is what is known as the rainy season. The rest of the year rain seldom falls. One cannot live in a tent all the year, but must provide better shelter for the rainy season. So hut building occupied the first few months. We had no wagon and no oxen, nothing but two little donkeys, which had been brought out with us from Bulawayo, and we did not know how to make the best use of native help. The poles used in the construction of the huts were cut and carried to the place of building by natives.

As the manner of building was quite foreign to an American, Brother Engle took occasion to examine other huts, built by Europeans, so that he was enabled to build very good ones for the mission. He was alone and, to make the work lighter, we women assisted, and used hammer, saw, and trowel, brought stones for building chimneys, raked grass, and assisted in thatching. The huts are built somewhat as follows:

A trench about fifteen inches deep is dug the size and shape of the desired hut. In this are placed, near together, poles from the forest, space being allowed for doors and windows and sometimes for fireplace. The poles are cut out so as to extend about eight feet above ground. Large ones are sawed lengthwise for door posts and window frames. Some flexible poles are nailed around the top and about halfway up the side, so that the walls of the hut are firmly fastened together. Longer poles are then used as rafters, these being firmly fastened to the walls and nailed together at the top. Small, flexible ones are also used as lath to fasten the rafters together and upon which to tie the grass in thatching. The grass used for this purpose grows in abundance among these rocks, and sometimes reaches the height of eight feet. The women cut this and bring it in bundles, glad to exchange it for a little salt. It is first combed by means of spikes driven through a board. It is then divided into small bundles; the lower ends being placed evenly together, and the bundles tied closely together on the lath with tarred rope. The next layer is placed over this like shingles, so as to cover the place of tying. When completed the thickness of grass on the eaves of the roof is from four to ten inches. Then follows the plastering. The mud or plaster is made from earth which had been worked over by white ants. This, pounded fine and mixed with water, makes an excellent plaster, and when placed on the walls it soon dries and becomes very hard. The native women put this on the outside with their hands, as the walls are too uneven to allow the use of a trowel. Similar earth, mixed with sand, is used as mortar in building with brick and stone. The floors also are of this earth pounded hard and polished.

The windows have either small panes of glass or muslin stretched on a frame, and the doors boast of imported timber brought from Bulawayo. Each hut is about as large as an average-sized room. It is difficult to make them larger on account of the scarcity of suitable material in this part of the country. The walls are whitewashed on the inside, and some have a white muslin ceiling. Much of the furniture is of our own manufacture and is made of boxes or of native poles draped with calico.

When completed the rooms looked quite cozy and comfortable, so that we felt thankful for such pleasant homes in connection with our work. The first year there were four of such huts built, kitchen, dining-hut, and two sleeping-rooms.

Dealing with the natives while building these was not always easy. Sometimes difficulties arose through not being able to make the natives understand, so that we could not always place the blame on them. When grass was wanted for the thatching a contract was entered into with one of the headmen to furnish one hundred bundles for five shillings ($1.20). The grass was brought until there was about half the specified amount, then the pay was demanded. This was of course refused. The man brought a little more and then he stoutly affirmed that he had fulfilled his part of the contract. After considerable delay and, being harassed by the headman, we finally paid him. After all, he may have been honest in the affair and a mistake may have been made in the beginning; for the word for *one hundred* and that for *much* were similar except in the prefix. He may have understood that he was to bring much grass, and he certainly did that.

Again, when the first hut was to be plastered, arrangements were made with certain women to plaster it for a stated amount. They brought a number of others along to help them plaster; and when pay day came, the total amount of pay demanded was about double the original agreement. There was such a noisy, unpleasant demonstration that day, that we learned our lesson, and we were very careful so to arrange matters that the difficulty would not occur again.

Matopo Mission—March, 1899.

Our living at the time was of the simplest. Nearly all kinds of eatables could be procured in Bulawayo; but they were very expensive, and there was no way of bringing them out except by native carriers, or by trusting to the friendly assistance of the white traders at Fort Usher. Sometimes it fell to the Elder's lot to walk the thirty miles to Bulawayo in order to purchase supplies. There was no need, however, for us to do, like many a missionary in the wilds of Africa has done, deprive ourselves of wheat bread and ordinary groceries. These we always had, but we were more economical in their use than we would have been at home. We had no milk, except tinned milk, no butter, and very little meat, and no gun to procure game. But we had chicken and could occasionally procure meat from the natives. Of course at first there were no vegetables to be had, except such as we could at times procure from the natives—corn, sweet potatoes, pumpkins, and peanuts, but these were scarce.

Elder Engle, alive to the value of the soil and the need of wholesome food, at once secured fruit trees and set them out, including a number of orange trees. He also bought a small plow and with the two donkeys broke land and planted vegetables. One native, who continually stood by us during those early days, was Mapipa, our nearest neighbor. He was a powerfully-built Matabele and reminded one of the giant of Gath; for he had six fingers on each hand and six toes on each foot. He had been quite active in the Rebellion and was wounded in one of the battles. He could always be depended upon in work, and Brother Engle greatly appreciated his assistance.

Perhaps some one who reads these lines may wonder whether building, farming, and such manual labor is missionary work. Did not the Great Missionary, according to all accounts—I say it in all reverence—take an apprenticeship in the carpenter's shop where He "increased in wisdom and stature and in favor with God and man"? Did not the Apostle Paul, undoubtedly the greatest of His followers, unite tent-making with his missionary work? Should then we, such feeble imitations, belittle manual labor, even though it falls to our lot as missionaries? Any one going to the mission field should not, if he is to be successful, decide in his own mind that he is going to do certain things, he should be willing to do whatever the Lord gives him to do, of spiritual, intellectual, or physical labors.

There are so many sides to missionary work, and who can tell which will result in the greatest good? To preach Christ and lift Him up that others may see and accept Him is undoubtedly the central thought of the Great Commission. The ways of exalting Him, however, are so many and so various. Christ must be lived among the people before He can in truth be preached to them. The heathen of Africa cannot read the Bible, but they can and do continually read the lives of those sent among them. If these do not correspond to the Word read and preached among them, they are keen to discern and judge accordingly. If the Christ-life is lived before their eyes, day by day, many will eventually yield their hearts to Him, even though, they may for a time resist.

CHAPTER SIX

Educational and Evangelistic Work

The natives were eager to see inside the new huts. When they had an opportunity to look at the whitewashed walls and the homemade furniture, they stood spellbound, and the first word that broke from their lips was "*Muehle*" (pretty).

They had another and more personal interest in seeing the huts completed. They had been told that, as soon as the goods were moved out of the tent, school would be opened. Both large and small were exceedingly eager to learn, or at least they thought so. They had never seen books, and writing was like magic to them. To put down some characters on paper and from those to spell out their names when they next visited the mission was little less than witchcraft. Both old and young like to be known. They are pleased if their missionary pronounces their name and seems to know them when they come a second time.

School opened October 11. The first boy to come bright and early was Matshuba, together with two of Mapita's girls. This little boy, then about thirteen years old, had been a very interested spectator of all that occurred from the time the mission opened. Day after day he would be on hand, and his bright eyes and active mind took knowledge of everything that was said or done. His father, Mpisa, then dead, had been one of the most trusted witch doctors of the King, and had been held in great respect by all of the natives in that part of the country. This boy was very eager for school, and the first morning he and Mapita's girls begged us to allow only the Matabele to attend school, and not the Amahole, or subject races. This furnished an excellent opportunity of teaching them that God is no Respecter of persons.

The first morning of school twelve bright-looking boys and girls entered the tent and sat down on the floor, curious to know what school was like. It was a momentous time. It was the beginning of a work the result of which human eye could not foresee. How the teacher, who had often stood before a far larger and more inspiring-looking school in a civilized land, trembled as she stood there before those twelve little savages in the heart of Africa! She knew that those bright eyes were reading her thoughts, and realized that she came so far short of the "measure of the stature of the fullness of Christ." The special burden of the prayer that morning was that, as these dear souls learned to read the Word, the Light might enter their hearts and they yield themselves to God.

The second day eight more were enrolled, and the third day fourteen, and by the end of the month there were forty in all. Sister Heise and I were kept busy during school hours as the pupils were taught to sew as well as to read and write. Cleanliness is a rare virtue with them, so they were told to wash before coming to school. As new ones entered the school the admonition was repeated, with the statement that we wash every morning. Mapita's little daughter, Sibongamanzi, with shining black face, which showed that she had been heeding the command, looked up brightly and said, "Yes, but you are white and we are black." She evidently had thought that, if she washed every morning, she too would become white, but she had concluded it to be a hopeless task. Mr. Anderson said that some of their children thought that if they ate the food of white people, they too would become white.

This, our first schoolroom, was very primitive. It consisted of a tent 16 x 16 feet. In front there was a box which served as a teachers' desk and as a receptacle for slates, pencils, paper, books, and sewing. Other boxes served for teachers' chairs. There were two easels made of poles; one supported the blackboard and the other the charts. The blackboard consisted of a few small boards nailed together and painted black, and the charts were of cardboard, 18 x 24 inches in size. There were ten of them printed on both sides with syllables, and Tebele words and sentences. These had been printed by homemade stencils and pen, and had occupied our leisure time while we were hut-building. The floor of the tent was covered with straw, and the pupils sat on this without seats or desks. They knew nothing of the comforts of the schoolroom in civilized lands and thought they were well supplied.

Since we had no primer at the time, the Gospel of St. John was given to them as a textbook when they had finished the charts. To enable them to read and understand the Word of God was the aim of the school work and the Bible the Textbook throughout. After they had learned to write the letters of the alphabet, their copy usually was a verse from the Scriptures. They were also taught to memorize certain portions in connection with the daily worship, and hymn singing.

The pupils compare very favorably with white children in their ability to learn, but few of them come regularly to school. To most of them school is just a side issue, some place to go when there is nothing else to be done. Some have an idea that they can learn to read in about a month, and when they find that it requires months of weary, patient effort at meaningless characters, they give up in despair. Others are ridiculed by the older people for throwing away their time at such useless work; "There is no money, no beer, no food in it and they are dunces to go."

Again, some are grown, and being past the age when mental effort is easy, they soon become discouraged. One big fellow stumbled along until he had mastered the chart after a fashion. Then, to his delight, he was given the Gospel of St. John to read. Day after day he struggled along over the, to him, meaningless syllables and words. Still he persevered until it gradually dawned upon him that the printed page meant something. He looked up one day with a most delighted expression on his face and exclaimed, "This book is talking to me!"

The native cannot be said to be very persevering, owing to the fact that all his life, in his untaught state, he goes on the principle that the world owes him a living. His needs are few and often they are supplied by nature. When he comes up against a difficult problem of any sort, his usual answer is, "It will not consent." For this reason arithmetic is always difficult for him and his progress in it is very slow. One day I was endeavoring to show a girl how to make the letter *b*. After a vain effort to make it properly, she exclaimed, "My pencil will not consent to slide that way."

The sewing hour probably was the most interesting time to all. They expected to receive the garments after they had finished sewing them and had worked for the cloth with which they were made. The dearest wish of their hearts was to have a garment to put on. And that is not strange, for in the cool morning air they come shivering, and at noon the hot sun burns their bodies. We might have made the garments and donated them; but that would not teach them to work and would have done them more harm than good. A native always appreciates most that upon which he has bestowed labor or money; so both boys and girls learned to sew. It was rather amusing to see them, in the absence of other garments to which they might pin their sewing, place it between their toes. It was also interesting to watch the different expressions when at last the garments were finished and they could clothe themselves.

Matshuba put on his suit; then, folding his hands, said in a quiet and contented manner, "Now I am not cold any more." Amuzeze, when he had finished his garments, put them on, and taking a good look at himself stepped off as proudly as if he owned a large estate. Sibongamanzi kept her dress for Sunday. At home she would carefully fold it, and putting it in an earthen jar cover it up for safe keeping.

In the meantime services on Sunday had not been neglected. At the opening of the work none of the missionaries could speak the language, but they could read it after a fashion. So, from the very first Sunday after the work opened, endeavors were made to instill into the minds of the natives that one day out of seven was a day of rest and worship. To them all days were alike—workdays, rest days, or carousal days, as they chose to spend them. Sad to say that even the few that went to work for the white man saw little or no difference between the days of the week. It falls to the lot of the missionary to teach the significance of the fourth commandment as well as the rest of the decalogue. On Sunday the people were invited to assemble under the shade of a friendly tree, and a portion of the Scriptures was read to them and hymns sung. They are great lovers of music, so that in itself was an attraction. The first congregation was very small. Sometimes there would be only Mapita and his family, five or six in number. As the nature of the meetings began to dawn on the native mind, others would assemble with us, but in the first few months, or until the opening of school in October, not more than twenty-five congregated at one time.

Acquiring the language is always a tedious, though important, part of foreign missionary work. The missionary sees the natives about him, day by day, and longs to tell them something of Jesus and His love, but is unable to do so, especially if he be a pioneer in the work and without an interpreter as we were. We had been endeavoring to study the language from the Zulu books on hand, but on coming face to face with the natives it was discovered that the set phrases we had acquired seemed as unintelligible to them as their words were to us. There were several reasons for this. One was that we had not learned the proper pronunciation and accent, and another was that their dialect differed somewhat from the Zulu, which we had been endeavoring to learn. Another, and far weightier reason, and one which, to our sorrow, we did not discover until some time afterwards, was that some natives did not speak the correct language to us. Those who had been accustomed to speaking to the Europeans had invented a jargon of their own, which they seemed to think especially adapted to the mental capacity of white people. This medium of communication is known as "kitchen Kafir."

It consists of a small vocabulary, chiefly of Zulu words, simplified and divested of all inflections—and grammar, it might be said. This dialect, which is especially distasteful to linguists, is invariably used by many natives in addressing white people for the first time. It is the common language of the kitchen and the shops, between master or mistress and their native servants. It has also of later years spread much among the natives themselves where various tribes meet and converse. Its use has become so general over South Africa, and even in parts of South Central Africa, that it has, not inaptly, been termed the "Esperanto of South Africa." Undoubtedly it lacks much of the elegance of the real Esperanto, but is in daily use by more people. Not only is "kitchen Kafir" spoken between whites and blacks and between blacks themselves, but sometimes, when a common language fails, something akin to this is used between even the white people.

Not so many of the natives in the hills had come into contact with Europeans before our coming among them, yet there was sufficient "kitchen Kafir" among them to confuse the newcomers and make it necessary in after years to unlearn many of the things they first acquired.

Learning the language is trying, especially without a teacher, and many blunders and misunderstands occur; but it is not the least useful of missionary experiences. People on first coming into contact with raw heathendom are seldom capable of doing much preaching to them in such a manner that the native can understand and appreciate.

While one is learning the language, he is also learning to know the native himself, his surroundings, and modes of thought. By the time one is able to converse with the native, he also knows better what to say to him. One thing, however, it is always safe to do from the time the missionary enters the field of labor; he may always read the Word, if he has it in the language. The unadorned Word is always safe and suits all conditions of men.

Gradually we learned to speak the language, sentence by sentence. How our hearts burned within us those days to be able to tell the story of Christ and His love! Usually the dull, darkened look on the faces of the few present would cause the speaker to feel that he had not been understood, or that there had been no answering response. Then occasionally a dusky face would light up, as if a ray of light had penetrated a darkened corner, and the speaker would be encouraged to renewed efforts to make the subject plain. Thus, Sunday after Sunday, the effort would be renewed.

It was not only on that day, however, that some of the older ones heard the Word read and an attempt at explanation given. Morning and evening worship was held in the native language, and often a larger number, in those early days, gathered about us on workdays than on Sunday. The door was always open and everyone was invited to enter at time of prayer. After school opened, and it became better known which day was Sunday, and that the services were held in the tent, the attendance gradually increased.

Our feelings, as written at the time, were somewhat as follows:

> We realize more fully every day that much wisdom and grace is needed in dealing with this people. If we did not have such confidence in our Great Leader, we might at times be discouraged, for the enemy of souls is strong here in Africa and human nature is alike the world over. When the truth is driven home to their hearts, they are quite ready to excuse themselves. Thus we find it necessary to get down lower and lower at the feet of Jesus and let Him fill us continually with all the fulness of His love and Spirit, that there may be no lack in us.

In his own eyes the pagan African is always a good, innocent sort of person. He has done no wrong, has committed no sin, hence has no need of forgiveness. One of the first requisites seems to be instilling into his mind a knowledge of God and His attributes. This must be "precept upon precept," "line upon line," "here a little and there a little." Time after time this thought of God must be reiterated until it is burned into the consciousness of the hearers. We are told of one missionary who, for the first two years, took as his text, Sabbath after Sabbath, "God is." And it would seem to be a wise course to pursue. The conception of a Supreme Being Who is holy, omnipotent, omniscient, and omnipresent, and cannot look upon sin with any degree of allowance, to Whom all must render an account, needs to be indelibly impressed on the native mind. Until they realize that "all have sinned and come short of the glory of God," it seems useless to preach Christ as a Savior to them.

Missionaries soon realize that they cannot sit down and wait for the people to come to them. They must go out into the streets and lanes of their villages and "into the highways and hedges and compel them to come in." Kraal-visiting forms a very important part of the Gospel work. Sister Heise and myself went among them as much as possible. We went chiefly on foot, and many miles were traveled in all kinds of weather, so that the people might be instructed in the things of God. At first these visits could be little more than a friendly call and the speaking of a few broken sentences. These wild children of nature were quick to respond to the interest that prompted the visits, and would always welcome the visitors. As soon as we were within sight the children would come to meet us and pilot us to their parents. When we left they would again accompany us a little distance, perhaps to the next kraal. Who shall say but that these early journeys, in which little of the Gospel was given, was not as fruitful of results for God as later ones? Back of those black exteriors are human hearts waiting to be touched by the finger of love and human sympathy, ready to imbibe the milk of human kindness. They know something of the natural love of parent to child, and *vice versa*; but they need to realize that there is such a thing as disinterested love in their welfare, and by this means be led to realize in some little measure the *wonderful love of God*. In this, thank God, we had no need to simulate love. A spark of the Divine love for them had entered our hearts before we even set foot on Africa's shores.

It is difficult to understand the expression of a missionary who visited Matopo some time after the work was started, and who in his own field of labor seemed to have been used of the Lord. He said one day: "I cannot say that I love these people. I do not love that child," pointing to a little girl at some distance in front of him, "but I realize that Christ loves them and desires them to be saved, hence my work among them." This seemingly cold sense of duty may answer. If, however, the pagan African once realizes that disinterested love prompts our treatment of him, he is generally most pliable and teachable. Without something of the Divine love work among them must be hard indeed, for there are so many trying things to be met with day by day.

After a time it was discovered that the donkeys might be made use of in kraal visiting. I well remember our first experience at this mode of travel. We had no saddles, so we placed blankets on the backs of the donkeys and fastened them with surcingles of our own manufacture. Sister Heise was an expert rider, while I was quite the reverse. Our first trip was to a kraal about five miles distant, the home of the chief, Hluganisa. Two boys, Matshuba and Sihlaba, accompanied us as guides. All went well on the trip over. We were very kindly received by the people and afforded an opportunity to give them the Gospel. The village was up among the rocks, and as donkeys are expert climbers they had no difficulty in making the ascent, or descent, either, but on the return journey I could not keep my place, and was sent over the donkey's head on to the ground. My companion, when she saw that no harm was done, rather considered the accident as a good joke, and I joined in the laugh at my own expense. The boys failed to see any fun in it, and seemed greatly to resent the laughter.

Some time after this we made another journey of about the same distance in the opposite direction. The reason for this second visit was as follows: Among our pupils was a nice, modest-looking girl about twelve years of age. She belonged to Mapita's family, and seemed to be an affectionate and well-behaved child. She was absent from school for a few days, and on inquiring we learned that she had gone to the home of her intended husband. Greatly shocked, we made further inquiry, and were told that Mapita had sold her to a man who had already one wife, and that he lived about five miles away. It was our first experience with heathen marriage, and we determined to hunt her up and if possible release her. We looked upon this child as a slave or prisoner.

Taking the donkeys and our two boys, we again started out one morning. The path was not familiar, even to our guides. It wound around among the rocks and we were in great danger of being lost. Immense boulders were piled up in all sorts of fantastic shapes, and a white person could easily be lost among the hills and perhaps never find his way out, but the native will always find his way. Once we found ourselves on the top of a nearly perpendicular rock, and dismounting reached the bottom only with great difficulty. The boys inquired the way of a native in his garden, but he regarded us with suspicion and remained silent. Since the close of the rebellion, when the natives hid themselves among these rocks, they have been very suspicious of white people, for fear some one may desire to capture them. It was only after repeated assurances by the boys that we were missionaries, and their friends, that he consented to direct us.

Finally we reached the home of Buka, the man who had taken little Lomanzwana. His kraal was situated up among the rocks in one of nature's fortresses. Here, in this desolate place, in the midst of densest heathendom, was the girl. Her husband was a cripple and very pagan looking. But what could we do amid such rock-bound customs as held these people? Nothing. With hearts lifted to the Lord in prayer we tried to point them to the Lamb of God. The man regarded us with wild-looking eyes, and listened with seemingly dull, uncomprehending ears to our stammering tongues. When he was asked a question, he looked at those about him and wanted to know what sort of an answer the missionary desired; then he would answer accordingly. In another hut was a very old woman, the mother of Buka, who was an imbecile and was fed like an animal. We retraced our steps with heavy hearts, but for many a day the memory of that visit haunted us.

As for the girl, the man did not pay sufficiently promptly to satisfy Mapita, so he finally took her home. Later she was sold to a man who paid a large sum. Here they quarreled and the girl returned home, and the pay had to be given back. It is needless to say that the girl was thoroughly demoralized by this time. She was finally disposed of to another man.

In February, 1899, Matshuba came to stay at the mission and attend school. Ever since the mission had opened he had been a great help to us in acquiring the language, and as he could understand us more readily, he often explained our meaning to others. He knew too just how many Zulu words were in our vocabulary, and in speaking to us he adapted himself to our limited understanding. He also gradually acquired the English. He made rapid progress in school; and as the Light came to him he accepted it. He did not do this all at one bound, but, as it were, according to his capacity to understand the meaning of the Atonement and kindred themes. The day came when he saw himself a great sinner, and he repented in truth. He was the only boy staying at the mission for a time, so that many and various duties fell to his lot. These he performed faithfully, except that he was somewhat careless in herding the donkeys, and lost them.

One evening he came to the door of our hut in great perplexity and said that he would like to have a talk. He came and sat down on the hearthstone, then said, "I prayed this morning, but the donkeys were lost at any rate." By his language he evidently thought that if he prayed the Lord would do the watching. This gave us an opportunity of telling of David, the faithful shepherd boy, and of the "Great Shepherd," who told us to both "watch and pray." The boy then told something of his early life. Among other things he said:

"Father used to tell me to go and watch the gardens so that the animals would not come and take our food. I did not watch well and the animals destroyed the crops and father was grieved."

"Are you sorry now that you did not obey?"

"Oh! yes, indeed," was the reply. "If I might live that time over again, I would be a better boy."

He continued, "When father was sick they said he was bewitched. So they tried to find out who had bewitched him. Once, before he died, he said that he would like to see a missionary. *Umfundisi* [Missionary] Engle should have come sooner, before father died."

"Matshuba, did you ever hear of Jesus before we came?"

"Yes, Missus," he replied, "I heard His Name once, and I wanted my mother to go where there was a missionary; then the Lord sent you."

Here was this dear soul, groping in the night and reaching out for something better than he had known, he knew not what. When the Light comes to him he is ready to accept it. There are many other such boys, and girls too, all over Africa, who are waiting for some one to bring them the Light. Is it you? There are many other old men to whom the message will come too late unless some one makes haste and brings it.

Matshuba had many hard battles to fight, and often have we heard him out among the rocks praying for help and victory. I well remember the first day on which he prayed openly before the school. Almost the hush of death fell upon all, for it was a new era to them. One of their number had learned to pray like the missionaries. There was no hut at first for him to sleep in, so he lay in the tent. One morning he came out, his face all aglow. He said, "I saw Jesus last night. He came and stood before me. He was tall and bright looking."

Some months after he came, another boy, Tebengo, came to stay at the mission. He, too, had been attending school and desired to be a Christian. Bright, impulsive, but easily misled, in his instability he was just the opposite of the more steadfast Matshuba. There were also others of the schoolboys who were stepping out into the light, and among these were Kelenki and Siyaya, who were Mashona people. Their home seemed more heathenish than some of the others, but these boys, with others from their kraal, appeared earnest in the service of the Master.

A Sunday-school was also opened this first year and proved quite interesting to the younger ones. On the first Christmas Day the natives were invited for services and about ninety came—the largest number up to that time. After the services they were invited to a large, unfinished hut, and all were treated to bread and tea and some salt. Father and Mother Engle sat down among them and partook of bread and tea with them. This greatly delighted all, and it was just as much of a pleasure to our elder and wife, who always enjoyed mingling with the people. The rest of us saw that all were served. The people were very thankful for the treat, and all expressed their gratitude in a forcible manner.

CHAPTER SEVEN

Reinforcements, and Progress of the Work

The various departments of the mission were gradually enlarging, and as the work increased the burden fell more and more heavily upon Elder Engle. It will be remembered that efforts were made to secure an assistant for him before we left America, but without success. In April, 1899, however, we gladly welcomed into our midst three new missionaries from America. These were Mr. and Mrs. Clifford Cress and Mr. Isaac Lehman. They were able and consecrated messengers, and a valuable addition to the work. With them came also several large boxes of clothing, cloth for the sewing school, and other goods which had been donated for the mission. About this time also the Board sent out some farm implements, a large Studebaker wagon, a two-seated spring wagon, and a bell for calling the people to services. More donkeys had already been purchased by Elder Engle, so that the question of traveling, and of bringing out supplies from Bulawayo, was most satisfactorily settled.

Shortly after this we also had the pleasure of welcoming Mr. and Mrs. Van Blunk, of the Christian Holiness Association. These had come to make their headquarters near us and engage in evangelistic work. We had now quite a little company of Christian workers—nine in number—and had very inspiring and encouraging English services, as well as those in the native tongue. Although Brother Van Blunks were under a different Board and their work was in a measure separate from the rest, yet they were spiritual and consecrated missionaries and of great assistance in exalting Christ among the people.

On account of the large increase in the number of workers, it was necessary also to enlarge our dwelling place. During this season five new huts were erected, including those for the natives, making the mission premises look like a little village. A building for church services and school was also greatly needed. During the entire rainy season these had been held in the tent, which was proving inadequate for the growing congregation. So Brethren Engle and Lehman, with the assistance of the natives, erected a very respectable looking church building of poles and mud, 16 x 30 feet. It was furnished with plank seats and good tables, and Brother Van Blunk donated glass for windows. Long poles of native timber were then secured and a framework was made for the bell. This being hoisted and fastened in place could be heard at many of the kraals. It also assisted in informing the people of the Sabbath.

At sunset on Saturday evening it was rung a long time to inform the people that the morrow was the Sabbath, and that they should lay aside their work and prepare for rest and service. Later in the work some of us agreed to take that time for secret prayer in behalf of the people, that the Lord might incline their hearts to come to the house of the Lord. After there were a number of native Christians, they too joined us in prayer, each going to his private place. One evening we were greatly impressed to see Mazwi, the boy who was ringing slowly, down on his knees, as if, while he was calling the people to prepare for worship on the morrow, he was also calling upon God to persuade them to come. We were often made to feel too that the Lord especially honored some of those prayers.

The sight of so many people about us being destitute of clothing had greatly touched Brother Engle's heart, and he had written to America about it. The result was a large box of clothing generously donated. He gave each of the headmen and the chief a shirt and a pair of trousers, and told them to come to services. They seemed to be, and no doubt were, very grateful for the favor bestowed, and a very few made good use of the garments. Others came once or twice clothed, and then nothing more was seen of them or their clothing. In less than a year these latter ones came again and asked for clothes, stating that they had nothing to wear to church. It is needless to say that by this time the missionaries had learned their lesson, and those desiring to be clothed had to work for it. A number did come and work for clothing and were well paid, but what they did with the clothing was often a mystery. Shirts they generally liked and appreciated, and sometimes the other garments would be sewed up in a wonderful manner and do duty for a shirt or coat, or they would answer for a grain bag.

Day by day we were learning the nature of the people about us, and were obliged to adjust ourselves to our changed understanding. They are all children and must be dealt with accordingly. The missionary soon finds that he not only needs much of the love that "never faileth," but also a large supply of patience continually in his work. He must also be firm in his dealings with the natives and make them know their place. They will respect him all the more if he does this in the proper spirit. Old children are more difficult to handle than young ones, as they are more unreasonable and more set in their ways. They generally do not feel under any obligations to keep their promises to you, but they fully expect you to keep yours to them, otherwise they will lose confidence in you.

When one first goes to the heathen and sees them in their ignorance and superstition, seemingly lacking everything to make them comfortable, he is led to speak much of Christ and His love, thus seeking to win them. They begin to say within themselves, "Well, if He loves us, He will do us no harm, so we need not trouble ourselves about Him," and they continue, as vigorously as ever, to seek to appease the malevolent spirits, who they think are seeking to harm them. Then the missionary thinks he should pursue another course. He soon becomes somewhat discouraged and disgusted with their indifference and hypocrisy, and is often led to the opposite extreme, and dwells much on hell and condemnation, which tends to harden his hearers. Finally he reaches a golden mean. He realizes that these poor souls about him have had no opportunity of rising above their degrading surroundings, and he must take them as they are, and seek by the ability which God giveth to live the Christ life among them and lift them to a higher plane of living.

Matopo Mission Church in 1899. Built by Elder Jesse Engle.

The Sunday-school had been chiefly for the younger ones, but we concluded to add a class for the older people. This was greatly appreciated by some of them, especially Mapita. It began with few in number; but as time passed it gradually increased in attendance and interest. Mapita seemed so eager to learn in those days, and would often look with longing eyes into the Kingdom, and the very joy of the Lord would seem to be reflected in his face, but he was afraid to step over. He gained a great deal of knowledge of the Scriptures too, and he was not slow to tell other people.

All the services were more or less informal, and any one was free to ask questions; yet in the Sabbath-school class many felt more at home and often expressed themselves freely in regard to the difficulties in the way of their becoming Christians. One day, after we had explained the lesson, Nyuka, a witch doctor, said:

"I believe all you say, and that Christ is able to save us, but what can I do? My hands are tied. I have five wives."

Nothing had been said about a plurality of wives, but intuitively he realized that it was a formidable obstacle in his way. We could only tell him that if he really reached the place where he desired to be saved, the Lord would open the way for him.

As question after question arose in the class, the answer often given would be to open the Bible and read a portion suitable for the question. One day, after this had been done several times, one of the men exclaimed, "It is no use to argue any more; that Book knows everything." The difficulty generally was that, although they believed the Word, they were not willing to take the Way. The darkness seemed too dense, the effort required was too great, the transformation was too absolute for these old people, rocked in the cradle of paganism for generations. It is the younger generation that are chiefly benefited by the mission work. Sometimes some of the others, seeing this, will say, "I am too old; you should have come sooner."

Then again the missionary sometimes meets with a Caleb or a Joshua. He receives some encouragement, from even the old. Allow me to give an account of a visit made at this time:

We are going to visit an old queen. It is not our first visit to her, but we are informed that she is ill at present and her friends are fearful that she might die, as she is very, very old. Sisters Heise, Cress, and myself are going. We carry a little bread, cocoa, and a New Testament. She is living at the kraal of Mapita, our faithful helper. He also has been sick with fever, but he is somewhat better today, and is sitting out of doors by the fire, where his wife and children are preparing their evening meal. This consists of peanut gravy, kafir-corn porridge, and pumpkin. After greeting these, we pass on to the hut where the queen lies. We sit down on the ground, so that we may look into the little opening which serves as doorway. The woman in charge invites us to enter, and we crawl into the hut. In the center of the hut is a fire with four large stones around it; the smoke finding its way into our eyes or out through the straw roof, for there is no chimney and no window. Near this fireplace lies the poor old queen. Her bed consists of a large hide spread on the hard, polished earthen floor, and a block of wood serves for a pillow. A blanket is thrown over her body. We offer the cocoa, which the sick one gratefully accepts, but the bread is refused. We then go to her side and try to point her to the Lamb of God, which taketh away the sin of the world, and tell her of the home prepared for all those who love God. She tries to listen, and sometimes responds to the question asked. Of course our knowledge of the language is still imperfect, and it is more difficult for the old to understand than for the young. When the sick one does not fully comprehend, the nurse, who is Matshuba's mother, explains. Sitting here by this old woman, and seeing her stretch out her thin hands to the warm stones at the fire, we forget that vermin surrounds us or that our clothes might become soiled; our hearts only overflow with a desire to let a flood of light into the soul of the poor one before us. As the talk continues she does seem to grasp some of the spiritual truths, and she gives a more ready assent to the questions asked:

"Do you desire us to pray for you?"

"Oh! yes," she exclaimed with feeling. "I always love to have you pray to Jesus for me."

Kneeling there we offer prayers that the Lord would speak to this dear soul and prepare her to meet Him. Her farewell word and clinging clasp of the hand on our departure cause us to feel that light is breaking, and that she, in her feeble way, is, by faith, taking hold of Christ. Once before, when we visited her, she too offered up her feeble petition.

We emerge from the hut and stop a few minutes to speak with Mapita and his family, and offer up a word of prayer. The sun has already set, so we hastily bid them adieu and start for home, but not before they have sent their respects to Father and Mother Engle.

Thus ends one of the many visits we are called upon to make. But who is this old queen, amid such unqueenly surroundings? She was one of the numerous wives of Mzilikazi, the founder and first king of the Matabele tribe. He had a large number of wives, not fewer than forty or fifty, and this was one of them. The natives here claim that she was his chief wife and the mother of Lobengula, the king. We think that, however, is very doubtful, although the husband of the woman where she stays was one of Lobengula's most trusted men.

Mrs. Cress Giving a Lesson in Cleanliness.

This poor queen in her younger days had no doubt plenty, with slaves to wait upon her and do her bidding. Now, in her old age, she tries to work for a living by cultivating the soil, and growing her own food. If her change of fortune is instrumental in leading her to Christ, she is richer than she knows. She will not have all her good things in life. We have been trying to help her also in temporal affairs.

She arose from this sick bed and afterwards visited us. One day, when we were again speaking of Christ, her face lighted up and she exclaimed, "I am happy because Jesus lives in here," putting her hand on her breast. We feel, as Sister Heise expressed it, "One would look upon her as one of the first fruits of our mission work in Africa."

Although the work among most of the older people thus far appeared to make little progress, if we may judge by their lives, yet a number of the pupils were steadfast. As far as could be ascertained they had accepted Christ as their Savior and were walking out in all the light they had. Since they were eager to follow the Lord in all things it was considered advisable to baptize some. Accordingly, after the little church was completed, they were examined as to their faith. In August, 1899, nine boys and one girl were by Elder Engle led into one of those sparkling streams and dipped three times into the name of the Trinity, and thus put on the Lord by baptism. It was a time of great rejoicing and encouragement to the missionaries when this was done, and they could gather around the table of the Lord, with some dark-skinned brethren, who had so lately come out of pagan darkness. Although these were but babes, yet the missionaries felt that the Lord had set His seal upon the work.

It might seem that we were somewhat hasty in thus so soon receiving into church fellowship. The mission had been opened only a little over a year, and our imperfect knowledge of the language, as well as of the native character, made it scarcely possible for them to be well instructed in the things of the Lord. There was no cause to think, however, that they were not honest and sincere so far as they knew. There was a radical change in their lives, and some were steadfast, but others had not fully counted the cost and soon fell back, if indeed they were really saved. One of the oldest, who was over twenty years of age, stood well until he went to work for a European, who made sport of him, and the boy gradually fell back into his former habits. Great pains were taken to lead them on to know the Lord.

During this year the war known as the Boer War began in South Africa. It was a conflict which seemed inevitable between the wealthy English mine owners and their Dutch rulers. We are perhaps safe in saying that heavy taxation without sufficient representation was the chief cause of the war. The first event of importance in connection with it was the siege of Kimberley, the great diamond field, and the headquarters of Mr. Rhodes at the time. This occurred October 14. The war then spread through other parts of South Africa and to the border of Rhodesia, but did not extend into it. English troops were, however, stationed there to repel an invasion should one be attempted.

The war did not directly affect us, but indirectly it did. By the siege of Kimberley, and later that of Mafeking, and the destruction of the railroad our line of supplies from Cape Town was cut off, consequently prices in Rhodesia rose very rapidly. Sugar was soon two shillings (48c) per pound, flour about three guineas ($15) per one hundred pounds, and other groceries in proportion. With little money on hand, and the prospects of receiving more under such conditions uncertain, famine might have stared us in the face. There was no need to be uneasy, however; the Lord and the forethought of Father and Mother Engle prepared us for such an emergency. Shortly before this the Charter Company had placed some cattle on the mission farm, and we had the use of milk. Butter, eggs, and vegetables for a time brought a very high price in Bulawayo market, and with all these the mission was supplied. The little spring wagon, drawn by four donkeys, went to Bulawayo nearly every week for a time, taking in produce which brought a high price, and we were in turn able to pay a high price for groceries and food for the table; so that, during the darkest days of the war, all our needs were supplied.

Occasionally disquieting rumors would reach us that the Boers were about to force their way through and come into Rhodesia. The natives themselves were not a little interested in the outcome of the war. They had no newspapers or system of telegraphy like the white people, but they had a means of gaining news which to them was much more effective. This was by means of communication among themselves. How they so quickly secured news of the various engagements in the south and the result of each engagement was a mystery. We on our part, situated among them as we were, and conscious that there were many who were still seething under British rule, could not avoid wondering what might be the outcome were the British defeated. On the other hand, many of the natives seemed to prefer British rule to that of the Dutch. They chose to remain as they were rather than change masters.

CHAPTER EIGHT

Extension of the Work Followed by Dark Days

Verily, verily, I say unto you, Except a corn of wheat fall into the ground and die, it abideth alone; but if it die, it bringeth forth much fruit.—St. John 12: 24.

Matopo Mission was only one little light in the surrounding darkness, and it was hoped that other stations might be opened in time. So after Brother and Sister Cress came, or as soon as they had some little knowledge of the language and of the work, they desired to open another station. After looking the country over, they felt led to a place up among the hills near the kraal of Buka, of whom mention was made earlier in these pages. There were a number of kraals in the immediate vicinity, and the location seemed a good one, except that it was somewhat near Matopo Mission. They decided to move out in November, and at that time they, together with the tent and supplies, were taken to their new station. Unfortunately a heavy rain came on while they were on the way and the ground was thoroughly soaked before they had an opportunity to pitch their tent. They concluded, however, to remain at their place and build. It was named Entabeni Mission.

The building progressed satisfactorily, and they held services on each Sunday for about two months or a little over. They felt encouraged in their work and the natives interested. At the Christmas holidays they came to spend the time with us, and we had a very enjoyable time with the natives. The third week in January, 1900, a messenger arrived to inform us that Sister Cress had been stricken with fever. A conveyance was immediately sent to the place to bring her to Matopo Mission, and by the time that reached their mission Brother Cress also was sick. Both were brought to the mission and made as comfortable as possible. At first no one considered their illness serious, for our party had thus far been enjoying good health since the work opened. Other complications set in in connection with Sister Cress' illness, and she gradually grew worse. For twenty-four hours she lay unconscious and then rallied and seemed quite bright. We were all present—Engles, Van Blunks, Sister Heise, Brother Lehman, and myself—when she rallied. She requested that prayer be offered for her recovery. This was done and we felt that she would gain strength, but it was not to be. In half an hour that sweet young life passed to be with God. This was February 8, 1900. All through her sickness she felt perfectly resigned to the Lord's will, whether for life or death.

We felt that we could not spare this saintly woman, so well fitted both by nature and by grace to shine for God. She had laid her all upon the altar for Africa, and often expressed herself that she wanted to spend her life in behalf of this people. She had been in Africa only nine and one-half months, yet she had entered heart and soul into the work of the Lord, and was rapidly acquiring the language, so that she could converse with the people. She had formed some of the women into a sewing class, uniting this work with religious instructions, and endearing herself to all with whom she came into contact. She loved the people and was willing and ready to undertake any kind of work that came to her. She was especially gifted in prayer, and it was always an inspiration to the rest of us to listen to her heartfelt petition. Why the Lord thus early in her missionary career took her to Himself, we know not; but when the things of earth shall be revealed, when we shall know as we are known, then all will be clear.

Brethren Engle and Lehman made a coffin; we covered it within with white muslin and without with black cloth, and thus laid the body away. Mr. Eyles, of Bulawayo, was interested in the mission and occasionally visited us and spoke to the natives, since he had good command of the Zulu language. On this occasion he consented to come out and preach the funeral sermon. The chief men of the people carried her to her last resting place beneath the Umkuni tree, and they mingled their tears with ours. The occasion was made more sad by the fact that the husband was still ill and unable to view the corpse or attend the funeral.

During the sickness of these two people we greatly appreciated the presence and help of Brother and Sister Van Blunk, who still lived near the mission. Both were very kind in assisting to care for the sick and also in the last sad rites. Shortly afterwards they moved to Bulawayo and made that the headquarters of their evangelistic work.

Elder Engle and Donkey Team at Matopo Mission.

Brother Cress recovered from his illness, but concluded that it was best for him to return to America, and wrote the Board accordingly. He felt his loss keenly. The work in general resumed its normal condition until the last week in March, when our bishop and overseer, Elder Engle, became sick. He had been very busy with the work, and in his frequent trips to Bulawayo, sometimes in the rain, he may have exposed himself. His condition did not seem serious, and he was not obliged to keep his bed continually. On April 2 he walked to a garden near by, and when he returned he again lay down. He ate heartily of the dinner prepared for him, after which his wife came to the dining-room and ate with us. At the close of our 3 P. M. dinner she went to her room, but returned at once and asked me to fill the hot water bottle and come over. I did so and found Brother Engle having a heavy chill and speaking the Zulu language rapidly, seemingly unconscious of our presence. We endeavored in every way to help him, but soon found that he was rapidly becoming paralyzed. Sister Heise and Brother Lehman were called and a consultation held. It was decided to send a messenger to the fort, ten miles away, and from there telephone to Bulawayo for a doctor. Brother Cress had left that day to go as far as the fort on his way to Bulawayo, and he was also to be informed.

All night we watched by the Elder's bedside, but there was nothing that could be done. Brother Cress arrived near noon the next day, but the doctor did not arrive in time. That was a dark time as he lay paralyzed and unconscious in the little mud hut he called home, far from his children, far from the comforts of civilization, with none of his family or relatives, save his devoted wife, by his side. As it became evident that the end was near, that heroic mother, who had been such a worthy companion in all his labors, stooped over and imprinted on his face a kiss for each of their seven sons in far-away America. At 5 P. M., April 3, he breathed his last. Thus, in less than two months from the date of Sister Cress' death, Elder Engle also was called home. The loss of our sister was great, but this seemed to be a still greater blow on the mission.

He was so absorbed in the work, and no sacrifice was too great, no labor too hard, for him to endure. Perhaps, if he had spared himself a little more, he might have been able to continue longer in the work. Who knows? The language was difficult for one at his age, yet he was making heroic efforts to acquire it, and could make himself pretty well understood. We have seen him, after reading the Word, stand before the people, with the tears running down his face in his great love for them and in his desire to help them to Christ. And the natives knew that he loved them and they in turn loved him and greatly lamented his departure. The language of many of them might be summed up in that of one woman. As she stood by his coffin, weeping, she said:

"He was good to me. He gave me salt, he gave me calico. What shall we do without him?"

It seemed that his life work was finished. He had had the desire of his heart, in that he had been permitted to reach Africa and see a work started in the wilds. He had been privileged to see something of the travail of soul by beholding some step into the Kingdom. Now he had gone to hear the welcome message, "Well done, good and faithful servant ... enter thou into the joy of thy Lord."

This time it was Brethren Cress and Lehman who made the coffin. There was no lumber on hand, but they removed some from the hut doors for the purpose. Again we covered it to contain the form of our elder. Mr. Eyles could not meet with us at this time, and the Van Blunks were away; but two of the officials from Fort Usher were present, and a number of natives, not so many, however, as at the previous time. No doubt they were becoming suspicious of this oft-repeated death. The white men present, together with some of the natives, carried the body to its last resting place beside Sister Cress. Brother Cress spoke in English to the white people present, while the natives were addressed by the writer from 2 Tim. 4: 7-8.

The devoted wife had been wonderfully sustained by a Higher Power through all this sad scene. She had been called here, far from her home and family, to lay away her husband, but she realized that she was not alone. When, however, the funeral was over, the effects of the shock and of the strain through which she had been passing were manifest. She too took her bed with the dread African fever.

MATOPO CEMETERY. Elder Jesse Engle. Mrs. Cress. Mrs. E. Doner. Elder Jacob Engle at his father's grave and Elder John Sheets.

The Seventh Day Adventist missionaries, who had been so kind to us when we first came to Bulawayo, sent letters of condolence as soon as they heard of our bereavement, and offered the services of their physician, should we need him. In this emergency we sent for him to come and see Mother Engle. He rode the fifty miles on horseback to come to minister to her and to give us instructions as to how to treat the disease. This was something which we greatly needed and appreciated, and it has been of great service to us in later years. He would accept no compensation for his long and tiresome journey. Such are the big hearts one finds in the interior of Africa. They are enlarged to take in more of the Spirit of the Master. All was done that could possibly be done for Mother Engle, so that she might gain her health sufficiently to return to America with Brother Cress. She continued to have relapses of the fever for three months, and it was not until July 19 that she was able to make the journey.

Brother Cress' stay of sixteen months in Africa had brought great loss to him, but the Lord had sustained him. We were sorry to lose him as well as Mother Engle in the work. She never felt called of herself to go as a missionary, but only to be with her husband. When he was led of the Lord to go forth, she most cheerfully bade farewell to her family and all that was dear to a mother's heart and went with her husband, neither of them knowing whether they would be permitted to see their family again. She was not merely a companion to him, but a most devoted helpmate, not only in all that can possibly mean in civilized lands; but larger still, in the heartaches, the weariness, the loneliness, and the discouragements that come to a missionary.

How often the names of their loved ones would be spoken by these two! How they would linger over the letters that came, and yet never a word of complaining or regret that they had left all for this. When Elder Engle died we felt that we had lost a father; so, when she left for America, we realized that the mother and homemaker was gone.

Before their departure a most important event transpired. I refer to the marriage, on May 1, of Mr. Isaac Lehman and Miss Alice Heise, by Rev. Van Blunk. This was to have taken place earlier, but was delayed by the sorrowful events through which we were passing. Even the day of the wedding was saddened by a most serious relapse of Mother Engle, and we felt quite anxious on her account. This was the first opportunity for the natives to see something of a Christian wedding, and we believe they were impressed with the difference between a Christian and a pagan marriage. Brother Lehman was a consecrated young man and had from the first taken hold of the work along all lines with zeal and readiness. He had also made rapid strides in the language. Sister Heise, too, ever since the opening of the mission, had been a most able and efficient worker, so that both were well equipped to do effectual service for the Master.

All of us accompanied Mother Engle and Brother Cress to Bulawayo, where they rested for a day and then took the train for Cape Town, while we returned to continue the work. For a time nine white workers had been at Matopo Mission, and in less than six months the number had been reduced to three. Those left, however, were not discouraged. May 23 of the same year one of them wrote to the *Evangelical Visitor*:

> "He that keepeth thee will not slumber." This is the Father's promise to all His dear children, not only to you who are sheltered in Christian homes, but also to us who are in the wilds of Africa. We have just as much faith in the promise today as when to outward appearances everything was more secure. Your hearts with ours have no doubt been torn by the sad messages which have crossed the waters during the few months just past, and some one may be even tempted to doubt whether it was the Lord's will for us to come to Africa. Beloved, does England doubt the outcome of the deadly conflict raging in South Africa because she has already lost thousands of men? Is her courage failing? No; far from it. Money and men are continually pouring into the country and soon the independence of two states will be a thing of the past. Shall we as Christian soldiers have less faith in the King of kings? Shall we give up the conflict because two have fallen by our side? No; not if all men forsake us, for with God we still have a majority. While our hearts feel bereft by the departure of our beloved colaborers, we still have

confidence in our Great Captain, and we know that He never lost a battle.

CHAPTER NINE

The Battle Is not Yours, but God's

Wherefore take unto you the whole armour of God, that ye may be able to withstand in the evil day, and having done all, to stand.—Eph. 6: 13.

The missionary going among the heathen must realize that he is about to engage in a warfare, and that the conflict will be fierce and long. He is assailing the great enemy of souls in his stronghold. The fight is on continually and one must keep armed for battle. More important yet than this the missionary should remember that he is under orders and that the work is not his but the Lord's.

The loss of our fellow-soldiers was most keenly felt, and there were some severe tests to face. The work had become disorganized by the continued illness and the deaths, when all our energies had been needed in caring for those about us. Encouraging letters, however, came from the homeland and the Mission Board, so that we realized that prayers were being offered in our behalf and in behalf of the work. We also expected that reinforcements would be forthcoming in the Lord's own time. So, under the leadership of our Great Captain, the army was again set in array and the conflict continued.

We were pleased to note that the people stood by us nobly in this extremity, even though Satan had put forth every effort to defeat the work. Some who had started to follow the Lord saw that they had become indifferent and renewed their covenant. There were four boys who were staying at the mission at this time, and they came one evening and said they would like to have a talk. This was not so strange, as we often had little confidential chats with them. On this particular evening they came in and sat down. Then, without any preliminary remarks, Matshuba arose and made a complete confession of his past life. He then sat down and Kelenki arose and began to do the same. I said,

"Boys, if you desire we will call Brother and Sister Lehman, that they may hear likewise."

They replied, "Yes, Miss, do so, for we desire to confess everything and have all wiped away, and we do not want to repeat our wrongdoings, for we want to be ready when Jesus comes."

So one of them called the Lehmans, and beginning again they arose, one by one, and told of their past life. When each one had finished he would turn around and inquire of the rest if he had told everything. Three of them were baptized members, and they evidently had been having a meeting in their hut and became concerned about their condition. They had not been guilty of any new sins, but were in doubt as to their standing before God, and wanted pardon and cleansing. They had taken 1 John 1: 9 very literally. When the confessions were finished we all knelt in prayer; and after we had prayed, they too most earnestly besought the Lord that they might be set completely free from their past life. When they arose to their feet their faces were shining and they said "God had heard and answered."

Then, as they sat there, they told of their old lives and of the lives of the people about us, until we felt that we were just beginning to know the people among whom we were situated. Conditions which, up to that time, they had been timid of telling, for fear of their people, they now boldly and fearlessly exposed, and they seemed to be done once and forever with their heathen past. Our hearts went up in gratitude to the Father, and our eyes were opened more and more to see the real need of this people and the obstacles in their way of becoming Christians.

People reared in Christian homes, with an entire Bible which they can read from childhood, with the privileges of church and Sunday-school, with good literature and hymns and many other advantages which might be mentioned, cannot possibly, by any stretch of imagination, put themselves in the place of those who are deprived of all these; and not only that, but who, from infancy, have been in an atmosphere of ignorance and superstition, reeking with influences the most foul and loathsome imaginable. Then, too, is it to be wondered at that when people, who have been brought up amid surroundings the most helpful possible, spiritually, and the most conducive to growth in grace, grow lean in soul and backslide—I say is it to be wondered at that the Christians in heathen lands, in their desperate struggle against such adverse and degrading surroundings, sometimes relapse into heathendom? Not only is it not to be wondered at, but it is positively surprising and a great cause for rejoicing among missionaries, that so many grasping hold of the Everlasting Arm do once and forever shake off the bog and filth of the bottomless pit and stand as monuments of His power to save to the uttermost.

During the dry season of 1900 an aggressive campaign against Satan and his followers among the rocks and strongholds was begun, for we felt that the Lord would have us press the battle to the gates. During the rainy seasons, when people are busy in their gardens, and when there is a great deal of sickness, both school and evangelistic work suffer, so that it is necessary to make the best use of the dry season. As soon as the crops were gathered the school at the mission increased in numbers and interest, and Brother and

Sister Lehman opened a school at the village of Chief Hluganisa. They rode back and forth day by day, and when they were unable to go two of the boys were sent to teach. The attendance and interest there were encouraging.

What of this chief, who had so kindly received the missionaries two years before? It would be a pleasure to be able to report that he had opened his heart to accept Christ as his Savior, but such was not the case. He was very ready to receive the gifts of the white man, whether from officials, missionaries, or any one else. He was also quite willing that the school should be started in his village; for would not this make his people wiser and more able to secure the good things of the earth? But the white man's religion, he would none of it for himself. He was a most troublesome beggar from first to last. Elder Engle, had made him a present of a very good blanket, with which he was greatly pleased, but he seldom came to services. When he came to the mission it was always with the expectation of asking and receiving something.

One day he came to pay us sort of a state visit, and a little later his three wives followed in order of their rank. We were desirous of treating them all kindly after their long walk to pay us this visit, so Mother Engle concluded to give them bread and tea. A plate of bread, together with a quantity of tea and sugar, was placed before them. We expected, of course, that all would receive some. The chief appropriated everything; emptied all the sugar into the tea, drank all, and ate all the bread. When they started home the wives went first, the lowest in rank preceding, to prepare everything for their lord and master, who followed at his leisure. One day one of the missionaries, tried by his cupidity and avarice, gave him a straight talk. He did not return for some months after this, not until the funeral of Sister Cress. Until this day he continues to be a rank heathen, greedy, and superstitious, and a lover of wives and beer.

All three of us by this time were fairly well prepared in the language, and some of the boys were beginning to be helpful in evangelistic work. Early in the season the Lehmans, with one of the men as guide, made a tour to the southeast of us in a section not yet visited. They reported an interesting and profitable trip and met the people from six different kraals. As it was a section of raw heathendom, they were surprised to find, at one of the kraals, a woman who joined heartily in the hymn sung and was familiar with the words. On inquiry they found that when a girl she had lived at the house of Rev. Thomas, one of the first missionaries of Matabeleland. He had a station at some distance north of Bulawayo, and his memory is much revered by those natives who knew him. The brother and sister had the fortune, or misfortune, to be present at a beer drink. This is their way of getting a lot of work done: They make a quantity of beer; then call in their neighbors to help work, paying them with beer. It is surprising how much beer they can consume at such times. They often become quite boisterous and even intoxicated, and frequently quarrel and fight as a result of their debauch. On this occasion the men were friendly, but scarcely in a condition to receive the Gospel. The travelers returned tired, but rejoicing in the Lord because of another opportunity of sowing seed.

The life of a missionary is not full of exciting adventures and encouraging incidents. It is very ordinary at times and very crushing at others. The ups and downs would soon wear him out did he not take fast hold of God and, looking up by faith, keep saying to Him, "Lord, this is Thy work. Do Thou bear the burdens, the joys, and the sorrows that keep crowding thick and fast upon me, and let me be only Thy instrument and Thy weapon of warfare." I remember, during the first year, I at times felt I was not burdened enough for the souls about me, and once spent long hours of prayer, asking that the burden might rest more heavily. I retired to rest. The next day the Lord answered the prayer of His messenger. I thought it would crush me to the earth, but the lesson had been learned. He knows how much we can bear, and we should always say, "As Thou wilt."

In our visits among the people one day is much like another, but they must be made in order to keep in touch with them. August 17 I wrote as follows:

"One more day's work for Jesus,
   One less of life for me,
But heaven is nearer and Christ is dearer,
   Than yesterday to me.
His life and light fill all my soul tonight."

This being Saturday, I arose early to go out among the people. After taking some food, I started a little after sunrise with Sihlaba as guide. We went to visit the kraal of Siponka, about two miles distant. These people have been on my mind for some time. They are good-hearted but veritable heathen, and care only for the good things of this life. They are entirely too indifferent to come either to school or church, although two, who were members, live here. The downward influence is too strong for even them, and seemingly they have done according to the proverb.

Early as it was in the morning, the people were nearly all away, but we found at home two men, some women, and boys and girls. There was an opportunity for giving the Gospel to them, and the Lord greatly helped in the presentation of His Word. They gradually became interested and seemed at least to have greater light. May the Lord send home the truth into their hearts!

   Siyaya (one of the backslidden boys) went along with us to the home of

Amuzeze (another member). Here there were a number of women, one man, and some young people. They were more willing than usual to listen, also more able to understand, and Amuzeze took part in prayer.

From there Siyaya also went along to Umvunzi's home. Poor boy! he followed us around, seemingly hungry for the Word, but helplessly overcome by the gross darkness surrounding him. At this last place there were only a few present. The men from all these kraals had gone a long distance to buy goats. Here the powers of darkness were so great that I could not shake off the feeling and have victory in speaking. I wonder what my spiritual status would be at the end of the year, if I were obliged to live long amid such surroundings; and yet I have Christ and His Spirit in my soul and much of His Word written in my heart, while these poor ones have only generations of paganism back of them.

We then turned our faces homeward, moving in something of a circle and coming first to Seba's village. This is not far from the mission, and yet it is our first visit to this place. The people seemed very glad to see us, and some here had the privilege for the first time of hearing the Gospel, and were eager to catch every word. While we were speaking, a native, carrying poles, was passing, and he put his poles down and entered to listen. He was a stranger to me. A tall fine-looking fellow he was. He informed us that he had moved near and was building a hut. Mapita and his wife also had entered during the services. Seba invited us to remain for dinner and eat of their *inkobe* (boiled corn), but it was not yet ready, so thanking him for his hospitality we continued our journey.

First, the stranger invited us to go over and see his wife and the hut he was building, which was only a short distance away. We did so and here we met two women from our nearest kraal. We then proceeded on our homeward way, and had gone only a short distance when we met John (a Christian) and his brothers, who followed us home.

On the way we stopped a few minutes at Mapita's home to see the children, and then reached the mission at midday. The boys remained a short time to talk. I then tidied my hut, made a dress and gave it to a little girl, and entertained a number of native women. After our three o'clock dinner and worship I read and studied the language, and here it is evening and the close of a very enjoyable day.

This account has been given, not because there was anything unusual about it, but because it is typical of many Saturdays on the mission field, and some of them have been days of the most exquisite enjoyment we have ever known. Such days never seem to become monotonous. One forgets the long and tiresome walk if he finds eager and interested listeners at the end. Even if some steel their hearts against the Word, there is still the consciousness to the messenger that he has done what he could. Then again much of one's time on the mission station is spent talking to the natives who come. They may not be anxious for the Gospel, but one always hopes some word or message may sink into their hearts.

The first few years of the mission, the country was occasionally visited by locusts, sometimes in such large swarms as almost to darken the face of the sky. These were not the seventeen-year cicadas, which some people are pleased to term locusts, but large grasshoppers, various kinds of which made their appearance to the great destruction of crops and vegetation. Sometimes the corn and the kafir corn would be stripped. Again, an immense swarm would come suddenly and alight—so that in a very short time the whole face of nature would be transformed from a bright green to a reddish brown, the color of the locusts—and would then as suddenly fly off without doing much harm. Wherever the locusts settled for the night, the natives would be there early in the morning with their nets and catch them for food.

The year 1900 was especially one of these locust years. During the dry season, the adult locusts selected suitable places, remained to feed for a time, then deposited their eggs in the earth and died. As at this time the insects cannot fly, the natives catch them in large numbers and carry them home for food. One such swarm settled about two miles from the mission, and thither day after day went the women and girls to catch them. They would put them in bags or large baskets and carry them home. One could often see ten or twelve women walking through our premises, each one carrying on her head a bushel or more of locusts. They would cook them in large earthen pots, then spread them on the rocks to dry, after which they would go for a fresh supply. When the locusts were dry they would be stored away for food. In eating them the natives would remove head, wings, and legs and eat them somewhat after the manner of dried herring, and considered them a great delicacy, saying, "They are our meat." We have partaken of them in this manner and found them not unpalatable, and they are certainly a cleaner food than many things eaten in civilized lands. The natives' favorite way of preparing the locusts, however, was to stamp them in a stamping block, then cook them, together with ground peanuts, into a gravy to be eaten with their porridge.

Although many of the locusts had been safely stowed away in the native storehouses, during this year, yet numbers remained in various parts of the country to lay their eggs in the ground. When the rains came and softened the ground these eggs hatched. After a colony hatched, the little wingless larvæ, or hoppers, started forth as an army, all going in one direction. These armies were generally about a rod or two in width and much greater in length, and woe to the young garden that came in their way! They would spread over it, devour the tender shoots, and then proceed in the same general direction in which they had been traveling. The natural grass and herbage of the country was too tough for them to eat. Not only one but several such armies coming from different directions passed through our gardens that season, and some of the cornfields had to be planted two or three times. One was finally left unplanted, while our potatoes and many of the garden vegetables were destroyed. At first we endeavored to fight them with fires when they were seen to be approaching a garden, but this was soon found to be useless. The missionaries felt the loss of their crops and vegetables, but their loss could not be compared with that of the poor natives, many of whom could not procure grain for a second planting, and they had nothing else to depend upon.

During this year we were seriously contemplating an advanced step in the work, by opening the way for more boys and girls to come as boarders. They would thus be given a Christian home and be trained to work and to habits of cleanliness. Up to this time the largest number staying at one time was four boys; and one girl had come lately. The day was not far distant when it would be necessary to erect better and more permanent dwellings, as the huts were already showing signs of decay; and if more boys could be received and these trained to make brick and assist in building, it would be an advantage both to the boys and to the mission. As the year drew near to a close there began to be a desire on the part of some of the older boys to attend school and perhaps come to stay with us. We knew enough of the native character to believe that it was best not to throw out any special inducement, as it is always best for them to desire a thing for themselves and to be fully persuaded in their own minds so that they might not be wavering.

On New Year's Day, 1901, after the close of the services, a boy, probably nineteen years of age, stood at the open door of my hut with rather a wistful look on his face. He was well dressed and had been working for white people, but had shown no interest in school or in the Gospel up to this time. Something in his face that day prompted me to say,

"Ndhlalambi, when are you coming to stay at the mission and give your heart to the Lord?"

He promptly replied, "I am coming one week from tomorrow."

Afterwards, in giving his experience, he said, "While I was working at the mines I became convicted of my wrongdoing and made up my mind that I would come to the missionaries and go to school and give my heart to Jesus. When I came I was afraid to ask and the Lord told Miss to ask me."

He did come and did yield his heart to the Lord, and seemed to settle it in his mind, if one may judge by subsequent actions. "I care not what course others may take, but as for me I will serve the Lord." He made a good confession and was always ready to step out into the light as it shone on his pathway. His way, however, was not an easy one. He met with violent opposition at times from an irascible pagan father, and persecution in various ways, but he stood firm. A special test came to him a year or two after he started to school. One day he came in great distress and said,

"Father is very angry with me. My mother's brother died and left me a lot of cattle and other property, and my parents wish me to go and claim the property. But if I go, they will have a big dance and claim to call back the spirit of my uncle and ask him his will about the property, and they will want me to take part in their worship. I desire to follow the Lord."

I said, "If you do not go perhaps you will not receive the property."

"That makes no difference," he replied. "I love the Lord more than I love the cattle. Only pray that father will not be angry with me for refusing to go."

Later he came with his face all aglow and said, "The Lord has heard our prayers. Father is not angry with me any more."

In school he was slow but persevering, and in work likewise. He had his faults, and seemed at times to be lacking in humility, yet he never seemed to waver in his determination to follow the Lord.

Several other young men also applied for admission, among whom was Gomo, a brother of Tebengo and Muza and Emyonleni; also two younger boys who were already Christians, Masikwa and Madhliwa. There were now nine boys, and several months afterward three girls came. These girls were trained by Sister Lehman to do housework. The work was looking quite encouraging, for all showed an interest in desiring to become Christians.

As this rainy season came on, it could not fail to remind us of the loss and of the trying times of the previous year. Some of our number thought it best to go to a more healthy place until the rains were over. This, however, would almost necessitate closing the work, which was not to be thought of.

In the midst of the rains, in March, Sister Lehman took down with the fever one day and on the following day her husband was also laid low. The buildings at Matopo are in a healthy place, yet during the rainy season one is always more or less exposed to fever, either by traveling and sleeping out, or even by going down to the gardens in the valley in the evening. At that time we did not understand so well how to check or combat the fever as in later years. So the sick ones grew worse and required my constant attention day and night for about ten or more days. Fortunately the boys were good helpers, as there were no girls at the time. Matshuba was able to take charge of the school; Ndhlalambi and one of the little boys could help me in the kitchen and sickroom; Gomo did the washing outside of the window where I could see and direct; and the other boys attended to the gardens.

As the sick ones grew worse we sent a boy for a doctor, but on account of the damp, rainy weather, he delayed several days before coming, so that the fever was broken by the time he reached the mission. It was a trying time and one of looking to the Lord on the part of the sick and the well ones. To make matters worse some of the boys became quite ill, and we were unable to give them the attention they needed. One day Kelenki, who was very low, managed to crawl to the kitchen and begged to be allowed to lie there by the stove. Mrs. Eyles kindly came out from Bulawayo when at last the doctor was able to reach us. She remained for a week during their convalescence and cared for the sick. This gave me a much-needed rest and an opportunity to turn my attention to the boy, who was still quite ill and needed help. It was a day of rejoicing when our brother and sister and all were restored to health, and we were thankful that the Lord had mercy upon us, lest we should have sorrow upon sorrow.

During the time we were passing through these afflictions, another difficulty was staring us in the face, which threatened, if possible, to be more serious than any which we had yet been called upon to meet. This was the land question. Mention was made that we were looking toward the erection of more permanent buildings. We had sent to the Board for money for this purpose; also for money to survey the land. Up to this time the 3,000 acres upon which the mission had been located by the government, had not been surveyed. It had been given only as a reservation for mission purpose, and permission had also been granted that the missionaries could stake off a plot of 3,000 acres and make a diagram without going to the expense of employing a government surveyor, as that kind of work is costly in Africa. For this purpose, the year previous, four of us, Brethren Engle and Cress, together with Sister Heise and myself, started out to stake out the land, supposing, as we had been informed by the official who located the mission, that the two beacons north of us were the limit of the surveyed territory. We climbed hills, went over precipices, and waded swamps under a hot August sun and made a diagram of the desired farm, only to find at the close that the result was not satisfactory to the government. It was necessary for a government survey to be made, and this had not been done; but we had sent for money for the purpose, and the money had just arrived.

The day on which Sister Lehman took sick, two Europeans brought some cattle and put them in our pen, from which the company's cattle had been removed the previous year. They did not ask for permission to place these cattle on the mission farm, and to us it seemed rather a bold step. They informed us, however, that they thought a mistake had been made in locating the mission, and that we were on surveyed land. They stated that they were not certain in reference to the matter, as the owners did not know the exact boundary of their farm.

The Charter Company, of Rhodesia had, especially at the close of the war, made large concessions of land to companies, syndicates, and individuals. These grants often comprised many thousands of acres, and in many instances the owners, in the early days, did not know the location of their land. They simply sent out a surveyor to measure and stake off the requisite amount and erect beacons; then the land was left entirely unimproved. If they were fortunate enough afterwards to know the boundaries of the farms, they often sent out an agent to collect tax of the natives living on it. The best of the land being disposed of, very little remained for farmers, who would have improved the land, or for missionaries, who would both improve it and instruct the natives. No doubt the government, when too late, realized their lack of wisdom in making some of these grants, as it greatly retarded the work of building up and developing the country.

This was the condition of affairs when Matopo Mission was located. We had, however, no intimation that a mistake might have been made in the location, until informed by the two Europeans previously mentioned. One of them desired to collect hut tax for the company owning the land, but this he could not do, as he was not certain of the boundaries, and the company, at the time, was not willing to bear the expense of having a surveyor come out to locate the land. It is needless to say that it was a dark and trying time for the missionaries. If we were on surveyed land, we might have to change the mission site and much of the work already accomplished would be lost. Again, how were we to find out where we were? If a wealthy company did not care to bear the expense of locating their land, how much less able were missionaries, whose purses, at the best, are never too full! Should we go to the expense of sending for a surveyor to locate us, we might be forced to move the mission, and the outlay incurred would benefit the company alone. We were in these wilds; could we succeed in locating ourselves?

As usual, when difficulties thus confronted us, we looked to Him who never fails. Any one in the mission field has often reasons to be thankful for the varied training and experiences of the home land; for no knowledge or previous experience of whatever sort comes amiss when he is out where there is little outside help. We had studied, hence had a little knowledge of surveying. Would that knowledge help us here in these fastnesses?

Mr. Jackson, the magistrate at Fort Usher, who had always been a friend in need, was appealed to. He did not know the boundaries of the farms in the immediate vicinity, but he knew the location of one important beacon several miles north, for he had had occasion to settle a difficulty in reference to it some time previous. So, with this knowledge to begin with, we went to the government surveyor and secured a diagram of all the farms in the vicinity of the mission. Thus equipped, and securing a compass, we started for home. Brother Lehman made a temporary chain, and together with some of the boys we went to the beacon pointed out by Mr. Jackson. From this a survey was made south, and it was discovered that the mission was on a tract of land known as "Matopo Block," owned by the Bulawayo Syndicate. This was a farm of 25,000 acres, and it was about twelve miles long. As there were no beacons for a distance of seven miles on the south of the mission, it was not difficult to understand how the mistake was made in the location. By further survey we discovered that we were on the extreme east end of this farm, and a line drawn nearly southeast from the beacon north of us would give the mission the required 3,000 acres. Another surveyed farm lay adjoining this on the east.

We had located the mission, but it remained to induce the government to arrange with the syndicate and give them land elsewhere in exchange for the amount promised to the mission. It is needless to enter into the details of the slow process necessary for settling the difficulty, for any one dealing with the affairs of government knows something of the tediousness and red tape required. Letters were addressed to both the government and to Mr. Rhodes, who was then on his estate near Bulawayo. The government officials met the question in a spirit of conciliation and fairness, promising to do all in their power to bring it to a satisfactory settlement. We were asked later to make further survey, to be certain that we had given the correct location. At one time it appeared that the exchange could not be made, and we were requested to look up another location. Looking to the Lord, we made another appeal, which resulted, in September of the same year, in the mission being allowed to retain its location. At first this was to have been only a reservation, but the final papers, which were not made out until late in 1902, resulted in giving a ninety-nine-year lease, which was much more satisfactory.

CHAPTER TEN

Reinforcements and Industrial Work

It is not the mere preacher that is wanted here. The bishops of Great Britain, collected with all the classic youth of Oxford and Cambridge, would effect nothing by mere talking with the intelligent people of Uganda. It is the practical Christian tutor, who can teach people how to become Christians, cure their diseases, construct dwellings, understand and exemplify agriculture, turn his hand to anything, like a sailor—this is the man who is wanted. Such an one, if he can be found, would become the savior of Africa.—Henry M. Stanley.

During the progress of the land question and the negotiations with the government, important changes were taking place in the personæ of the mission. In June of 1901 we were pleased to receive much-needed reinforcements in the persons of Mr. Levi Doner and Miss Emma Long. Accompanying them were Mr. and Mrs. Jacob Lehman, who were on their way to engage in mission work at the Compounds in Johannesburg. On account of the war they were not yet permitted to enter Johannesburg, so they came to Matopo for a time.

At the same time Brother Isaac Lehman and wife thought it best to go to Cape Town for a rest, as she had not fully recovered from her attack of the fever. We were very sorry to lose so valuable colaborers at this time, for they had the language and experience in mission work, and it always requires time for new missionaries to take hold of the various duties. I especially felt the loss of Brother Lehman, as I was the only one left who could speak to the natives. Brother Doner, however, made rapid strides in the language, and soon acquired a working knowledge of it, and was also a willing and efficient messenger along all lines. Very early in the work he was laid low with fever, but he recovered. Then Sister Long was quite sick for a time. These experiences, coming so early in their missionary career, were somewhat discouraging.

The mission family was steadily increasing. A number of other boys had come to stay at the mission and become pupils and industrial workers. From the very first in receiving boys at the mission station, it was our plan to have them in school three and one-half hours and the rest of the time, which was five or six hours, they were engaged in some industrial work. As the natural inclination of the native is toward laziness and filthiness in personal habits, we were opening the door and taking all who desired to come and giving them a home, our aim being to take them out of their degraded home surroundings and give them the threefold training, spiritual, intellectual, and industrial, all of which seemed necessary to help them become strong, established Christians.

These natives, for sanitary and other reasons, are always given their own separate huts, away from the Europeans; they have their own native food and live their own life. Some of them are appointed to grind and cook their food and do the work of their kitchen. It could not be otherwise in such a country. Even the most civilized natives as a rule prefer to eat by themselves. The missionaries sometimes accept the hospitality of the natives in their homes and eat of the food set before them, but even there the natives will wait until the missionaries have finished eating, or else they will eat in a separate place.

Since the pupils have time to do considerable work, they receive, in addition to food and schooling, a small sum of money sufficient to clothe themselves; and on Saturday afternoon, after washing their clothing, they have the time for recreation and mending their clothing.

Up to this time the industrial work of the boys had been chiefly on the farm and in the gardens; but now a new line of work was being introduced, that of brickmaking. Brother Doner desired to start in this work at least. It was at this time somewhat of an experiment, as the various kinds of soil had to be tested so that he might know which was best suited for this purpose. It was also too late in the season to spend much time in this work. A few thousand of brick were made; and as rains threatened to come early, they were hastily built into a kiln and burnt. A beginning had been made, however, and some knowledge of brickmaking gained.

During November of this year an event occurred which was second to none in the history of the work. I refer to the arrival of Elder and Mrs. Steigerwald, sent out to have charge of the mission.

We had been looking forward and hoping that some one might come in this capacity. In the meantime we were carrying on the work as well as we were able during the nineteen months since the death of Elder Engle. The brother and sister took hold of the work courageously from the first. It is not an easy task to begin mission work in heathen lands, among a strange people, strange tongue, strange surroundings and ways of living. It is no less easy to step into a work already begun amidst such different surroundings and new ways of doing things, and find the work pressing in on all sides. Such were the conditions that met Elder Steigerwald from the first, but it soon became evident that he was equal to the task.

Constant changes in the mission field are trying, both to the people and to the missionaries themselves. Here two had been called away by death, four had returned home (including Brother and Sister Van Blunk), and the two Lehmans and their wives had gone to Cape Town. The people could not help feeling these changes and scarcely knew what to expect. The changes seem to have been unavoidable, yet it makes the people suspicious of those who remain. The natives, like all those in heathen countries, love to think that their missionaries have come to stay and be one with them. The true missionary bears much the same relation to his people as the parent does to the child; for they are his spiritual children. Then too the language is not mastered in one, two, three years, or even in a longer period of time. In fact, many do not master it in a lifetime, so that all these changes could not fail to have their effect on the work and the natives, and render the position of Brother Steigerwald a difficult one.

His first important work was to unite in marriage, on Christmas Day, Brother Doner and Sister Long. There were many more natives present on this occasion than at the previous marriage to witness the ceremony and to congratulate their missionaries.

Money had been forthcoming for permanent buildings which were greatly needed. The huts were not only showing signs of decay, but some were damp and unhealthful during the rainy season, and even became mouldy at times. It was evident that, however convenient and useful they had been in their time, their day was fast passing away, and for the comfort and health of the missionaries something more permanent must be erected. The rains had started before Elder Steigerwald's arrival, so no more bricks could be made until the rains were over. Brother Doner was busy with the farming, and this left Brother Steigerwald free to make preparations for building.

There is an abundance of fine granite stones and slabs in the vicinity; and as the new year of 1902 opened, he had these hauled together for a foundation. During the rainy season, whenever the rains stopped for a time, he built at the foundation of the house. Although he had natives to assist, yet he found the work to be very heavy and taxing to his strength, but by the end of the rainy season he had a most excellent foundation for a house laid. Then he and Brother Doner, with the help of the schoolboys and some other natives, made and burnt a large kiln of bricks and were ready to begin the house.

Matopo Mission House. Front View.

The brethren in Africa can tell you that building on a mission station in the wilds of Africa is quite a different affair from what it is in civilized countries, or even in the cities of Africa. In these latter places, a man, desiring to build, buys his timber, his ready-made brick, and other material. Then the stone masons come and lay the foundation. The bricklayers, carpenters, plumbers, plasterers, and painters all follow in their order, together with their helpers, and the work is completed in an incredibly short space of time. On the mission field all this usually falls to the lot of one man, from the blasting out of the stone for the foundation and the brickmaking until the building is completed. He is mason, bricklayer, carpenter, plumber, plasterer, all in one. That one often is not a trained mechanic, or even a practical one, but many times he comes direct from the farm, schoolroom, or pulpit. With the many duties of a missionary pressing in upon him, sufficient to occupy all his attention, he must in addition undertake the laborious task of building a house, and even make most of the furniture with which it is fitted up.

Some one may inquire, is it not possible to secure skilled workmen to do the building? Yes, in some instances this can be done; but the high cost of living in Africa raises the wages of skilled mechanics to such an extreme height as to make it practically impossible for the missionary to employ them. Again, he has around him raw natives, who need to be taught to work, and his ambition is to do mission work in connection with his building.

Elder Steigerwald was equal to the emergency, and together with the help of Brother Doner and the natives, he completed the house in a little over a year from the time he began to haul the stone. The house is large, having nine good-sized rooms, with a fireplace in each one. There is a broad veranda nearly all around it and an iron roof over the whole, and it is a building that would be a credit to any one. The building is high and dry and has good board floors in four of the rooms, which add much to the healthfulness of it. Brother Steigerwald could no doubt tell you, if he would, of many days of arduous toil, which threatened to undermine his health; of many difficult and perplexing questions which confronted him in the process of construction; of lying awake at night, planning how everything was to be accomplished; especially how he was to build three fireplaces opening into one chimney and all have a good draft—a feat which he most successfully accomplished.

There were natives who lightened some of the heavier parts of the work, but to train these to perform their work properly is often a greater task than to do it one's self. This training must be done, however, if the missionary is faithful to his trust of developing the native character along useful lines as well as in giving him the Gospel. One of the officials, in making a report of the work, stated, "Here, at least, are missionaries who believe in teaching the natives the dignity of labor." This is the course pursued at all our stations. To train them properly is no easy task. It requires much wisdom, patience, firmness, and love. One meets with many discouraging results and often with great ingratitude on the part of those instructed; yet in the end it pays, if natives are ever to be brought to a more civilized plane of living.

There is one thing which operates strongly against the natives respecting labor. The average European, on coming to Africa, even though he may have been a day laborer and hard-working man in the country from which he came, soon sees that the more menial tasks fall to the natives; and when he takes the hoe or pick or shovel, he is told, "We do not do that here. Let the nigger do it and you oversee." The majority do not need a second invitation, and so such work is relegated to his black neighbor. The native soon sees, or thinks that he sees, that the white man regards manual labor as beneath him. This training is exactly what the African finds in his own home. He leaves the distasteful and hard tasks to his wife and the younger members of his family, while he sits down and enjoys himself. He is thus confirmed in his belief that labor is degrading.

Not so with the missionary. He works continually along many lines, and seeks to teach the native by his example, as well as by precept, the dignity of labor, and that only indolence, dirt, vice, and kindred evils are degrading. It is true that on account of climatic conditions and the many duties falling continually to men and women on the mission field, they are obliged, as their field of labor widens, to leave many lines of work to the natives they have in training. If they did not do this the spiritual part of the work and their own health would greatly suffer in consequence.

Perhaps some one might ask, Do those ignorant blacks ever learn to be cleanly and do their work properly? Yes, some of them respond in a surprisingly short period of time to faithful, energetic, yet patient training, and become real helpers to the missionary, both in the house and outside. Some, in addition to handling the oxen on the farm, also learn to use hammer, saw, chisel, and plane, and work side by side with white mechanics in certain lines of work.

While the house was being built at the Matopo Mission, Matshuba, still quite a young lad, was an interested spectator of everything that was done, and he himself did carefully whatever he was able to perform. When he found a small piece of lumber which was not likely to be used, he would say, "Mufundisi [Missionary], may I have this?" If permission was granted he carefully put it away, but said nothing. After several pieces had been obtained, he asked permission to use tools and work-shop on Saturday afternoon, when other work was stopped. He worked away in the shop, asking questions of no one. After a few weeks had passed he finally surprised us by showing a neatly-made chair, patterned after one that had been purchased in town. He gradually learned to do all kinds of work, as well as to build himself a good dwelling house.

There are almost insurmountable difficulties, however, in the way of teaching the trades to the natives as a means of earning money. The cry of the country is for industrial schools and for native skilled labor, but almost in the same breath the European will tell you that he will not work side by side with the native in the same line of work. A gentleman in Bulawayo had a contract for a fine, large building. His mechanics were white, while the blacks were the attendants. Being in need of more skilled labor, he sent south to the more civilized portion of the country for a native mechanic, and of course paid his way to Bulawayo. The white mechanics absolutely refused to work with this native and threatened to strike. The only course left for the contractor was to pay the native some wages and his fare home. This was no heathen native, but one who had grown up amid civilized surroundings, and no doubt his parents also were civilized.

We do not wish to criticise such mechanics, for here, in a land where the blacks so far outnumber the white population, there are many things to be considered. But with these facts staring the missionary in the face, there is little inducement for him to spend a great deal of time in training natives. The only course left which will give the native any chance at all in some sections of the country is for a contractor to have all native mechanics. He might then be employed by the more broad-minded Europeans, but be boycotted by others. Notwithstanding these difficulties, industrial training in its broadest sense is very important on the mission field, and it is encouraged by the governments. It enables the natives to improve their condition and way of living and to earn more money.

While these changes and the industrial training were in progress, the intellectual and spiritual part of the work was not neglected. New boys were continually coming, and some who came during these years were destined to be of help in after years. First was Nyamzana, who began to follow the Lord before coming as a boarder. Although not so quick in books as some, yet he was a faithful and devoted Christian, never giving his missionaries any uneasiness as to his spiritual standing. There were also Nkwidini, Mlobeka, and Mahlenkle. The last named was a nephew of the late king, and he had begun to attend school when the Lehmans were teaching at the kraal of the chief. He was an exceptional native, most steady and unassuming, ready and willing for any task assigned him. I have mentioned these names because they with others already referred to were among our future evangelists and teachers. Nor do I wish to forget Kolisa, a son of Buka, whom we visited up in the hills.

Not all, however, continued to remain at the mission. Some left, never to return. Others went away to work for a time, that they might obtain more money and then return again to enter school. The new boys as they came generally showed a desire to leave their old heathen lives and become Christians. Others were a cause of great anxiety to us. There were times of heart-searching and crying out to God, which showed that His Spirit was still at work in their hearts. One after another would come and confess their temptations and failures, and ask for prayer and help that they might be more victorious over evil. Some would receive definite help and blessing, while others seemed, for some reason, unable to take hold of the Lord by faith. Often we would feel greatly encouraged over the progress some were making, and look forward to their becoming able helpers and soul-winners for Him, only to have our hopes and expectations suddenly dashed to the ground. This was all a part of our training as missionaries. The Lord was teaching us by these experiences to take our eyes off individuals and fix them upon Him. He was also giving us sufficient encouragement, day by day, through some who were steadfast, to enable us to realize that our labor was not in vain for the Lord. There were a number in the inquirers' class, and in July, 1902, three more were baptized by Brother Steigerwald. Of this number were Ndhlalambi and Nyamazana.

The attendance at school was not as satisfactory as could be desired. The authority of the parents being paramount in the home, if there was anything to be done, such as digging in the gardens, herding, keeping the animals from the gardens, or running errands, the children must stay at home and attend to it. An early morning school was also started for those who could not attend at midday, and this enabled some of the herdboys to attend.

The parents were especially opposed to their daughters attending school, because they became unwilling to marry the old men to whom they were betrothed. As we mentioned previously, several girls did come to stay at the mission. One of them was Ganukisa, a daughter of the king. She was a very nice, modest girl and proved a great help in many ways. She also became a Christian and member of the Church. Another girl, Zwadini, ran off from home twice and came to us, imploring us to save her from the man her parents were forcing her to marry. We tried to buy her freedom, but to no avail, and she finally was forced to return home and marry the choice of her parents. At this time we had no right by law to interfere in these matters, however much we longed to free some of these dear girls from their lives of slavery. It required time and prayer and much looking to God before a certain amount of freedom of choice was granted the daughters, and then it came through an action of the government.

In the school some were making good progress. English and some other branches had been added to the curriculum, but the Bible continued to be the chief Textbook, and some were acquiring a fair understanding of it. Natives have generally a keenness of discernment and a clear grasp of the subject, so that it is necessary for the teacher to be well prepared for any question that may arise. The one who was first at the mission was a philosopher and a keen thinker. Nothing seemed to escape him. I have heard him deliver most excellent sermons and bring far more out of a Sunday-school lesson than the ordinary teacher. One day in reading the book of Isaiah, he came to the eighteenth chapter. He knows nothing about Ethiopia, but after he had finished reading, I inquired what people the prophet referred to. He thought for a moment and then exclaimed, "I believe he means us, the black people."

CHAPTER ELEVEN

Continuation of the Work

Furlough

The missionary, however robust he may be, cannot keep at his work all the time; for he generally works seven days in a week and fifty-two weeks in a year. After a few years of such labor it is necessary to call a halt, if one does not wish to break down altogether. New missionaries can take much of the burden, yet those who have something of the language and can speak to the people must be ready in season and out of season, to talk, interpret, explain, as well as to have heart-to-heart talks with the people.

I had now been actively engaged on the mission station for four strenuous years and was greatly in need of a rest and change. The Board at home, as well as the missionaries on the field, had been urging me to go south for a few months. The only difficulty in the way was the need of some one to take the school, and so we had been looking forward to the return of Brother and Sister Lehman from Cape Town to take charge of it. They, however, had been looking on the fields for mission work at the Compounds on Johannesburg, and had decided to go there. As a last resort we decided to ask Matshuba to do the teaching. He was capable of doing it, and he was also becoming able to do some interpreting from English into the vernacular.

Before this happened an event occurred which more or less concerned all South Africa, and especially Rhodesia. I refer to the death, on March 26, 1902, of Cecil Rhodes at his home, Groot Schuur, near Cape Town, the place where he had so kindly received Brother Engle on our first coming to Africa. It had been his request to be buried in Rhodesia, the country that bore his name. In the Matopo Hills was a beautiful spot which he had discovered and to which he gave the name, "View of the World." This is about fifteen miles from Matopo Mission, as the crow flies, but over twenty-five miles by wagon road. Here, on the summit of a large granite hill, in the heart of Matopo, is the spot he selected to be his last resting place.

When the body was brought to Bulawayo, thousands of people, both white and black, vied with each other in paying a last tribute of respect to him who had done so much for the development of the country. The natives realized that they had lost a friend that could not be replaced; and the white people believed that no one could carry out so successfully many of the public affairs with which he was associated. When the funeral procession reached the burial place, the heavy casket was raised to the top of the granite hill. Into the solid rock a grave had been cut, and into this the casket was lowered. The grave was then covered by an immense granite slab, on which was fastened a large brass plate with this inscription: "Here lie the remains of Cecil John Rhodes."

A part of his property was left for the improvement of the country to which he had devoted his time and talents. His two large estates in Rhodesia, together with an annuity, were bequeathed to this country; and his fine and well-built estate near Cape Town was given over for the use of the government of Cape Colony, but the grounds are continually opened to the public. The Rhodes scholarships for various countries, including two for each State in the United States, were given with a hope of cementing nations together. He wished no monument to be erected over his grave, but near the place is the Shangani Monument to the memory of those who fell in the Matabele War. The grounds have been beautifully laid out and a well-built road extends from Bulawayo to the grave. On his estate at Cape Town is a granite monument seventy feet long, built near the seat overlooking both the Atlantic and the Indian Oceans, where he used to sit and lay his world-wide plans. There is a sad feature connected with his life, like that of many other men whom the world calls great. While he made so much provision for earthly things, there seems to be no evidence that he made provision for eternity.

During this year there also died near us a native who had been more or less interested in the work, by the name of Fusi. He had been a prominent soldier under King Lobengula, and also remembered the first king, Mzilikazi. He loved to talk about the good old days, and could tell of a visit that Rev. Moffat, the father-in-law of Livingstone, once made to this country. He said, "I remember Chete [Rev. Moffat] quite well. I was just a young man at the time and King Mzilikazi treated Chete nicely. He said to me, 'Go and milk a cow and bring some milk for the missionary.'"

This old warrior, however, never showed any desire to become a Christian; but he was always glad to have his people attend school, and his youngest son was one of the first communicants. The native finally became sick with dropsy, and when we visited him during his sickness, he said an enemy had bewitched him, adding:

"Before the white man came into the country we put all the witches to death and we were well. Now we are not allowed to kill them and we must suffer."

Later we again visited him. When asked if we should sing for him, he replied, "Yes, sing one of the old hymns you used to sing when Missionary Engle was alive." We did so, and he too joined his quavering voice in the chorus. He also listened most attentively to the Scripture reading and comments that day, and joined us in prayer. What thoughts these things stirred in his heart we know not, for that was the last time we saw him.

In July of this year the time finally came for our furlough. I took a ticket from Bulawayo south to Port Elizabeth. This was shortly after the close of the Boer War, and all along the railway in the south were to be seen the blockhouses erected to guard the railway from destruction. Here and there were the demolished farmhouses and the orchards and beautiful groves that had been leveled to the ground. Worst of all were the many graves—mute testimony to that saddest of all human employment, human butchery. Kimberley already was recovering from this terrible siege. This was still a small town, its chief attraction being the great masses of blue earth surrounding it. This diamondiferous blue rock is mined far down in the earth, where it had been formed under great pressure; and when brought to the surface, the combined action of rain and sun slakes it somewhat like quicklime. It is then washed, which removes the lighter earth, leaving the diamonds and other precious stones.

From this place I went to Port Elizabeth, which is 1,200 miles south of Bulawayo. It is the principal seaport of Cape Colony, as it furnishes a shorter and more direct route into the interior than Cape Town does. This is a town of about 35,000 inhabitants, but there is nothing especially inviting about the place except its thriving business. It has been said of it: "Out of sand-hills and scrub, Anglo-Saxon energy has created a town that, for cleanliness and health, and for the handsomeness of its business buildings, is second to none in South Africa." After a stay of a few days at this place I took the steamer *Norman Castle* for Durban, where the greater part of my vacation was to be spent.

Durban is the seaport and largest town of Natal, and has nearly 70,000 inhabitants. The business part is low and often quite hot, but the part known as the Berea is high and cool, and has many fine dwelling houses. Natal is more thickly populated than other parts of South Africa. It has a most luxuriant vegetation and varied and picturesque scenery, and well deserves the appellation, "Garden of South Africa." In this warm, moist, subtropical climate of the coast many delicious and tropical fruits are grown. This is the home of the Zulu tribe of Africans, of which the Matabele are a branch.

My special purpose in coming to this section of the country to rest was to make my furlough as profitable as possible, and to gain information helpful for mission work. Missionaries had been in this section of the country the greater part of the nineteenth century. The American Board had started their work some time in the '30s, and this formed an excellent opportunity of seeing some of the fruits of missionary labors.

I spent some time at an English Mission under Mr. Eyles at Imbezana, at a

Free Methodist Mission and girls' school, Fairview, and at four missions of the American Board—a boys' school at Adams, a large girls' school at Inanda, and one at Umzumbi, and also visited their work at Durban, in charge of Rev. Bridgeman. At all these places I was most hospitably entertained and given every opportunity for studying the work. It was an inspiration to see what God had wrought among these erstwhile heathen. Here were large boarding-schools, and natives living like white people in neat brick houses, built by themselves. Here were missionaries, like Mrs. Edwards and Mrs. Bridgeman, grown old in this soul-saving work, and yet so attached to the natives and the work that they could not think of leaving the country.

Natal, like Cape Colony and the Transvaal, can no longer be called heathen Africa, as so many of the natives are civilized. The large cities of white people are built in modern style, with all the latest improvements, electric lights, street cars, telephones, and the like, and since then automobiles. There are also many white farmers, as well as small towns of white people, throughout the country. Missionaries of many societies are here in this densely-populated and easily-accessible district of Natal. This is considered one of the greatest fields for the overlapping of missionaries, perhaps, to be found anywhere, yet all seem to have plenty to do.

With all the advantages for improvement which the Africans here possess, I was surprised to meet, within a mile or two of one of the oldest mission stations, natives with paint and grease, and when the evangelists go to the homes of the people they still find some raw heathen. Some not only do not and will not accept Christ, but they also prefer their dirty, indolent, ignorant way of living to that introduced by civilization.

At Durban I took the train to go north to Johannesburg, a distance of 480 miles. The war had been over for some time, yet it was still necessary to procure a pass to enter Johannesburg. This I procured through Brother Lehman, who was then at Johannesburg. People were flocking thither as fast as they could procure passes and trains to carry them. The trains were crowded every day, and one was obliged to book ahead in order to secure a seat. This ride to Johannesburg is a delightful one, so far as the scenery is concerned, but the winding railroad is exceedingly rough and uncomfortable. One passes through a landscape most beautiful and varied, from the green, grassy hills of the coast, through mountains and valleys, to the high, rolling veldt of the Rand, where the famous gold reefs of South Africa are to be found. In this journey one leaves the sea level at Durban and gradually rises to the height of 6,000 feet at Johannesburg. It is said of this place: "In 1886 the site was nothing but a bleak, bare plain, that could have been bought for one hundred pounds. Then came the discovery of gold reefs east and west for sixty miles, and stores, public buildings, and churches sprang up with marvelous rapidity." This is now the largest, richest, and most modern city of South Africa, and the Rand is this sixty miles of gold-reef mines.

At these mines are many thousands of natives from all parts of South Africa, and when they are not at work they are confined in large enclosures known as "Compounds." This furnishes the missionary an excellent opportunity of doing mission work among this conglomerate mass of natives. The great variety of languages is one hindrance in the way, but if the missionary is able to speak one of the chief divisions of the Bantu family of languages, such as the Zulu, he can generally find some native to interpret for him into other languages.

In this mission field we found our beloved colaborers, Brother and Sister Isaac Lehman, who had just come from Cape Town and were becoming settled in their new home. A dear little girl, Faith, had come to bless their home and cheer their hearts. Brother Jacob Lehmans also were engaged in mission work here, as well as our dear Sister Swanson (nee Hershey), who had left us at Cape Town to come to this place. As our Board had no mission station here at that time, these were all laboring in connection with an undenominational mission in charge of Mr. A. W. Baker. All were actively engaged in mission work. It is a broad field and is a great opportunity for giving the Gospel to the heathen. However, one has the same obstacles to encounter as in the native village, *i. e.*, the indifference of the people. While we would be having a service in one part of the Compound, other natives would be dancing within sight in another part, and often be making such a noise as to disturb the meeting. One difficulty with the work is that the natives often remain at the mines only six months or a year, not sufficiently long to get them established. Much good is, however, being done; schools are established to teach the natives when they are not at work, and services are held regularly at various places. Natives, accepting the Light, carry it to other parts of Africa, and sometimes become teachers of their people.

After spending a most enjoyable month at this place I again returned to Matopo Mission, after an absence of three and one-half months. It was a pleasure to get back to the old battle ground, for it was still the most beautiful spot on earth and its people the dearest. Great changes had taken place during our absence. Then the foundation of the house had been laid and the brick burnt, but now an imposing structure met the eye and the house was rapidly being completed. It looked as if the missionaries had come to stay and were to have a comfortable place to live in.

The school was progressing favorably under Matshuba's management, and all parts of the work seemed encouraging. As there was continually some difficulty about the stability of some of the industrial pupils, it was decided to divide the school year into two terms of five months each, with a month's vacation intervening in which the pupils could return home if they so desired. This worked well and seemed more satisfactory to all. The one who had been teaching was retained as pupil teacher and was also permitted to take advanced work.

"Here lie the remains of Cecil John Rhodes."

There was again opportunity for me to visit in their homes. So, accompanied by some of the boys or girls, we made long excursions on foot among the people, sometimes walking from eight to twelve miles and meeting many people. Because so many missionaries had left them and did not return, they were not a little pleased to see me back, and, native-like, were inclined to make flattering speeches. One day we visited nine kraals, and everywhere had attentive listeners, and the people seemed to be hungry for the Word. At another time we went to Sibula's village for the first time, where we met and gave the Gospel to over one hundred people. They had never been visited before and seemed anxious for a school. Later they built a schoolhouse, and Nyamzana was given to them as a teacher.

One day when we were out to the kraals we happened to come to a beer drink, where they were having a digging-bee.

They said, "Why does not Missionary Steigerwald invite the people to come and dig his large gardens? He is so busy with building."

"Will you come if he invites you?" we asked.

"Certainly we will," they replied.

When we reached home we told Brother Steigerwald what they said, and he at once thought it a splendid opportunity for getting his corn planted. So he appointed a day and sent out invitations to the people. One hundred and sixty-four adults with their hoes came and digged and planted an eight or ten-acre lot. It was an interesting sight to see that many people digging in one place. They would usually sing a native song, and with their hoes keep time to the music. They performed this piece of work without pay, and of course received no beer, but a generous supply of bread and tea was furnished them, which they greatly enjoyed. These Matabele are always very ready to come out to work when invited, and in this respect they were a contrast to some natives. When hired to do work, however, it was necessary to make them keep their promise and come at the time appointed, and also finish their work.

Sister Steigerwald was much amused at Sibongamanzi shortly after she came to the mission. My hut needed replastering, and Sibongamanzi was engaged to do the work. The appointed day arrived, but the girl did not come according to her promise, and as the work was urgent I employed another girl to do it. The next day Sibongamanzi came to do the work and was quite disappointed to find some one else had accomplished it.

I said, "Why did you not come yesterday according to your promise?"

"I am sure a person has a right to change her mind," she replied.

"Yes, I think so, too, so I employed some one else."

In school one is obliged to use the English word for such articles as slate, pencil, and paper, since there is no word in the language for these things. When Steigerwalds came, there were also a number of boxes of goods sent out; and in unpacking these a pencil fell out. Sister Steigerwald picked it up, and handing it to Masikwa, said, "Here is a pencil." He was most delighted, and came and said, "The Inkosikazi [Mrs.] can speak our language already. She said 'Pencil.'" Sister Steigerwald, together with the other sisters, had their own experiences in teaching natives in the kitchen and housework, as well as in sewing. She proved most capable and patient in training various ones to be cleanly and to do their work properly.

The services at the mission were well attended at this time, and sometimes we were obliged to have an overflow meeting. Natives would come fifteen miles to be present at the Sunday services. "Our little church is too small," said some. "We need a new one."

Our congregations were gradually emerging from barbarism, and their appearance on Sunday was often quite striking. Some of the boys and young men would come, clean and neatly dressed in European clothes, including hat and shoes, and exhibit good taste in the selection of their clothing. Some again came well dressed but without shoes; others would appear partly dressed, but anxious to display all the clothing they had. Perhaps on a sweltering, hot day some would don a heavy winter overcoat reaching below the knees, or a heavy suit of bright red flannel. Another would have on a coat turned wrong side out to show all the colors, and a vest outside of this, while a number continued to wear the purely native garb of skins. A few of the girls were neatly clothed in dresses; others in short skirts with or without a cloth thrown over their shoulders. Some of the women's clothing was very modest and picturesque.

Natives, especially at this stage of their advancement, do not as a rule dress according to the weather, for to them clothing is more or less a matter of ornamentation and they don it accordingly. One must be very careful about placing special emphasis upon clothing, as the native is naturally vain, and when he is able to be better clothed his vanity often increases. He soon thinks that if he is clothed he is a Christian, or if he goes to school and learns he is a Christian. He is quite ready to put on these outward semblances of civilization without yielding himself to God. If the missionary is willing to accept the outward form of Christianity, whether of clothing or ceremonials, he may soon have a large membership. He must continually guard against these things, and seek to know the inner life of those about him, and their daily walk; nor is it always easy to ascertain what is beneath the surface. Hypocrisy is not at all unusual.

Early in our work there was a native who came occasionally to our services. He had worked in Bulawayo and attended one of the native churches sufficiently long to gain a smattering and lingo of Christianity. He came clothed in black broadcloth and carrying a book under his arm, and withal seemed a person of some consequence. He was a brother of one of our boys, and we were informed that he could read. One day in church, at the close of the services, he asked permission to say something, and not knowing what was coming we gave him permission. He arose and began to read out of his book and then talked. Again he read and talked in a preaching way until he was finally requested to sit down. As we were suspicious from his manner in regard to his ability to read, we took occasion to test him and found that he knew absolutely nothing about reading. What he gave had been memorized, and we learned that his life too was decidedly corrupt. This taught us how necessary it was to be careful of the stranger who came and claimed to be a Christian.

December 26, 1902, there was a most welcome addition to the mission family in the person of a little son to Brother and Sister Doner. This was the first white child at the mission, and it was quite a curiosity to the natives. Of course every one must have a look at it, and happy was the one who might touch or hold this wonderful white baby.

CHAPTER TWELVE

Looking on the Fields

Say not ye, There are yet four months, and then cometh harvest? behold, I say unto you, Lift up your eyes, and look on the fields; for they are white already to harvest.—St. John 4: 35.

We moved into the new house early in 1903. This left the huts empty, for our increasing family of boys. As soon as the rains were over for this year, Brother and Sister Steigerwald and myself felt led to make a tour of exploration in the interests of the work. Matopo Hills or Mountains extend northeast and southwest for a distance of about sixty miles. Between the hills and Bulawayo there is a mission station and work had been carried on for some years, although there were at this time many raw natives to be seen. Through the hills and south for a long distance there were as yet no missionaries except our own, and as our mission was on the north side of the hills, we desired to go through them and explore some of the south side.

In June we arranged to make the trip, taking our large wagon on which was a canvas top, which was drawn by donkeys, consequently progress was slow. Three of our boys accompanied us. We were obliged to go west about nine miles before a road could be found leading through the hills. This wagon road was exceedingly rough and stony and very little traveled, and the donkeys slowly wended their way in and out among the hills which continually surrounded us and seemed to close us in. Frequently as the immense piles of rock seemed to stretch across our path in front and bar further progress, we would be led to exclaim, "Truly, there is no way out of this," but on we went and the way continued to open.

The tediousness of the journey was relieved by the exceeding beauty of the scenery as it gradually unfolded before our eyes. In the first of the trip are to be seen the immense bald hills of solid granite, similar to some in the vicinity of the mission. Soon the scene changes and the eye is greeted on every side by lofty ridges, consisting of immense boulders piled up in all sorts of fantastic shapes, by the Great Architect, and from out of every possible crevice grow trees and shrubbery of all sorts. The dark green of the foliage, interspersed with the varying shades of grey, yellow, red, and green of the rock, forms a picture of surpassing loveliness. Baboons, large and small, would make their appearance on the jutting rocks, as we passed along, and bark at these intruders into their peaceful domain.

As the hills abounded in game, and Elder Steigerwald was a good shot, we did not want for meat on the journey. So, while the donkeys were grazing, fires would be built and pot roasts and many sorts of delectable dishes would be prepared and eaten with relish. Natives are generally happy if they have plenty of meat to eat; so on this journey Tebengo declared that they would be longing for the fleshpots of Egypt when they returned to the mission. Next to meat, their favorite dish was Graham flour made into a loaf by means of water and a little salt, then baked in the hot ashes.

South of the hills we left the beaten track, which proceeds east to Gwanda, and started south to the open country, which is known as Mapani Land, named from the large amount of excellent hardwood Mapani trees which grow here. Very few natives were seen on the journey through the hills, but in this rich, open plain of the south there were numerous kraals. The natives received us gladly and readily consented to have services; and as there were no missionaries in this part of the country, many of the people had the privilege of hearing for the first time the Story of the Cross. On this trip we came to the home of Holi, a rich and prominent native. His wife is a daughter of King Lobengula and a sister of Ganukisa, who lived at the mission. Here we were very kindly received and Holi presented Elder Steigerwald with a fine fat sheep.

From this point we turned west and north through the hills by a different route. Along the way we visited some places of interest, especially the "View of the World," where Mr. Rhodes was buried. Thence we proceeded east and south to the mission. We had been absent about two weeks, had traveled over one hundred miles, and had had a most pleasant and profitable trip. It had also been a change from the labor and routine of the station.

Brother and Sister Doner had for some time been contemplating opening another station, and they concluded during this dry season also to make a tour and explore the country, as well as do evangelistic work. They made preparations to spend a month in this way, taking the wagon and several boys. Little Oliver, who was then only seven months old, also went along, thus early in his life learning what trekking in Africa meant.

They went south over the same route we had taken, and it was on this trip, if I mistake not, that the present site of Mapani Mission was selected. They spent a very delightful month and came home quite enthusiastic over the prospects of opening a new work and eager to launch out at once. Permission did not come from the Board, however, in time to open that dry season, and the work had to be postponed another year.

During this year word came that one member of the Executive Board had passed "over the river." Dear father died the latter part of March. It was a double loss to some of us; for we should now miss not only his fatherly letters, but the wise counsel that he gave in his capacity as a member of the Mission Board. He always seemed to have such a keen insight into the work, and wrote about it as if he had been on the field and knew exactly our surroundings.

Matopo Mission Church. Built by Elder Steigerwald in 1905.

The work at the mission continued to go along as usual, and two more united with the Church, and everyone found plenty of profitable employment. One feature of the work, not yet mentioned, but which always requires much of the missionaries' time, is medical work and the care of the sick. The natives accept the miracles of healing, mentioned in the Scriptures, without question, and the sick frequently asked the prayers of the missionaries. There were several instances of remarkable cases of healing without the application of medicine, when the native could be led to take hold of the Lord by faith. On one occasion a native came for Elder Engle, from a kraal about five miles distant, where a woman was very sick and had eaten nothing for several days. She was very low indeed and seemingly unconscious of what was going on about her and her friends were weeping. Brother Engle felt led to anoint her and pray for her. The next day they came to say that the woman was much better and was eating, and they declared that the missionary had raised her from the dead.

At another time one of our Christian girls was sick with such a disease that we knew we could not help her, and she desired prayer. We granted her request and she was healed immediately, even to our surprise. Some time after

Brother Doner had come, an elderly native was quite ill with lung trouble, and his people had been trying in every way to heal him. They appealed to us, so we made the case a special subject of prayer and he was healed immediately, and told everyone that Jesus had healed him. A mother also wished us to pray for her child, who was very ill and seemed ready to die at any minute; it too was healed at once. Other instances of help might be cited; but we give these, because we see that He is the same Christ yet today and often shows His power, saying unto the sick, "According to your faith be it unto you."

Back View of Matopo Mission House, Showing Granite Hill Beyond.

Why He does not always choose to manifest His power in this way I know not. I am giving things as I found them. At first we were more or less loth to use medicine, and some of the early losses may have been owing to this fact. We believe also that He receives honor in helping the missionary make use of remedies to relieve the suffering of the sick. With the natives sickness is always the result of witchcraft or the influence of their ancestral spirits. If one can by means of remedies, under the blessing of God, show them that this is not true, he is doing much to overthrow some of their superstitious beliefs. So the sick are visited in their homes and ministered to, and many come to the mission for treatment. Sometimes the disease may be such as will not yield to treatment, but the gentle sympathy and the delicacy for the appetite are always much appreciated, even from some sources least expected. The missionary necessarily becomes physician and nurse to his people, and it brings him into contact with them and relieves their sufferings and thus paves the way for ministering to their spiritual needs. He who neglects this part of the work makes a grave mistake. Many missionaries, who had done little medical work at home, have by a willingness and desire to learn, become quite proficient in healing on the mission field.

Elder Steigerwald has been much used in this line of work. Many and various cases have been treated by him most successfully. In addition to the sick who come for medicine, there are generally some who remain for a time at the mission to be treated.

During this dry season, as usual, kraal visiting occupied much of my time outside of school hours, and many long and enjoyable trips were made to all the villages surrounding us. During these journeys the Lord was also reminding His messenger of some things that had been almost forgotten. He was showing the large fields yet beyond where the people were in pagan darkness and the Light of Life had not yet penetrated, and where missionaries and teachers were greatly needed.

In the Matopo Hills.

The reader of these pages will remember that our call had been to the far interior of Africa, where Christ had not been named. When Matopo Mission was started it was felt that here was my place to begin work, but that the time would come when the Lord wanted me to press on farther in the interior. This thought kept following me, and in the second year of our work at Matopo, on my speaking to a friend of the call to press on farther, the question was asked, "You do not intend to go alone, do you?" My reply was, "No, I do not think that will be necessary. Perhaps the Lord will raise up others who desire to go beyond the Zambezi." Also, while Brother and Sister Van Blunk were at Matopo, the question of going north was often mentioned, for their eyes were likewise looking in that direction.

As time went on, however, and the work at Matopo increased, I entered more and more deeply into it and became absorbed in my surroundings. The children and also the older people occupied a large place in my heart and crowded out for the time being all thought of anything else. The Lord had to take His own way of cutting me loose and again lifting up my eyes to the fields beyond, and I could not doubt but that His time was near at hand. On the other hand, what a struggle it was to be willing to leave these! He, however, showed me most strikingly one day that when I was willing to lose these children there were others waiting to be found; and when the work was given into His hands, He accomplished that which to me was impossible.

First, the pushing out of the work must be presented to the Board and the home Church and their consent and aid solicited. Permission was given to return to America, and as Conference drew near, it seemed as if the Lord's time had come for me to do this. Together with my colaborers, we made it a special subject of prayer, and felt that I was to start at once. So, on March 25, 1904, I left the mission for America. Sister Emma Doner, as she bade me good-bye, said weeping, "If I did not know of a truth that it was the Lord's will for you to go at this time I could not say good-bye." That was the last time I was permitted to look into her dear face. Brother and Sister Steigerwald, together with several of the boys, accompanied me to Bulawayo, where I took the train for Cape Town.

I shall not dwell on the events of that journey to America, for many things connected with it are too sacred to find way into public print. It is sufficient to say that it was a time of severe sifting and testing, but of such sweet fellowship with the Father, that I would not blot it out of my life, if I could. I learned, in truth, what that meant, "With God all things are possible." After it was over one of God's children greatly desired to hear of the trip home, and when told, he was quiet for a time; then he said, "I believe it was God's preparation for going farther into the interior. I believe the way will open."

America was reached just in time for Conference in Ontario. We were sorry to learn that Elder S. Zook, the Treasurer of the Foreign Mission Board, had in the meantime passed away in February. We greatly missed him who had always been such an able pillar in the Church and missionary work, for his farsightedness and wise counsel had smoothed the way in many a difficulty. The old fathers were thus passing away and the work was devolving upon younger shoulders, but they were equal to the task. The Executive Board now consisted of Brethren J. R. Zook, Chairman; Eli M. Engle, Secretary; and Peter Climenhage, Treasurer, two of whom had been connected with the foreign missionary work from its inception.

A report of the work from the field met with an enthusiastic reception, and it was requested that the churches all be visited and an account of the mission work be given. Permission was also granted for an appeal to be made for pressing the work on into the interior, both for workers and funds.

In the meantime Miss Sallie Kreider had gone to Africa to engage in mission work, and Elder and Mrs. John Meyers and Miss Lydia Heise had also gone there on a visit. Brother and Sister Doner, with some of the mission boys, had gone to Mapani to open a mission station in August, 1904. At first Brother Doner was troubled with fever, and much of the hut building fell to Ndhlalambi; then Sister Doner became quite ill, and Sister Kreider hastened down to assist in caring for her, but she passed away. Thus three precious lives had been sacrificed for the people and the work. Brother Doner was desirous of taking the body and laying it by the side of the others at Matopo. This was unusual in a hot climate like this, where interment is usually attended to at once, and the natives too object to carrying a dead body, so there was much parleying before they would consent to take hold of the bier and carry it. The way over the hills was much shorter, but it was also much more difficult. It was an exceedingly trying journey for all of them, and only the grace of God could have sustained them through it; but Brother Doner had the comfort and satisfaction of seeing his loved one resting in the little cemetery beside Sister Cress and Brother Engle.

Sister Doner's stay of over three years in Africa was almost a continual struggle, one might say, against disease, and heroically she bore up under it. Her constitution was naturally not very rugged, and this malarial climate aggravated her disease, as it is sure to do with any one who is not strong. She was afraid to write home and inform her friends of the condition of her health, lest they should insist upon her return to America, and that she did not desire. She loved the work among the heathen, and we believe she had her desire in laying down her life in their behalf, rather than return to America where she might have lived for a longer time. Little Oliver continued to thrive, but as Brother Doner's health was great impaired, it was deemed advisable that he return to America on furlough and, after placing Oliver with friends, regain his own health. So in the spring of 1905 he left for America, and Ndhlalambi was left to care for the work just started at Mapani.

In America the work was progressing; a number had volunteered for the foreign field, and four were ready to go to Africa at once; these being Mr. and Mrs. Harvey Frey and Misses Adda Engle and Abbie Bert. Over $2,000 had been donated toward pushing the work on into the interior. This was offered to the Mission Board, but they concluded that it was best to leave it in our hands toward the opening of the work. Of the four new missionaries who were going to Africa, none were pledged to the interior work except Sister Engle, but we still hoped others would be ready to go.

We reached Matopo Mission August 1, 1905, and rejoiced that the Lord permitted us again to return. Some very noticeable changes had taken place during our absence: Brother Steigerwald had been busy making improvements, and a fine, large brick church, with an iron roof, had been erected. This was much needed and it added greatly to the appearance of the mission premises. The women, about eighty in number, gladly offered their services free to put in a fine polished earthen floor. A number of the class members had been baptized, and Matshuba was doing well in the schoolroom, where Sister Kreider was also doing some teaching.

Mapani Mission, 1907.

Ndhlalambi had been holding on faithfully at Mapani Mission. A number there had accepted Christ and he had formed them into a class for instruction. It was thought advisable for Sister Engle and myself to spend the remainder of the dry season at Mapani and help in the work there, so we turned our faces in that direction. We were there two months and helped in the various lines of work and visited some of the people in the surrounding neighborhood. Some of the converts were very encouraging at that place. At the time in which the rains usually open we returned to Matopo. On the way down we had gone by wagon road, but on our return four donkeys had been sent down, two for pack saddles and the other two for Sister Engle and me to ride, and two boys came along to assist in the homeward journey.

Kwidine Taking His Aunt to Church. Matopo M. Hospital.

We left Mapani Mission at sunrise and took the shorter journey across the hills, the same path along which they had carried the body of Sister Doner the year previous. It was a most difficult trip for us and we had to marvel how they could have possibly made the journey. We were obliged to stop on the way and let the donkeys graze and eat, and did not reach the hills proper until afternoon. As the climbing was difficult and there were many trees and shrubs growing out from between the rocks, it was difficult for us to keep our seats, so we dismounted and walked. The pack saddles would frequently be nearly brushed off the other donkeys. Once one of the donkeys in attempting to go up a steep rock fell back and became fast in the rocks. The boys removed the load and carried it up; they then extricated the donkey and after much persuasion got it on the rock and again placed on the load. By the time we reached the summit, darkness had overtaken us and we were obliged to make the descent in the dark. We knew not where we were going, and were frequently in danger of broken limbs or becoming fast in the rocks. We were very thankful when at last at eleven o'clock we reached the mission without any serious accident. This was one of Sister Engle's first experiences in Africa, but from her composure through it all one would judge that she expected such things.

Christian Wedding Reception Near Matopo.

Ndhlalambi remained on at the work in Mapani most of the time for one and one-half years, and when Brother Doner at last returned there were some nearly ready for baptism. Not long afterwards thirteen were baptized there and proved faithful Christians.

Brother and Sister Steigerwald had now had four very strenuous years of work at Matopo and were in need of a change. So, while the new workers were at Matopo, the way was opened for them to go to Cape Town over the rainy season. Here they had a good rest and returned in April, 1906, quite refreshed, ready to take up their duties at their station. Brother Doner also returned from America at the same time and was ready to resume work at Mapani.

There had been some pupils attending school at Matopo Mission, from Mtshabezi Valley, south of the hills, but about fifteen miles east of Brother Doner's station. These had strongly urged that a mission be planted in their midst. Brother Steigerwald promised them to consider the matter, and at the opening of the dry season Brother Frey went to see that part of the country. He was much pleased with the outlook and felt led to open work there. This is the origin of Mtshabezi Mission which was started in July, 1906. The phenomenal success attending that work since helps to confirm the belief that it was a work of the Lord's own planting.

CHAPTER THIRTEEN

The Religion of the Matabele and Subject Tribes

In order to understand a people properly one must know something of their religious beliefs; for all the important actions of their lives rest upon their religion. Find out what a person believes and you have a pretty good idea of his character. A native is loth to talk about his religion, and will, unless he fully understands and trusts the questioner, often evade answering directly questions asked upon this subject. It is somewhat difficult to dissociate the religious beliefs of the Matabele from those of the first inhabitants of the country, as the two are so closely interwoven.

It would seem that all the natives, with whom we have come into contact, have some conception of a God, however vague that conception may be. They do not as a rule discuss Him and His attributes among themselves, and so differ greatly in the attributes ascribed to Him. They often prefer to deal with and worship the lesser spirits, especially the shades of their ancestors with whom they are somewhat familiar, than a great God Whom they do not know and Whom they fear, for the shades they think can intercede for them. The native is really very religious, but prefers to take that religion found ready to hand rather than to make an attempt to fathom that which he does not understand.

The Matabele when asked who their god is will readily respond that it is the King Umzilikazi. They say, "He gave us the country and everything we have, and our customs and laws, and him we worship." This can be easily understood from the belief of the Zulu tribe, of which this is a branch. The Zulu will say that Umkulukulu (the oldest or first one) is the one to be worshiped, as he gave all the rest their religion and customs. As their ideas of worship were very elastic, there was no difficulty in including other departed spirits in the list of those worshiped. All who left them could intercede for them in the spirit world; hence, when the old queen was buried, the woman who washed her face just before burial said, "Go in peace and speak a good word for us to the king, and to those who have gone before, so that we too may find a place and not be found fault with."

This very fact, that their religious beliefs are so elastic, makes missionary work often the more difficult and discouraging among them. They will quite readily accept the God one preaches, and Christ as the Savior of men, but to their way of thinking this does not interfere with their worship. This fact was forcibly thrust upon me one day in coming to a kraal near the mission that had been frequently visited. The people here had much light and often came to the services, and their son Masikwa was a baptized member. On this occasion we found the older people worshiping the spirits, and said to the woman,

"How is this? We thought that you worshiped the Lord Jesus."

"Oh! yes, we do," she replied, "He is the Big Spirit and we worship Him too."

It was not at all difficult for her to include Him among the number of spirits to be worshiped. She was willing to accept all who might be able to help them, and even give Him a large place alongside of the others. The fact that He had been on earth and died only added to the conception that He was like the rest. The force of the resurrection idea she had not grasped. It will be readily seen how difficult it is to inculcate the idea of one Supreme Being Who alone should be worshiped, and Who is a jealous God and will brook no rivals.

On the other hand, the belief in an intercessor has its useful side in giving them the Gospel, for we endeavor to impress upon their minds that Christ is the Great Intercessor, Who "ever liveth to make intercession for them," a risen Savior, not a dead One. The great question here is, "Intercede for what?" Sins they do not claim to have. To them religion has nothing to do with morals, for neither if they live pure moral lives are they the better, nor if they are base and licentious are they worse when they come to die. The spirits whom they worship are of their own conception and have the same loves and hates. As Mr. J. W. Jack says: "Down all the ages to the present time so frightful have been the abysses of depravity, the intolerable cruelty, the extravagances of nameless lust associated with religion, that if the veil were lifted, Christianity could not bear the story." The raw native will tell you that lying, stealing, murder, and adultery are bad, but they do not look upon these as having anything to do with their religion.

Again, the very fact that they are so tolerant in their religious views, and so ready to include all, led the Matabele early in their history to adopt the religion of the conquered tribes. The oldest and, to them, the most powerful and most widely-worshiped of these heathen deities was Umlimo. This was the name of one worshiped by the Makalanga. He was supposed to have his abode in the Matopo Hills, several of which places are still pointed out. If one may judge from the information received from the natives, the worship greatly resembled that of the ancient Greek oracles. When any important question of the tribe was in need of solution, or even when individual questions arose, they would go to the hill or cave in which the Umlimo was supposed to have his dwelling place, carry a present, perhaps of beer, meat, or other food, and, placing it on the rock, remove to a respectful distance and then make known their wants. They said the answer would come from the very depths of the earth.

It is said: "The answer was given by means of ventriloquism and, as the speaker was inside the cave and invisible, the voice appeared to the inquirer to issue from the very bowels of the earth. The extreme ingenuity of the device will be better appreciated when it is known that the spirits of the departed are universally believed by the natives to dwell in an under world. For a ventriloquist to practice his calling as a diviner in the foregoing manner is probably not unworthy of that oracle which Socrates himself felt it necessary to consult at Delphi."

In this way they would inquire as to the cause of drought, rinderpest among the cattle, locusts, and the like, and they were told that these came through the white man. In speaking of their worship some would acknowledge that a priest dwelt in the cave and received their offerings, and that he would consult Umlimo and give forth the answer in sepulchral tones to the worshipers. This god was also worshiped at the opening of every year by a great dance, so that he would send an abundance of rain. One special place of worship was in a large cave in the midst of the Makalanga country. As this was said to be only about five or six miles from Mapani Mission, I had a desire to visit the spot and see what it was like. Setyokupi, one of the first Christian girls at Mapani, offered to accompany Ndhlamlabi and myself to the cave, as she lived near the place but had never visited it. We started early one morning to the home of Setyokupi, which was several miles from the mission, and from there continued our journey to the cave. It was much farther than we had anticipated, and we walked quite a distance before reaching the immense kopje, or hill of stone, in which the cave was. Then our way wound round and round among the rocks for a long distance. Setyokupi saw that the task was greater than she had anticipated, and fearful of losing ourselves, we asked a young lad, whom we met in the neighborhood, to guide us. After reaching the cave we were obliged to climb forty or fifty feet up the side of the rock before we could enter.

It was a large cave, extending back into the rocks, and would have formed several good-sized rooms. We had understood that the worshipers generally took a present and left it in the cave. This was frequently a branch or twig of a tree; consequently there were to be seen in it many dried leaves and branches of trees, the thought in their mind in this connection being no doubt similar to that of the olive branch of peace. There were also a few old ornaments and cloth, but nothing of value. Here it was said the people came to have their yearly dance and pray for rain. Everything on the inside was quite old, and it looked as if the place had not been visited lately, but we were informed that there was another and more important place of worship in the vicinity in which there was a pool of water. This we did not see, nor did we learn of its location. The day was fast passing and we were obliged to hasten back to the mission.

At this time, 1905, Europeans had already been fifteen years in some parts of the country and the natives about Matopo Mission were always quite willing for anyone to be present at their religious festivals. Many were beginning to throw off some of their old superstitious ideas, and some were accepting Christ; so there was no thought of impropriety in our making this tour of investigation. The account of it no doubt came out through the little boy who accompanied us, and although these natives in Mapaniland were more raw than those about Matopo Mission, perhaps nothing further would have been thought of the visit, had the rains come on that year at the usual time. Unfortunately they were exceptionally late, not really coming until the first of January, and the people were becoming desperate. It is always necessary for the heathen to let the blame rest somewhere, and as the witch doctors and diviners generally hate the missionaries because of their loss of custom and prestige, so they naturally put the blame upon our visit to the cave. I never learned that they placed the blame upon myself, but they did upon those who accompanied me. Ndhlalambi's life was really in danger that year and his people were much concerned for his safety. He, however, did not seem concerned about himself and continued to go back and forth and see about the work at Mapani. Several years later Setyokupi, who is a most devoted Christian, had to bear the blame from the older people for a similar drought, the years of plenty intervening being overlooked. We as missionaries, however, always try to be careful not to stir up unecessarily the opposition of the natives.

According to some of the older natives Umlimo is worshiped under various names; in fact, there is a trinity. In the hills to the south is the father, Shologulu. He is stern and unbending and is to be greatly feared. In the east is the son, Lunzi, who is kind and easy to be entreated. The mother, Banyanchaba, is in the north. Just how much tradition, handed down from Christianity, is embodied in this idea cannot be ascertained, but the belief is quite ancient.

Again, some of the natives say that certain of the people at times claimed to be Umlimo and to have the power ascribed to him. One of these was a woman whom the king, in order to test her power, put in a hut near him. He convinced himself of her false pretenses and punished her accordingly.

In a general way natives do not concern themselves about a Supreme God. Some, of course, will readily say that He made everything. Again we have inquired of others,

"Who made the trees, the rocks, the grass?"

They will answer, "We came here and found them already created, so we did not concern ourselves to inquire who made them."

This indifference or spiritual laziness had much to do with their religion. On another occasion we were speaking with a native living near Mapani Mission, and were telling him that he ought to repent and accept Christ as his Savior. To excuse himself he said:

"He made me. He brought me into the world and it is His business to boss me up."

He really meant to say, "I am here by no choice of my own. He made me. I am His and He has a right to do as He pleases with me."

This idea of fate runs through all their beliefs. They have no volition of their own. Everything that comes to them, whether of accident, sickness, ill luck, or whatever it may be, is the result of malevolent spirits which are in league against them. In fact, all their worship is one of the propitiation of the malevolent spirits. Good spirits will not harm them.

One day in the Sabbath-school class, where questions were freely asked, one of the older men said, "Since I hear you tell who God is and what He likes, and who Satan is and what he does, I see that our god, whom we have been worshiping, is Satan himself."

The *amadhlozi* (spirits of the departed) are constantly besetting their path, causing sickness or misfortune, or else helping them to do what they desire. Their expression, for ill luck is *Angi ladhlozi* (I do not have any spirit). When sick they send for the witch doctor to tell where the trouble is. He may say that one of the spirits thinks he had not been properly treated and wishes a goat. The goat is brought and killed, and a small portion of meat is used with medicine for the sick, but by far the greater part of the meat is generally appropriated by the witch doctor himself, who was no doubt more desirous of it than the shades.

If health is not forthcoming for the sick, he is certainly bewitched. This is generally the belief when one dies or is suffering from an incurable disease. The witch doctor then takes his "bones" and "smells out" the supposed witch, and he is very careful to select as his victim one who is not very popular in the community by reason of his wealth or other circumstances. This one is accused of bewitching, and is ignominiously put to death, and all his property confiscated.

Since the occupation of the country by the English much of this killing of supposed witches is done away with, but there are still violent deaths, which looks suspicious. Since our stay at Matopo there was an instance of an old woman being drowned, which was traced directly to the witch doctor and he was punished. There were also several instances of supposed suicide by hanging, which looked as if there might have been foul play, but which could not be ferreted. It is not unusual for the old or infirm to be gotten rid of in this way, especially by the ordeal of drinking poison.

It would be unjust to say that their doctors never use remedies; in fact, they have many herbs which they use and some of these are very efficacious. In fever we have seen them administer a greenish-looking powder of a native herb, which tasted much like quinine, and we were surprised once to see a native physician pass through the mission premises with a wallet full of various kinds of herbs. He had a pass from the magistrate to practice among the natives, and he proudly opened his wallet and displayed his drugs. Notwithstanding that they have these remedies, yet, in practice, this is often so mixed with charms and other superstitious ideas, that it is difficult to tell wherein the real remedy lies. A witch doctor, who lived near us and who had much light, exclaimed one day, "I can give medicine, and if the Lord says the sick will recover, he will recover; if He says the sick one will die, he will die; my medicine cannot save him."

When one treats a native in his home for any disease, it is always difficult to induce his people to follow the prescribed treatment; for they desire often to use their arts as well. A case of scurvy was at one of the villages, and they came to the mission for help. We went over. The boy had been losing blood for several days and was very weak, seemingly in the last stages of the disease. They had been using their arts, but to no avail, and had come to the mission as a last resort. Elder Steigerwald reproved them for waiting so long, and took hold of the case, hoping still to save him. After looking to the Lord for guidance, he managed to get the bleeding stopped, but to see that everything was properly carried out one of us remained for a time at the kraal. When he was thought to be out of danger he was left with his people, with strict injunctions to do just as they were told. When the patient was next visited it was found that the people had again brought out their charms and put them about his head, and it was necessary to frighten them thoroughly before they would follow instructions.

Parents are always very anxious to have their children at home if they become sick. This may partly be owing to natural solicitation on the part of the parents, for they love their children as well as white parents do, but it is also due to the fact that they cannot use their divinations properly except at home. Then, too, if they die, they are always anxious that their people die at home. In this way we often had great difficulty in keeping at the mission some who were sick and needed care.

One of our boys was very sick and we had been unable to help him, and both he and ourselves were looking to the Lord in his behalf. He was a good Christian and perfectly conscious all the time, and quite ready and willing to die if such was the Lord's will. His parents lived near and had been trying to take him home, but he did not wish to go; and we too thought it best for him to remain under our care. When he became very low, it was necessary to inform his parents. The father, who was a very violent and wrathy man, was determined to take the boy home, but we felt sure that a move at that time would be fatal, and told the father so.

He replied, "I'll take him home if he dies on the way. I'll not have it said that my child died and was buried away from home." And it was with great difficulty that he could be prevailed upon to let the boy remain. The Lord heard our prayer in his behalf and he recovered.

From what has been written it may readily be seen that the African believes in the immortality of the soul; that the souls of the departed take cognizance of what is done on the earth by the survivors; and that they have power over those who dwell on the earth to help, harm, or intercede in their behalf. They also believe in transmigration of souls, that the spirit of the departed often enters a snake, bird, lion, rhinoceros, or other animals, each of these tribes having its own especial animal. This does not necessarily imply that the soul remains in these forms. Frequently they speak of the animals as only a medium through which the spirit appears to its friends.

The Matabele revere the snake and will not kill it. The first year of the mission a long snake entered one of the huts, that was in process of erection, and climbed up near the roof. I told one of the boys to knock it down and kill it. He recoiled from the idea and refused. Thinking he was afraid I took a hoe, knocked it down and killed it. When other natives came to the mission the incident was related to them by the boys and they expressed great surprise. I rather supposed that they were surprised at my prowess, until one woman who knew me better than the others exclaimed, "Were you not afraid to kill it? Perhaps it was one of your friends." I then found out that the snake was an object of reverence.

Matshuba said that when his father was ill a snake entered his hut and he exclaimed, "That looks like a child of mine, it is so pretty. It is your brother, Matshuba."

"Is that the reason," we inquired, "why so many people are afraid to kill snakes?"

"Yes," he replied, "they think their friends come to visit them in this form."

Again, once while out kraal-visiting we were speaking to some people who were working in their garden. Some one came from their kraal with a message of some kind, and soon all was commotion and hurry.

I inquired, "What is the matter? Where are you going?"

They answered, "Two snakes have entered our hut and we must go and see them."

"Will you kill them?"

"No, they are probably some of our friends, who have come to visit us," was the reply.

The people were also accustomed to use a goat in their worship and then drive it away on the veldt. I know very little of this ceremony, except that when it was told to me, I was forcibly reminded of the "scapegoat" of the Israelites. Each family also has a sacred ox or cow among the herd. They do not worship images, and are surprised to find that there are people on earth who do. Two of the boys in reading their Bibles one day learned for the first time that some people worship images made by men's hand, and they were as much surprised as any white child could have been.

"Do they answer their prayers?" inquired they. "Can they talk, or do they know anything? Is it something like we make cattle out of mud to play with?"

We are accustomed to despise people who worship animals, and it is certainly not very elevating; but they are God's handiwork, and are they not superior to many of the hideous images of idolatrous nations? When these people do worship, the object of their reverence is not the animal, but the souls of their people who they think enter the animals.

Spiritualism is a legitimate product of their beliefs. I can best illustrate this feature of their worship by giving an instance which came to our notice in the year 1900. It was a religious dance. The chief actors had come from a distance and the worship was in honor of one of their dead relatives, the aim being to bring back the soul and hold conference with it through one who acted as medium.

We felt to avail ourselves of this opportunity of seeing something of their worship, that we might have a better understanding of the same. The mother of Kelenki, one of our converts, participated and she, heathenlike, was anxious to have her boy take part, but he of course refused, as he had always done when urged to join with them. It was only about two miles from the mission, so Brother and Sister Lehman and myself went over for a short time. We entered the village at about 3 P. M. and found about one hundred people assembled. They had just been drinking beer and were feeling quite good. As many of them knew us, they greeted us quite pleasantly, nothing loath to see us on this occasion, provided we did not interfere in their worship.

One of the most noticeable features at first was the evident attempt at ornamentation on the part of the women, especially the older women who were to take active part in the proceedings. We might add that only the older people took part in this dance, and that the ornamentation of the body is always a noticeable feature of their worship. Their dress, or rather undress, consisted of a short skirt of dirty, greasy leather, covered with a heavy embroidery of bright-colored beads. The rest of the body was ornamented with beads and heavy brass rings, neck, waist, arms, and ankles being heavily laden. The headdress consisted of a broad band of beads artistically put together.

Our attention was soon drawn to three women seated on the ground before one of the huts, each with a large drum made from a hollowed log, over one end of which was a skin tightly drawn. On this drum they were beating with their hands and accompanying the sound with low, plaintive singing. Presently a man, who proved to be the leader, or medium, stepped out, beating at the same time on a drum made of a broad wooden hoop, over which was stretched a piece of skin. He was a tall, athletic-looking fellow, clothed in a short skirt similar to that worn by the women. He had many yards of blue cloth wrapped about his body and a yellow scarf thrown over one shoulder. The drum which was beaten with a stick produced a sharp ringing sound, and he danced with a peculiar backward step, keeping time to the beating of his drum, and sang, calling upon the shades. To this the women, beating the drums or tomtoms, would respond. A number of other men with similar drums joined him in the dance, and the air was filled with their melody.

This was continued for some time, when all suddenly ceased and disappeared within a hut and continued their dance within. We were invited to enter, and after creeping through the low doorway we found ourselves in a hut about eighteen feet in diameter, with a somewhat higher roof than is to be found in many native huts. The performance was similar to that on the outside, except that others joined in the dance, but all danced alone. The actions and contortions of the body became more and more rapid and violent, and there was also leaping and jumping, the heat and violent exertion of the body causing the perspiration to flow freely.

The medium finally worked himself up into sort of a frenzy and announced that a spirit had entered the door. With this he pretended to enter into conversation, but as he spoke in the Shuna language we did not understand him. The dancers all finally rushed out on the rocks and the leader fell down exhausted. After their return the same motions were continued, but a new feature was added by women entering, having native-made bells tied to their ankles, and these added to the general din. The motions of all were more or less similar, and even when the actions and contortions of the body were the most violent, they were somewhat rhythmical. The noise was deafening in the extreme, and would have surely waked the dead were such a thing possible. In addition to a dozen drums and the bells, there were yelling, whistling, and singing. A huge battle-axe was handed around from one to another, and part of the time was dangling on the neck of the leader. Sad as one felt at the delusion under which they labored, he could not but be impressed by their evident earnestness, and only wished it might be expended in a better cause.

They did not forget our presence, and no doubt we did interfere with the freedom of their actions. The medium came toward us several times, beating his drum. Thinking he might be annoyed at our presence we spoke to the headman, but he hastened to assure us that we were welcome to remain. In fact, he as well as many others in the kraal, seemed to be spectators rather than participants in the worship.

They finally became quiet and the medium again claimed to converse with the departed, and this time one of our boys interpreted. Of course both questions and answers were given by the medium. Among other things he said: "I see a spirit enter the door. It says, 'Who are these white people? Are they the people who killed the Matabele?' No, they are missionaries and like the black people." It seemed evident that not only the spirit but some of the strangers present were somewhat afraid and needed assurance that we were harmless.

We returned home sad at heart for their heathendom. We were informed that this worship continued until late in the night and two days following. There was much beer drinking and immorality, so that even some of the heathen in the kraal were thoroughly disgusted.

The Matabele do not use drums in their religious dance like the Mashona. Once when we were out kraal visiting we happened to come upon some of these worshiping at Fusi's kraal. We stopped only a few minutes to see what they were doing, and were greatly shocked by the hideousness of their looks and actions. The very stamp of the bottomless pit seemed impressed upon their features.

Heathen worship, heathen dances, and hideous rites are becoming less and less in the vicinity of the mission, for the natives are fast losing faith in their old religion. The missionaries need a great deal of patience, forbearance, and firmness in dealing with the perplexing problems in reference to the natives' beliefs, but in the end God's cause is sure to win.

CHAPTER FOURTEEN

Some of the Customs

Custom is so interwoven with and dependent upon religion that it is almost impossible to dissociate the two, so there is a difference of opinion as to what constitutes custom and what religion. Whatever the natives believe or practice has in their estimation been given them by their god, even to the ornaments of their bodies. As Rev. W. Chapman says, "The most satisfactory way of changing native customs is by changing his religion." On the other hand, take away the native's religion and the restraints which often accompany it, and place him in a modern city, with its so-called modern civilization, without the restraining influences of the Christian religion, and a monstrosity of evil is often the result.

From infancy this inexorable law, custom, assails him. He must not step aside from the laws of his ancestors or he will suffer the consequences. If twins are born, they must be put to death. If a child cuts his upper front teeth first instead of the lower, again death is the penalty. Not because the mother does not love her child. It is just as dear to her as the child of Christian parents is to them, and generally no amount of money will induce her to part with it, but this infant is departing from the customs followed by its ancestors, and if its precocity leads it thus early to change the customs, what will it not do as it becomes older? It is a monstrosity and must be dealt with accordingly.

If the child is a girl, it may at any time after birth be betrothed or sold to a man for his wife, and a part or all of the pay be given to the parents to bind the contract. This intended husband may be already middle-aged or old, with several wives. That is to his credit, because it frequently means that he is rich or a man of importance in the community. An old, gray-haired man living near the mission had nine wives when we arrived on the scene, some of whom were just young girls. However, one frequently meets with heathen natives who have only one wife.

The would-be bridegroom sends some one to the father or guardian of the girl to ask for her hand in marriage. He consults his relatives in reference to the matter, but even if they disagree, he may give his consent, for he alone receives the pay. This may be in the form of cattle, sheep, or goats, or even money in later years, and the amount of pay the man can or is willing to give had much to do with the father's consent. Of course the girl has no say in the affair, and may not, until she is older, know who her intended husband is. If she is small, he waits until she is about grown before the actual marriage takes place, but in the meantime she is looked upon as his prospective wife and is often thoroughly demoralized before marriage.

Before the missionaries or Europeans came to the country, it is doubtful whether the girl rebelled much as to what disposition was made of her, for one choice was about the same as another, only so that she might become a married woman. In their eyes it was almost a disgrace to be unmarried after they had reached the proper age.

It is said that when the time came for her to be married she would say, "I am grown and want to marry." At first her people refuse, but finally they give her a hoe and showing her a piece of raw veldt say, "Show how you can dig, so that we may see whether you have strength to perform the work of a wife." She takes the hoe and shows her strength by vigorous work; for is she not to take the place of oxen or donkeys for her husband and plow and sow his gardens? This is no exaggeration, for more than one native has been heard to exclaim, "These are my oxen," pointing to his wives, the chief difference being that whereas the oxen get some time to rest and eat, the wife gets little, as she must grind and prepare the food in the interim of digging.

When the day set for the wedding arrives, a number of girls of about her own age are called and they have a feast, often of goat, after which they accompany the bride to the home of the bridegroom, an old woman, carrying a knife, leading the way. Here they are assigned their places and various ceremonies. The wedding lasts several days and ends in a feast, and very often much immorality is connected with it. During a certain stage of the ceremony the bride runs and hides, not again making her appearance until she is found by the others.

So-called marriages sometimes take place without any pay being given for the wife, but in such instances the children do not belong to or are not under the control of their parents; they belong to the father or guardian of the wife, as she has not been paid for. It may thus be seen that the giving of pay is not an unmitigated evil, as it leaves the children in the hands of their natural guardians, the parents. With the wife the pay is merely changing her from the ownership of her father to that of her husband, and if she should leave her husband, the pay or part of it must be returned to him.

It frequently happens that a man takes a wife according to native marriage without paying for her, and afterwards, if he desires to retain her or her children, he pays the father for her. A native in the vicinity of Matopo had, in this manner, taken five wives, at various times, without paying for any of them. When some of his children became of an age that his wives' parents desired to take them, he took steps to secure them by paying for his wives. One, however, whom he did not like, he drove away without paying for her.

These things show that the marriage vow is exceedingly loose and leads to much immorality. Several years after we came to Matopo Hills a law was passed by the British Government, allowing the girls some freedom of choice in regard to the marriage question, and it is now possible for Christian girls to choose Christian husbands.

A man will have a hut for himself and one for each of his wives, and the more wives he has, the greater his importance in the community. I think that it is safe to say that an old heathen's ambition is to have many wives, each with her hut, about him, many sons, who too, with their wives, add to the number of huts, and many daughters, that he may sell them for cattle or sheep and thus increase his flocks and herds. He also likes to have nephews, younger brothers, and other relatives with their wives come to him and swell the number of huts. This makes a large number of huts, large herds, and he becomes an important headman; or if his followers increase sufficiently he may become a chief. These huts, built near together and often enclosed with a fence, are what constitute a kraal. This is a Dutch word and applies only to native villages, but there may be only three or four huts and it still be called a kraal.

Their huts are built of poles and mud, much as described in the making of our own, except that the huts of the raw natives are much lower, without windows and with a doorway only about three feet in height. Sometimes no poles are used in the construction of the walls, but they are moulded of earth from the bottom up and are well made. The floor is made of ant-hill earth, well pounded. This is then covered with a thin coat of black earth and polished with stones until it looks not unlike a nicely-polished wooden floor. The Matabele build much better huts than some of the subject tribes; these latter are good farmers, but often have most miserable-looking huts.

Matabele Kraal near Matopo Mission.

There is no furniture proper in the huts. The bed consists of a mat or hide spread on the floor at night. During the day this, together with the blankets, is rolled up and tied to the roof of the hut. The pillow is made from a block of wood, and there are no chairs, a small mat answering for this purpose. They have earthen pots for cooking and brewing beer and for various purposes. They have many kinds of nicely-woven baskets, and gourds for carrying and dipping water as well as for drinking vessels. There are also the necessary stamping block and a large flat stone on which the grain is ground. The wash basin is the mouth. The mouth is filled with water, which is allowed to run in a thin stream on the hands until they are washed, and then the hands are filled in the same way to wash the face. I was greatly interested once in the operation of bathing twins. This mother had sufficient light to keep her from killing her babies because there were two of them. She spread a blanket on a large rock in the sun. Then she took a gourd of water and filled her mouth. (It is surprising how much water they can hold in the mouth; practice aids greatly in this, no doubt.) She kept the water in her mouth a short time to take off the chill, then picked up one child, held it out and, with a thin stream of water pouring from her mouth, washed the entire body of the child thoroughly. After this ablution she laid it on the blanket in the sun to dry. She again filled her mouth and taking the other baby repeated the process and also placed it on the blanket. The children were evidently accustomed to such baths; for they took it all quietly, and perhaps enjoyed it as much as a white child in a bath tub of warm water.

Polygamy is not necessarily opposed among some of the heathen women.

They will frequently tell you, "I like my husband to have more than one wife; then I do not need to work so hard." It is, however, a source of much dissension and rivalry among them and a cause of much favoritism among the children. One day Gomo was reading the story of Joseph and Benjamin. He exclaimed, "That is just like our people. The children of the favorite wife are loved more by the father." Of course polygamy is one great drawback to the introduction of christianity, but we believe that it has had its day and that in many places it is becoming less in practice. Each wife cooks of her own food for the husband and places it before him. He, with older boys, eats what he desires and leaves the balance, if there be any, for the wife and her children. If he has many wives a number of dishes are often placed before him during the day, and he can eat that which he prefers. Or, if there are several men in the kraal, they often all eat from one dish, and from each dish as it is brought to them by the various wives, while the mother and daughters eat from a separate dish.

Their chief occupation is farming, and they grow corn, kafir corn, millet, sweet potatoes, peanuts, ground peas, melons, citrons, and pumpkins. They generally hull the grain and then stamp or grind it into a very fine meal or flour. This they put into boiling water and make a very stiff porridge, or mush. Their favorite food seems to be this porridge, eaten with meat into the broth of which ground peanuts have been cooked. They generally have chickens, sheep, goats, or cattle, and often hunt or trap game. Their usual way of eating is to allow the food to cool a little and then dip the two front fingers into the porridge, take a little and dip it into the gravy and then put it into their mouth. They also greatly relish green corn, eaten from the cob or cut off and ground on the millstones. This milky meal is then made into a loaf and placed into a kettle and thoroughly steamed. This is their best substitute for bread, and in its season it is considered their most dainty dish, and with a little salt it is quite palatable, especially if not much grit has combined with it in the process of preparation.

The African is fond of his beer, which also is made by the wives. For this purpose they use any of the grains grown by them, but they prefer kafir corn or millet. This is moistened and put in a warm place until it sprouts. It is then ground or stamped and the meal is cooked into a thin porridge and put into large earthen pots, where more water is added, also the yeast or dregs of a previous brewing. It is then allowed to stand in a warm place and ferment, and before drinking it is usually strained through a loose bag of their own weaving. The native will tell you that their god showed them how to make the beer, and I have no doubt but that he did.

It is needless to say that it intoxicates and is the cause of frequent brawls and fights among them, and it is not unusual for the missionaries to be called upon to help settle some of these disturbances. It is less difficult to convince the Africans of the evil effects of its use than it is some Europeans. The latter will often tell you that the native thrives and works better if allowed his beer. Missionaries are not wanting who think it is best not to interfere with their native Christians having their beer. Our missionaries, however, have no difficulty in inducing the Christians to discard the use of it, and we believe the sentiment against it is increasing among the missionaries in general. In a native Conference held at Matopo Mission in February, 1914, the question of native beer came up. Of course all were opposed to members drinking it, but the question was in regard to the Christian girls, who were minors, assisting in the making of it, since they are under the jurisdiction of their heathen parents. The older native Christians were in favor of more stringent measures than even the missionaries.

In order to show what an enlightened Christian native can and will do if he has the power we need only refer to the work of King Khama. He is the King of Bechuanaland, the country just west of Southern Rhodesia. His father was a heathen king and a sorcerer, but Khama embraced Christianity in his youth, and in the midst of most bitter persecutions from his own father and others, he stood true. The people finally recognizing his ability chose him king in place of his father in 1872. Then his difficulties began in another line. If he was to be the chief of the country, it must be founded on the principles of the Gospel. All imported liquor was prohibited from crossing the border, nor was native beer allowed to be made.

Matabele Women Stamping Grain.

It was a fierce battle with some of the natives themselves, for they were not all Christians and did not readily yield. This domestic trouble, however, was nothing compared with the battle he had to wage with unprincipled white traders and even with government officials, for the country was under the protection of England, and they had some voice in the management of affairs. But Khama won the day in such a struggle as would have dismayed many a stouter heart. According to Mr. J. H. Hepburn, Khama wrote to the British Administration as follows: "I dread the white man's drink more than the assegais of the Matabele which kill men's bodies and is quickly over; but drink puts devils into men and destroys their souls and bodies forever. Its wounds never heal. I pray your Honor never to ask me to open even a little door to drink." Words worthy of a native Christian hero, indeed; a hero that could not be bought, that could not be bribed or frightened by the liquor men.

The Government of Rhodesia is rather favorable toward native beer, yet we owe it much for prohibiting imported liquor sold to natives within its territory. Perhaps (who knows?) Khama's firm stand in his own territory may have been an influence in keeping Rhodesian natives from securing imported liquor.

Mention was made before that the native way of getting work done is to make a quantity of beer and invite their neighbors. They do this in digging and preparing the ground for sowing, in weeding, in cultivating, and in threshing. While a little beer is given during the work, the greater part is kept back until the work is completed, perhaps as an inducement for them to persevere unto the end. If then one, in evangelistic work, comes upon such a company early in the day, they are not much the worse for drink and will often listen attentively.

Once Sister Steigerwald and I came to a place where a large company were busy weeding. They had a large garden to weed and did not greatly desire to stop for service, but we promised not to keep them long, so they gathered under the shade of a tree. On opening our Bible our eye fell on the "Parable of the Tares," which seemed quite suitable for the occasion. They listened most attentively to the short talk, and as illustrations taken from their gardens and work always seemed better understood and appreciated, we made use of such entirely in the application. After singing and prayer we told them they might return to their work. We sat still and watched them awhile, and as they worked and pulled out the weeds, we could hear them talking to one another and saying, "Yes, the bad things Satan sows in our hearts are just like these weeds, and they need to be rooted out or they will destroy us."

On another occasion, one Sunday morning, there were no natives from one of the large kraals present at the services, and we felt to pay them a visit. Ganukisa and some of the boys accompanying, we went to the place in the afternoon to hold service. We always tried to impress upon the people that they should not work on Sunday, and many were heeding, so on this occasion we were surprised to find about seventy-five of them having a digging. As we drew near, they had just finished the work and were about to surround the huge beer pots for a "good time." We knew by the time they had consumed all that beer they would scarcely be in a condition to receive the Gospel. What should we do? We never like to ask the natives to do anything unless there is some probability of its being carried out, for one is likely to lose influence over them. Could they be persuaded to leave their beer pots and let us talk to them first? We could not make them do it, but God could, so looking to Him we said,

"Leave the beer and come out under the shade of the trees while we talk to you."

"Oh, no," they replied, "let us drink the beer first and then we will come."

We knew that if they did their drinking first some of them would not stay for the service, so again, with somewhat more authority, I repeated the request, and at the same time, together with the Christian natives who accompanied, moved toward the shade. It was almost more than we expected, but the Lord moved upon their hearts to leave the beer untouched, and come to listen. The Lord especially anointed some of our native Christians for the service and they gave forth the Word with power. One of them referred very strongly to their desecration of the Sabbath. At first they sought to justify themselves, but as the truth was pressed home to them they said they would never do it again. At the close a number of the older men for the first time in their lives prayed and pleaded for pardon. The old women who had invited them to work seemed especially concerned and promised not to repeat it on Sunday.

When they thresh they also invite a lot of their neighbors. They place the grain on a large flat rock and then strike it with a straight stick. Once I was present when a large number of the Amahole, or subject tribes, were threshing. They were decked out with all their ornaments, and being divided into two sides were placed opposite to one another, like two opposing forces in battle array. Each being armed with his threshing stick, they performed a mimic battle with the grain lying on the rock between the two lines of battle, each one alternately driving the other before it and at the same time beating the grain with their sticks. They also sang their war song, of how the Matabele overcame them and impaled them alive, and of the dire vengeance they would inflict in return. The interlude would be occupied by a sort of ballet dancer among them. The whole was exceedingly heathenish, but not uninteresting; and as for the grain, a large amount of it was threshed.

While much of the work falls to the women, some of the native men are quite diligent in digging in their gardens; but they generally wish to sell their grain and secure money to pay taxes for themselves and their wives. The women, in addition to growing most of the food that is eaten, often help to furnish the tax money. Of course to the raw native dress is a negligible quantity.

The people are always generous, and the food in the kraals is shared with the strangers. No one needs to go through the country hungry unless there is famine, and even then they will often divide the last morsel. When the stranger comes among them, they always bid him welcome, and it is etiquette to let him remain for at least one day without asking him any questions as to his business among them.

Even in respect to continually begging, which is so obnoxious to Europeans, the native is not so rude as it would appear. They are not slow to ask one another, and they have often surprised me by saying that they felt flattered to be asked for articles, as it showed that they had something which the other did not have and they had an opportunity to help. A native likes to have plenty, but he does not want to have his gardens surpass too much those of his neighbors, in productiveness; neither does he want his herds to surpass others too much, for fear he may be an object of envy to those around him and a victim of malice, or be accused of witchcraft.

There always seems to be a great attachment between the mother and her children all through life. This does not hinder the big, stout boy, however, from lying around and living on the bounty of his hard-working mother, and on the other hand the heathen boy will often exert himself to aid his mother and pay her hut tax, and she often lives with her son when she becomes old.

The native women generally shave their heads with a piece of sharp glass. It is a laborious and painful process and needs to be done by an expert, but in the end it is well done. The married woman always leaves a small tuft of hair on the crown of her head. This is her sign of wifehood. The raw native has no means of keeping record of his age, so we must always guess at it.

Matabele Women Digging.

The government is patriarchal and the younger are generally respectful to the elders, and all are more or less polite to one another. Their very name implies this. The surname is handed down from father to child, even the wife retaining that of her father unless she is married by Christian marriage. The surname is also the *isibongo*, or thank word. By that I mean that it is what they say if they wish to thank for any favor. Among themselves they do not say "I thank you" for any favor received. Suppose Muza Sibanda would give another one something. The recipient on receiving it would say "Sibanda" instead of "I thank you." Again, in addressing another, if one wishes to be polite or respectful he will use the last, not the first name, or he may say "Father," "Mother," or the like. I at first thought them somewhat rude in not thanking properly, but soon found that it was often the result of not knowing what to say. One day I gave a piece of bread to a little fellow about five years of age. He hesitated, then looking up into my face, said, "*Isibongo sako sipi?*" ("What is your thank name?") If a native is given anything, all the others present will join in thanking, for a favor to one is a favor to all. The mother will often use the thank name, or surname, as a term of endearment to her child. After she has a child she is no longer known by her name, but if the child is Luju she is known as the "mother of Luju."

If one falls or meets with an accident, however slight, all the rest will say "*Pepa*" ("Beg pardon"). If one enters the kraal of another, he enters the hut and sits down near the door without saying anything. Presently he says "*Eh! kuhle*" ("Peace"), about equivalent to saying, "Peace be to this house." It is not a salutation, but a polite way of announcing his presence. The occupant of the hut then responds by saying, "*Eh! sa ku bona*" ("We see you"). In reality, however, it is equivalent to saying "How do you do?" to which the other responds.

It is a real treat to hear two old natives conversing together, especially if they are unconscious of one's presence. Their gossip may not be very elevating, but it is always carried on in a polite and interesting manner. The Tebele language is most beautiful and expressive, as its liquid syllables roll off the native tongue, and it is always most correctly spoken—no errors in grammar among them.

This would not be complete without mention being made of death and burial. In burial the various tribes differ somewhat among themselves. Among the Matabele, when one dies the friends come and prepare the body for burial by placing it in a sitting posture with the knees brought up near the face. They clothe it in the garments which it owned, and wrap the blanket about it, tying the body firmly in this position with the face exposed. It is then left sitting in the hut, together with some of the women mourners, while the men go and select a place for burial, generally at a little distance from the kraal, unless the deceased should be headman. They make the grave more or less circular in form, and near the bottom a slight excavation is made in the side for the reception of the body.

The body is then placed on a blanket or large hide and carried out to the grave, the friends following and mourning. A gourd filled with fresh water is brought, and with this a near friend or relative washes the face of the dead, at the same time giving it a message to kindly remember them to the king and to speak a good word for them. The two men standing in the grave receive the body and place it in the excavation with the face toward the east. They fasten it in position with stones and then fill in the grave with earth. On top of the grave are placed stones and the property of the deceased, together with branches of trees, perhaps to protect it from the wild beasts, for the grave is somewhat shallow.

As children do not have any garments which they can call their own, they are often buried without anything being wrapped about the body. Once, when a little son of Mapita died, Sister Doner and I went over to the burial. The little body was lowered into the grave quite bare and they were about to put in the earth. Sister Doner could not stand that, so she hastily removed a large apron which she had on and told them to wrap that around the little body before throwing in the earth. They did so, but no doubt would have preferred keeping it for themselves before it had been defiled by coming into contact with the dead body. When Kelenki, one of our Christian boys, died in his home, they wanted to know what to do with his books, and one of the other Christian boys said he thought they had better leave them for the living.

After burial they all go to the river and wash, for death means defilement. The women are the chief mourners, and they assemble early in the morning, fill the air with their wailing and then return home until the following morning. This is often done for four consecutive mornings. In the interim the relatives sit about the kraal, quiet and with little talking, except to answer the condolences of their friends, who come from time to time to sympathize with them. There is no feast, as among some natives. In fact, for a time little food is cooked or eaten except that brought by neighbors.

Some of the other tribes lay the body down in burial, and often place it in the crevices of the rocks. If the deceased is headman of the kraal, he is generally buried in the enclosure and often inside his own hut, and the people usually remain there for a year and then, after a period of worship, the kraal is abandoned. The wives go to be the wives of the brother of the deceased, unless they be old, when they usually live with a son or daughter.

About fifteen miles from the mission, in the direction of Bulawayo, is the grave of the first king, Umzilikazi. It is in a large kopje, between some immense boulders. On the top of the grave, or in the immediate vicinity— since one cannot point out the exact spot of the body—are many wagon loads of rock thrown in to fill up the cavity between the boulders. There are also wheels and the remains of broken wagons and other property once owned by the king, and probably bought from the white men in his emigration from Zululand to this country. I cannot give the exact date of this king's death, but it was at least more than fifty years ago. As he was considered the god of the Matabele, this grave was often no doubt a place of worship by the tribe, but we have no knowledge that it has been worshiped in late years. Perhaps it somewhat fell into disuse after Umlimo, the god of the Makalanga, was considered so powerful.

FIFTEEN

Later Visits

The missionary stands to the native for religion and education, for all the help he may get to make his life cleaner, more moral, and more in keeping with ideals of the white man at his best.—M. S. Evans.

In the year 1910 it was my privilege, on returning from a furlough to Natal, to again visit Matopo, after an absence of nearly four years. Bishop and Mrs. Steigerwald were at that time in America on furlough, and Brother Doner and his wife, who was formerly Sister Sallie Kreider, and Sister Mary Heise were in charge of Matopo Mission. When I reached Bulawayo I found Brother Doner waiting to convey me to the mission. It was indeed a pleasure again to visit the place and to look into the faces of those natives who had grown very dear by reason of my long stay among them. Here it was my privilege to come into contact, for the first time, with raw heathendom, and to have the joy of seeing light enter darkened minds and souls born into the Kingdom. So it occupies a tender spot which later experiences cannot touch.

There had been improvements made since I had left. Prominent among these were two substantial brick buildings, a house for the boys and one for the girls, and there were thirty-three boys occupying the one and three girls the other. There is a nice little band of believers at this place, some of whom I wish especially to mention. First is poor old blind Ngiga. Shortly after Elder Engle's death we found him at a kraal, destitute and afflicted, with no one seemingly to care for him and give him food. We carried or sent food to him for a time, and gave him a blanket, and he gradually gained strength. Thinking that exercise would do him good, Brother Lehman encouraged him to come to the mission for his food, as he was only a short distance away. He had lain for so long without exercising his body that at first it was with great difficulty that he reached the mission, but being supplied with food, he grew stronger and was enabled to walk the distance easily and to help himself a little. Some time after Elder Steigerwald came he treated him for his disease and built a hut and brought him to the mission to stay, as the loathsome disease with which he was afflicted had left him about blind. He, however, was converted and has been received into the Church. It is a pleasure to hear him now testify to Christ's saving power, and to praise the Lord for bringing the missionaries. Truly, the Lord is no Respecter of persons.

Again, let us go to Buka's house. My readers will remember Buka, whom

Sister Heise and I found upon the rocks eleven years before when we went in search of little Lomazwana. Yes, it is really he whose life and home looked so black to us that day. He moved to within about three miles of the mission, and his son Kolisa came to stay at the mission and go to school. The father became sick and Brother and Sister Doner visited him and ministered unto him. Then they built him a hut and made him more comfortable. He finally became a paralytic and unable to help himself, so Brother Steigerwald assisted them to get a home on the mission premises, and gave them gardens, so that they are now quite comfortable. The oldest daughter also accepted Christ, then the mother followed, and these two with the son are now members of the Church.

My first Sunday at Matopo, in company with Brother and Sister Doner, I visited this home. A smile of recognition at once lighted up the face of the invalid father; and though he could not speak, the family interpreted the sounds he made. After he had expressed his welcome he said that though his body and speech were paralyzed, yet his heart was all right. During another visit he tried to explain how Jesus was dwelling within, and how glad he was that when he got "over there" he would not be sick. One could not help feeling that he had learned to know the Lord. Truly, affliction had proved a blessing to him.

Building the Boys' House at Matopo, M. S.

Boys' Brick House at Matopo Mission.

There was a good school at Matopo, with Sister Heise and Matshuba as teachers. Brother Doners were very busy overseeing this work, as well as their own station at Mapani Mission, and they kindly took me to that place to see something of the work there. Nyamazana had had charge of the mission at Mapani for about six months and was doing good work, especially spiritually. He is Spirit-filled and alive to the responsibility resting upon him. He had charge of the Inquirers' Class and Sunday services, and the natives say that he preaches powerful sermons. He has a nice Christian wife, who is a help to him. There is a company of earnest believers at this place. Brother Doner erected a large brick church and a brick dwelling-house, which added greatly to the appearance and comfort of the work, and he deserves much credit for the work accomplished alone and single-handed in building.

The first Friday in each month has been set apart by the missionaries in Africa as a day of prayer and fasting. On the Prayer Day in May of that year we were permitted to meet with the believers at Mapani Mission. Over seventy were assembled. They included the members of the Church here and those of the Inquirers' Class. We had a most precious waiting on the Lord and heard many soul-stirring prayers and testimonies. Many seemed to be reaching out for a greater fulness of the Spirit, while others were overflowing with the joy of the Lord. The work was most encouraging and the members steadfast, and the Lord had been pouring out His Spirit upon some of them in a marvelous manner, and our hearts were made to rejoice with them.

We also spent a few days visiting some of the people and the schools taught by Brethren Nkwidini, Mlobeka, and Nyamazana. All three of these teachers were our former pupils and had been converted at Matopo.

Brother and Sister Doner then took me to Mtyabezi Mission, after which they returned to Matopo. Mtyabezi is the mission station of Brother and Sister Frey, and a little over a year after it was opened Miss Elizabeth Engle also came to help in it. This was my first visit at the station, and I was made to rejoice at what the Lord was doing at this place. The buildings are pleasantly located at the foot of an immense kopje, which towers high above them in the background. A neat-looking brick church had been erected by Brother Frey, and well-built huts in which they were living at the time.

A Native Christian's Home. Matshuba's.

Sister Frey had been doing the teaching, but at the time of my visit, Bunu, one of their pupils and converts, was teaching and doing excellent work. On Thursday Sisters Frey and Engle and myself went in the wagon to visit some members about eight miles distant, where we met with a warm reception among those who were Christians. At one place there was a Christian woman about sixty years of age, who seemed so happy in the Lord and so eager to make us welcome and comfortable during our stay. We were surprised to find in one of the kraals a native dressmaker who owned a sewing machine and had all the sewing she could do for her dark-skinned neighbors. The sisters have been teaching their girls and women to sew.

In the evening about thirty natives, most of whom were believers, gathered around our campfire to hold service. We spoke for a time, and then a number gave a clear testimony to the saving power of Christ. We had to contrast this little company with some other gatherings which we have seen and heard in the hours of night in darkest Africa, where beer, the dance, licentiousness, and all forms of devil worship made night hideous. One can best understand what the Gospel message is doing for the people, if he first sees something of paganism.

On Sunday at the mission there was a very impressive time, and when the altar call was given a number came forward. There were truly penitent hearts, among whom were a number of young men seeking to get right with God; also some girls and married people. Here was a woman whose husband had two wives, and she was much persecuted at home, but she wanted to follow the Lord, and piteously, in the midst of her sobs, she inquired what she should do. Then a Magdalene confessed that she had fallen into grievous sin, and like the one of old came with bitter tears to the feet of Jesus. Another's way was made hard on account of the unfaithfulness of her husband, and so on. But the one whose experience seemed the most touching was a woman of nearly sixty years. Her married daughter, who is a Christian, had been much in prayer for her mother, and so the woman came and with utter abandonment, seemingly, threw herself at the feet of Jesus, weeping and confessing her sins and saying, "I am a dog. Pick me up, Lord."

At the opening of 1913 we were permitted to make another visit to the missions in this vicinity. This vacation was to be only a month, and as I had in the meantime been cut off from association with white people, except those at the mission, I concluded to spend the first few days in Bulawayo. The place had grown since we reached it, nearly fifteen years before, and although the growth had not been so rapid it was of an enduring, steady kind. The place is laid out on broad lines, with broad streets and roomy dwellings—no need for skyscrapers here. There are many fine, substantial-looking business blocks, and as one goes into the suburbs he sees many elegant, well-built dwelling-houses. There are fine churches, a good hospital, museum, and library, and two large government school buildings, each with a good dormitory attached. One of these is for boys and the other, which is on the opposite side of the town, is for girls. Here, as in all parts of South Africa, there is some industrial work in connection with the schools. Bulawayo has also many excellent stores and shops, so that one may purchase almost anything required, not only in the line of provisions, household goods, and clothing, but all lines of farming implements and many kinds of machinery. The heavy wagons, drawn by great rows of oxen, donkeys, and mules, are still to be seen, but there are also many dainty one-horse traps, as well as two-horse conveyances, and a large number of automobiles and motorcycles.

There is attached to the town a large native location, for the heavy part of the work as well as the housework is about all done by native boys. They are all called "boys." In the eyes of their white employers the native seldom becomes a man. He may be an old boy or a young boy, a little boy or a big boy, but he is always a boy. On the other hand, in the eyes of many Europeans it is almost an insult to speak of their children as boys. In the early days one of the missionaries, in speaking to an old European lady, said something about her boy. She straightened herself proudly and with emphasis said, "My son." At the mission one day a native woman was begging very hard for a piece of cloth, and to strengthen her request she said, "I am your boy," evidently meaning that she belonged to me.

Mtshabezi Church and School.

Mtshabezi Mission in 1910.

Although Bulawayo is the largest town in Southern Rhodesia, there are others, such as Salisbury, Gwelo, Victoria, and Gwanda, which deserve mention. Farmers are scattered throughout the country, especially along the high, rolling plain between Bulawayo and Salisbury. There are many valuable gold mines and many old gold workings to be found in various places. The most noted is Great Zimbabwe, near Victoria. It is said: "The ruins cover a large area, and on an eminence are the remains of a fortress, the walls of which are thirty feet high and ten feet thick, and built of cut stones put together without mortar, so closely-fitting that a knife can hardly be inserted between them. Smelting crucibles, with gold in them, ingot moulds, and spears have been found." Some think that the Sabeans from Arabia worked these about 3,000 years ago. This is thought by some to be the "gold of Ophir." Ruins on a smaller scale are to be found in various places. Not far from Mapani Mission we saw a circular wall made of wedge-shaped stones, nicely fitted together. The country is also rich in iron ore, and at Wankie is the great coal-mining district. All these places furnish abundant work for all the natives of Rhodesia, and are also centers for mission work.

January 1, I was again taken to Motopo Mission, not with the slow, patient donkeys of fifteen years ago, but with the swifter mules. Many changes have taken place among the natives surrounding the mission since 1898. On our first entering this valley the natives had just fled and hid themselves away in these rocks at the close of the Rebellion. They were then very poor, without flocks and herds, and had few gardens, and very little of the land had ever been brought under cultivation. Since then the natives have gradually come out of their hiding-places and settled down to their work. Under the influence of peace and better teaching their surroundings have greatly changed. There are more natives near the mission than at first, and they have sheep, goats, and cattle, and some of them have plows and oxen to draw them, so that they can plow their large gardens. Every available place near the mission has been brought under cultivation, but not in the old, laborious way with human oxen, so that the wives are not the slaves they once were. Of course, in the absence of the men at work the women often hold the plow, but they have more time to keep house. One of the officials affirms that the best way of doing away with polygamy is by introducing civilized ways of farming.

The people began by bringing their oxen to Brother Steigerwald to be trained, and then he helped them to procure plows, and they still come to him for help in trouble. The 3,000-acre farm is far too small for all who desire to live near the mission. If he had twice the amount of land it would soon become filled with natives, who would thus be near the mission and under the influence of the Gospel.

Let us visit some of the houses and see what changes have taken place. Here first is the home of Matshuba. As he was first in the fold, he is worthy of first notice. He lives in a small, neatly-built brick house, with a well-swept yard inclosed by a fence. Inside the house are homemade bedsteads, chairs and tables, and here is Matshuba the same as of yore. He is older and has fought many battles since that first day when, as a little boy, he came and watched the newcomers. He has found the conflict severe and almost overpowering at times. It has left some scars, but, praise God! he has come off victorious at last, and in a more humble spirit he is following the meek and lowly Savior. He is Elder Steigerwald's right-hand man and is capable of turning his hand to almost any kind of work. He can take the blacksmith tools and mend the large three-disc plow; he can make use of the small engine and grind the meal for the native food, or do any other kind of work about the place. Best of all, he can go out and tell the people about Jesus. He had hoped that the elder's many-sided ability might be his, and he seems to have had his wish. He could secure much larger pay as an engineer in the mines, but he feels that his place is in the Lord's work. May he have our prayers that he may always find God's grace sufficient.

Mtshabezi—Baptismal Scene.

Here too is his wife, Makiwa. She was also educated at Matopo Mission, where she learned not only in school, but also in the kitchen and sewing-room, that she might know how to take care of her home and family. A faithful helpmate she has been to her husband and a blessing in the Church. Here are their little boy and girl, whom they are bringing up in the fear of the Lord. This old woman, also neatly dressed, is Matshuba's mother, long a slave to her old religion, her superstitious ideas, her beer and her tobacco. Now she has accepted Christ as her Savior and He has cleansed her and she is in the Church. And this bright-looking girl is her daughter, Sixpence. She was only about four or five years old when we came to Matopo. Now she is a tall, fine-looking Christian woman and well taught. She has on a neat-looking black dress which, Sister Steigerwald tells me, she cut and sewed without any help from the missionaries. Yes, this is a Christian home, from which we hope and pray that the evils of heathendom have flown forever.

There are others. First is Anyana, long a faithful helper of the mission, and his wife, Citiwa, also one of our girls. Then comes Siyaya, who had some falls, but he has at last got his feet on the Rock and is helping to tell others of Christ. Mahlenhle is also here. He is the same faithful boy as of old, one of those who never give their missionary any uneasiness. He is always ready and willing to do what he can, which is not a little. He teaches, he preaches, and interprets for others, or he can go out and handle the oxen and see to the farming. There are also many new ones in church and school, several of whom are assisting in teaching. There are forty-two boys staying at the mission for school, and a number coming to day-school. Sister Heise has plenty to do, for she teaches both early morning and midday, and is doing excellent work. There are about 150 regular attendants at the Sunday services. The majority of them are young men and women and children. Almost all are respectably clothed and are seeking to know the Lord. The girls who desire to stay at the missionaries' and be trained are now sent to the Girls' School at Mtyabezi Mission. There is a large sewing class at this place for those who wish to learn. Two new missionaries, Brother Levi Steckly and Sister Cora Alvis, are also assisting in the work at Matopo.

I went out among the people, eager to secure a snapshot of a kraal, as they formerly were, but I failed. They are all better built and more cleanly than formerly. In every village there are some who wear European clothing, for even if they have not accepted Christ as their Savior, some have put on the garments of civilization. There are, of course, many among the older ones who have not changed much, and who have always hardened their hearts and stiffened their necks against the truth. This has been the condition of the world ever since the Fall, and it will no doubt continue until all sin and wickedness shall be put under foot and He shall reign in righteousness. If the command had been "Go into all the world and make disciples of every creature," missionaries would have given up long ago in despair. Miss Carmichael, in her work, "Things as They Are in Missionary Work in Southern India," says, "It is required in a steward that a man be found faithful. Praise God! it does not say 'successful.'" The same will apply to missionary work in Africa.

During the year of our visit the rains were unusually late, and, as the harvest had been quite light the previous year, some of the people were in great need of grain. Brother Steigerwald was doing all in his power to get grain out from Bulawayo for them. The six mules were hauling out every week to the extent of their strength, for farmers are not allowed to take their oxen on the road, for fear disease may spread among the cattle. As the wagon returned from Bulawayo with fifteen 200-pound bags of grain on it, the people, who had been watching for its return, hastened to come to the mission to purchase. Grain was expensive, about seven or eight dollars a bag; but as soon as it was unloaded it was sold. Their people must have food, and many of the able-bodied natives had been away to work and thus procured money, and perhaps a month's wages would buy one bag of grain. Others were trying to sell some of the cattle and sheep for grain. Although many of these old people who were buying had not accepted Christ as their Savior, yet they have absolute confidence in His messenger, Elder Steigerwald, and they come to him in their difficulties, knowing that he has a kind heart. He is their father, as Sister Steigerwald is their mother.

A love feast had been announced for Mtyabezi Mission the middle of January, and arrangements had been made for all the white workers and as many of the native converts as possible to attend. Mr. Steckly and Mr. Hemming went across the hills, twenty-five miles, on foot, and the rest of us went by wagon around on the road—a distance of about forty-five miles. This road was down through the hills in the direction of Mapani Mission. We started on Thursday morning, sleeping out on the veldt during the night, and reached Mtyabezi on Friday afternoon.

Brother Freys were at that time in America on furlough, but the work was ably carried on by Brother Walter Winger and his wife, formerly Abbie Bert, and Sister Elizabeth Engle. This is now known as our Girls' School. Twenty-five girls were then staying at the mission, and they are being trained in housework and sewing, in addition to school and outside work. They are also supplying some of our Christian boys with Christian wives, and Christian marriage is taking the place of heathen rites. In addition to these there was a good-sized day-school, which was under the excellent management of Miss Sadie Book. There were also several large out-schools in connection with this mission. A large brick house was nearly completed and they were at the same time living in it. This part of the country south of the hills was especially suffering from drought at this time. Although this was in the middle of what should have been the rainy season, yet no rains had fallen, and the entire country was bare, not a blade of grass was to be seen, and the grain sown had not yet sprouted. Brother Winger was busy with his wagon, getting grain out from the station ten miles away to help the people.

This was the first love feast in Southern Rhodesia that I had been permitted to attend for nearly seven years, and I had looked eagerly forward to this gathering. The joy of seeing the natives assemble for the occasion was too deep for words. First to come were some of the communicants from Matopo Mission on Friday evening. The sisters were walking in front, Indian file, with their blankets and Sunday clothing tied up in a bundle and carried on their heads, and Sixpence leading the way. Following these were the brethren, with Matshuba bringing up the rear. It was now sundown and they had walked twenty-five miles and were tired, so they were shown their places for the night, and after eating their supper, and prayer, they retired. The next morning early a similar crowd came from Mapani Station, fifteen miles distant. A number also gathered from the vicinity of Mtyabezi and out-schools on

Saturday morning. The little church could not hold all and an overflow meeting was held on the outside. There were also a number of members who could not be present.

Saturday morning was devoted to a short discourse and self-examination meeting, followed by testimonies. It was an inspiration to look over the crowded house and listen to the earnest testimonies following one after another in rapid succession. Often four or five would be on their feet at once, and yet there was no confusion or disorder, as each one quietly waited for his time to speak. We had to say to ourselves, again and again, "What hath God wrought!" We could not avoid contrasting the early days of nakedness and midnight heathendom with this enlightened, well-dressed company before us. In fact, the contrast was so marked that one could scarcely bridge the chasm even in imagination.

Girls at Mtshabezi Mission.

In the afternoon seventeen from Mtyabezi Mission and its out-schools were received into the Church by the right hand of fellowship. On account of the drought and lack of water in the streams, the baptism was deferred until a later date. There were several others who made application, but after examination it was thought that some were not ready. On Saturday evening the natives had a meeting of their own and were addressed by Myamazana, while the missionaries had an English service and were addressed by Bishop Steigerwald.

On Sunday morning we again gathered to observe the ordinance of feet-washing and to commemorate the sufferings and death of our Savior. There were over 300 natives gathered together, nearly all of whom were either members or inquirers. The native communicants were 129 and the white ones eleven, making 140 in all, and these assembled in the Church while the rest were addressed by Mahlenhle and others on the outside. We had now a better opportunity of looking into the faces of those who had been received into Church fellowship. As our missionaries are in close touch with their people and know pretty well their private lives, we knew something of the company before us.

It was indeed an intelligent and respectable-looking company of men and women, one to be proud of, if I might use the term. Its respectability did not depend so much on the fact that they had thrown off the undress of paganism and had donned the garments of civilization. That is not necessarily an adjunct of Christianity, nor is it all due to Christian influence. While the missionaries have been laboring these years to win souls to Christ, many civilizing influences have been at work throughout the country, some of which have been previously mentioned. Stores with European clothing are to be found everywhere, and many natives discard their heathen garb for civilized clothing and yet know absolutely nothing of Christ and His power to save. Some of these well-dressed natives about the towns have learned far more of the evils of civilization than of its virtues, and hide under their new dress an even blacker heart than they did under their old pagan exterior. Then too we are sorry to say that intelligence in the sense of having been at a mission station and learning to read does not necessarily make them Christians. Some of these also, to the great sorrow of their teachers, have made poor use of their knowledge.

It is because the missionary sees this, and knows only too well the many pitfalls before their unwary feet; it is because he realizes, as probably no one else does, what it means to these poor souls to be so suddenly brought from the dense darkness of heathendom into the glaring lights of modern civilization, and how unprepared they are for it all, how little they know to shun the evil and choose the good; it is because he knows how helpless these are who have suddenly broken loose from their old tribal laws and customs—some of which were beneficial—and have been cast on the untried sea of strange and bewildering surroundings, without any anchor to hold or compass and chart to guide them—I say it is because the missionary knows all this and much more that he can rejoice over such a crowd of fine-looking, stalwart men and women as were gathered there that day to commemorate the sufferings and death of our Lord.

He sees in the company before him Christian homes, free from ignorance and superstition, free from witchcraft and pagan worship, free from the beer, the filth, and degradation of their neighbors. He sees in this company, homes free from the licentiousness and vice so common not only among their heathen neighbors, but, sad to say, also among some of their white ones. The missionary can rejoice that here are men and women who have the Anchor in their souls and are standing as beacon lights to their heathen neighbors and friends. It means much to them on the one hand to break off from their old heathen lives; it means much on the other not to be allured by the evils of the white man's civilization and the inducements so often thrown out to lead lives of sin. To come out from all these and accept Christ as Savior and be true to Him would seem to be an almost Herculean task, and much greater than those in Christian lands are called upon to perform. But we know that it has been and is being accomplished. While one feels to rejoice over these sheep, at the same time he bears a heavy heart for those other ones which have been devoured by the grievous wolves.

The missionary is about the only force that makes for righteousness among the natives, and he would often feel that his task was an impossible one did he not continually realize that he is only under orders of Him Who is sure in the end to win. Lest some may think that I am overestimating some of these things, let me again quote Mr. Evans, who is an authority on native affairs from a governmental standpoint. He says:

"What is effecting the most profound change in the native is his contact with the white man at all points, and this change is proceeding with ever-accelerating speed. The fundamental difference between these changes and those wrought by the missionaries is that, in the former there is little building up of any salutary influence to take the place of the old wholesome restraints, whilst in the latter religion and morality are inculcated and replace the checks weakened or destroyed."

The work in Southern Rhodesia is by no means completed; it is only fairly begun. The natives are just beginning to see the advantages of Christian teaching, and are calling more and more loudly for schools, and they are eagerly availing themselves of the opportunities afforded. There is a large field to work and the time is opportune. Let every one of God's children ask himself what his duty and privileges are in taking possession of the country for God. Our people should have at least one more station of white missionaries here as well as others for native workers. Shall we leave to themselves these people, who are emerging from centuries of darkness, to the influence of a corrupt civilization? Our missionaries are laboring to the extent of their ability and the means at their disposal. The work can advance only as it is backed up by the people of the homeland, together with their prayers and money. Something depends upon you, my reader, whoever you may be. What part have you had in the winning of these souls? What part are you going to have in those yet unborn into the Kingdom?

PART TWO

MACHA MISSION

"Lo, I am with you always, even unto the end of the world"

—Matt. 28: 20

CHAPTER ONE

Bound for the Zambezi

Africa is a gigantic and dark continent. In fact, it is several continents in one. Although nearly every one seems to know something of its immensity, yet very few persons realize it unless they have resided for a time in some portion of its vast interior; even then their knowledge of it is likely to be quite vague. For centuries travelers of various nationalities sought to penetrate it, many of whom perished in the effort, while others brought back wonderful stories of peril and adventure.

It remained for David Livingstone, however, to unearth the secrets of Central Africa and to expose to the gaze of Christendom something of its condition and needs. He inspired missionaries to press into the narrow opening thus made, and to carry the light of the Gospel to the millions bound in chains of darkness and blackest midnight. Messengers have been heeding the call and have been kindling fires, one here and another there, in the darkness.

In dealing with missionary work in Africa we must continually keep in mind the fact that the natives are much scattered. The population cannot definitely be ascertained, but it is variously estimated at from 130 to 150 millions of people. These are scattered over a territory equal in area to the United States of America, Europe, India, and China combined. In certain portions, such as the Sahara and Kalahari Deserts, there are very few natives, while the lower plains and river valleys support a large population. These alluvial plains, where nature affords an abundance of food with a minimum of labor, offer great inducements to the easy-going Africans. Here they settle in large numbers, not greatly inconvenienced by the unhealthfulness of the locality. Pampered by the amazing prodigality of nature on all sides, so that they need not exert themselves much for food, and requiring little clothing in this mild temperature, they settle themselves to the enjoyment of their animal natures.

The missionary, as he enters these swamps, which are reeking with malaria and other death-breeding diseases, takes his life in his hand; for Africa has the unenviable reputation of being the "white man's graveyard." It is true the medical fraternity are fast solving some of the problems which confront everyone entering the country, yet many difficulties still lie in the path of the missionaries who desire to settle in the more densely populated regions.

In the old days of Dr. Livingstone and his immediate successors, it required almost a small fortune to penetrate Central Africa. In addition to this the way by wagon or by native carriers was long and tiresome, and the traveler was subject to delays by swollen rivers, dying oxen, and many other things. He was often in danger of his life by wild animals or still wilder men, so that some never reached their desired goal. Even after missionaries had succeeded in establishing mission stations, they suffered much in health from exposure and lack of comfortable homes, and they were obliged to live on the coarse native food much of the time, on account of the difficulty in procuring supplies, even though they might have had sufficient money to procure better food.

At the present day the railroads are eliminating much of this difficulty. Their advance is accomplishing more than any other agency in opening up the continent to the Gospel. They are extending right into the heart of the country, making use of the plateaus on which to build, and bringing the necessities of life and even many of its luxuries within reach of the white inhabitants.

In the year 1904 the Cape to Cairo Railroad was completed as far as the Victoria Falls on the Zambezi River, a distance by rail of 1,642 miles from Cape Town. This part of Africa as far as the Zambezi is generally known as South Africa. If one examines a map, it is easy to be seen that in size it is a very inconspicuous part of the African Continent; but in point of modern civilization and twentieth-century methods of doing things it compares very favorably with any other country. Especially can this be said of the towns and vicinity, but there are yet many natives who are without the Gospel. On my return to Africa, in 1905, the railroad was being extended north of the Zambezi, the objective point at that time being Broken Hill, making a total distance of 2,016 miles from Cape Town.

The facts just mentioned had nothing to do with our call to interior Africa, for that came before we knew what the actual conditions were and before the railroad north of Bulawayo was built. The opening made by the railroad, however, had much to do in making the advance practicable at this time.

After our return from America we engaged in the work at Matopo and Mapani for nearly a year, and continued looking to the Lord to ascertain His will as to the time of opening the new work, for we were hoping that there would be other missionaries ready to move out. Money was on hand for the purpose. This meant something. While I was in America, as the needs of pagan Africa were set forth, one after another would slip a bill into my hand, saying, "I too want a share in pushing on that work into the interior of Africa." What did it all mean—the lack of workers, the ready money and the intense longing in my own soul to carry the Light to those people? We had now waited a year with no prospects of others being ready to go.

Victoria Falls Bridge.

Brother Steigerwald was sending to America for a large Studebaker wagon, and he advised that one also be ordered for the forward move, that both might be sent out together. These arrived in May, 1906. Ndhlalambi had felt called some time before to carry the Gospel beyond the Zambezi. Although he was quite young, he was proving to be a very steadfast and useful helper, both at Matopo and at Mapani Mission. When they were opening the latter station, Sister Emma Doner wrote to me—as I was in America at the time—and said, "Ndhlalambi is such a good helper in erecting our buildings, as Levi has been quite sick. Perhaps the Lord is preparing him so that he can build for you in Interior Africa." At that time, however, I little thought that it would be necessary to rely upon him for that work.

The time drew near when a decision must be made, either to move out or to postpone the opening of the work for another year, and much time was spent out among the rocks alone with Him. From a human standpoint it appeared to be a hazardous undertaking to enter such a new country, and many obstacles were in the way. I had been invited to spend the year at Mapani Mission, and was quite ready to do so, providing that was the Lord's will for me. On the other hand, if He desired that the work beyond the Zambezi be opened this year, all power is in His hands; it would be a small affair for Him to go before and prepare the way. The more we looked to Him to ascertain His will the stronger the conviction became that the time was at hand. Sister Adda Engle also expressed herself as being ready for the work. The rest of the missionaries were requested to make the matter a special subject of prayer. They did so, and a few felt that an onward move was to be made; but the majority said they did not have a clear understanding of the Lord's will in reference to it.

It was hoped that Brother Steigerwald might be able to accompany us to open up the work; but there were so many lines of work engaging his attention at the time that it was impossible for him to leave. He, however, fitted out the new wagon with a strong body and a fine large tent, 6 x 13 feet over the whole, and as far as possible put everything in readiness for the journey.

Our company included, besides Sister Engle and myself, the two native Christian boys, Ndhlalambi Moyo and Gomo Sibanda. The latter was going chiefly for the manual labor. They were both trustworthy and we knew they could be depended upon. It was again the 4th of July when we started on this northern journey, just eight years from the day on which we had left Bulawayo for Matopo. Brother and Sister Steigerwald and Sister Frey accompanied us as far as Bulawayo, expecting to aid us in purchasing supplies and to assist us in getting started north. Mr. Jackson, the English magistrate at Fort Usher, gave us letters of introduction to the Civil Commissioner and the Administrator of Northern Rhodesia, as the country north of the Zambezi is called.

Unfortunately it was found, on reaching Bulawayo, that much of the business could not be attended to that week on account of holidays, so that our friends were obliged to return to their station. The Monday following was a busy and trying day on account of the many things to be attended to and the long distances to be traversed. We wished to purchase supplies for the greater part of the year, for we knew not what awaited us and where the next would come from; and it was also necessary that all the goods be sent on the same train on which we went. Everything was finally accomplished, and July 10, 1906, found all our supplies, about 2,800 pounds in weight, and the wagon, on the train bound for Victoria Falls.

As Sister Engle and I entered our compartment on the train and began to move northward, many conflicting emotions stirred within us, and it was with much trembling and looking to the Lord that we went forward. We knew not what opposition confronted us; for we had been informed by those who knew something of the country that the officials might not allow us to proceed farther than the Zambezi River. Only the consciousness that we were under Divine orders gave courage to proceed. We had the promise, "Commit thy way unto the Lord; trust also in Him and He shall bring it to pass," and we were resting in it.

The journey of 280 miles to Victoria Falls is through new territory. There were no towns—nothing but small station houses—and the country is wild and in some places quite jungly-looking and infested by numerous wild animals. At Wankie we passed through the region of the coal-mining district, where there is a large vein of coal which is a most valuable adjunct of the railroad. Victoria Falls was at that time the terminus of the government-owned railroads, and the limit to which regular trains ran; and we could not avoid wondering what was awaiting us beyond that.

As we stepped off the train at Victoria Falls a gentleman approached us, and introducing himself as a forwarding agent, inquired if he could be of any assistance to us. He inquired if we were not from Matopo Mission, and at the same time stated that he had met Mr. Steigerwald in Bulawayo. What a surprise and relief it was to us, for he seemed to be God's especial messenger, sent to help us on the way. When he learned of the situation he at once set our minds at rest by the assurance that he would attend to everything and see that the goods and wagon, as well as ourselves, were safely taken across the Zambezi River to the town of Livingstone, seven miles on the other side. The railroad at this time was completed to Broken Hill, 374 miles farther north, but trains were run only occasionally. We were obliged to wait at this place two days before an engine could be procured to take us over to Livingstone.

Main View of Victoria Falls, 1¼ Miles wide.

An opportunity was thus afforded of viewing that magnificent sight, Victoria Falls, which was discovered by David Livingstone in 1855, but of which little was known until comparatively late years. This surpassingly grand bit of scenery is considered by some people to outrival that pride of all Americans, Niagara Falls. In dimensions, at least, it certainly does surpass the American wonder. The Zambezi is 1,936 yards wide where it takes its mighty plunge of 400 feet into a vast chasm below, only to be turned into clouds of spray again and rise perhaps a thousand feet into the air. Rainbows play about it, forming a scene of wonderful beauty and grandeur. The rock over which the river flows has a gigantic V-shaped crack about 300 feet wide, into which chasm the water plunges. The opposite wall is unbroken, save at one place where it forms a gorge 300 feet wide, through which narrow channel all the water of the falls, over a mile wide, escapes. Along this opposite wall of rock is "Rain Forest," so called because it is always dripping and, needless to say, the vegetation here is most luxuriant. Six hundred and sixty feet below the gorge is a railroad bridge, 650 feet long and 420 feet above the water, the central span being 500 feet. The view of these falls greatly changes at different seasons of the year. To see them at the height of their magnificence, one should visit them at the close of the rainy season in April, as at that time the volume of water is much greater. At the close of the dry season, in October or November, when the water is shallow, the Falls are often much broken in some places. As this is one of the greatest of the sights of South Africa, thousands of tourists visit the scene, and a hotel had been erected near the railroad at this place.

Our agent informed us that on July 13 an engine would come and transfer ourselves, together with the goods and wagon, to the Livingstone station on the north side. For this purpose the wagon and goods were loaded on an open truck, and as there was no passenger car, we too climbed up into the wagon, on the truck, and in this manner crossed the Zambezi on that railroad bridge, 420 feet high. At Livingstone the car was met by another agent who, with his boys, assisted by ours, unloaded the car and placed the wagon under the shade of a tree. Here it was fitted up as a dwelling-place for Sister Engle and myself for the remainder of the journey. It was a home on wheels. We praised the Lord that He had cared for us this far on our journey and permitted our feet to be planted on the north side of the river. Oxen could not be taken beyond the Zambezi for fear of carrying disease, so it was necessary that some be purchased before we proceeded farther.

This part of the country, like Southern Rhodesia, is under control of the British Charter Company, but with a separate government. Unlike that, it does not belong to the English by right of conquest, but through concessions granted by Lewanika, the King of Barotseland, and paramount chief of the country, for the purpose of exploration and development. The country is occupied by three main tribes—the Barotse, living along the Upper Zambezi and west of Victoria Falls; the Baila, or Mashukulumbwe, as they are often called, living along the Kafue River and north, and the Batonga, on the plateau between the Kafue and Zambezi Rivers and east.

Those familiar with his life will remember that this is part of the country explored by Dr. Livingstone during his first and second great missionary journeys through Central Africa, from 1853 to about 1860. The Barotse at that time were subject to the Makololo, who had emigrated from Basutoland and settled along the Upper Zambezi. The Makololo warriors were also responsible for the death of the first party of missionaries to this part of the country. I refer to the expedition under Price and Helmore, sent out in 1859 in response to Dr. Livingstone's urgent call. Nearly all of this party of missionaries died from poison administered by these natives, to the great sorrow of the African explorer. His memorable prophecy, "God will require the blood of His servants at the hands of you Makololo," was soon fulfilled. It is said that just four years afterwards the Barotse arose against their rulers, the Makololo, and slew them and asserted their independence.

It was in this part of Africa too that Livingstone first saw some of the evils of the slave trade, and in 1873 he wrote to Mr. Gordon Bennett: "When I dropped among the Makololo and others in this central region, I saw a fair prospect for the regeneration of Africa. More could have been done in the Makololo country [which is today known as Barotseland] than was done by

St. Patrick in Ireland, but I did not know that I was surrounded by the Portuguese slave trade; a barrier to all improvement.... All I can say in my loneliness is, may Heaven's richest blessing come down on every one, American, Englishman, Turk, who will help to heal this open sore of the world." A very remarkable circumstance connected with this utterance is that he evidently did not imagine at that time that the healing was to come first from yet another country, France. Just six years (in 1879) after those memorable words were uttered, Rev. F. Coillard settled in Barotseland. He and his heroic wife deserve of all people in this part of the country to be called Livingstone's successors.

These natives could speak the Suto language, and as the Scriptures had been translated into that language for years, those books could be used here among the Barotse, just as Zulu could be used in Matabeleland. In the opening up of that work, Christian natives from Basutoland, a thousand miles farther south, volunteered to accompany Coillard. It is said, "Just on the border of Barotseland one of these native evangelists, Eleazer, died. 'God be blessed,' he exclaimed, when he knew that he must give up his heart's desire of preaching Christ to the Barotse, 'God be blessed! the door is open. My grave will be a finger post of the mission,'" as quoted by James Steward. So that it may be seen that consecrated Africans also did their part in helping to heal this sore. Coillard and his successors have ever since carried on a most far-reaching work in Barotseland. About twenty years after the work was opened, Brother Engle had the great pleasure of accidentally meeting this venerable messenger of the Cross, Mr. Coillard, in a store in Bulawayo. His hair then was white, but he was as intensely interested as ever in his work, and was in a hurry to be back to his field of labor. As, at that time, there was no railroad farther than Bulawayo, he had to travel about 300 miles by ox-wagon and then by boat on the river. The labors of the missionaries and the advantages of good government have accomplished marvelous results in bringing peace and safety to this valley, yet even at this late date there are not wanting those who, if they dared, would rejoice to resurrect the old slave trade.

Among the Baila tribe the Primitive Methodists of England, after encountering many difficulties along the way, had begun a work in 1893 at Nkala, and a few years later at Nanzela. In 1905 they also opened one at Nambala, about seventy-five miles north of the Kafue. Although they were doing excellent work, they had as yet been able to reach only a small portion of the Baila tribe when we appeared on the scene. There were no missionaries among the Batonga tribe living on the plateau between the Zambezi and Kafue Rivers, until 1915, when a mission was opened about 175 miles northeast of Livingstone by Mr. Anderson, of the Seventh Day Adventist Mission. This was just one year before we reached the country. Livingstone in his journey had passed through much of this country, including Kalomo, Monze Tete, and the Kafue River.

CHAPTER TWO

From the Zambezi River to Macha

The town, Livingstone, was, in 1906, quite small, and consisted chiefly of government buildings, postoffice, native stores, railway station, and shops. Some of these buildings, especially those owned by the government, were well made and ant-proof. The town was at a short distance from the railway station and seemed to have been built on a hill of yellow sand, which sand was so deep that walking seemed almost impossible, and riding was very little improvement over walking.

Our first step was to call on the Commissioner, Mr. Sykes, and present the letter of introduction. He met us in a friendly and accommodating spirit, but gave no encouragement to proceed on into the interior, owing to the newness of the country and the unsettled condition of the natives in some places. His version of the work accomplished by missionaries was not very flattering, but that did not deter us in the least, as one generally becomes accustomed to hearing such things. He, however, did not offer to throw any obstacles in the way of our progress, but stated that it would be necessary for us to have an interview with the Administrator (governor) at Kalomo, the capital of North Rhodesia. He expressed his willingness to do whatever lay in his power to aid us in the undertaking, and advised that the purchasing of trained oxen for drawing the wagon be left in his hands, and he would see to it that good ones at a fair price were secured. This generous offer was most gratefully accepted. We were also invited to his home, and were most hospitably entertained by his estimable wife and his sister, and were made to feel that as yet we were not beyond the reach of civilization. They were living in a well-built mosquito-proof dwelling, which had been made in England and sent out ready to be put together.

The next day a European brought to our tent ten trained oxen, with a note from Mr. Sykes, that he had proved these and found them satisfactory. The price too was below what had been expected. Thus equipped we were prepared to proceed to Kalomo, a distance by wagon road of nearly one hundred miles. A boy was employed to lead the oxen and a native government messenger was also sent along as guide. Gomo was to do the driving, but the man of whom the oxen had been purchased said he did not think the boy knew much about driving oxen, and so it proved later. There were occasional passenger trains running north through Kalomo, and some of the people at Livingstone had advised us to take the train that far and let the boys bring the wagon. Others, however, thought it best for us to stay by the wagon and supplies, as there was no suitable hotel at Kalomo, and it would be over a week before the wagon could reach that place, so we decided to remain with our supplies.

The wagon was heavily laden, the roads were rough, and rivers bridgeless. About ten miles out from Livingstone, in going over a piece of rocky road, the reach of the wagon broke and further progress was impossible. Had the drivers been accustomed to this wild country, and the accidents incidental to it, they might soon have made another reach with timber from the forest surrounding us, as they often did in later years. At that time, however, we were helpless. What was to be done? There was only one course open, and that was to take the wagon back to Livingstone and have it mended. Some of the party remained with the wagon and supplies and the rest of us walked back to Livingstone to see what could be done. The question wanted to force itself upon us, Were we after all mistaken as to the Lord's leadings?

Mr. Sykes was again the Good Samaritan, when he heard our story. The next morning he sent out conveyances to bring all back to Livingstone, and he and Mrs. Sykes insisted on our occupying the guest house until our wagon was repaired. There were no hotels in the place, and we were informed that prospectors and others often made use of the government house for an indefinite length of time. They said they were glad the accident had not occurred forty or fifty miles out, beyond the reach of help. We too felt deeply thankful that it had been no worse, and in a short time we were made to rejoice that there had been an accident; for it was soon evident that it was a blessing in disguise, and God had permitted it for a purpose. There were two roads to Kalomo, and neither was much traveled at the time. We learned that the one on which our guide was taking us was not well supplied with water, was infested with many savage beasts and the tsetse fly, which kills oxen, so that it was altogether unsafe for the journey.

While we were waiting at Livingstone this second time, a great deal of information was gleaned in reference to the people and country north of Kalomo, called the Mapanza Sub-district. We learned that the people there were quiet and peaceable and that there were no missionaries in that section of the country. We also met a gentleman from Kalomo, who proved of assistance when we at last reached that place. Again information was received that a number of wagons under Mr. King were proceeding north to within a short distance of Kalomo, and if we could travel in their company, all difficulties in regard to the route, the finding of water for the oxen, and dangers along the way would be at an end. A driver accustomed to the country was also secured to take the wagon as far as Kalomo. Thus equipped we again started. As we left Livingstone, Mr. Sykes exclaimed, "I feel more in favor now of your going on than I did the first time."

On the first day out our wagon came up with Mr. King's company, which consisted of five large wagons, all heavily laden with goods and each drawn by eighteen oxen. They were traveling north to within twenty-five miles of Kalomo, and thence west and north to Tanganyika. We might have delayed a year and not have found so good an opportunity of traveling by wagon to Kalomo. We followed this train of wagons and had no anxious thought in reference to the journey. Traveling by ox-wagons is done chiefly at night, or from very early morning until 9 A. M. Then the oxen are outspanned and allowed to graze and rest during the heat of the day, while the travelers cook, eat, and rest. Late in the afternoon the oxen are again inspanned and they travel until about 9 or 10 P. M., when they stop for the night. One or two large fires of logs are built at each wagon and kept burning through the night to ward off wild beasts from the oxen. Animals are afraid of the fire; especially do lions love darkness rather than light, their favorite nights for prowling being the dark, rainy ones. This king of beasts, although the strongest, is by no means the bravest. He does his loudest roaring in the midst of his native haunts, far away from harm, and when near his prey, human or otherwise, his tread is most stealthy and catlike.

Before retiring for the night the natives, especially, cook and eat. They often do with a small portion of food during the day, but before retiring they like an abundance of good porridge and meat. They then retire to rest, their favorite place being around the huge campfires. Sister Engle and I were very comfortably situated in the tent of the wagon. Two other difficulties likely to meet travelers in this part of the country are scarcity of water and the tsetse fly. If the latter is met with it is necessary to make the journey through the infested district entirely by night. Since the uninitiated are not familiar with the location of these districts, the oxen are often bitten without their knowledge, and death is certain, for as yet no remedy for the bite has been discovered. As for water, that is one of the great difficulties on these African plateaus, and at one time we were obliged to travel seventeen miles without seeing any. Since oxen, with heavily-laden wagons, travel slowly, this required the oxen to be inspanned three times before water was reached. Mr. King rode a horse and went in advance to look for water and camping places, and also for game, which generally furnishes a large proportion of the food, both for white people and black ones on such trips. We ourselves would be favored with a piece of delicious venison after such excursions. Water in casks was carried along from one watering place to another for cooking and drinking purposes, but it is never drunk without being boiled or made into tea, and even then it is often very muddy-looking.

Mr. King was familiar with the country, and had formerly traded with the people in the vicinity of Macha, north of Kalomo, so that he could furnish all necessary information about the Mapanza district, to which we desired to go. This was the first time we heard the name of the place which was destined to be the future mission station. The information received from him proved invaluable later on, when the question of location was being considered. As the way thus opened, step by step, we were continually made to feel that the Lord was guiding and causing all things to work together for good toward the opening of the work, and our hearts were filled with gratitude for His many favors.

The last forty miles of the journey were made alone, as we did not care to travel on Sunday, and the other wagons were soon to leave and proceed westward. We reached Kalomo August 1, after a journey of nine days. This place, although the chief seat of government, could not be designated a town. It was rather a scattered camp, containing two small stores, a postoffice, and the dwellings and offices of the government officials. The railway station was about three miles distant. Here the fate of the undertaking was to be decided, as to whether we should be permitted to proceed or be turned back. That morning in worship the Lord gave us Isaiah 41: 10 for a promise, which greatly encouraged our trembling hearts. We had now been absent from Bulawayo four weeks and had received no mail, as it had been ordered sent to this place; so the first journey was to the postoffice. I went for the mail alone, and inquired first for myself. The clerk exclaimed, "And Miss Engle, too?" and handed out a bundle of letters, all carefully laid together in a place by themselves. Evidently we were expected, and visitors were not common, especially women.

It was necessary first to meet the secretary of the Lands' Department, so in the afternoon Sister Engle and I proceeded to his office. He had heard of our coming and absolutely refused a place in Mapanza district on which we might locate. His reasons were more or less plausible, and we were not wholly unprepared for his answer. We learned afterwards that we were not the only persons who had failed to receive encouragement from this gentleman. He added, however, that they could not hinder our proceeding farther if we felt so inclined. He suggested our going to Broken Hill, the terminus of the railroad, 280 miles northeast, as there were some white inhabitants there. That no doubt would have been a good opening for a mission station, as there were no missionaries there at this time, and only one between Kalomo and that place. It did not, however, seem to be the Lord's will for us to proceed that far, and since there would be a new set of officials there to deal with, our reception might not be any better. After sending our letter of introduction to the Administrator, we turned toward the wagon to consider and pray over the affair, realizing that a more perplexing problem than a broken wagon was facing us.

We had not proceeded far when a gentleman came to inform us that the Administrator, who is the highest official in the country, requested an interview. We were kindly received by the honorable gentleman and given an opportunity of explaining in what part of the country we desired to open a mission station, and the condition of the natives in that section. He said that he saw no serious difficulty in the way, and that he was in favor of allowing us to proceed and select a mission site. He affirmed, however, that the unhealthfulness of the climate was the most serious obstacle; and, since it was late in the season for us to put up a mosquito-proof dwelling before the rainy and unhealthy season came, he thought it best for us to select a place and then go south until the rains were over. Otherwise we might be stricken with fever, a deadly type of which, known as black water fever, is common in this section of the country. We promised to consider seriously his advice, if a proper dwelling could not be secured before the rains came. He then directed us to the civil commissioner of that district, who especially encouraged the undertaking, expressing his belief that we would encounter no difficulty among the natives, since he was familiar with and had jurisdiction of Mapanza district. He said, "The field is before you, and as there are no other missionaries there, it is yours to occupy." He also gave a letter to the magistrate at Mapanza and a native messenger to show us the way.

It was with thankfulness too deep for words that we returned to the wagon. God was again verifying His wonderful promises. Praise His Holy Name! Part of our freight had been sent to Kalomo by train, so after procuring that from the station, we proceeded north about sixty miles through Macha and other places to the camp of the official at Mapanza. When about half the distance was traversed we unexpectedly came upon a Dutch family living there all alone in the wilds. They had not been there long and were not permanent settlers, but we managed to purchase from them some fine imported chickens and some banana sprouts, all of which have proved to be a most useful addition to our mission property.

The natives were much scattered in a portion of the country through which we passed until we approached the vicinity of Macha. Here they were much more thickly settled, and also from this on to the camp at Mapanza. At the latter place the official was not at home. While waiting for him we concluded to visit some of the natives and went to the village of one of the most prominent chiefs of this district, Mapanza by name. There were thirty-five huts in the village. In the center of this was a large cattle pen, and around it and the outside of the palisade the huts were built in a circle, all opening toward the center. As we entered this enclosure we were greeted with clapping of hands on all sides. This is the native way of saluting their king and government officials and sometimes other white people. In this instance the uniformed government messenger accompanied us, and no doubt gave prestige to our visit. The people of the village received us in a friendly manner, but since their language was unintelligible to us we soon returned to the wagon.

The time of the official's return was uncertain and we preferred not to locate in the immediate vicinity of the camp, so it was thought advisable to return a short distance and select a mission site. Some of the rivers through which we had safely come proved more difficult on the return journey. Gomo had been driving since we left Kalomo and did excellent work; but he found the Myeki River here at the camp very difficult to cross. There are long, steep hills on either side of the river, and in addition to this the bed of the bridgeless stream is quite deep. Our oxen had done splendid work on the long journey from Livingstone, but in recrossing this river they seemed unequal to the effort. After struggling awhile one finally lay down and refused to move. This was a new experience for us, but perhaps not for the boys. Gomo used every inducement to make it rise, but to no avail. To our amusement he finally, as a last resort, bit its tail. It was up in an instant and the wagon moved on. We have since learned that oxen are often more stubborn than that one, especially new ones. They sometimes lie down and nothing will induce them to move. They will endure fire and even death itself.

We drove back and carefully looked over the various locations, and after asking the Lord for direction, we finally decided upon our present site on the bank of the Macha River, or rather on the hill above it. The tent was removed from the wagon and placed on poles and prepared for occupancy. This place is about fourteen miles from the camp at Mapanza, and was reached August 17, a little over six weeks from the time we left Matopo Mission. We had traveled in all about 485 miles, about 170 of which was by ox-wagon. Our journal of the time records:

"In all the Lord has wonderfully given us health and strength, and no harm of wild beasts or wilder men has befallen us. The journey had been far more successful in every way than we had anticipated, and we praise the Lord that at last we are settled."

CHAPTER THREE

The Opening of the Work at Macha

In selecting a location for the mission, the desire was to secure a place sufficiently high so as to be at a distance from the low swamps, breeding malaria and other deadly diseases, and yet near enough to the river so as to have access to water. We desired also to have land in the vicinity suitable for agriculture and industrial purposes in general, and for the growing of fruit and vegetables. Then again, in addition to the above requirements, the object of our coming to the country was not to be lost sight of; *i. e.*, the natives themselves. We desired to have easy access to them so that they might receive the Gospel. All of these requirements were prayerfully considered and we believe met in the location of Macha. As eight years have passed since then, our convictions have only been strengthened that it was the Lord's choice for the work.

As near as can be estimated the location is about 16½° south latitude and 27° east longitude, and is about 4,500 feet above sea level, so that, although it is within the tropics, the altitude causes the climate to be pleasant the greater portion of the year and as healthful a site as can be secured in that section of the country. Along one side of the 3,000-acre mission farm is a small river, which gives name to the locality, and the tent was pitched over half a mile from this river. The place afforded excellent facilities for agriculture and fruit growing. Especially can bananas and citrus trees be grown without irrigation. The country is rolling and there are numerous rich valleys capable of supporting many natives. There are wagon roads which have been made by traders who go through the country and buy grain of the natives in exchange for cloth, ornaments, blankets, and clothing. There were no surveyed farms in this vicinity, and the only farmers near lived over twenty miles from Macha, but numerous villages of natives are within walking distance and wagon road.

At the opening of Macha Mission there was a station of Primitive Methodists northwest at a distance of at least sixty miles, and the one of the Seventh Day Adventist Mission at about the same distance northeast. With the exception of these two places one might go a hundred miles in any other direction and not find a mission station, so that we could certainly feel that we were not intruding into the territory of any other missionaries. The natives in this part of the country had heard absolutely nothing of Christ, and they knew not what missionaries were or how they differed from other people.

Our little tent, 6 x 13 feet, was sufficiently commodious for eating and sleeping, but all the work had to be performed on the outside in the shade of a large tree, near which the tent had been placed. Beneath this tree also our supplies were piled off the ground and away from the destructive white ants, of which the ground was everywhere full. We had no cookstove then, and all our cooking was done over an open fire, while bread was baked in a large, flat-bottomed iron pot with long legs. This was placed over a bed of live coals, while coals were also placed on the iron cover. Some very good yeast bread came from that iron pot, novel perhaps to Americans, but familiar to Africanders. Many people traveling through the country made use of the ant hills as bake-ovens.

The Christian boys who accompanied us, as well as some younger ones who came for work, camped at a short distance from the tent, and at night slept around the fire until huts could be built for them. Before the mission site had been agreed upon two young boys came and asked for work. We took them, and one of these has been one of our most faithful helpers. As grain was plentiful in the neighborhood there was no difficulty in securing food for the natives. Many of the older people, men and women, came to see and welcome us. Every effort was put forth toward erecting buildings before the rains came on, but as fires had swept over the country and destroyed most of the grass, it was evident that our chief difficulty would be in procuring thatching grass. This difficulty was obviated by a man at Mapanza, who was erecting a house for the commissioner, offering us for a small sum a lot of grass that he had on hand. Some time later our journal is as follows:

> These have been busy days; much work has been crowded into them. Building and making furniture have occupied the attention of all of us, and everything has had to be done with native material and few tools, which have increased the amount of labor. The poles had to be hauled five or six miles and some of the grass for thatching was brought fourteen miles. Ndhlalambi has been a faithful and excellent workman. He is not as quick as some, but few natives would have succeeded in making better buildings, as he is careful and painstaking in all he does. Gomo is just the opposite; he is just as willing, but is no builder. He has, however, been very useful in hauling poles and grass, and mud for plastering, and he performed a splendid service in venturing among the Baila (a warlike tribe north of us) and purchasing for us two cows. Sister Engle and I have been bending all our energies toward helping with the building in the more technical parts, so that the work might be accomplished as soon as possible, and we have been spending some of our time in making furniture. There has been no difficulty in securing natives to work for us, and they have all worked faithfully under

Ndhlalambi's supervision.

There seems to be nothing to mar the work and location thus far, except the savage beasts, which prowl around at night, a terror to the domestic animals and to ourselves. When we pray, "Keep us from harm and danger," it is a more genuine prayer than formerly. Many nights the howls of the wolves and hyenas are to be heard, and one night some of the boys awoke to see in the firelight the eyes of a hyena glaring at them. Some of the natives built a high, strong pen for our cattle, and the first night they were enclosed in it a lion tried to force its way in, as indicated by the spoors the next morning. Leopards have also been seen. These evidences, as well as the stories told by others, convince us that there are wild beasts in the neighborhood, yet the Lord is able to keep and has thus far kept us from harm.

The 91st Psalm was very precious in those days.

These first buildings were constructed in a manner very similar to those at Matopo Mission, except that it was thought advisable to build the main part of the house all in one, so as to obviate the necessity of going outside in passing from one room to another—a very important consideration in such a wild country. The scarcity of grass limited the size of the house to a certain extent. It was 26 x 14 feet, with a veranda around three sides to protect from the sun and rain, and was divided into three small compartments opening into one another, the small doorways being closed by curtains. As there was no seasoned lumber to be had, there was only one outside door, and this was made from one of the boxes in which the goods had been packed. A table was manufactured from another box, and the bedsteads, as well as nearly all the rest of the furniture, were manufactured from native unseasoned timber and draped with calico. A muslin ceiling was a necessity to prevent the sawdust from falling from the rafters.

On the inside of the house the walls were carefully plastered up against the thatched roof, and the openings for windows were closed by fine wire gauze netting to exclude mosquitoes. An important question was how to make a screen door for the only outside door of the building, as unseasoned timber would not answer the purpose. The pole of the wagon had been broken soon after our arrival at Macha, and one from the forest put in its place; and since this broken piece of timber was of hardwood and sufficiently long for a door frame, we decided to make use of it for that purpose. It was sawed and with considerable labor made into a frame and proved quite satisfactory. Sister Engle, who was always patient and painstaking in her work and full of resources, deserves much credit for this and many other things with which the house was equipped. That screen door is still doing excellent service after a lapse of eight years. After it was finished it was found that to fit it into the door frame so as to make it mosquito proof was no small task. The door frame had been manufactured from unseasoned native timber and was greatly warped. After much chiseling and shaping even this feat was accomplished, and the result was a mosquito-proof house, for that season at least. Mosquito nets for the beds had also been brought along.

A small kitchen was also built and a hut for the native brethren before the rains came. The grass, stumps, and underbrush were cleared off all around the buildings and at some distance from them. This is customary in this part of the country, and it is done for the purpose of removing the hiding places of mosquitoes, snakes, and the like. Although more natives were employed the first few months at Macha than at Matopo, we experienced no difficulty in dealing with them; perhaps because we were more familiar with their character, and our native Christians too were quite capable of understanding them.

During the progress of the work, the advice of the Administrator had not been forgotten, as it was our earnest desire to do that which was best, and we looked to the Lord for guidance. It seemed advisable to remain. Contrary to his expectations, a mosquito-proof dwelling-house had been constructed, and the work which was started would certainly have suffered if we had gone away. The boys who had accompanied us were in every respect proving themselves capable and reliant; the natives were quiet and respectful; and not the least difficulty in the way of our return was the long, dangerous trip to Kalomo to reach the railroad. We had safely come that way once, yet we dreaded the long trip back, perhaps because we did not believe that it was the Lord's will for us to make it. The post was brought to our door by the government messenger as he passed on his way to Mapanza, and a trader near offered to bring out from Kalomo any needed supplies.

All our needs thus far were abundantly supplied by a loving Father. All praise to Him Who "is able to do exceeding abundantly above all that we ask or think." Even in our most sanguine expectations before coming to the country we had not thought to be so well provided for. He in His infinite wisdom and forethought had gone before and prepared every step of the way; He had opened every door and enabled the mission to be thus planted in raw heathendom where Christ had not been named. The location proven by years of trial could not have been improved, for He makes no mistakes. The call and the desire for the extension of His Kingdom, which He had put into our hearts before ever Africa was reached, was thus being fulfilled. He had done and was doing His part; what more could we ask? Yea, we were weighted down and humbled by the multitude of favors which He was showering upon us. The only thing to mar our peace at this time was the consciousness that our friends and some of the government officials were uneasy on our account. We saw no cause for fear, and were conscious that the continued prayers ascending in behalf of ourselves and the work were availing before God, and that we were at the place where He desired us to be.

After the buildings were completed and the rains came the boys put forth every effort to dig some of the ground and plant grain and vegetables. This had to be done by hand, as the plow had not yet arrived.

In the many duties incident to starting a new station, the spiritual part of the work was not neglected. A little visiting among the people was done both by Sister Engle and myself and by the native brethren. An attempt was also made each Sunday to instill into the minds of the people something of the sacredness of the day. Since a number of natives came daily to work at the mission, they were informed that we did not work on Sunday, but worshiped God instead. It was thus not difficult to assemble twenty-five or thirty on Sunday for services. These were always married people, with the exception of the few boys who were staying at the mission to work. The younger people, and especially the girls and children, were conspicuous only by their absence. It was the same at the village; none except men and women were to be seen, so that at first we all concluded that there were no children in the neighborhood. Later it was learned that these and all the unmarried girls ran and hid when we approached a village.

We could invite the people on Sunday, or we could go to see them in their homes, but to speak to them was a more difficult affair. There was the same difficulty in the language as at Matopo, but with a difference. There we had a translation of the Bible, dictionaries and grammars, and could at least read the Word to them. Here we were among the Batonga, and their language, although belonging to the same great Bantu family of languages, was quite distinct from that of Southern Rhodesia. There were no translations, no dictionaries, at the time the mission opened, so that the task of acquiring it was no small one. We soon realized that we had not sufficiently appreciated our blessings in Southern Rhodesia. Here it was necessary to have notebook and pencil continually on hand and write down the words as they fell from the lips of the natives; nor was it an easy task to decide upon the spelling of the words; especially was there difficulty in distinguishing the letters *l* and *r*. The same word as it fell from the lips of one native would seem to have an *l*, and as spoken by another it would be *r*. Of course there were many similar difficulties.

One of our first aims was to secure the expression for "What is that?" "*Chi nzi echo?*" and with that as a basis the names at least of many things could be learned. Then too it is not so difficult to learn to use expressions common in everyday duties and the material things about one; but to secure a suitable vocabulary for instruction in the Gospel is generally a difficult task, and missionaries differ widely in reference to terms for spiritual things.

The native vocabulary is by no means meager, and one is often surprised that people living such seemingly narrow lives as they do have in constant use such a copious vocabulary. Their thoughts as a rule can be expressed in fewer words than in English. For instance, they will say bona, to see; *bonwa*, to be seen; *bwene*, to have seen; *bonana*, to see each other; *boneka*, to be visible; *bonela*, to see for; and *bonesha*, to see clearly, and some verbs have additional forms. Again, in the use of verbs, such as *go*, they will have different words to express various phases of it: *Ya*, to go; *benda*, to go stooping, as after game; *fwamba*, to go quickly; *endenda*, to go for a walk; *ambuka*, to go aside, or astray; and so on for eighteen different words.

The especial difficulty of the missionary is to secure the proper words to convey spiritual conceptions not generally met with in their comprehension; such as, *faith*, *holy*, *save*, *cross*, *heaven*, and even in the word for God there is often a difference of opinion among missionaries as to the word to be used. Among all tribes there seems to be a word for God, but the conception upon which it is based is so degrading that one often hesitates to make use of it in referring to the Holy and Omnipotent One Whom we have learned to revere. Two opinions are prevalent among missionaries in reference to some of the words. One is to make use of the words already found in a language and to seek to build up upon those words a new conception altogether foreign to the native line of thought. Others think that it is better to introduce a new word and attach the desired meaning to it. I think it is safe to say that the former is the method generally employed among translators, but whether it is in all instances the best method is open to question.

Natives very quickly learn the language of other tribes, and so it was in this instance. Our native Christians soon acquired this language. A few of those working for us could after a manner speak that "Esperanto of South Africa," "Kitchen Kafir," and this enabled them from the first to understand one another, in a slight degree at least, and gave them a common basis from which to pass to the Tonga language proper, spoken by the people about us. As Ndhlalambi, who took the name of David, had felt the call definitely to give the Gospel to these people, and had had experience in evangelistic work, both at Mapani and at Matopo Mission, he was able in a comparatively short time to give the Gospel intelligently to the people, and also to assist us in acquiring the language. Of course this was by no means accomplished in a few months, or even in a year, for it was often difficult for even him to secure the proper words in spiritual language. These helpers too had their difficulties in the work, and had their misunderstandings with the natives. One day one of them was quite discouraged in an attempt to make some natives understand properly, and he exclaimed, "I have a great deal more sympathy with the white man now in his endeavors to make the people understand, and to teach them how to work. These people seem so dull to me, and I know why our masters became so out of patience with us."

There was at first no attempt at opening school; but stencils and cardboard had been brought along, and with these charts were printed in the syllables and sentences of the language as nearly as we understood it. Sister Engle made use of these charts in teaching, by the light of the campfire in the evenings, the young boys who had come to work for us. Our two native helpers also continued their studies and were instructed whenever there was time for it after the buildings were completed.

As the first Christmas drew near, a query arose as to how it should be observed, and whether services should be held, since no one could yet speak very well the language. David and Gomo were eager for services, saying that they would put forth every effort to speak to the people about Christ. We longed to give the people something on that day as an expression of our good will, but could not see the way open to do so. At Matopo Mission salt was always given, but in this part of the country salt was very expensive and there was only a little on hand, and we were not prepared to give them meat, as we had little opportunity of procuring game for ourselves. Services, however, were announced for the day, and early in the morning some natives began to arrive, curious to know what the day was like.

In the morning Sister Engle and I were sitting at the table on the veranda, eating our breakfast, speaking of the plans for the day, and expressing a wish that there was some food to set before the people. While speaking, we heard a goat bleat, and presently two natives, one of whom was carrying a goat on his shoulders, came toward us. They put the goat down on the ground before us, saying as they did so, "The Chief, Macha, sent you this as a present." Here was the answer to our wish and unuttered prayer. Another native headman a short time previously had also presented a goat, and we had bought one, and these three would be sufficient for the dinner. Our praises ascended simultaneously, and we realized that the promise was again verified, "Before they call, I will answer; and while they are yet speaking I will hear."

The native brethren entered heartily into the preparations, and with the assistance of the others, they soon had the animals killed and dressed, and in the cooking kettles. Fortunately there was cornmeal on hand which also furnished sufficient porridge. We rejoiced as we saw the people coming that there was food to set before them, even though the Gospel messenger could not be given satisfactorily; but there was still a greater and more blessed surprise in store.

There were ninety-six grown people assembled, chiefly fathers and mothers, heads of families, and these were all seated along the veranda and in the shade of the tent. David took up the subject of Christmas and its origin by first reading it from the Zulu Testament, which, of course, they did not understand. Before he had read much the Lord sent a first-class interpreter, in the person of a Mutonga native who had worked for some time in Bulawayo, and there learned to read and speak the Zulu language and to understand the Gospel. He was not, however, a Christian, as we learned, but he proved a most ready and excellent interpreter for the day; and as the message was given in Zulu, he as readily interpreted it into the vernacular of the people.

The Lord especially anointed our brother David for the message that day, and he most ably and feelingly presented the wonderful story of the birth and life of our Savior and His great mission in the redemption of the world. Perhaps the unique opportunity had some effect upon my feelings, but it seemed to me that I never at any other time heard the subject so well handled before a congregation of natives as it was on that day. The native men, especially, listened most attentively throughout that long discourse. Tears came into my eyes as I looked upon those seamed faces before me, those middle-aged and elderly men who, for the first time in their lives, had an opportunity of hearing of Him Who had come to earth nineteen hundred years before to redeem them. How much of the *makani mabotu* (glad tidings) they grasped at the time it is difficult to ascertain.

At the close of the discourse some of the rest of us spoke for a short time on the same theme, and also explained the cause of our being among them. Then after a hymn and prayer they were given their food. A bountiful dinner had also been prepared for ourselves, a portion of which we handed over to the two helpers who had so faithfully labored to make the day a success. It is needless to say that they too thoroughly enjoyed their dinner. In every way this first Christmas was one long to be remembered, with nothing to mar the perfect harmony of the occasion.

CHAPTER FOUR

School Work. Reinforcements

Up to this time nothing had been said about school, except that a few boys had been taught in the evenings. There was no word for it in their language, and learning had no meaning or attraction for them. They only desired to work and earn money.

The first herdboy came before the mission was located, and to him we gave the name "Jim," as we did not fancy his native name. He remained with us three months and then returned home and his cousin Tom came to herd. Both of these boys manifested a great interest in what they heard, and Tom was the first one to express a desire to be a Christian. Another little boy ran off from home one day and begged permission to remain at the mission. His mother immediately followed him and told him to go home. He refused, and sitting down by a tree he put his arms around it and clung to it; but the mother tore the poor little fellow from the tree and dragged him away. Aside from these, very few children made their appearance during the first five or six months of the mission, and no girls came for a much longer period of time. The older people were friendly from the first, but we often felt that some of them inspired their children with a certain amount of fear of the newcomers.

January 1, 1907, the people were informed that we wished to open a school and that they should come to learn. By this we had in mind a day-school, where the pupils would come in the morning and return home at the close of the session. It had been impossible to build a schoolhouse, since nearly all the grass had been burnt off before our appearance on the scene. We, however, set up the little tent and built a straw shed at one end of it for a temporary schoolhouse.

As school and its advantages had no meaning to the people, no one came. Then too it was the busiest season of the year. One, two, three weeks passed, and still no one desired to learn. January passed and half of February; still no scholars. This was a new experience. At Matopo the children could scarcely wait until school opened, and they were the pioneers there and gradually drew the older people to take an interest. Here it was quite the reverse; the children were afraid of us, and would run away, screaming, to hide in the tall grass when we approached their villages. What was to be done? As usual we began to look to the Source that never fails.

The middle of February it was thought advisable to have a week of prayer. All work was laid aside and the time was spent by the Christians in interceding at a Throne of Grace, for we felt that perhaps we had been too much occupied in temporal affairs. In the midst of this week of prayer, on February 19, Macha, the chief, came, bringing his little boy, about twelve years of age, and said, "Here is my son. I should like to have him stay with the missionaries and learn to read and to work." Here then was a direct answer to prayer. The chief of the district had set an example to his people by thus bringing his child. This was a signal for others, Apuleni, another boy of about the same age, came the next week, and Mafulo and Kajiga followed; also others. Jim and Tom came to remain and attend school, and by the end of the year there were seventeen boys in all staying at the mission.

These were nearly all boys from ten to sixteen years of age; a few were older. None who applied were refused if they were willing to abide by the regulations; and industrial work was at once inaugurated in connection with the school. They were to be taught in school three and one-half hours, and work early morning and afternoon, receiving, in addition to their food and instruction, some clothing, and blankets for the night. They were to remain at least a year before they could take the clothing home with them. This stipulation was made to teach them stability and prevent them from coming sufficiently long to secure clothing and then leaving before they had properly earned it. The arrangement proved very satisfactory. The few taxpayers who entered the industrial school were given a small sum of money, provided they completed the time agreed upon. They always had Saturday afternoon as a half holiday, when they were to wash and mend their clothing and have the remainder of the time for recreation.

It was always our aim to make them understand that they were expected to earn what they received by giving labor in return. We had no sympathy with pupils who desired to learn and lie about and be idle the rest of the time. Several who desired to bring their food and remain at the mission without working were not allowed to do so, as we thought it would prove detrimental, both to themselves and to the rest. We preferred a dozen industrious and stable boys to many times that number who were lazy and indifferent. It is true some of the smallest could scarcely be said to earn their way at first, but they were at least taught habits of industry. In their homes many of them spent their time in an indolent fashion, their muscles being flabby and unused to exercise; and often, when they came to us, they were too lazy even to play at recess. Gradually they brightened up and took hold of the tasks assigned them. One day one of the mothers came and inquired about her son, a boy about thirteen years of age, and she was told that he was digging in the garden.

"Kanyama digging?" she asked, in great surprise. "Why, he does not know how to work."

The first rainy season was quite pleasant, and it passed with very little sickness among our workers. It gave us an opportunity also of learning something of the fertility of the soil on the mission farm. Much of the land, and especially that in the valleys, was unusually productive, and the grass grew to the height of ten feet. Our aim was to make use of the rainy season to instruct the boys in agriculture and horticulture and to raise sufficient grain and other food at least for their consumption; and more than that, if possible, so that the expense of keeping a number of boys would not rest so heavily on the mission. This first season very little food was grown, because there had been no land ready for sowing, but the plow came in January, and Gomo was enabled to break two large gardens ready for sowing the following year.

Macha Mission Huts, 1907.

As soon as the rainy season was at an end, building was again undertaken by David and Gomo, together with the assistance of the native men and schoolboys. Thatch grass had to be cut and poles hauled and seasoned. The Matabele women were always eager to work for cloth, salt, or money, but the Batonga women were not. It was impossible to make satisfactory arrangements with them, either to cut grass or plaster, so that the men and boys were obliged to do this also in connection with the rest of the building, and they performed the work very satisfactorily.

As there was only one small hut for the schoolboys, the first building this second year was a hut, 13 x 16 feet, for their occupancy. Then a building answering for church and school purposes was erected. This was 16 x 30 feet, with a large veranda in front, and was an excellent building of the kind. The seats were made of bricks, built up in rows and plastered over, and the floor was made of earth, pounded hard and plastered. Another building, 14 x 20 feet, of poles and mud was also built, and was divided into two rooms. It had a veranda all around it. We were expecting missionaries out from America, and this last hut was for their accommodation. These three buildings were all respectable-looking ones and required a great deal of time and labor, so that David and Gomo were very busy and deserved much credit for their efficiency and perseverance. In addition to the outside work the schoolboys were instructed in sewing, and two of them in housework.

The school at first was very poorly equipped, as we had nothing but the homemade charts and a few slates, and knew not where our books were to come from, since we did not know the language sufficiently to make any. Some of our needs in this respect were also supplied later. In the latter part of 1907 Rev. E. W. Smith, a missionary at Nanzela, published an excellent "Handbook of the Ila Language." This was a grammar and dictionary combined, and the language was closely allied to that of the Tonga. We secured this book about a year after we had reached Macha and found it very helpful in acquiring the language, since the grammar and many of the words of the two languages were similar. He also published in that language an excellent first reader and a book of over one hundred pages of Bible stories. This latter book is a very faithful account of Genesis and Exodus, and contains some of the more interesting parts of later Old Testament history. Not long after, there was also published a book of questions containing the essentials of Christian belief, and also many quotations from the Scriptures. With the exception of the mode of baptism this was so essentially like our own faith that it could be used to excellent advantage in Inquirers' Classes.

All of these books proved of inestimable value to us in school and church work. The pupils in the school proved bright and studious, and before the end of this year some had started in the service of the Lord.

It was almost impossible for us to spend much time out among the natives during the rainy season, since the rivers were often swollen and difficult to cross, and the grass was high, rendering walking difficult and even dangerous on account of savage beasts lurking about. It is true we seldom saw any of these animals, but that they were in the vicinity we had no reason to doubt. Once when David was on top of the church, putting on the rafters, a native from a neighboring kraal called to say that three leopards were after his sheep. Our boys all ran to hunt with spears and clubs, and some of them had a glimpse of the animals as they disappeared in the tall grass. Another morning some of the men on coming to work reported that they saw four lions crossing one of our plowed fields. Occasionally we would hear a lion roaring on the opposite side of the river, so that there was no reason to doubt the presence of danger.

Northwestern Rhodesia, where we found ourselves, is essentially the home of wild and savage beasts and game of all kinds. In addition to smaller animals there are the duiker, reedbuck, hartebeest, sable antelope, eland, kudu, and many other varieties of game. The forests are full of apes and baboons, and the gnu, the zebra, and the buffalo are to be found. The mammoth elephant roams at will in herds or singly, the rivers are full of crocodiles, and the larger ones abound in the ungainly hippopotamuses. It is the paradise of hunters, and many avail themselves of the opportunity for sport thus afforded; others for the gain to be had from ivory and hides.

The fact that there was not only game, but that there were also dangerous animals lurking about, may have been the chief reason why we never succeeded in starting a day-school at Macha. It was scarcely safe for children to go alone back and forth to school. Even men seldom traveled far alone, and they always went armed. A native would carry three or four assegais, and many were supplied with guns. It is surprising how much game they managed to kill with those old blunderbusses.

As stated previously, the presence of animals had much to do with the amount of kraal visiting carried on. Sister Engle and I went, however, quite frequently after the grass was burnt off in June, accompanied by some of the schoolboys. As we neared a village, our approach was always heralded by the barking of dogs and the screaming of children as they ran away to be out of reach of the *mukua* (white person). Every village is supplied with its quota of dogs. One day I counted twenty-four in one small village. Nor is their presence unnecessary in this animal-ridden country, as they often succeed in driving off ferocious animals from the herds, and they help supply their master with game. They are, however, generally so lean and starved looking that one would like to see a "Society for the Prevention of Cruelty to Animals" among the natives.

It was a long time before we could get a sight of the girls in the kraals around us. Once, in company with Apuleni, we went to his home, and here as everywhere we were warmly welcomed by the older people and given an opportunity of telling them of the Savior, as well as our limited vocabulary would allow. While we were sitting there talking to some of the older people, Sister Engle said she thought there were some girls in a hut near by. I arose to investigate. The older people saw the move and laughingly told the girls of my approach; but it was too late for them to escape. As I reached the door I saw five girls in the hut, some of whom were nearly grown. Some began to scream and hide their faces, and others sat trembling, not daring to look up.

They appeared as if they were afraid of being torn from their home by violence. Two of these were sisters of the boy who accompanied us. It required much tact and patience to finally gain the confidence of these wild children surrounding us, and to help them realize that we would do them no harm, but we at last won the day.

During this dry season of 1907 word was also received of a threatened native uprising. Our first information of this condition of affairs was received from some officers who had come from the Transvaal and were passing through on their way north on a hunting expedition. They said that they did not know how serious the difficulty was, except that some of the Europeans northeast had been ordered into the government camp. The natives around us were quiet and law-abiding and gave no indication that they were dissatisfied. They themselves were not of a warlike nature, and they had in the past been harrowed and many of them ruthlessly killed by the Matabele, the Barotse, and the Baila, each in their turn, and they were now enjoying peace and quiet under the beneficent rule of the English. They knew that they would gain nothing by rebelling against the English, and the only condition that would cause them to rise would be fear of their powerful neighbors. For this reason we could see no cause for fear. They were, however, not ignorant of the trouble in the country, and confided to David that Lewanika wanted to fight. The powerful tribe north of us, the Baila, were probably as dissatisfied as any. David at first did not tell us what he had heard, for fear of alarming us, and we too said nothing to him at once. Later, however, he told us and we gave him our information. The danger at that time seemed past, and we would have allowed the affair to rest; but it was learned that our fellow missionaries were uneasy on our account. So we wrote to an official at Kalomo to inquire if they anticipated a native uprising. He wrote, assuring us that whatever danger there might have been, there was no more serious cause for alarm.

Macha Boys and Schoolhouse.

In September of this year a young man from Cape Town came to assist in the work. He was a nephew of our friend and benefactress, Mrs. Lewis, and had been impressed with the importance of pressing on the work into the interior; hence his presence at Macha. He suffered so much with fever, however, that he concluded it was best to return south after a stay of only a few weeks at the mission.

On November 10 our long-looked-for colaborer, Mr. Myron Taylor, reached Macha. This was a welcome and much-needed addition to our number. The new building was ready for occupancy, and Brother Taylor entered enthusiastically into the work before him. He came just at the opening of the rainy season, and perhaps entered on the work with too much vigor; for in the latter part of December he was laid low with the dread African fever, and for a time his life was despaired of; but the Lord raised him up. During that, his first rainy season, he had frequent relapses of the fever and saw very few well days until the season was at an end. He was not, however, discouraged, but continued at the work whenever his health permitted.

The boys who came to attend school remained, and others also applied for admission, so that by the end of this second year there were thirty-two staying with us, and they were becoming quite useful in the work, and best of all were going on to know the Lord, and were formed into an Inquirers' Class.

This second rainy season was in some respects a repetition of the first, except that there was more land under cultivation, and we ourselves were better supplied with fresh vegetables and more nourishing food, and Brother Taylor with his rifle could furnish us with game. We were at this time becoming more familiar with the pests with which we had to contend in this tropical Africa. We thought we had learned something of the ravages of the white ants, or termites, while at Matopo, but the experience there was nothing compared to that at Macha. This is not in any sense intended as a scientific treatise; yet even from a missionary point of view one needs to know something of the difficulties in the way. One cannot be long in America without realizing that the ordinary reader is woefully ignorant of some of the most common experiences of the Africander, and in nothing is this more noticeable than in the ravages produced by the white ants. The species to be found in Africa is unlike that found elsewhere and is much more destructive. A knowledge of the presence of these pests also seems to help solve some of the characteristics of the natives in this section of the country.

These white ants are of various kinds and sizes, but they are similar, in that they build great nests of clay which extend above the ground from one or two to twenty or more feet. These nests are known as ant hills, and in this part of the country some of them are not unlike hillocks. They are all honeycombed within and down deep into the earth, and are the homes of the various members of the community, consisting of the large, bulky, wormlike white queen, an inch or two in length, the savage, warlike soldiers, and the small, inoffensive-looking workers. There are also winged ones which leave the earth in great numbers at the opening of the season after the ground has been softened by the rain. These soon lose their wings and again enter the ground at various places to form new colonies.

The white ants can work only under cover, and exposure to light and the sun is generally fatal to them, so they build small clay tunnels underneath the ground or on top where they desire to work, and through these they pass to and fro, carrying particles of food to store it away. They prefer dry food, such as wood, leather, paper, clothing, straw, and vegetation as it is becoming dry, although if these articles are not to be had they have no objections to attacking growing trees or plants. Many trees in our young orchard have been destroyed by their ravages. These ants are to be found all over South Africa, but as one approaches the equator they are more numerous and destructive and the hills are larger.

At Macha, boxes, shoes, clothing, everything had to be kept off the ground floor. If this precaution was not observed, perhaps in a single night a clay coating would be formed around the sole of a shoe and it would be greatly damaged. Sometimes they would find their way up the leg of a box and begin destroying the clothing or articles within. As I came out of my room one morning, the noise of the sentinels of the ants gave signal to the workers of the approach of danger. This led to an examination of some bookshelves which were supposed to be safe out of the reach of the pests. Wet clay was found to be all along the end of the bookcase, and the end books on each shelf were partly eaten, all the work of one night. Our bedposts had to be put on zinc or into old tin cans to keep the ants from making their way to the top and soiling the bedclothes. Several times they started to build an ant hill on the floor of the hut, and one morning a small hill of wet clay nearly a foot in height was to be seen, the result of one night's labors.

Nor did they confine their ravages to the floor and the articles placed on the floor; walls and grass roof were full of them. No article could be hung on the wall with safety. There was a ceiling of muslin in the house, yet one day Sister Engle, on going into her room, found an army of white ants marching around on the counterpane of her bed, having fallen from a broken clay tunnel in the roof. In addition to these pests, we were greatly annoyed by insects boring into the soft wood which formed the rafters. During this season the sound made in the quiet hours of the night by these insects sawing caused one to think the entire hut was alive. The ants would carry their clay tunnels into the opening made by the borers and complete the work of destruction. For a time the ceiling became so heavy with falling sawdust and clay, that it was necessary to open it about every two weeks and remove the dust, which almost filled a small tub each time. Many more incidents might be cited. We were forced to admit that, at least during the rainy season, a large portion of our time was occupied in protecting our huts and goods from the ravages of the ants.

The Last Invitation.

Their work did not stop with the house. We would think that the grain and meal were placed high and secure out of their reach, only to find that they had formed a channel and destroyed a lot of grain. At first when some boys came for school there was no suitable place prepared for their accommodation, and they were obliged to lie on the floor. They would occasionally come and show where the cuticle had been removed from some portion of the body during the night. In the garden there was also difficulty in protecting the growing crops. The cornstalk would be eaten off and fall to the ground, where the ants would complete the work of destruction; so that from the time corn began to be filled until it was ripe, it was generally necessary to keep several boys most of the time gathering the fallen corn. Continual vigilance was needful, or in an unguarded moment something about the place would be destroyed.

The varieties of ants in the country are many and diverse, but we will mention only one other kind, to which we were introduced during the early days of the mission. One night some of the boys said they could not sleep on account of ants coming into their hut. We supposed they referred to large black ants, which often came in armies and made a raid on white ants to carry them off for food. These black ones are very troublesome when disturbed, and the boys were told to occupy another hut for the remainder of the night. Again the boys spoke of being disturbed and showed some small, reddish ants with vicious-looking heads, which were marching in a straight line through the yard. But these looked innocent and little attention was paid to the matter. Then one morning a hen and two young guinea fowls, confined in a pen, were found to be dead and covered with these insects. We concluded that they had died and the ants were eating the carcass, but the boys assured us that the ants had killed them. The pen was immediately burnt, together with as many of the ants as possible. Another night the sheep began to bleat most piteously. The lantern was lighted and the boys called to see what was the difficulty, and while waiting for the boys I approached the pen. Almost instantly needles seemed to penetrate my body in various places. I gave the lantern to the boys to let out the sheep, while Sister Engle and I hastened to the house, where she helped to remove the vicious little insects. After that experience there was no further question in my mind as to whether those ants could kill fowls or other animals.

These are called the army ants. Once it required two days for an army of them continually on the march to pass through our yard. Fortunately we have not been troubled much with this variety since that time, but in some parts of Africa they are very numerous. Human bodies are sometimes thrown to them, and even live ones, as a punishment in supposed witchcraft.

We had been in correspondence with some of the Primitive Methodist missionaries at Nanzela, from whom we had purchased books for the school and ourselves; and we were eager to visit them and learn something of their work. About the 1st of May we arranged to make the journey of sixty miles and pay them a visit. Brother Taylor was here to take charge of the journey, so we took the wagon with the ten oxen and a number of schoolboys, as well as David, leaving Gomo in charge of the mission during our absence. This was a new and untried road in a northwesternly direction, and required four day of hard traveling to make it. On the way we occasionally had an opportunity of preaching Christ to the natives.

The kindly welcome received from Rev. and Mrs. Price, who were then at Nanzela, more than repaid us for the tediousness of the journey. We spent a most delightful four days at their mission and learned to know something of our neighbors and of the work being accomplished at this oldest station in this part of the country. They were working among the Baila, and also some Barotse who were living in that section of the country. The trip, however, proved a most unfortunate one for us, as we were informed that we had passed through a small district of the tsetse fly on the way. The result of this will be given in another chapter.

On account of the presence of these pests, as well as for other reasons, a very common method of travel and transportation in this part of the country is by native carriers. A native will carry fifty pounds of goods, so that it requires forty persons to transport a ton of goods. This means is employed by officials, and it is somewhat more expeditious than by wagon. It is often not very satisfactory, however, and it is difficult to secure natives who are willing to carry, unless they are almost forced into service. The wages too, eight cents a day, is small, but where the tsetse fly abounds this is the only safe method of transportation.

CHAPTER FIVE

Additional Reinforcements. Preparing to Build

In June, 1908, we were pleased to receive additional reinforcements in the persons of Mr. and Mrs. Jesse Wenger, who had lately arrived from America and felt called to the work at Macha. Accompanying them were Elder and Mrs. Steigerwald, who came to pay us a visit and to see about the work.

There was now a strong force of missionaries at the place, and it was thought that better and more permanent buildings should be erected. The mission had been in progress nearly two years, and David and Gomo had been active both dry seasons in erecting buildings—and they were good buildings of their kind. From what has already been given, however, of the ravages of the white ants, it can easily be seen that such buildings were very unsatisfactory and of short duration. To make others of the same kind would require the missionaries to be continually building.

My opinion in reference to missionaries' houses and surroundings had gradually and materially undergone a change since I first entered the mission field. My firm conviction on entering had been that missionaries should be as approachable as possible, and that they should endeavor to get on a level with their people; not in their dirt and filth, not in their ignorance and degradation, but, leaving out these essentially objectionable features, they should seek to imitate as much as possible Him Who had no certain dwelling-place and went about doing good. He became one with the people wherever He went, "Made Himself of no reputation, and took upon Him the form of a servant." He of course is the Great Exemplar, after Whom the missionaries, His messengers, are to pattern. The true missionary should and does esteem it a privilege to endure any necessary privation and hardship in the cause of the Master Whom he loves and seeks to imitate. Otherwise it would be impossible to carry the Gospel to the heathen. But our God is a wise God, and has promised wisdom to His children and to His messengers, which He expects them to use on the mission field as well as elsewhere; so that they may adapt themselves to their surroundings and do that which will best advance His Kingdom.

The missionary goes to his field of labor. He builds himself huts of poles, mud, and grass. He does this carefully, that he may protect himself from the weather, the wild animals, and from the mosquitoes which bring fever. He provides his hut with furniture, manufactured by his own hand, so that it looks quite cozy and comfortable, and the poor natives as they look inside may conclude that if heaven is no better than this, it is at least worth striving for.

The missionary himself for the time feels quite satisfied and happy in his surroundings and concludes that the place is good enough for anyone.

He opens his door and invites his dear dark friends to enter and sit and talk with him—a privilege which they greatly appreciate and the missionary also enjoys. Are not these the people for whom Christ died? Are not these the poor people to whom he is bringing the privileges of the Gospel? He loves to embrace every opportunity of getting into their hearts, and he feels keenly everything which separates and tends to form a barrier between them.

Time passes, and the rainy season comes. Perhaps the huts become damp and even mouldy in places, and gradually, as the ants continue their ravages, the walls crack and other difficulties arise. He is forced to be continually on his guard to protect himself. Mosquitoes enter, and he is incapacitated for work, by fever and other sickness. His health becomes undermined and his appetite gives way. The coarse food of the natives, if he has been using it, becomes distasteful and hurtful. Perhaps, if there is no way out of the difficulty, his life pays the penalty and his work on earth for God and the natives is stopped. This is no fancy picture. It has been repeated over and over again in this great "White Man's Graveyard."

Suppose, however, that by taking plenty of quinine and having considerable vitality to start with, he survives and continues successfully to combat disease; he soon finds that he must build a separate hut in which to meet the natives, or his house will be overrun with vermin and he cannot live in it. His hut, too, soon becomes a hiding place for snakes, rats, and lizards. He may pick up a piece of furniture and find a cobra lying beneath it, or go into the little kitchen and find a deadly puff adder beneath the cooking kettle. Even if he has in building kept as near to the natives as possible, they are in no haste to get rid of their filth and improve their manner of living. They have not yet seen the advantages of exerting themselves to that extent, unless they are members of the mission family and compelled to wash. Even then they may have conscientious scruples in reference to the matter, as one of our best boys at Matopo did. He was frequently remonstrated with for not keeping his clothing clean. He said that clean clothing made him feel proud.

Again, the missionary soon sees that his hut is going to pieces, and he must go over the laborious task every two or three years of building another, and at the same time constantly fight the ants, so that his life is one of long struggle with disease, pests, and building. When and how is he to give the Gospel? He concludes that he must make brick, build a house, and put on an iron roof, that it may be better protected from the mosquitoes and furnish good rain water. He makes a tank, so that he may have good drinking water instead of the muddy, disease-laden stuff which comes from the river. It will make more work for a time, but when completed he sees some result of his labor.

These reasons, any or all of them, are sufficient in the eyes of the missionary for building a good, substantial house, but there are other reasons, quite as patent to him, but they may not be to one who has never been in his place. The natives like to see their missionary build good dwellings, for then they think he has come to stay, and because he has come to stay and is willing to work and to train the natives, he sometimes has a better house than some of his white neighbors. And we are loath to think, as some affirm, that it is a reproach to be better housed, if he himself builds it.

There is another and more subtle reason for a good house, and one which the writer could not enter into until the last few years. If one has access to a town he has an opportunity to see other civilized places and has a change of scenery and companionship, which is both interesting and beneficial. Especially is this so to one who is continually surrounded with uncouth barbarism in its many forms. When, however, one is far removed from all civilized associations and sees nothing that is beautiful and uplifting, week after week, month after month, year after year; when all this time only dirt and squalor meet the eye as he steps off his own premises, his range of vision becomes so narrowed, his brain so benumbed by the monotony, that he feels he can endure it no longer. He is not tired of his services for the Master; he is not tired of the dark faces surrounding him; but his spiritual vision has become so befogged that, as he rises before the people to give them the message, he feels that he cannot give what he longs to. He cannot even take hold of God by faith in prayer as he did, and he must get away for a change.

But what has this to do with a good house? Just this: If one has a good home and pleasant surroundings, good and helpful literature and a few of the things which minister to the æsthetic as well as to the spiritual part of his nature, he has a change, at least, in his own home, and when he can snatch time, from the many duties which continually confront him, for a little quiet, the surroundings are pleasing and restful. He is then just that much better fitted to cope with the opposite conditions, and he can cope with them for a longer time and do better work for the Master. On the other hand, missionaries are human and make many mistakes, and we in the mission field need also to guard against the other extreme of spending too much time in beautifying our surroundings and making ourselves comfortable, to the neglect of that God-given message.

Even under the best of surroundings, physically, the missionary has enough to contend with. Circumstances over which he has no control, difficulties which far outweigh any already mentioned, meet him on every hand. As Rev. Stewart, of China, says, "'Agonia,' that word so often on St. Paul's lips—

what did it mean? Did it not just mean the thousand wearinesses, and deeper, the stirrings, the travailings, the bitter disappointments, the deaths oft of a missionary's life?"

The natives often are so indifferent, so disinclined to exert themselves, that, after months and years of weary, persistent labor among them, the missionary often feels that little is accomplished. He dare build hopes on none but God, and must accept seeming success or defeat as alike from Him. This continual drain on his system is quite sufficient, without having to combat with poor dwellings, poor food, and unhealthful surroundings.

After the Brethren came, they concluded to start at once to make the preparations for building. Elder Steigerwald had had experience in this line of work, so he generously offered to start the rest in brickmaking. After a few weeks' visit he and Sister Steigerwald returned home and Sister Engle decided to accompany them for a change. David and Gomo also had been absent from their people for two years and wished to return, the former for a visit and the latter, perhaps permanently. We were very sorry to see all these leave at once, even for a few months, and especially David, whose assistance in the language and in interpretation was greatly needed.

Making Brick at Macha.

Brick Kiln. Mr. Jesse Wenger and Helpers.

The Brethren Taylor and Wenger, with the assistance of the schoolboys and some other natives, moulded and burnt a large kiln of brick. Brother Taylor attended to the moulding and Brother Wenger to building the kiln. This gave the boys training in another line of industrial work, and at the end of about six weeks a lot of excellent brick were ready for building. Unfortunately there was no money on hand to build a house, for the Board had not been informed of our needs in this respect, since brickmaking had been undertaken rather suddenly. It was therefore necessary to postpone building a house until the next dry season. Brother Wenger, however, erected two small brick buildings, with thatched roofs. One was for grinding and storing grain, and the other a two-roomed cottage. In the latter a room was fitted up for the occupancy of himself and wife, so that we were prepared for another rainy season.

One thing which was a serious handicap in the building and work that season was the condition of the oxen. After our return from Nanzela, in May, the oxen gave no indication of being bitten by the tsetse fly. Nearly a month later they were driven to Kalomo, a distance of about forty-five miles, and brought out a heavy load of goods on the arrival of our colaborers. They were also made use of in hauling sand for brickmaking; and in July, when Brother Steigerwalds returned home, they were again driven to the station. This time they made use of a new road and went east to Choma Station, a distance of only about thirty-six miles. By this time the oxen were showing signs of being bitten, and as there was no cure for them, they gradually became weaker and died, one by one, until we had lost nine, the last ones not dying until about six months after they were bitten. The fly injects a parasite into the blood, which gradually absorbs the red corpuscles, hence the lingering death.

It was a serious loss to the mission at the time, as they had been in use almost constantly in farming, hauling, and bringing out supplies. In the Syracuse plow it was necessary to use all ten of the oxen in this heavy clay soil, and also in hauling the wagon.

We still had a few, but there was not sufficient money on hand to purchase others at once. With eight ill-matched oxen, Brother Taylor undertook to go to Choma in November for the purpose of bringing out a six months' supply of goods and provisions, which had been sent up from Bulawayo. He took along five of the largest schoolboys to assist in carrying the goods across the bridgeless rivers. To add to the difficulty of the trip, grass was scarce at that season of the year, so that there was little food for the oxen. A little rain also fell while he was away and made the road muddy.

On returning with the load he was able to get within twelve miles of home when the oxen could go no farther. He sent four of the boys each with a load of goods to the mission, and a call for help. Several native men and about twenty schoolboys were sent to his assistance, and after they reached the wagon, Brother Taylor concluded to endeavor to come a little nearer home before resting for the night. Each of the natives carried a load, and he himself carried one hundred pounds of flour and drove the oxen. They came about two and one-half miles farther and then camped for the night. A fire was kindled, but as the night was dark and misty the fire burned low. The boys lay around this and Brother Taylor on the open wagon. He was aroused several times during the night by a disturbance among the oxen. Thinking it was caused by one of the new oxen which had given him some trouble, he arose at three different times during the latter part of the night to quiet them, but the darkness was too great for him to see what was the trouble. The last time it was dawning a little in the east, and he thought he discerned the form of an animal moving toward an ant hill in the vicinity. The boys were aroused and soon had a fire; and as the morning came they discovered by the spoors that two lions had passed along within a few feet of where the boys lay and had gored one of the oxen during the night. These were what Brother Taylor had been trying to chase. The reader can imagine the thankfulness of all of them, as well as of ourselves, when it was discovered how wonderfully the Lord had preserved them all from harm. We rejoiced when the goods as well as Brother Taylor and the boys were all safely at home, but the heavy wagon had to remain for a time on the veldt before it could be brought to the mission.

When the news of the misfortune to the oxen reached America the Lord inspired some of His children to send special donations for the purchase of others, and even before an account of the trouble had reached there some had heard of the need by way of the Throne and had sent money.

CHAPTER SIX

Evangelistic and Other Labors

During this dry season the spiritual part of the work, together with school and kraal-visiting, was not neglected, even though most of those who could speak the language were away.

There were thirty-two boys in school, and they were doing good work. A translation of the Gospel of St. Mark had been printed by Rev. Smith, and an Ila hymn book by Rev. Chapman, of the same mission, and these were both very useful in our work. After our boys had finished the Ila books, we concluded to allow them to continue the Scriptures in the Zulu Testament, as it is always easier for the natives to pass from one native language into another than from English into their language. We found later that this use of the Zulu Testament proved very satisfactory, both to ourselves and the boys. Since we were familiar with that language, and they readily acquired it, their knowledge was of great assistance to us in translating portions of the Scripture into their tongue, and they were soon capable of interpreting for Elder Steigerwald and others who came to us from Southern Rhodesia. Here, as at Matopo, every day and all the day were the Scriptures studied and Christ held up, and morning, noon, and night we met in worship and explanation of the Bible. The great aim, both in school and out, was to produce sincere and ripe Christians, who should become teachers and evangelists of their people.

Macha Mission Dwelling House.

Other studies were gradually introduced. Arithmetic seems to be always a difficult study for most of them, but some of them compared very favorably in that branch with others whom we had instructed. They had their own peculiar way at first of announcing whether their problems were correct or not. If they were correct the pupils would answer "*Wa pona*" (it is alive), and if incorrect they would say "*Wa fwa*" (it is dead). Although they sat side by side in the schoolroom and could easily look on the slates of their neighbors, they were generally very honest and independent in their work and did not attempt to copy.

English also was introduced after they could read understandingly their own language. The opportunity of learning English is a privilege which all natives covet, as it seems to be more important in their eyes and more European. In some respects this *importance* is one of the objectionable features about teaching it. Then too the native often is dull in learning it, but we need interpreters, and the value intellectually of this and arithmetic and kindred studies is not to be despised. English often aids the native in securing better positions with better pay when he goes to work among the Europeans; for go, at least for a while, he will. Some Europeans prefer natives who can speak and understand a little English. On the other hand, some white men, who have themselves a little knowledge of the native tongue, prefer, for their own purpose, that natives do not understand English. They want the native to understand only enough to go at their bidding and "keep his place," which is somewhat similar in their eyes with the lower order of animals. This class is forever a foe to the missionary and to the education and christianization of the natives. If one who has to some extent been educated, goes out into the centers of civilization and there, swallowed in the maelstrom of vice which surrounds him, imitates his new white teachers, they will point to him and say, "Yes, there is one of your mission boys. That is what missionary work does." Many a well-meaning native, who was making a fair progress toward Christian life, can trace his downfall to such teachers. If that class of Europeans would remain at the centers of civilization, it would still be more tolerable for the missionary, but often the towns are too moral for them, and they seek to go into the region of raw natives. As one glibly remarked, "When it becomes too civilized for me here, I'll go farther inland."

Mr. Naylor, who has had an opportunity of studying at first hand the work all over Africa, says, "In Africa conscienceless trade, social vice, race hatred, and religious intolerance have freer scope because so far removed from the restraining influence of Christian public sentiment."

This seeming digression from the subject can be excused only on the ground that it is one of the most difficult and perplexing problems the missionary has to face, and every one coming into the country in such a capacity is certain to meet it in one form or another. We are pleased to add, however, that the missionary also finds Europeans who are generous and helpful and favorable to the work; and the number of this class is increasing, as the aim of the missionary and the results of his efforts are more clearly understood.

The attendance at church services was constantly increasing, and those present on Sunday sometimes reached 140 in number. Kraal-visiting also was carried on as opportunity afforded. Before Sister Engle left we had made a visit to Mianda, the home of Tom and Jim and of several other of our boys. This was about seven miles from Macha and too far for some of the older people to walk to services. As the boys were still with us, those in the kraal had not yet received any light. They appeared to be much pleased to see us, but when we attempted to point them to the Savior they seemed so dark and so unable to grasp spiritual things. This was especially true of Tom's mother, who sat in a little dark hut and was afflicted with a very sore eye. She had such a hopeless expression on her face, that the picture haunted us for many days afterwards.

When Tom, who had accepted the Light as far as he knew, had been at the mission fifteen months, he desired to return home, and did so. A few months after he had returned to his home, one day, in company with two of the schoolboys, I went about four miles from the mission to visit some of the people. Quite unexpectedly we came upon Tom's mother in one of the huts. She was there visiting some of her friends. As usual, I began telling her of

Jesus, and her face brightened immediately as she exclaimed:

"Oh, yes! Siwesi [Tom] told me that. He said we should not worship the spirits any more; we should only worship God above [pointing upward]. He reads from his Book and sings and prays. I enjoy hearing of those things." This woman had never been at the mission, and this was the first indication, apart from the boys staying with us, that we had of Light entering the home. Her eagerness and evident sincerity showed plainly that she believed and was accepting the truth, and that the Light was coming through one of the schoolboys. The contrast between this picture and the first sight of this woman was so marked, and the joy of realizing that a ray of Light was entering one home at least, was so great, that as I retraced my steps homeward I kept saying to myself, "It pays, it pays."

Brother Taylor felt especially called to spend his time in evangelistic work among the villages, and whenever he could snatch time from other duties pressing upon him he went out among the people, and in this manner a number of villages were visited.

Many of the people at this time were destitute of food, as the previous season had not produced good crops. Many of them were living on fruits, roots, and plants, and much sickness was the result. With our large family, and only a moderate supply of grain, we were unable to give them much assistance, but we did what we could. Had they been willing to bring their small children to us we would have cared for them until other food was grown. One mother did bring her little boy, Halikumba, who was four or five years of age and nearly starved. He enjoyed his new home so much, and the abundance of food it supplied, that he would run and hide if he saw his mother come for fear she would take him away. He was such a little mite of humanity that we were afraid of placing him in the huts with the other boys, and for a time cared for him in the house.

David returned to Macha in January, 1909, ready to enter again with enthusiasm into the work, and Brother Taylor concluded that the way was now opened for him to spend additional time in evangelistic labor, so he decided to take several boys and spend some time among the Baila north of us. This is a bold and warlike tribe, living in large villages, and much addicted to drink, dancing, and carousals. Rows, and even murders, are not infrequent among them, and it required some courage to venture into their territory. The Lord gave the Brother open doors, however, and some attentive listeners, and we believe seed was sown that will bear fruit in eternity.

He had some difficulties to encounter, which were not so pleasant. It is a low, flat country; and as he was there in the midst of the rainy season, heavy rains flooded the country on all sides, so that he was frequently obliged to wade the water in going from one village to another. After two months of arduous labor, his health gave way and he was carried back sick to the mission. It required some time before he fully recovered from the exposure and hardships of the trip.

These experiences are not pleasant, but they are incidental to the country, and every missionary feels that he should be ready at all times to endure for Christ's sake and the salvation of souls what men are going through every day for money or a home.

Brother Wenger also had been suffering greatly in health while at the mission, both from nervous disorders and from fever. Notwithstanding this, he decided to begin building a house, since the rains were about over and funds had been received for this purpose. David also was ready to help in the work. With the assistance of the boys they brought together stones and began the foundation. Near the mission there were very few building stones, but this need had been supplied in a rather unexpected manner. The brethren had undertaken to dig a well the previous season, but on coming into contact with a great deal of stone, which necessitated blasting, they went down only forty-five feet and finally concluded the task was useless. The only beneficial result of their labors was the stones which had been taken out of the well, and which furnished a large part of the material for the foundation of the house.

Eld. Steigerwald and Mr. Doner with Carriers on Their Trip North of Macha.

Brother Wenger laid the foundation of a house 41 x 16 feet, with a wing 18 x 10 feet, and began work on the brick. Unfortunately, while this was in progress, his health gave way repeatedly, and he and Sister Wenger concluded that it was advisable for them to leave for Bulawayo and finally for America, and David continued to work at the house. Brother Taylor had sufficiently recovered from his illness by this time to be able to take the Wengers to the station. He then waited there a few days for the train from the south, and brought back with him Elder Steigerwald, Mr. Doner, Miss Engle, and Gomo, all of whom we were expecting.

He was absent from the mission eight days, and during that time I had an attack of fever and was obliged to be in bed for a week. This was my first attack, and as it was quite severe, it enabled me to sympathize better with those who had been sick so much. We were very glad to welcome Sister Engle and the rest back to work. The two brethren from Bulawayo were on a tour of exploration north, but they generously decided to stay and assist Brother Taylor to finish the brick work of the new house. This timely assistance was greatly appreciated by us all, and that part of the building was completed in two weeks, after which they proceeded north.

The special object of their trip was to look at a location north of the Kafue River, where a missionary had died not long before. This missionary had started a work in this unhealthy region, and his life had paid the penalty. Some friends of his, notably Mrs. Lewis, of Cape Town, had desired our people to examine the place, and, if thought advisable, to continue the work, and Brother Doner was willing to do this if they concluded that the opening was a good one.

They made the journey on foot, accompanied by Matshuba and native carriers from the vicinity of Macha. They passed through the very heart of the territory occupied by the wild Baila, and visited the new station at Kasenga, which had just been opened by Rev. Smith. He and his heroic wife had started this station in the heart of the Baila country and in an unhealthful locality, not considering their lives dear unto themselves, only that they might take the Gospel to these people and continue the translation of the New Testament, which Mr. Smith had already begun.

Crossing the Kafue River in a Native Dugout.

Near this place the brethren crossed the broad Kafue River and proceeded in a northwesternly direction toward the railroad. They found the mission station and the place where the missionary had died, and heard some of the children sing a hymn which the missionary had taught them. They were not very well satisfied, however, with the location, and returned to Macha by a different route. They traveled on foot a distance of perhaps 250 miles, and were absent from Macha a month. They could not understand the language and had some trying experiences from wild animals and wilder men, but the Lord graciously preserved them from all harm. They then returned to Bulawayo to continue their labors.

In the meantime Brother Taylor, with the aid of the native brethren, was progressing very satisfactorily with the house. It contained four fair-sized rooms and a pantry, and had a broad veranda on three sides to protect the walls from deterioration by sun and rain. These walls were twelve feet high, with a drop-ceiling of muslin two feet below the eaves, to serve as a protection from the fierce rays of the sun and to furnish an air chamber. On top of the foundation and underneath the brick walls were placed strips of zinc, soldered together, to prevent the white ants from forcing their way through into the walls and thence onto the timbers of the roof. The floors were of earth, pounded hard and well tarred to keep out the ants. The large glass windows were quite a relief from the small holes in the old house. Later the windows and the greater part of the veranda were screened. The house was in every way most satisfactory, except that it was not quite proof against the white ants. Cement floors and steel ceilings would have been preferable, but the cost was prohibitive.

Batonga Chiefs and Headmen.

Sister Engle's return gave us an opportunity of continuing the kraal-visiting, and we made use of it in gaining an entrance into other homes. At Kabanzi village, about nine miles away, services had been held more or less regularly ever since the establishment of the mission, and Sister Engle and I decided to take the tent and spend a week at this place and hold some Gospel services. Gomo and a number of the boys accompanied us and built a hut for the use of those coming here to conduct services. This week spent among the people was a most delightful one, and beneficial physically, especially to myself, since I was feeling the effects of my three years' stay in this climate. The people attended the services well, and seemed greatly interested as they sat around the campfire and listened to the Message.

In other homes too there was beginning to be a change, for the girls were coming out of their seclusion and listening to the old, old Story, and some were even venturing to the mission on Sunday. Some of the older people also appeared interested, and made a show at least of desiring to be Christians.

This does not imply that the kraals around us were fast accepting the Gospel as a result of the three years' labor among them. No, the devil was plying his trade at our very doors. Almost nightly one could hear the tomtoms beaten in connection with their worship, or as an accompaniment in their immoral dances; for none of their worship was omitted by the older ones, at least in their homes. The missionary work was just begun, and perhaps none of the present workers would live to see the day when these things would cease in the villages. The false religions and customs which have been so deeply imbedded for centuries would require patient, consecrated labor for years, and even generations, to uproot. One must be willing to go on, day by day, although he may see little or no fruit of his labors, knowing that the Great Husbandman will care for the seed sown.

First Baptismal Scene at Macha. Native Congregation Not Visible.

The work thus far, however, had not been without its visible fruits, as the stability of some of our boys gave ample testimony. The number staying at the mission had now grown to forty. These were some of the called-out ones from the various kraals about us. Each had sent its quota, and although some had come and gone, the great majority stayed on from year to year. As the Light came to them they came and confessed their sins, forsook their old life and accepted Christ as their Savior, showing by their lives that they were His. Some of these were about grown; others were still quite young, but we hoped to see the day when some of them would become teachers and evangelists of their people.

Wedding Dinner at Macha.

Word had been received that Elders J. N. Engle and J. Sheets were to be sent out by the Mission Board to visit the various stations and report on the progress of the work. In November, 1909, just after we had moved into the new house, they, together with Elder Steigerwald, came to pay us the long-looked-for visit. Their visit was greatly enjoyed and we believe was a blessing to the work of the Lord. To Brother Sheets the boys gave the name "Happy," no doubt because he frequently used the word and also showed it in his manner. Two important events occurred during their stay, which deserve special mention.

The first was the marriage, on November 4, of Mr. Taylor and Miss Adda Engle. The natives were invited to this ceremony, and about 350 accepted the invitation. Several chiefs came with their people and arranged themselves in groups, eager to see what a Christian wedding was like. The marriage ceremony was performed by Bishop Engle, who was a son of the first bishop to Matopo Mission, and also a cousin of the bride. Bishop Steigerwald delivered an excellent and instructive discourse to the natives on the importance of the occasion and the tenets of Christian marriage. This was interpreted into the vernacular by David and was listened to most attentively by the natives present. It was their first opportunity of learning this phase of Christianity, and it was an important event from a missionary standpoint. Christian marriage and the principles it stands for generally require a long time for inculcation into the hearts and lives of at least the older natives, but many of the younger ones very readily accept it, as the many Christian marriages performed at our older stations testify.

At the close of the ceremony, and after the missionaries and boys had offered their congratulations, the rest of the natives congratulated in their own way, which was by the clapping of hands. Some also began cheering with the mouth, but this demonstration was checked. Brother Taylor had arranged to give them a feast of beef and porridge, and this they greatly enjoyed, as it is to some the great aim of life; namely, to have plenty to eat.

The second important event was the occasion of the first baptism at Macha, in which ten of our boys were baptized by Brother Steigerwald in the Macha River, and received into Church fellowship, thus showing to their heathen neighbors that they had forsaken their old lives. A beautiful feature of this was that some of the parents and older ones met them as they came out of the water and seemed to rejoice with them in their new life. There were others who were eager to take the step, but it was thought they had not yet sufficiently counted the cost.

We then had the privilege of surrounding the table of the Lord together with these who had been so lately snatched from heathen darkness. These were the first fruits of Macha and reminded one of Professor Drummond's experience in Nyassaland. He says: "I cherish no more sacred memory of my life than that of a communion service in the little Bandawe Church, when the sacramental cup was handed to me by the bare black arm of a native communicant—a communicant whose life, tested afterwards in many an hour of trial with me on the Tanganyika Plateau, gave him perhaps a better right to be there than any of us."

The missionary too is often made to feel, as he sees some of these humble, black followers of the Lord, and thinks how far they have come, and how steadfast the lives of many of them prove to be, that He Who sees and tests all hearts may, with Mr. Drummond, conclude that they have a better right to sit around the table of the Lord than any of us.

CHAPTER SEVEN

Other Missionary Experiences

The experiences of a missionary are so many and so diverse that nothing should surprise him. To give these experiences, with too distinct a line of demarcation, would not place the work in its proper setting, for they often come piling one upon the other and cannot be separated.

I had now been north of the Zambezi nearly three and one-half years, and was in need of a change, so when the delegation from America left I also went along to the station. Brother and Sister Taylor accompanied us to Choma Station on a little wedding trip, and then returned to carry on the work at Macha, while David took charge of the school. Elders Engle and Steigerwald went north on an exploring trip as far as Broken Hill. Brother Sheets went to Bulawayo and I to Natal.

On the way south an accident occurred which was quite unusual, even for this animal-ridden country. After the train had passed the Zambezi River and Wankie Coal Fields, in the evening about eight o'clock there was a lunge in the train and a lady in the same compartment with myself exclaimed, "There must be an accident of some kind." The train soon came to a sudden stop, and it was evident that something had happened. People began running about in the darkness, a large bonfire was soon built near the front of the train, a bulky form was visible, and word came back that we had struck an elephant. Great excitement prevailed. Gomo also was on the train, returning to his home, and he came back to our compartment and said, "Come and see the elephant. I'll take care of you."

I went forward with him and found a huge elephant lying beside the train. Its two hind feet were crushed, as the engine, tender, and service car had passed over them; otherwise it was unhurt, and at times made violent efforts to stand upon its front feet. At such times the crowd of people would suddenly take flight, to be out of harm's way, and a box-car near by was in danger of being demolished. No one on the train was supplied with a large rifle, suitable for elephant hunting, but small ones kept up a lively fire, until perhaps three dozen were emptied into the huge bulk before it succumbed.

The engine had been derailed by the violence of the shock, and it would require some time before we could proceed. Judging from the spoor it was evident that the elephant was one of those large ones that roam the forests alone, and it had run quite a distance on the track before the engine struck it.

It was an immense animal, and the large ears resembled a cape lying back over the shoulders.

There were a number of natives on the train, who were going down to work in the mines about Bulawayo, and they wished to begin at once on the feast of meat before them, but the authorities thought it best to put them at working the large jacks used in moving the engine back on the rails. All night long bright fires of logs were kept burning to light up the scene and work. The engine finally was in place, and the natives eagerly hastened to cut out large pieces of elephant meat and to roast it over the great beds of coal left from the campfires of the night. Soon, however, the train began to move, just twelve hours from the time of stopping, and the natives, with their raw or half-cooked meat, hastened to enter their car, and we moved on, having had a share in one of the most exciting railroad trips of the season. The tusks of this elephant finally found their way into the Bulawayo Museum.

The Elephant That Derailed the Train.

The tusks of the African elephant often are quite large and heavy. I once saw in a European home three pairs of tusks from elephants lately killed by a young farmer. Of one pair of tusks each was five feet long, eighteen inches in diameter; one weighed one hundred pounds and the other five pounds less. We are informed, however, that some have tusks still much larger than these.

It is unnecessary to give the details of this, our second trip south to Natal and Johannesburg, and my visit to our mission stations in the Matopos have already been mentioned. I was absent six months and felt thoroughly rested and ready for the work again. On my return to Bulawayo, however, I learned the sad news that the native who had come south on the train at the same time as myself had, since he was at home, fallen into sin. We were all deeply grieved over this, and he confessed and wept over his condition, but appeared discouraged and unable to take hold of the Lord by faith for pardon and cleansing. There were several others in his home who had once confessed Christ and had backslidden, and they no doubt had their influence over him. The Lord is still able to redeem him, and may he have our prayers. Such are some of the heavy burdens the missionaries have to bear.

On my return in June, 1910, Misses Mary Heisey and Elizabeth Engle accompanied me to Macha to pay a visit to that place. Brother Taylor met us at the station and conveyed us to the mission, where we were greeted by a crowd of boys and five girls, who had joined the mission family, with the clapping of hands and the firing of a rifle. We rejoiced that we could again return to our field of labor.

Macha Mission School, Boarders, 1910.

In the new house and improved surroundings every one had been well and the work had been moving forward in all its departments under the efficient management of Brother and Sister Taylor. Not only had these girls come to stay at the mission, but David had prevailed upon a number to attend day-school, at least part of the time. Sister Taylor, in addition to her many other duties, had formed all these girls into a sewing-class and was endeavoring to teach them to make garments for themselves. This was the first opportunity that had been given of instructing girls in sewing, and she had made remarkable progress also in instructing them in their work about the house.

Naturally they do not know what cleanliness is, either about their person or in their homes. They seldom wash, they go half-clad, and smear their bodies with paint and grease, and often let the dogs lick clean the few dishes or pots which they possess. If their hands are wet or dirty, the posts of the veranda, blocks of wood, or floors are used as towels to wipe on. They see no reason for continually washing a lot of dishes, sweeping floors, and keeping the house in order; and they open their eyes in astonishment to see white sheets and tablecloths put into the water to be washed. The few articles of clothing to be seen in their homes are generally so thickly coated with grease and dirt as often to render it impossible to distinguish the color. Many times they do not have any soap, and even if they do have, they object to washing their clothing for fear it will wear out. And yet these young girls, reared in such homes had, in these few months, made rapid progress and were becoming quite proficient in assisting with some of the work of the kitchen. Sister Taylor's great patience in teaching them was bearing fruit.

Brother Taylor had, in connection with his other duties, made a large galvanized iron tank to hold rain water. This was large enough for 1,700 gallons of water, and was greatly needed, as the river water which we were obliged to use was very muddy part of the year. He had always maintained that he was no mechanic, but another missionary, Rev. Kerswell, who had had experience in mechanical work, said on seeing this tank, "Mr. Taylor, you say that you are no mechanic; but if you made this, you are one; for no one but a mechanic could perform such a piece of work."

Macha Wagon and Oxen Near an Ant Hill.

While the sisters were with us Brother Taylor and wife arranged to take them on a trip north, so that they might have an opportunity of seeing something of the country and the natives. For this purpose the wagon was again fitted up with the tent and camping outfit and the ten oxen inspanned. A number of the schoolboys were permitted to accompany them for a holiday, but the regular driver for the wagon did not go along. They spent some time at the two large villages of Kabanzi and Simeoba, holding services and conversing with the natives, and then proceeded toward a village farther north. The grass was long, the road new, and darkness was coming on when they approached the village. As frequently happens near a village, there was a large opening in the ground from which clay had been taken to plaster the huts. This was partly hidden by the long grass, and had not been noticed in the gathering darkness. Brother Taylor had gone in advance to look out a place for camping, and some of the boys were driving. The wheels of one side of the wagon went down suddenly into the excavation and the wagon was overturned, the tent being under the heavy wagon. The accident might have been very serious for the women, but fortunately there were two large boxes in the wagon and these prevented the weight of the wagon from resting on them and they escaped without any serious injury, but the tent was of course ruined. Brother Taylor said that, as he hastened to the wagon, he heard a boy on the rear end of the wagon yelling lustily; so he felt satisfied that that one was not dead, and he turned his first attention to those who were making no noise.

When the sisters returned to their fields of labor, David again returned home, this time to be married and bring back a wife from Mapani Station.

The spiritual condition of the pupils continued excellent. There was a spirit of inquiry among them and a searching after God at times, as the Spirit was poured out upon them. Some prayed through to victory and a definite knowledge of sins forgiven. Those who had been with us longer were instrumental in bringing the newer ones to seek pardon. The spirit among them was such that any one who did not care to be a Christian generally did not remain long at the mission. At this time also we were favored with special donations and enabled to equip the school better and give more attention toward the training of teachers.

It will be remembered that one of the special needs was a translation of the Scriptures into the language of the people. The books already in use, prepared by Rev. Smith, were in the Ila language. This was sufficiently allied to the Tonga for use at Macha; and it is always an advantage in the mission field to unify the languages as much as possible, so as to reduce rather than increase the number of languages.

St. Mark was already in print, and Mr. Smith, together with some of his colleagues, was putting forth great efforts to translate the entire New

Testament into Ila. At their urgent request I consented to be on the revision committee, for they desired to make the translation as intelligible as possible to the Batonga, so that it could be used all over Northwestern Rhodesia, with the exception of among the Barotse, where the Suto language was in use. Matthew was soon in print, and the entire New Testament is at present in the hands of the publishers. The translators deserve much praise for their laborious task and the creditable manner in which they have performed the much-needed translation. The Word cannot be properly disseminated among the people unless the pupils have it in their own language as they go out among the villages to teach.

Placing native teachers in their homes seems to be the best method of reaching the majority of the people, and especially the girls; and some of the pupils were sufficiently advanced to begin teaching, yet they were somewhat young to go out into their dark, dark homes and stand alone for God. Notwithstanding this, before the end of 1910 several schools were opened in the nearest villages, and the teachers boarded at the mission and went back and forth to teach.

On Christmas week of this year a sad and unfortunate affair occurred, which threw a gloom over the community. My readers will remember the Chief Macha, who sent a goat the first Christmas, and who was the first to bring his little boy as a pupil in school. To all appearances he was a friend of the work from the beginning, and he was nearly always to be found in his place at the services on Sunday. He had even expressed a desire several times to be a Christian. We knew his life had not changed, but he had evidently lost faith in some of the old pagan beliefs, and his influence was worth much. He was a man of importance in the neighborhood and the owner of a herd of cattle, which was quite large from a native standpoint.

Simeboa's Village, Viewing the Strangers, Misses E. Engle and Mary Helsey.

On the day before Christmas word came that he had gone to the hills and could not be found; again that he was found dead, killed by a lion. His son at once went home, and I, together with some of the girls, soon followed. On the way to the village we met a native woman, who informed us that he was already buried, and on our arrival at the place we found that those who buried him had gone to the river to wash. While we were sitting there several of the people came to speak to us, and we noticed that some of the men spoke together in a low tone. Their answers to some of our questions were somewhat vague; but as there was no suspicion of foul play, we thought no more of the matter and asked no further questions.

After the people returned from the river, the wailing began by about thirty or thirty-five men walking back and forth; brandishing their assegais and guns and crying "*Mawe!*" At the same time the women stood about the grave, wailing and calling upon the dead. The sight was somewhat fearful and might have alarmed a stranger, but since the majority of these were from the adjacent kraals and were acquainted with us we feared no violence. In the evening Brother Taylor and the boys went over to show their sympathy, and the next day services were held there. All this time nothing further was learned except that the chief was killed by a lion. The English official from Kalomo, who, with his messengers, happened to be in the neighborhood at the time, received the same version of the cause of the death as we did. According to native custom, the brother of the deceased assumed his title and appropriated his cattle, and the affair, as far as it concerned ourselves, was dropped.

About three weeks later Lupata, another chief, who lived near, together with one of his men, and Kaiba, a nephew of the deceased, came to inform us that Macha had been murdered. They said that he had been murdered while out on the veldt, and an attempt made to hide the body. A number of natives went to search for him, Lupata among the number, and when they discovered the body they saw at once that a murder had been committed. The brother of the murdered man enjoined the rest to secrecy and promised to give Lupata some cattle if he would not tell the missionaries or officials of the crime. Lupata, although very fond of cattle, of which he had only a few, did not jump at the bribe. He said that he and Kaiba desired to inform me on the day of the funeral that the chief had been murdered, but the brother said, "Do not talk about it to the white people," and they had been silent for fear of offending him; as natives never like to gain the ill will of their fellows.

We might have heard nothing further about it, at least for a time; but the brother was afraid the crime might leak out, and he still hoped to silence the affair by giving the other chief some cattle. To do this he was not willing to take of his own cattle, which he had taken from the murdered man, but tried to take those of Kaiba, who was a good, unassuming native. Kaiba greatly resented this disposition of his property, and wanted to take the matter to the magistrate at Kalomo. He and Lupata came to inform us of the murder and wished us to inform the magistrate by letter. Lupata said, "I do not want his cattle and I think you should write and tell the *Mwami* [magistrate] of the murder." Both refused to state who they thought was the murderer.

Brother Taylor wrote an explanation of the affair and Kaiba carried the letter to the magistrate, the brother and two other natives accompanying. This was the first intimation the magistrate had of foul play, and when he put the question to them they readily acknowledged that the man had been murdered. The brother, however, who had always been opposed to everything good, and had a very evil countenance, showed the cunning of his master; and he and one of the men accompanying put the blame on the third. This one acknowledged his guilt, saying that he and the other had killed the chief and the brother had sent them. We were informed later that the brother sent them three times before they became willing to perform the deed. Of course all three were put behind the bars.

It was a case of alleged witchcraft. Several children had died in the kraal under peculiar circumstances, and the blame had been laid by the brother, who was a witch doctor, on the chief. We prefer to think, from what we know of the two, that the brother was the guilty one in each instance, and was desirous of the chief's property and position.

Sisters Engle Crossing the Tuli River in the Matopo Hills.

During this rainy season it was thought advisable for Brother and Sister Taylor to go to Bulawayo and Matopo Mission for a much-needed rest. She went in November and he followed in January, 1911. At the same time David returned with his wife, Mankunku. Mankunku is one of the converts from Mapani Mission. She is a sincere Christian girl, and has proved a great help and blessing among the women and girls at Macha ever since she came. These two, with myself, prosecuted the work at Macha for the next five months alone.

There were at this time forty-six boys and four girls staying at the mission, and it was necessary, not only to teach them in school, but to keep them profitably employed during work hours and out on the farm. Quite a fair amount of land was under cultivation, and Brother Taylor had planted grain, fruit, and vegetables before he left, the care of which gave the boys plenty of work to do during the rainy season. As soon as that was over David made use of them in getting grass and poles together for building, and as permanent buildings were to be erected they tried to secure hardwood rafters.

Although there were so many boys together, yet all manifested a nice Christian spirit. They were not quarrelsome, and they were obedient and faithful in their work. The chief difficulty with natives is that they are inclined to keep their eyes fixed on the missionary too constantly and do not learn to depend on God for their own spiritual needs. The missionary, as he realizes the responsibility resting upon him, often feels like exclaiming, "Who is sufficient for these things?" to lead all in the right way. He may rejoice, however, that he can continually say, "My sufficiency is of God." He must also by every means in his power get their eyes off of himself and fix them on God. Otherwise they will do what is right at the mission and fall when those props are removed.

June 16 I wrote somewhat as follows:

> Last Monday the wagon went to the Myeki River (about five miles distant) to get some thatching grass which the boys had cut there the week before. I thought it an excellent opportunity to visit Semani, who has been sick for some time and not likely to recover. I took along three girls and the two six-year-old boys and thoroughly dismissed from my mind home cares. We had a delightful ride over and a nice walk back, but best of all was the visit with Semani. He had accepted Christ while here at the mission and had often accompanied David in his kraal-visiting. He became sick, however, and we seemed unable to help him, so he desired to return home until he was well. He was always hoping he would recover and return to us.
>
> He has pleurisy and is continually growing worse, and it is evident that the end is not far off. He greeted me with a smile as I entered, and while we were speaking, I inquired "Is Jesus here?" The reply, with a bright smile was, "Yes, He is here." We continued to speak of the things of the other world and what the Lord has in store for His children, and through it all he seemed so ready both to talk and to listen. His old heathen mother sat there in sort of a dazed wonder to hear us speaking thus familiarly and without fear of death and transition. For her sake I then asked him if he were afraid to die. He quickly replied, "Oh, no, I am not at all afraid to die; I am ready."
>
> Later, when we bowed in prayer, he prayed, "I thank Thee, God, for Thy help and blessing. I have come through some hard places, but Thou hast given me victory. And, Jesus, if my time has come and You want to take me, it is all right. I'll gladly go with You."
>
> How we could rejoice that here was one who, only two or three years ago, was a raw heathen boy, now so happy in the Lord, and so ready to meet Him. If one soul is worth more than the whole world then our coming to Macha has not been in vain. His people had been wanting to "throw bones" and "smell out" the one who, according to their ideas, had bewitched him, but he steadfastly refused, for he has no faith in those things.

The Bottle Palm.

Later it was my privilege to again visit him, together with Mankunku. We had made a trip to a village beyond, where we remained for the night, and stopped with Semani, both going and returning. He was much weaker at this time and it was evident the end was near, and his friends had gathered and were ready for the wailing. We found him, although in great pain and with great difficulty in breathing, yet rejoicing and happy in the thought that he was soon going home. He could not lie down, but was supported in the arms of his mother, who was doing all in her power to help him bear his suffering. He was, however, able to take a little of the nourishment which we brought him. On our return the day following, he was still weaker. In the night his friends thought he was dying, when he suddenly roused and sang "*Jesu udi tu fwine*" ("Jesus loves me"). These heathen friends in speaking to one another the next day said, "His heart is white toward God, and that is the reason he can sing when dying."

Before we departed he requested Christian burial, so we left word for them to inform us at once of his death. Word came that same evening. Brother Taylor was at home by this time, and he and David, together with a number of the schoolboys, went at once to the burial, although it was night. They found the body prepared for burial and the people digging the grave. Brother Taylor said everything was carried on most quietly until services were over and the body had been buried; then the heathen part of the wailing began in earnest. His brother, while wailing, continued to cry out, "Semani, where has he gone? He has gone to the light. Oh! where has he gone?" It was the wail of gross darkness seeing a faint glimmer of light, but knowing not how to reach it.

The deathbed of our friends, surrounded with all the comforts this life can afford—soft beds, willing, low-voiced nurses, dainty food, helpful and spiritual ministrations—is often trying enough; here, however, was one deprived of all these comforts, with the exception of the occasional visits of his missionaries, lying or sitting on the hard floor, with only a mat for a bed, without even the ordinary decencies of life, much less its comforts, in a village and home wholly pagan; and yet he goes, rejoicing in his Savior's love, carried out of this dark hovel to behold things "Eye hath not seen, nor ear heard, neither have entered into the heart of man the things which God hath prepared," but He had already revealed them unto him by His Spirit.

CHAPTER EIGHT

Further Improvements and Industrial Work

Industrial work had from the first progressed very favorably at the mission. The majority of boys, as they came, stayed on from year to year and exhibited more tenacity of purpose than is generally to be found among the natives. Some of them had assisted in making brick for the house and in the building; others had learned to handle the oxen in the wagon and on the farm in plowing, harrowing, and cultivating, while a number were engaged in gardening, hoeing, and the general work of the farm. Even the youngest were not idle, although their labors did not equal the expense of their keeping. We were, however, growing sufficient grain and food to supply our large family so that they could be kept from year to year under Christian training without their proving a heavy burden on the mission financially.

In June we were pleased to receive Brother and Sister Taylor back from Bulawayo, and with them a blessing to the mission in the person of a little baby, Ruth Taylor. I use the term *blessing* advisedly, for this dainty little Ruth was indeed such to all connected with the work. These people had not seen a white child, and this one was an ever-increasing source of wonder and interest to the black faces around us. They would stand near her noting every move and commenting on everything they saw. Her soft white skin and spotless garments soon gave her a name. "U swezhiwa" ("she is clean or pure") the girls called her, and thus she undoubtedly looked by contrast. Her presence often attracted to the services people, especially the women, who otherwise would have remained at home; for in the eyes of some, all other interests paled besides this mite of humanity, and it warmed their hearts toward the entire work. When we went to the village she was again a center of attraction, and when we went alone the natives would always inquire about U swezhiwa and her mother. When prayer was offered by the boys for the missionaries, the child was never forgotten.

After Brother Taylor's return the preparation for building went forward with accelerated speed. This dry season of 1911 was an unusually busy one at Macha. A church was greatly needed, for the one which David had erected four years previously, and which appeared to be so well-built, was rapidly showing signs of decay. It was still standing, but the ants had riddled the roof to such an extent that some of the timbers were falling, piece by piece, sometimes to the danger and great annoyance of those within. On this account we decided that it was best to vacate it even before the new one was finished.

The boys' huts also were decaying, and we found it difficult to house the large number of boys staying at the mission. These thatched roofs are very heavy, and if some part of the wall becomes weak the huts may become dangerous to life.

One evening the boys of one of the huts came to say that the roof of their hut was breaking. We told them to take their blankets and clothing and go into another hut. They did so, and in the morning their own building was found leveled to the ground. As we viewed the sudden ruin we breathed a prayer of thanksgiving that no one was hurt. There had been about fifteen boys sleeping in that hut, and had they been inside some would have been killed or seriously injured. This enabled us to realize how dangerous huts were when partly eaten, and the need of better buildings.

On account of building it was fortunate that there was such a large number of boys staying at the mission, and that the majority were large enough to be of service, so that there was no need of employing outside labor. Brother Taylor was excellent in training boys along industrial lines, a quality which is especially useful and helpful on the mission field, both in the interests of the work and of the natives themselves. Some people are glad to use native helpers when they are trained ready to order, but they soon become discouraged when time and patience are required.

The native learns by doing, and often learns by his many mistakes. Again, he may be careless and consider accuracy unnecessary. He is nature's child, and everything he does for himself is in curves. His hut is round, his baskets are round, his paths are meandering, like the stream, for he, like it, goes in the path of least resistance. Straight lines and right angles are unintelligible to him, and he does not readily grasp such things, nor does he easily learn to make them. Patience, which is always a virtue, is, in industrial work among the natives, an absolute necessity. One who will not take time and teach them will accomplish nothing praiseworthy in this respect.

We said the native learns by doing; so he does, but it is generally by doing not once or twice but repeatedly. One of my first lessons along this line was when visiting in the home of an official. The lady had always lived in South Africa and had been accustomed to deal with the natives all her life. Noticing a basket of snowy-white clothes I inquired, "Who does your washing?"

She replied, "The boys; I send them to the river to wash."

"But how can you teach them to do their work so well?"

"If they do not do it properly," she replied, "I send them back to repeat it until it suits me."

This is the keynote of the situation. In addition to showing them how to perform a task, one must insist on their doing it just as they have been told. If they become careless or learn with difficulty, one should not become discouraged and go and finish the work—for this frequently is easier than to teach the natives—but should insist on their repeating the task until it is properly done. Some natives with very little instruction become experts at certain kinds of work. And sometimes even raw ones readily adapt themselves to housework with very little training. A lady in Bulawayo, who was a very careful housekeeper, had a native boy as servant, who was giving excellent satisfaction, yet she supposed that on her own exertions depended the work of keeping the rooms in order. Finally he concluded to leave her service, and she said she did not know until after he left how much work he had really done. He had been in the habit, early in the morning, before his master and mistress arose, of going over the house, cleaning and polishing mirrors and furniture.

Macha Mission Church and Boys' House Built by Mr. Myron Taylor.

Another native, whose name has been frequently mentioned in these pages, was exceedingly cleanly and careful in his personal appearance. His clothes were always well washed and mended, and he went on the principle that a stitch in time saves nine. He learned to do things by seeing others perform them and was able to do them well. Although coming from a raw heathen home he was called an exceptional native, even by those who had had long experience with civilized natives.

As a rule those who are careful and painstaking are generally slow, and many who are quick often do not perform their work properly. Some never seem to respond to careful teaching, and with others, many both trying and ludicrous blunders often occur. In the early days of Macha Mission we had a half-grown boy, by the name of Hamambile, helping in the kitchen. He was a good boy and seemed to be performing his work properly. One day several of the boys, who had been working on the farm and had soiled their hands, came into the kitchen. Hamambile was washing the dishes, so he generously stepped aside and invited the boys to wash their hands in the water where the dishes were being washed, and this they were vigorously doing when Sister Engle stepped in at the door. Nor did her presence in the least abash the boys, for they saw no impropriety in the act.

Again, during the last year some new girls had joined the mission family and were being initiated into the mysteries of housekeeping. They seemed to learn well and were doing their work properly, but one day Sister Doner, on looking out of the window, was shocked to see a girl out in the yard with the dishpan, washing her feet. She too failed to see anything out of place in her act when she was first spoken to. She said she was just making use of some of the nice soapsuds on the water, for she thought it was too nice to throw away. It can easily be seen that one needs to be continually watchful while teaching some of them. On the other hand, there is no doubt that the raw native considers the white man or woman very cranky and extreme when he insists on cleanliness and order about the work.

On account of the great need it was necessary to build both a church and boys' house in the one dry season. There was erected a substantial church, 42 x 21 feet, with a wide veranda in front, which was also partly walled up, and a boys' house, 55 x 16 feet, of five rooms, with a veranda all along the front. These were both of burnt brick with thatched roofs. All the hardwood timber for rafters and plates, and also the large amount of thatching grass, were procured by the boys the same season, beginning in March and April. The bricks too were made and both buildings were under cover by the 1st of December. This was all done with the aid of the school boys under the supervision of Brother Taylor, assisted by David. Part of the time the work was in progress during school hours, the boys who assisted at such times receiving full wages, as they are all eager to earn a little extra money. During the month of brickmaking, the boys donated their time as an offering to the Church.

After they had made the bricks, Brother Taylor started on the foundation of the church, and then trained several of the Batonga boys in bricklaying. Together with himself and David they laid the walls of the church, all the larger boys having a share in some part of the work. The walls of the building are high, are fourteen inches in thickness and well laid. When this was completed Brother Taylor left David, assisted by some of the boys, to put on the thatched roof, which too is an excellent piece of work, while he turned his attention to the boys' house. Nearly all the brick work of this building was done by the boys under his supervision, and at the same time he was directing some in sawing by hand and making door and window frames out of the native hardwood timber. Later some of the boys were instructed in thatching it.

When this boys' house, fifty-five feet long, was completed in January, the only thing in its construction that had been bought for the purpose was the zinc under the walls to exclude the ants. The doors were made of the boards of packing cases in which a wagon had been sent from America; the thatching was tied on with strips of animal hides procured from the natives. The bedsteads were made of poles procured in the forests and reeds from the river. These were tied with bark string, and over the top were placed animal hides also bought from the natives. Later the rooms were whitewashed and they, with the long veranda in front, made an excellent and clean-looking home for the boys. The church had imported doors and windows, as well as zinc and thatching twine. Otherwise the material was almost native.

Ruth Taylor and Her Mother. A White Child in the Midst.

It was a creditable year's work and Brother Taylor deserved much praise for the ability with which it was all managed and the boys trained. No doubt some, on reading these lines, might say, "I could never be a missionary if I had to build like that!" "Where there is a will there is a way," is just as applicable on the mission field as elsewhere. It is surprising what one can accomplish if he is willing to be used. Every one of the men on the mission field has done excellent work along these lines, as the well-built brick houses and churches on the six mission stations at the present day testify. Some at first declared that they could not build, but, doubtless, today they look with surprise and satisfaction on the work of their own hands. In addition to this they have every reason to be thankful for the great amount of missionary work they were able to accomplish in the building by training and fitting the boys to a higher plane of living.

After the buildings were under roof, Brother Taylor, who had always desired to devote more time to evangelistic work among the villages, felt that his way was opened to attend almost exclusively to that line of work. Previous to this he had held services at many of the villages, such as Mapanza, Simeoba, Kabanzi, Kabwe, and at almost all the important villages near as well as north among the Baila; but during the year following he went out with his tent and sometimes spent two, three, and even four weeks at one place, so that he might have an opportunity of giving the people a fair conception of the Gospel. He spent a month at Chungu, near a large village, over twenty miles from the mission.

He had visited the place before, but the people were not eager to listen. At this time he pitched his tent a short distance from the village and informed the people that he had come to teach them, and that those desiring to hear should come to the tent at such a time as best suited them. About 8 A. M. every day a fair-sized congregation gathered at the tent and heard the Gospel expounded to them. He had some very good meetings at that place, and the people became interested sufficiently to request a school.

During the year he found many open doors and gave the Gospel to a large number of people who had never heard of a Savior, and there were urgent calls to start new stations in the needy places. How one longs to see some one step in at the opportune time and plant lights in the midst of the darkness!

While this work was progressing David devoted his time to finishing the new buildings and overseeing the boys at work. A dear Christian lady had sent out money for seats in the new church, and he began to make them, and accomplished this task well, and the building was furnished with good, comfortable seats. Some of the boys, in writing to their friends who were away at work, said, "We have nice seats in the church and we do not become tired when we sit on them a long time." A good solid floor was also put in, and this was tarred and sanded.

In November, 1911, we again had the privilege of welcoming Elder Steigerwald to Macha. He had lately returned from a furlough to America, and his visit was like getting a glimpse of the outside world. The Mission Board had sent out with him for Macha a large two-seated spring wagon with canvas top, something just suited for this country and climate. It was a most welcome and useful addition to our outfit. Especially since there are roads all over the country to the principal villages, this was helpful in evangelistic work and in visiting the out-schools, which were on the increase. The old days of laborious tramp were more or less in the past, and a new era seemed ushered in. Brother Steigerwald put the wagon together and added a long, useful box in front. Four oxen were then inspanned and we tested it. It is indeed a most satisfactory and comfortable conveyance and adds much to the enjoyment of the work.

While the bishop was with us eleven more boys were baptized and received into church fellowship. The first ten were all standing true, so that our number had now increased to twenty-one. There were as yet no girls or women ready for baptism, but some were beginning to accept Christ as their Savior.

As the new church was nearly completed at the time of his visit, it was thought advisable to dedicate this also before his return. He gave a most excellent sermon on the occasion, and we were all strengthened by his visit among us.

CHAPTER NINE

The Native

The most interesting thing in Africa is the native himself; the more I see him and study him the more I respect him.—Bishop J. C. Hartzell.

I most heartily voice the sentiment expressed above. The study of the native is a most interesting one and worthy of the best minds of the age. The latent power and ability lying back of some of those crude exteriors is often marvelous, and the transformation often wrought by a few years of careful, sympathetic training far more than repays for all the labor expended.

From what has already been given in the preceding pages, some idea of the native character may be gleaned, and yet it is impossible to give in such a book an adequate conception of the nature of the natives. In fact, the only way to know them is to live among them, and then one can not be sure that he has the correct idea. The subject is so many-sided, so elusive, and above all so changing that it is doubtful if any one can tell all there might be given.

This twentieth century has produced three large volumes on the African native, which, in the estimation of the general public, seem to occupy a preeminent position among the many books continually written. I refer to "Thinking Black," by Daniel Crawford; "White and Black in South Africa," by M. S. Evans; and "The Essential Kaffir," by Dudley Kidd. The first is the work of a missionary who has spent twenty-two unbroken years in the heart of the African Continent. The second is the work of a politician who has studied the native problem deeply and sympathetically from a governmental standpoint and has given his opinions and conclusions in a clear and convincing manner. The third work might be said to have been written from an independent standpoint, and is by many Europeans in South Africa considered the best thing written on the native. One who has lived long in Africa might be inclined to differ with any one or all of these writers in some points, but they are all excellent and well worthy of careful study.

I was once speaking with an official who had had long experience in dealing with native problems, and whose opinions along these lines were sought after by others. I asked him, "Wherein do you think lies the chief difficulty in dealing with the native?" He replied somewhat as follows:

"I think it lies in this: that the native so readily responds to civilization and improvement, that he comes up to our highest expectation along some lines;

and then we, forgetting the generations of barbarism back of him, think he should measure up to our expectations along all lines. When he fails us at some particular point we become disgusted and do not give him credit for the advancement he has made."

There seems to be much truth in the above statement and it has often been a help to me in dealing with natives. There is something else also which must not be lost sight of, and that is that as much as possible they should be dealt with as individuals. Too often the white man thinks the natives are all made over the same mould, and that the characteristics of one are the characteristics of all. He will often not take the trouble to study their individuality, and perhaps he thinks they do not have any. This is not surprising. Europeans often visit New York, remain a short time and then return home, thinking they know Americans, and can be found prating of how Americans do. If people come to such superficial conclusions about such a heterogeneous mass of humanity as exists in the United States of America, it is not surprising that one or two natives in the eyes of many white people stand as a type of all Africans.

The writer has had an opportunity of studying the natives of four or five tribes and has come into contact in various ways with several other tribes, yet she feels that her knowledge of the native character is in many respects superficial and unsatisfactory. It has this to recommend it, however, that it is gleaned at first hand from many years' residence among the raw and semi-civilized Africans.

We have tried to show that the natives differ greatly in their ability to learn in school and out of it, in their habits of cleanliness, and in their readiness to receive the Gospel. As there was a large number of boys about us day by day, we found that they also greatly differed in disposition, as much so as white people, and it was necessary to study the characteristic of each in dealing with them. They soon understand if the missionary respects and trusts them; and they readily respond to such treatment and show by their conduct that such confidence is not misplaced. On the other hand, if they are censured for a fault, especially if they think the censure is unjust, they soon become careless and discouraged. On account of their secluded and simple life they, even the grown ones, are much like children when they first come into contact with white people, and they fail to understand why two persons should treat them differently—why two missionaries or two masters should not have the same way of doing things, the same generosity and the same dispositions.

Child-life of these dark-skinned Africans is in some respects not so different from that of their white neighbors, unless it is in its greater freedom. Until it learns to walk, the child spends much of its time on its mother's or older sister's back, tied by a skin with its face toward the mother. In the early days at Matopo, Matshuba once inquired how our mother carried us when we were children. We said she carried us on her arms. He nodded his head sagely and exclaimed, "That explains it. That is why your noses are long and straight and ours are flat."

Little Nurses. Mianda Village.

On the mother's back the child sleeps and coos and observes what goes on about it. Here it bobs up and down as the mother handles the hoe, stamps or grinds the meal, or goes about her cooking. Here it takes rides as the mother goes after wood or water, or on long journeys to visit her friends. Occasionally she removes it from her back, straightens out its cramped limbs, feeds it, and then places it on the ground to play. It has no garments to impede its progress, and so it soon learns to help itself, crawls about and picks up earth or whatever comes in its way and eats it, no one objecting.

As it becomes older the freedom is still greater, especially if it is a boy. There is no school to confine him, no hard lessons, no table manners, no daily washings, oftentimes. He runs, he hunts, he fishes, he plays often the long day through, together with the other little ones of the village. He has no clock to tell him the time of the day, except the great orb above him, and this he learns to read with surprising accuracy. As it sinks in the west, he comes with his assegais and faithful dogs, and with a rabbit or some birds, carried on a stick across his shoulders, proudly displaying his prowess in hunting. He makes bows and arrows, popguns, plays hockey and other games, makes clay animals, wagons, and many other things. In fact, some native boys are genuine artists, and it is a pleasure to watch them deftly mould animals of various kinds.

His sister will have her doll, made from a stick of wood, a corncob, or the like, and tie it on her back, like her mamma does. She plays at housekeeping, grinding, cooking, and imitating her elders, the same as her white sisters do. She is also expected to help take care of the baby and younger members of the family, as her brother is often expected to herd the cattle or sheep, for there are no fences to confine them. All of these children, however, often suffer from hunger, cold, and nakedness, and worst of all they generally indulge in many evils which cling to them and greatly retard their progress when light comes to them. They also become quite cruel and unfeeling about giving pain to animals and birds. Every accessible bird's nest is robbed and the young birds, partly plucked, are thrown, often while still alive, on the live coals to roast and furnish them a dainty morsel. When a bird is secured there is not the least compunction about plucking off all the feathers without killing the bird. Once, when I was lying sick in bed, the four girls staying at the mission came in laughing and carrying the fledgling of a secretary bird. It was about the size of a half-grown chicken, and had all the feathers plucked from it while it was alive, and in this condition it was still blinking with its big, solemn-looking eyes. The brother of one had brought it in this condition, and to them it was a good joke to see it thus.

As one enters the raw African's village and sees the native in the midst of his filthy and uncouth surroundings, lacking seemingly the very necessities of life, he readily concludes that the African is lazy, shiftless, lacking in resources, and exceedingly dull or he would have advanced further in civilization even before the advent of the white man. To a certain extent this is true, for even the native, after he is somewhat civilized and looks back to where he came from, has been heard to exclaim, "We must be the dullest people on earth. Others could read and write and knew something of civilization, but we Africans knew nothing." We need, however, but to look back to our own Celtic and Teutonic ancestry to see barbarism and illiteracy.

The African pagan cannot be said to be lacking in resources, however. He wishes fire and he goes and selects two suitable twigs of wood. Into one he cuts a notch and the other he points. Placing the first on the ground, he inserts the point of the other into the notch and twirls it rapidly between his hands until it strikes fire. At the same time he has on hand some inflammable substance upon which he places the fire and soon has a blaze. He can thus roast his fish or meat. He wishes cooking vessels; and the woman goes to the river and procures the proper kind of clay, which she mixes with water and works until it is the required consistency. She then takes a piece, and with deft fingers moulds it into a circle, and places it on a stone or piece of broken crockery. She adds more and more clay, carefully shaping it with her hands as she proceeds upward until the top is finished. Then she puts it aside for a while until the clay sets and becomes slightly dried, after which she carefully removes and turns it and moulds the bottom, and when dried she burns it. In this way she makes earthen pots of many kinds and sizes, from the dainty small ones, which are often nicely glazed and artistically marked, to the large, heavy beer pots, holding ten or twelve gallons.

Weapons for war, hunting, and domestic purposes are needed. The man goes to the hills and digs until he finds the iron ore. He smelts it and with the iron thus obtained makes axes, assegais, hoes, and other useful implements. He burns wood and makes charcoal for his forge. His bellows are made from the skins of animals and the pipes are clay tile; and the anvil and hammers are also pieces of the iron he has obtained. He moulds, welds, shapes, and performs all the work of the ordinary blacksmith. If his hoe wears out he will take the iron that is left and shape it into an assegai bristling with points. With three or four of these and a shield made of hide, he will go out to fight his neighbor, or perhaps he will have bow and steel-tipped arrows, which he dips in a poisonous substance to ensure their deadly work.

Or, if it is in time of peace, he makes use of his assegais and his faithful dog and supplies his household with meat. If he has been fortunate enough to secure an old blunderbuss of a gun, he tinkers at it till it works. He may not be able by law to buy any ammunition from the white man, or even lead to make bullets; but he will manage in some way to obtain some ammunition. Perhaps the chance possession of a nail, or solder melted from a tin can, will, by a laborious process, be turned into bullets, for time is no object to him when working for himself. In the same way he will secure some gunpowder or the ingredients for it, either by barter with his neighbors, who have been to town, or elsewhere.

He wishes fish, and he will spear or catch them with hooks, or his wife will, with willowlike twigs and bark strings, make a long troughlike net, and as the water subsides she will supply her household with fish. Both fish and meat are dried and preserved for future consumption.

Batonga Fisher Women.

The native wishes a hut to live in. He goes to the forest and with the axe cuts down poles and carries them home, and with his hoe digs a trench into which he places them. With some forked sticks he makes a neat doorframe. Thin, willowy poles are also brought and split through the center, and one piece is placed on the outside and one inside of the poles of the hut, and with bark strings he firmly ties these together and thus secures the poles in their places. They are also fastened at the top in a similar manner, so that the walls of the hut are firmly fastened together, for of course his hut is round. With his method of building he is wise in making it round, as it is more easily done and stronger when completed. The slender, straight poles for the roof are fastened together in the same way. These are often extended beyond the walls so as to form a veranda, which may or may not be enclosed. The wife takes her hoe or assegai and cuts grass to thatch the hut. She also takes some of the beautiful long grass, and with bark string makes a large mat to form a partition to separate the bed-room from the living-room. They need a bed and the man will procure forked sticks and fasten them firmly in the ground as bedposts, and on this with poles, reeds, bark string, and animal hides he makes a bed. Skins may also be used for blankets, and if they should be lacking in these they build a fire or place a pan of coals underneath or near the bed. Some Africans weave blankets and some make them out of the inner bark of the trees; others purchase from traders.

The native needs a chair, so he goes to the forest and, selecting a certain kind of tree, he cuts a suitable block of wood. With his little axe he hews and cuts until from a solid block of wood he makes a very respectable-looking chair, or stool, varying in height from six to fourteen inches. In the same way he makes spoons, stamping blocks, dishes, and other household articles. These he carefully oils to prevent cracking, and often colors and ornaments them. The natives along the large rivers make their own dugout canoes. A large gourd or earthen jar answers for a water bucket, one with a long handle for a dipper, a very large one with woven top is used for a churn, a long one as a butter receptacle, and a very small one for a snuffbox. A small piece of iron, nicely shaped and beaten thin, is snuff spoon and handkerchief.

A large flat stone, built in a clay receptacle with an earthen jar at the end, is the mill, and on this another stone is used to grind. The wife needs baskets. She procures palm leaves, bark string, reeds, and willows and makes baskets of various kinds: a flat one for a sieve, dainty little ones for plates for their stiff porridge, larger ones for grain, and still larger ones for reaping. She also makes mats of various kinds. Skins of animals do for clothing. They are so confident that this is the native invention, that one of the boys, in reading of the garments of our first parents, declared they must have been black because they wore skins. The girls' loincloth is made of bark string. Their clay pipes are often quite artistically made, and so hard that it is difficult to distinguish them from metal.

In all of these things just mentioned the native is in no way dependent upon the European; they are of his own invention and manufacture, except the rifle. It is not to be supposed that any one native makes all the various articles. There are blacksmiths, potters, basketmakers, and workers in wood, and the rest barter for or buy the things they need.

Given various colored beads, some fine and some heavy wire, a few buttons, shells, and ivory rings, and they are adept at adorning the body, at least according to the native's idea of beauty. In some respects the barbarous African's idea of ornamentation does not differ materially from that of her white sisters, the difference being one of degree rather than of kind. The American beauty thinks one or two strings of beads around her neck are quite the proper thing, and add to her charm. The African beauty will tell you that if one or two are nice, four or five are nicer. It is the same with the bracelets; the American belle is pleased with one or two on her wrists. The African is likewise, but she is better pleased with a dozen, only she adds utility to beauty and thinks that a lot of heavy rings around her wrists or ankles add to their strength and give her corresponding value in the eyes of the opposite sex. Then too she will tell you that her god told her to adorn herself thus, which is doubtless true.

What has been said of inventive ability applies more or less to all pagan Africans, although in different sections of the country they differ somewhat in their work. The Batonga, by whom we are surrounded, do not at present remove the iron from the ore, but there are many blacksmiths among them, and according to some of the old natives they were accustomed to smelt the ore. There are certainly evidences of iron workings in this part of the country. Brother Taylor made inquiry of an old native in reference to these workings. He said that many years ago the Batonga used to work them and thus obtain their own iron. Then their Barotse conquerors came and killed all the iron workers and told them to come to the Barotse and purchase their iron. No doubt this was done to weaken them in battle. (See 1 Samuel 13: 19-22.) In this instance the smiths remained, but they go to the Barotse to purchase hoes and pig iron. Since the old ones were killed, the younger generation were afraid to smelt the ore.

All the Africans brew their own beer. They also grow tobacco, which they both smoke and snuff, and they grow a kind of hemp which they smoke. Of course they raise their own food, and before the arrival of the white man some even procured their own salt.

As to the general character of the raw natives—for it is of them we are writing—we hesitate sometimes to tell what we do know. But the missionary, however much he may think of the Africans and enjoy his work among them, cannot, dare not, be blind to their faults. It has been said of them that they are naturally liars, thieves, and harlots; a hard saying, truly, but there is a measure of truth in it. As a people there is little or no reliance to be placed on their word, especially when they desire to shield themselves, their relatives, or even their tribes. Possibly a native may tell an untruth for the mere pleasure of it. This habit is so inbred that it is difficult to overcome it; and yet by careful religious training, and the power of the Holy Spirit, one is frequently surprised at the progress they make in speaking the truth under very trying conditions—that is, when they are led to see the evil of the opposite course.

Thieving is probably not so prominent, but it exists, not only, as some affirm, among the half-civilized, but also among the raw heathen. Every missionary, who has seen heathen accepting the Light and confessing their past, can testify to the truthfulness of this statement. Many instances of stealing among them can be cited. I was told by a farmer, who was living in the midst of pagan Africans, untouched by civilization or the Gospel, that one year he employed about 100 women to gather his corn. He suspected them of stealing, but said nothing until one evening, just as they were starting for home, he suddenly rode in among them and frightened them. The corn which they had carefully concealed about them was scattered in all directions.

Stealing, however, is not as common as lying; for while there does not seem to be a strong public sentiment against the latter, there is against the former, for the protection of their property. Those who flagrantly disregard this are branded as thieves and are sometimes punished. I know one native who was required by his heathen neighbors to pay ten hoes for visiting their grain bins. Generally, however, grain, either in the gardens or in the granaries, is not disturbed by others, and one may allow property to remain exposed year after year and it not be disturbed. The white man's law against thieving greatly assists the native in the enforcement of his law. We have found some very trustworthy natives, and none who have been with us any length of time have proven dishonest, and they are frequently sent to carry sums of money without in any way tampering with it.

As to other forms of vice what shall one say? One European has been heard to exclaim that "their morals are as black as their faces." That they are dark no one can deny, for from childhood up vice in many forms is common. It could scarcely be otherwise when one considers the filth and degradation of their surroundings, where a number are crowded like so many animals into a filthy hut, overrun with vermin and parasites of all kinds. Some will tell you that there are none pure. It is true that the lives they lead give little opportunity for anything elevating. Then too their lives are open to the general gaze; nothing is hid.

But take the modern city; dig it up from the foundation; open all its cesspools of infamy, crime, and debauchery, and such a stench will ascend to heaven that everyone beholding will cry out, "Babylon, the mother of harlots and abominations of the earth!" And yet this is the boasted twentieth-century civilization. Shall we, then, say that there are no Christians in that city, or that there are none living good moral lives who do not profess Christ? God forbid! All honor to the noble band of men and women in our cities who, in the midst of fearful odds, are living upright lives and helping their fellow-men.

I believe I can safely say, from what I have seen and learned of the inner life of the native, that in dark, heathen Africa, even before the light of the Gospel penetrates, there are those who are moral and pure, although the number is small. Then take the Christian natives; the life of many a one is a living rebuke to some who decry mission work, and it is too often because they are a living rebuke, that they are so fiercely hated by some Europeans. People usually find what they are looking for, and in Africa is no exception.

CHAPTER TEN

The Native—Continued

Beggars the Africans naturally are, and when the white man comes among them they are always eager to obtain all they can for nothing. They beg of one another; then why should they not beg of the white man, whose pockets are supposed to be full of money? Then too some of them think the white man does not need money to buy food, clothing, and other goods from the store. They will say, "You do not need money to buy things. You just write something on a piece of paper and send it to Bulawayo and the goods come." Experience has taught us that the greatest good one can do the native is to make him work or pay for everything he receives, unless it should be during a case of sickness or helplessness.

It is a common expression that the African is lazy; and yet even this must be accepted with a reserve and an understanding of his surroundings. Aside from the effect of the climate, much of their indolence and indifference is due to their smoking of hemp, a narcotic drug, similar to the *hashish* of eastern countries. This they grow, and it is a common practice for the older, and for even young boys, to smoke it. It seems to sap their very life and take away all the ambition to better their condition. Yet the native can and does work even in his home, when occasion demands. During the digging and growing season they are found out in their gardens, which are generally at a distance from the villages, from early morning until late at night, hoeing and watching their crops to protect them from the ravages of the animals and birds. During the hottest part of the day they generally stop for a time to rest and cook. It is useless to attempt much evangelistic work during this season of the year, except at night, for the villages are about deserted during the day.

They may, during the dry season, work for Europeans, but with some a short time of such work suffices, as their wants are few. As one fellow expressed it: "I have now sufficient money to pay my taxes. I only want to work long enough to earn money to buy a blanket and then my needs are all supplied." If they have food on hand, that is the extent of the ambition of some natives. They feel that then, during the dry season, or winter, they are entitled to rest, hunt, smoke, drink beer and palaver.

Frequently, however, they must build in the dry season, for one of their huts in this ant-ridden country lasts only a short time—perhaps two or three years —and then another must be built. This is no small task, but it is usually postponed until near the rainy season. In order to build, the native is obliged to make frequent trips to the forest to procure suitable poles and bark strings, all of which he must carry on his shoulders. His wife too is inclined to postpone cutting the thatch grass until it is nearly all burnt, and then it requires much more labor to find enough thatch than if she had done the work at the proper time. The rain usually is threatening, or even the first has fallen before the man begins the actual building, and then he and his neighbors hurry and put up the huts after a fashion. When asked why he does not build earlier in the season he naively exclaims, "Oh! I leave it until the rains come, so I must hurry and build it." In other words, he puts it off until he is forced to do it, willy-nilly.

As a rule the native is never in a hurry; he always performs his work deliberately. That is characteristic of the country, or climate, rather than of the individual, because no one in Africa seems to be in a hurry. We had our first lesson in this on the threshold of the continent. Just after we had reached Cape Town and had rented rooms, some groceries were bought and ordered to be sent to the house. They were very slow in coming, and we mentioned the fact to an American lady who had resided at Cape Town five years. She replied, "We are all slow in Africa, and in a few years you will become slow too." I cannot say that this has become true of all our missionaries, but this is the general effect of the country. The atmosphere, the heat, and the diseases, all have much influence on a person. To hurry and violently exert the body in order to complete a piece of work often brings on an attack of fever. Horses, mules, oxen, and donkeys are not as hardy as in temperate climates, and it requires several times the number to do the same amount of work, so that it need not surprise one that the natives, who, as far back as they know, have lived amid such surroundings, should be slow and indolent.

There are three natives in our nearest village, all able-bodied men of about 40 or 45 years of age. Two of them have four wives and one has three. Since the hut tax is ten shillings a hut, that means that one must pay thirty shillings (nearly $7.50) tax per year, and the other two forty shillings (nearly $10). They are all intelligent-looking natives. Two of them have been government messengers and know something of European life. Now they are at home year after year, for they seldom go away to work, because they are too lazy. How they secure their hut tax is often a query, and about the only solution that seems possible is that they beg some here and some there of natives who go away to work, and they may occasionally have a little grain to sell. Often they are short of food for themselves and their families. One of them at least has had his family out on the veldt, living on fruit and roots and what game he could procure, for two months at a time. These are extreme cases, and one must feel sorry for the women and children when crops fail, for they at least cannot go among the Europeans for work.

The natives differ greatly among themselves in diligence and training as well as in character and morality. While there are always some improvident ones, who live on the charity of their neighbors, yet some are exceedingly industrious the entire year. After their grain has been cared for they go to the towns to work and earn money, buy cattle and sheep, and in general enrich themselves. Workers in wood are always busy making articles to sell to their neighbors, and other artizans do likewise. The women also show the same difference of character. Some are always busy and forehanded with their gardens, their grass cutting, and cutting and carrying firewood to stow it away before the rains come. The same difference is to be found in the training of families.

In some of the homes the children are well trained along industrial lines, according to the native idea of training. The parents require them to work and bear a certain amount of responsibility in providing for the family and in caring for the herds. For instance, a number of our best boys came from a village called Mianda. They proved very helpful and skillful in work and became some of our best builders and teachers. Their parents were generally considerate when we had dealings with them. Sometimes we had as many as ten boys at once from that one small village, and the father of some would even help to see about his herds so that his children might attend school. If a boy was needed at home to help build or herd, the father would tell for just how long he was needed, and we might be sure that he would send the boy back at the expiration of that time. The children of this village were required to be obedient and work while at home, otherwise they were denied food. There were other similar homes. In the villages, even before Christianity enters, the natives look upon some of the customs of their tribes in various ways. Where there are large villages and many people, dances and carousals are frequent occurrences and much immorality results. Some of the parents forbid their children frequenting these places of amusement on account of the immorality.

Again, from some villages boys would come to the mission, stay only a few days and then leave, because they were obliged to perform a certain amount of work daily. We did not try to coax them to remain, for we preferred to keep only those who were willing to work—the others seldom amount to anything. Go into the houses of some such boys, and one would see them lying about, not willing to herd, much less dig. Perhaps the father will say, "Go and see about those sheep." The boy pays no attention to the command. The mother comes and scolds him and seeks to make him work, but with no better result; yet when food is prepared he is the first one to be around the pot and no one forbids him. From these instances it can be readily seen that African family training does not differ materially from European or American.

In many of the villages there are always some who desire to improve themselves and better their conditions. They have their gardens, but, work as they may with their primitive little hoes, they cannot make much headway; or there may be a drought and famine is the result. They go away and work for a time, and come home with a supply of clothing and some money. They come to their dirty homes and filthy surroundings, and their friends and relatives try to get as much of their clothing and money as possible. They gradually become more and more sordid in appearance, their clothing disappears, and we become disgusted with them for so soon leaving behind the outward marks of civilization. But how many months could we live their home life and be presentable in appearance?

Let us take Charlie as an example. He, with a number of other boys, went to Southern Rhodesia to work on a farm. He remained a year and received fifteen shillings ($3.60) per month, and he had to pay his way down and back on the train. He came home at the end of the year with a nice supply of new clothing and some money, and he looked as clean and well-dressed as a European when he came to Church on Sunday. He is a Christian boy and is trying to do what is right. Soon after his return home, his father, who is one of the three lazy men I mentioned, and extremely filthy in appearance, began wearing Charlie's clothes. First it was a shirt and a piece of calico; then another garment; then his nice grey coat. Charlie gave his little naked brother one of his shirts. He wished to marry, and this took all of his money. In a few months he presented quite a different appearance from what he did on his return home from Bulawayo, and we began to blame him, at least in our minds, and say that he should not allow himself to degenerate in this way. But most of his clothing is gone and his money is gone; he does not even have sufficient with which to purchase soap, so that he may wash the remaining clothing.

Says one, "He should keep at work and not come and sit down in his home." The work takes him away from home, and his wages are low, so that he must keep at it continually in order to maintain appearances. May he not have any home life at all? It is a perplexing problem, and were we forced to take his place we would no doubt conclude that the boy does remarkably well under the circumstances. While at home he works in his gardens and does what he can find to do for the white men near his home; then, as his needs increase, he again goes to Bulawayo to begin again. This is an actual occurrence and typical of many others. He may conclude to have no home life, but keep up the semblance of civilization, hang about the towns, and imitate many evils surrounding him, and in the end prove a greater menace to society and to the country than if he would, at least part of the time, live in his own home in a more primitive manner. Again, if he depends too much on the stores of the traders, he ceases to manufacture articles for himself, so that if he does finally settle down for himself, tired of the struggle, he is often more helpless than at first, because he cannot make the articles which his father made.

Is the native provident? or does he live from hand to mouth? Yes and no. I heard a man who traded with the natives say that in one year he bought about 1,000 bags of grain from them, giving in exchange goods from his store. Before the next crop was harvested, he had sold about all the grain back to them, at of course quite an advance in price. I have seen, near our own doors, natives sell to European traders grain, either for money or goods, from $1.25 to $2.50 for a two-hundred-pound bag and buy it back later in the same season for from $6 to $7 per bag. But these are extreme cases. In the latter instance a year of plenty was followed by a year of drought, and the natives were far from markets and at the mercy of local traders. Many of the natives had put in their granaries what would have tided them over an ordinary season, but the prolonged drought led them to want. Others had a comparatively poor crop the previous year and this caused a scarcity. Some did not need to buy at all, as they always look in advance for such emergencies and do not sell their surplus until certain of a new crop. Such natives, when they do sell, often sell to their native neighbors or exchange their grain for cattle. Such are generally very thrifty, while there are always some who are in want. In this too it may be seen that they are not unlike other people.

In fact, the Batonga taught their missionaries some lessons in caring for grain. We found that they store their corn in the grain bins without removing all the husks, and they shell it as they need it or near the end of the season. With the Kafir corn they do the same way, cutting off the heads and putting it away without threshing it. This was so different from the thrifty Matabele, who carefully shelled and threshed their grain, that the first time we visited one of the villages and saw their method we thought, "How lazy! We must teach them how to do their work properly." We soon discovered that in this hot climate the shelled corn was soon weevil-eaten, and that the shelled Kafir corn was almost ground to meal before the year ended. Now we are inclined to imitate the natives in this respect rather than they us. It shows too that the native adapts himself to the country and climatic conditions.

The African is a genuine lover of nature. He enjoys being out in the open air; he loves the bright rays of the sun. Everything around him is pregnant with meaning. Nature is his school, and he knows the habits of every beast, bird, or insect. In a measure he appreciates and loves the beautiful, even though at first he may smile at the white man's love for flowers. One day I inquired of an old heathen woman, who never came to Church, why they moved their kraal from the rock-bound place in which it had been, to the open plain. Her withered face brightened up, as with a sweep of her arm she took in the magnificent scene before her and exclaimed, "Is not that beautiful?" The native too shows good taste in the selection of clothing after he has become accustomed to civilized ways. We are inclined to think of them as being especially partial to bright colors. A few are, but my experience is that the majority are not. Many of the boys especially soon discard the native stores, where cheap apparel is sold, and frequent the stores for Europeans.

They love music and have several crude musical instruments. Their songs are generally of war, love, marriage, and the chase. They also have some songs suitable to their work. They of course have good voices for singing, and can be easily trained to sing well. They have their legends, their poetry, proverbs, and animal stories.

Natives, although very generous among themselves, are not inclined to be so to white people; perhaps because white people have not as a rule treated them so generously. If the native wishes to sell anything and is greatly in need of the money or clothing, he will often consent to sell for almost any price. It is the same with work; he will work very cheaply if he is eager to work.

On the other hand, if the need is on the part of the buyer, he will ask a very high price for grain or other articles and absolutely refuse to give for less, especially if the buyer is an European. With work it is the same. Even boys, after they have received a certain amount of education and religious training, are very slow to accept the idea that they should do anything for the white man from a sense of duty. There are doubtless some very good reasons for this. They, however, respect a master who is kind but firm, and it is best not to coax them. If they find that we are not dependent upon them, and can get along without them, they are more likely to conclude that they cannot get along without us.

The native is said to be lacking in gratitude to his benefactor, and there is some truth in this. One often spends much time and labor to train him along certain lines, with the hope that he will be of genuine service in the future. Perhaps about the time he is able to take the place for which he is fitted, he will often turn and, rejecting his benefactor, give the benefit of his training to some one who can remunerate him better. Naturally the missionary, or master, whichever it may be, feels grieved at this lack of gratitude. Too often, perhaps, the fault is on both sides, and we do not give him credit for the help he has been to us. Then too it is difficult to put ourselves in his place and see matters from his point of view. He has no idea of the value of our time or training and we sometimes spoil him in the beginning. Would not the best and safest way for the good of the native be to require him to earn his way as he goes? Let him always work sufficiently, if possible, to pay for the trouble it takes to teach him, whether in school or in industrial work, or in work pay him small wages at first and increase as he becomes more and more proficient. It may require a little of his time, but it has not spoiled him, and if he should conclude to go at any time, he has altogether or nearly paid his way in kind and one is none the loser.

The native, however, can, and many of them do, improve greatly along this line after they have become Christians. While naturally they are not inclined to be disinterested and generous to the white people, yet many of them become so and display a remarkable spirit of self-sacrifice in the Lord's service. Many teach year after year at a far lower salary than they could obtain elsewhere; and, not only in teaching but in other lines of labor requiring skill, they will work for the Lord for a much lower wage than they could procure elsewhere, as all of our missionaries can testify. Then too many of them often give largely of their penury for the advancement of the cause of Christ.

I was one day touched by the spirit manifested by a big fellow. He had come to the missionaries destitute of clothing, but anxious for an education. He was a hard-headed chap, both in school and out, and ran up against many hard places before he became pliable. He received, like the rest, a little money at the end of each term, but since he was in school three and one-half hours each day, his time for work was limited and his pay necessarily small. He, however, stayed at the mission and gradually obtained some clothing and money to pay his taxes. He also began to accept Christ as his Savior and from being a proud, obstinate fellow, he became more and more docile. At one time the amount coming to him was ten shillings ($2.40). His wardrobe was still scanty, but he took out for himself one shilling of the money received and brought the remaining nine shillings and said, "Here, I want to give this to the Lord."

Giving the Gospel to the natives in their villages, while it is generally a pleasure to the missionary, is not always an easy task. They soon learn to be very quiet and respectful in the church, enter quietly, take their places and go through all the outward forms of service, and also leave without being noisy or talking, perhaps because they are requested to do so. But when one goes out into their villages, even to the best of them, there are many side issues. The chief, if he is present and worthy the name, will aid in keeping order, and even if he is not present, the majority may sit quietly and seem to be listening; but perhaps the cattle get at the granaries and must be driven away, or the chickens go into the huts and eat the meal and must be watched; perhaps new ones are continually coming and must be noticed and greeted, if they are allowed to do so. Then the babies are so interesting to their mothers or those near them, or perhaps there is a mother with an older child at her side, and she does not wish to lose any time; so, during her enforced leisure, she is sedulously examining the child's head or ornaments for parasites. Perhaps over there, outside the hut door, is a man who has not had time to make his morning toilet, so he concludes to spend the time in dressing the long locks of hair around the top of his head.

One does not like to stop and reprove them, because the rest seem attentive and perhaps those are also listening, for the work they are engaged in is such a common one! Again, all may seem attentive and the missionary rejoices that the seed is falling into well-prepared soil, and he continues eager to drive the truth home to their hearts. He pauses to let it sink in—when lo! some one will make a remark wholly irrelevant to the subject he seeks to impress upon their minds; it may be in reference to some article of clothing he is wearing, or some of their own needs. His enthusiasm cools, for he perceives that some, and perhaps many, have paid little attention to the message.

Again, one may be speaking, and the chief or headman repeats what has been said, or he may ask a pertinent question, the answer to which brings out other questions, which serve to elucidate the subject. The other natives are led to listen; and while the discourse turns to be almost a conversation between the speaker and this one, yet the missionary goes away feeling that they have at least understood and perhaps have received some light. Sometimes, again, one may have only a few listeners and go away thinking nothing has been accomplished, but God has taken care of the seed sown.

I remember being out once with one of the Christian boys. We came to a garden where a woman and her daughter were working, and we sat and talked with them about Christ our Savior. This was the first time they had had an opportunity to hear. Years passed and the incident was about forgotten by both the Christian native and myself. That girl later, out of much tribulation found her way into the Kingdom. Her father was a hardened old heathen, and had sold her to an old man. He was going to force her to marry the old man, but she escaped and fled to Matopo Mission where, with Elder Steigerwald's help, she was set free. She returned home, and later an European offered oxen and wagon to her father for her. She steadfastly refused and kept herself pure. Today she is the wife of a native evangelist and one of our most valued helpers. She says her first knowledge of Christ was at that little meeting in the garden, where she and her mother were working, and her present husband and I stopped to speak with them.

CHAPTER ELEVEN

Some of Their Religious Ideas

Nevertheless He left not Himself without witness, in that He did good, and gave us rain from heaven, and fruitful seasons, filling our hearts with food and gladness.—Acts 14: 17.

The above quotation may apply to the African's idea of God in general, but it seems especially applicable to the Batonga and kindred tribes. Among these the word for God and rain are one and the same, *Leza*. This does not necessarily imply that they have no conception of God apart from the Rainmaker, but that conception is closely allied to rain and kindred elements in nature. They understand the name *Mubumbi* (Moulder or Creator) and *Chilenga* (Originator of Customs), but when speaking of the earth and vegetation, they will say, "Leza [God] made these things, because when leza [rain] comes, grass and vegetation spring up and grow, so Leza made them."

Of course their conception of Him, like that of all Africans, is very remote. He is their Creator, but to approach unto Him is like reaching out in the dark, in a vague sort of way, after something more powerful than themselves, something or some one they know not what. In times of great trouble, as in famine, fear, or when there is an earthquake or an eclipse, they will worship God, not necessarily by word of mouth, but by clapping their hands in reverence. They generally, however, like the Matabele, feel that they cannot approach God. He is too great and terrible, so they approach Him through mediators, such as departed spirits, prophets, and prophetesses.

Mr. Eddy, in "India Awakening," says: "Joined with these is the worship of dead parents, where spirits are dependent on their survivors for comforts, and who will avenge neglect or any deviation from custom. This belief is (1) a religion of fear, since most spirits are malicious; (2) a religion divorced from ethics, since spirits have no regard for moral ideas; (3) a religion of custom, since the worship rests on tradition and the spirits are apt to punish all departure from custom." This statement in reference to India can be as truthfully said of the pagan African.

The Batonga, many of them, build roofs or small huts over the graves of their dead. In them they will place skulls of animals and some of the property of the deceased. Their descendants come to this place, bringing beer and even water, and pour it out upon the grave in worship. If one has been considered powerful while alive, has been a great rainmaker, many people will gather around his grave in time of drought and pray for rain.

They have also their living prophetesses and prophets, to whom they turn in times of need. These claim that the soul of some powerful deceased one has entered them and bequeathed to them its power. In times of drought these prophetesses—for they are generally women—multiply rapidly. In a village of about thirty-five huts, near us, there were said to be ten prophetesses during the drought two years ago. The prophetic term of some of them is often very short, much depending on their seeming success as rainmakers. Sometimes the prophetess will make no claim for herself, but her friends will make it for her. The prophetesses are very often immoral characters.

Day after day people will come to the prophetess, as the time for planting draws near, bringing their presents of grain or money and their seed, that she may bless it and insure good crops. They come, sit down, reverentially clapping their hands and beseeching her aid. The hunter brings his gun, to receive medicine which will insure him prowess in hunting; a man comes asking for medicine for his sick wife, who is bewitched, and this medicine is to ward off the witchery. There comes from afar an old woman, who claims to have the power of making their grain last a long time by putting a certain medicine into it when cooking. She is believed and the medicine is bought and put into the food, and she rejoices in her pay. These heathens are always very gullible and readily purchase anything which appears conducive to their own interests.

One day I saw a number of natives going to a village to worship a rainmaker, so I concluded to go also and see what they did, for it was a village near the mission where the Gospel had often been proclaimed. As I reached the place the prophetess was in her hut, but a number of women and girls were outside, clapping their hands in worship. Their faces were familiar to me, and I could not avoid feeling sad to see how little influence the Gospel had thus far had on their lives. Finally the prophetess came out of her hut and was received with more clapping of the hands. She was a large, powerful-looking woman and gave orders like a queen, nor was she unqueenly in appearance. The worshipers were seated around a large hole or excavation in the earth, and had several dishes of grain which they had brought. They were told to sort the grain, selecting only the best and whitest; and I am informed that some of the grain, together with incantations, is dropped into the opening in the earth, but this I did not see. She came and greeted me and spoke a few words and then entered her hut. A man came to her for medicine for his sick wife, who was bewitched, and others went to consult with her. Finally I went to the door of her hut and spoke with her, inquiring why these people were worshiping. She said:

"They want rain. The spirit of a rainmaker who died a long, long time ago entered into me and they come for me to make it rain."

Knowing them so well, and being jealous for Him Whose ambassador I was, I asked, "Do you really mean to say that you can cause rain?"

Regarding me quite earnestly for a time she finally said, "No, I cannot cause rain."

"Why then are you deceiving the people and pretending that you can? God only can produce rain."

"Yes," she replied, "He alone can make it rain."

"Then come and tell the people that He only can cause it to rain and that they should worship Him."

She willingly complied, and coming out of her hut, she spoke to them very earnestly, telling them to worship God, as He alone could cause rain. As she claimed to be only an intercessor, and no doubt did this to please me, it did not necessarily interfere with her role as rainmaker. Even the most pagan among them acknowledge Leza (God) as the Rainmaker, and these only as His messengers. Since the people so readily transfer their worship from one to another, they also freely come to the missionaries to have them pray for rain. They have done this at Macha, and the Lord has graciously answered the prayers of His servants. This, however, does not seem to bring the native any nearer to repentance and God, and one feels loath to heed their request, except in the case of Christian natives.

With the Batonga, wailing for the dead seems to be essentially a religious requirement, and it is most religiously observed, so we venture to include it as a part of their religion. When the news of a death reaches a village, the people begin to wail at once, especially if they be relatives, and continue to do so while they are moving about, putting away their grain, baskets, and the few utensils they own, for a stay of several days. They may be heard wailing as they pass on their way out of their village to go to that of the dead. In a short time perhaps the entire village is deserted. We were once camping near a village of fifty huts, and news came that a relative had died at a mine near Bulawayo. In a few minutes nearly all the inhabitants were on their way to the house of mourning; for, although the body was buried about four hundred miles distant, they firmly believed that his spirit returned to his home and took cognizance of all they did. If a native is traveling along a path, and word comes to him of the death of a relative, he will begin wailing at once, and turning around proceed to the place of mourning.

Perhaps the reader will more fully understand what an African funeral is if he in mind accompanies us to one. Apuleni's father had been working in a mine in Southern Rhodesia. He became quite sick there and was brought home to die. We visited his home, and found that they had taken him to a temporary hut at some distance from the village. It is a very common practice for them to do this, especially if one is near death's door. His wife and daughters are near him, doing all they can to relieve his sufferings. His lungs are diseased and it is likely to prove fatal.

One evening word comes to the boy that his father has died. He immediately goes home, while Sister Engle and I conclude to go and see him buried. We have seen the wailings, but not the interment. It is already dark when the word comes, so we take the lantern and together with several schoolboys start for the village. We all go single file along the path for nearly three-fourths of a mile, down the hill, across the river, which is dry at this season. The night is quite dark and only lighted up by the flame of the lantern. Up the hill we go, on the opposite side, for over a fourth of a mile to the village. All along the path the sound of wailing comes to our ears. Sometimes it subsides and then becomes more violent than ever. Before death the deceased has been brought back to his hut, and as we enter the village the men are sitting around in groups outside and are quiet. We proceed to the hut of mourning, which is crowded with women and is dark, save for the light of the fire in the center, the flickering flames of which ever and anon light up the weird scene.

We stoop down and enter the low door. It is so crowded and hot that farther progress seems impossible, and yet we manage to work our way among the crowd, seated or standing and keeping up their doleful wail. Our object is twofold: We wish to see, and also to show our sympathy for the boy who has been with us so long and is a Christian, and we desire to see the sorrowing wife and daughters, for we know them well and believe that they will appreciate our presence and words of condolence. We finally reach the partition which extends over halfway across the hut. Near this lies a bundle about four or five feet long. It is a somewhat shapeless mass, wrapped with a number of layers of blankets and carefully tied. In the fitful light one might easily mistake it for a bundle of clothes, but we know without asking that this is the body of the deceased; for around it are seated the wife and daughters weeping bitterly, and lovingly patting the wrapping of the body. The rest of the women are mingling their tears with those of the relatives. We stoop and speak a few words of comfort to the wife, but it is little we can give; he had frequently heard of Christ, but refused to accept Him. As the fire flames up we can see Apuleni standing in the shadow, and he too is weeping bitterly, but more quietly. The boys who came with us make their way through the throng and going to him mingle their tears with his, and our own eyes overflow at the sight.

But this crowded hut, without windows or means of ventilation and with a hot fire, is unbearable, so we go outside, the boys following. Everyone on the outside is quiet or speaking in low tones. Sister Engle and I are given blocks of wood for chairs. From one of the groups of men the chief, Lupata, rises and takes his little hoe, and after he has made some measurements, he marks off the grave a few feet from the door of the hut of mourning. In the meantime wood and logs have been brought and several fires kindled, as night is nearly always cool. Around these fires the men sit in groups, but the fires do not make sufficient light, and some grass is brought from the roof of the hut and burnt near the grave for light, so the chief may see to do his work in digging out the first part of the grave. He then hands the hoe to another, who continues the work. The ground is very hard and the work proceeds slowly, and since they have difficulty in seeing, we place our lantern on a stamping block near them. This is gratefully acknowledged by the little group, and the digging continues.

It is an uncanny scene: The steady, dull thud of the hoe as it digs into the hard earth; the various campfires lighting up the dusky, grave faces of the men in their heathen garb; the steady wail of mourning in the hut near by—all leave an impression not soon obliterated. Thus perhaps an hour passes and several men have taken part in digging, the loose earth being removed by means of a basket; but the picking of the hoe has taken on a metallic ring, for the earth is stony. The chief asks for kafir corn, and a daughter comes and shells some and places a pan of it near the open grave. Frequently some of this grain is dropped into the opening, "to soften and appease the earth," they say, and the digging continues, though but little progress is made. Then the chief calls to the mourners, "Be quiet and do not make so much noise. Don't you know that the ground is hard and stony?" The noise subsides and the digging goes on. Soon the friends again begin their loud wailing, and since the ground is still hard and stony, the chief finally goes to the door of the hut and berates them soundly. "Be quiet! Do not know that you are making our work difficult by your lamentations? The earth refuses to receive the dead" (because you are loath to give it). They become quiet and the work continues. They think the very elements are arrayed against them, and the friends must propitiate the earth by a willing surrender of their loved one to its cold embrace.

It is now midnight, and from the progress made we conclude that it will take all night to finish the stony grave. We speak to the chief and he says, "Yes, the interment will not likely be before early dawn." We conclude to return home and have some rest. At an early hour we are awakened and reach the village just at dawn. The grave has been dug so that those inside can stand to their armpits. Then near the bottom a further excavation is made in the side of the grave, sufficiently large to receive the body. Two men remain standing in the grave while the body is carried out amid the lamentations of the mourners. It is gently lowered into the open grave and placed in the excavation in the side. Earth is handed down in baskets, and this is carefully packed around the body. Then comes the filling of the main part of the opening. As the ground is lowered the two men stamp it down with their feet, for of course they are not standing on the body. When it is nearly full, the men emerge and several with sticks carefully pound the earth as it is put in until the grave is full.

All this time the friends have been standing around weeping. When the grave is filled and all the rest of the earth removed, the head one calls loudly, "Water!" This is brought in a gourd and all the relatives and those taking part in the burial rush together; and as the water is poured out on the grave, they wash their hands in the falling water. The surface of the grave is by this time quite wet. The friends throw themselves on the muddy grave with their entire force, so that one would think bones might be broken. Some throw themselves repeatedly, and by the time they have finished, their bodies are quite muddy, but the top of the grave is pounded down as smooth as the surrounding earth, and by the time it is dry the uninitiated could not tell the place of burial.

Those participating then go to the river to wash, and the chief mourners paint part of their bodies with an ash-colored soil. Word has been sent to the friends and neighbors and the wailing proper begins. Men with assegais, axes, or guns walk back and forth crying "Mawe"; the women surround the grave, wailing and uttering various lamentations, such as "My friend." "The father of Apuleni." A wife will have on her head the deceased's hat; another will be carrying his assegai with the point bent; another his stool. All this time the son remained quietly weeping, taking no part in the heathen demonstrations.

An important part of the Batonga funeral is the sacrifice of animals, cattle, sheep, and goats. They think these have souls and accompany the deceased. The number killed depends upon the rank and the wealth of the one who died, although not all the animals sacrificed are his property. Relatives often bring of their own herds for the purpose. Some of the poorer class may have only one animal and small children none. At the grave of the murdered chief they sacrificed eight head of cattle; at that of another chief, a little farther away, there were twenty-two killed. The meat of these animals is eaten by the mourners. At the funeral which we have just described the man was poor. One of the relatives slew a goat, and an ox of the deceased also was killed. Later in the day, as the people began to assemble for the general mourning, several young men came leading an ox for sacrifice. They were decked out in a most fantastic manner, with pieces of bright-colored cloth and various colored paper cut in ribbons. As they arrived near the scene they made a rush for the grave, brandishing their weapons fiercely and seeming to fight the very powers of darkness.

One day Sister Taylor and I were present at the funeral of the daughter of a chief. She was already buried when we reached the place and two oxen had been killed. We had no sooner spoken to her parents and sat down than a number of cattle were driven into the enclosure, between the huts. An old native raised his spear and aimed at one of the cattle. The rest were at once driven out while that one staggered and fell. A woman stepped to the grave and loudly called to the dead that the animal was slain and its spirit was coming. It was a sickening sight. The wailing continued, and some of the people would run around the huts in a wild, scared manner, as if they were fighting something. The air is to them peopled with malevolent spirits, seeking to do them harm, and they must ward them off. If one is dying they often beat their tomtoms in a furious manner to ward off danger. Heathen death and burial is a sad thing. It must be seen to know how terrible it really is. The warlike Baila were accustomed formerly to sacrifice any one of another tribe who happened to be in the neighborhood at the death of a chief, for all strangers were enemies, and Gomo said he saw four or five human skulls on a tree as he approached one of their huts. The wailing is kept up for several days, especially at night, for it would seem that darkness adds to their terror of the evil spirits.

We have often endeavored to show them the folly of some of their beliefs, and of course the Christians take no part with them. Even many of the older people are losing faith in some of these things, but are continuing to keep up appearances for fear of the rest. The chief near us says he is not going to sacrifice any more cattle; he will keep them and train them for oxen.

Some are very eager to have white cloth in connection with burial, and one old man at some distance north of us, who has a son in Bulawayo, desired us to write to the son, telling him to bring him a white shroud for burial. Whether this idea has come in through the white man I am unable to say, but it has probably come through some natives who have been to the towns to work and there learned something of Christian burial. Among some half-civilized natives in some parts of Africa, the idea prevails that if one is put in a coffin, and has a Christian burial, he will go to heaven.

There is also a second and sometimes a third wailing, consisting of a beer drink and a dance. This too is generally held at night. The friends and relatives come together and the half-intoxicated mourners engage in singing and dancing. The actions are most lewd and disgusting, for these are often genuine carousals of the basest sort; but they are most religiously engaged in, and people who believe that the departed spirits have such power over the living, are loath to ignore any established worship of such spirits.

Shikazwa is the messenger of witches and is supposed to bring harm, sickness, or death to its enemies. This class of spirits they say never dwells in a human body. They are always disembodied spirits and mediums. The belief in witchcraft and transmigration of souls is similar to that of the Matabele and need not be repeated. The native, too, has firm belief in the efficacy of charms to ward off sickness or accidents and to bring good fortune, and the dispensers of these articles do a thriving business.

There are various other beliefs in the possession of spirits, which are not very well understood, and some of them seem to be comparatively new, even among the natives themselves. While I was in Natal, in 1910, a missionary was telling me of a difficulty they were encountering among the native girls. They became possessed with an affliction not unlike hysterics, and when it was started in a neighborhood it spread rapidly even among half-civilized natives. I say hysterics, because this lady was enabled to check its advance by punishing the first one who was afflicted in that way in her school. I had never witnessed anything of the sort among natives until my return to Macha in that same year. One day, while out kraal-visiting, I was surprised to see something of the same nature. They tried to keep the actions of the young woman, who was afflicted, from my notice, and hurriedly attempted to quiet her by silly remedies. When I inquired what was the matter, they quickly replied, "Nothing." The boy accompanying me said it was demon possession. This has spread over the country among the girls and young women. The natives called it *Masabi*. The older people do not care to mention it or, if they do, it is in sort of an apologetic manner. They claim that the spirit of some bird or other animal enters the person and causes her to act so strangely. The usual remedy resorted to is to beat the tomtoms to drive away the spirit. They claim that the so-called possession is comparatively new in the country, and that it came from a tribe northeast of Macha.

CHAPTER TWELVE

A Few of Their Customs

The Batonga are very dark in color, although not always black. Their features are regular and well formed, and the people are intelligent looking. Some of them are large, but as a tribe they are not as powerfully built as the Matabele. Their tribal mark amounts to almost a deformity. When a boy (or girl) is about fourteen years of age, he is taken to the native dentist. The head is put on the ground and held in place while the dentist with a blunt instrument knocks out the front upper teeth, usually four, sometimes six in number. The gums and lips become much swollen and inflamed by this barbarous procedure; but in time they heal, and the child is a Mutonga or Mwila, and this deformity proclaims his tribe wherever he goes.

The natives never care to have the process repeated. Other natives often go to their missionaries to have teeth extracted, but the Batonga seldom or never do. They prefer the suffering which comes from neuralgia or toothache. This barbarous custom, like many others, has nearly had its day, and many of the boys have already rebelled since they have come into contact with other natives or Europeans. It will require more time for the girls to break away from it, as they live more secluded lives, and have developed less independence of character than their brothers. A mother will tell her daughter that it is a shame for a woman to have upper front teeth. She should be like the cow.

They are all very fond of grease for their bodies, either animal fat or butter; and in this hot, dry climate this is not so objectionable, if they use it in moderation, by simply oiling the body to prevent the skin from cracking. Many of the women, however, use the grease to excess. They grind red ochre and, mixing it with the grease, paint their bodies, including their hair, red, which is their idea of beauty. In this perhaps they are more excusable than some others. Clay often is used in dressing their hair, and buttons, beads, and shell are sewed to their hair, as ornaments.

The men too take great pride in dressing their hair, and in this respect generally surpass the women. They shave part of the head and let the hair about the crown and back of the head grow long. This they straighten out, and it looks not unlike strings hanging from the back of the head. This is carried to extremes among the Baila. There the dude lets his hair grow and then goes to the hair-dresser who, with grease, hair, and other materials, builds it up into a chignon on the top of his head. With some, this chignon is only five or six inches long, but in the interior of the tribe it is said to be sometimes three feet in length. Brother Steigerwald on his trip north saw some of these long ones. Of course the head cannot help lying uneasy with such a weight.

Batonga Village with the Cattle Pens in the Foreground.

Among these people the clan, or perhaps I should say the kinsfolk, forms the unit. They all are closely bound together and each one more or less responsible for the others of his relatives. In marriage, death, sickness, or trouble, all are concerned in the affair. When difficulty arises the heads of each clan listen to the affair and settle the dispute. Perhaps the persons most interested may have no opportunity of expressing an opinion, especially if they be younger and unimportant members of the families.

An unfortunate accident occurred among some boys and one lost an eye. The one who caused the loss was not more to blame than the one who suffered the loss. It was purely accidental and without malice, and all who were spectators so regarded it. The one who suffered the loss desired that no attention be paid to the affair, but the father and elder relatives thought differently. They called a meeting of the heads of the two clans and discussed the affair with great deliberation, and in a most dignified and respectful manner. The boys were not consulted and there was nothing said in reference to its being an accident. An eye was lost and it must be paid for, and their custom is to require the one causing the loss to give all his property. In this instance the boy considered at fault was young and his father was dead, and all his property was three head of cattle and a sheep. His relatives said these animals would be given; but the other boy's father said, "No, that is not sufficient. I will accept them, but the affair will not be settled. When he acquires more property, I will take that also." This was what the deliberations hinged on. The faulty one would be unable to secure any more property; it would all be taken away from him, so his elders were willing to give what the boy had, only on condition that that would end the matter. It could not be settled that day, but later the other party agreed to take that and consider the affair settled.

Cattle Pen of the Batonga.

A little fire often kindles a great conflagration among them. Once a murderer was taken through our premises on his way to the magistrate. He had come from a distance and the difficulty was something like this: A native had a needle, and his neighbor borrowed it and lost it. The owner of the needle demanded and received an ox in pay. Some time afterward the borrower found the needle, and bringing it back to the owner wanted his ox back, but the ox was dead. The trouble finally resulted in murder.

In marriage the question of kinship also is prominent. Marriage is not merely the union of two people, or even two immediate families, but of two clans, and the prominent members of both must be consulted. If a man sees a girl whom he wishes to make his wife, he first consults his parents, and if there is any objection among his relatives the matter is dropped. If, however, they are satisfied, his mother goes to the mother of the girl and asks for her daughter. If the immediate relatives of the girl object a negative answer is given. If they look with favor on the proposed alliance, they consult the other prominent relatives, which may require considerable time. Some one may object because a relative of the proposed groom quarreled a great deal with his wife, or some one may affirm that he is lazy. Trouble that has arisen between the clans in the past, such as that relating to the boy's eye, may be a formidable obstacle, although the parties concerned may have had nothing to do with the accident or the settlement of it. If all are agreed, well and good. All this time the bride has had no voice in the affair and generally does not know what is transpiring.

A Batonga Family Traveling.

Betrothal among these people may take place when the girl is quite young, but generally not until the girl is from 14 to 18 years of age, and then it is of short duration, as marriage follows soon after it is found that all the relatives agree. The old people, especially the mothers, take the affair in hand, the interested parties merely following their instructions. The groom is told to be ready. Perhaps he has been looking forward and gathering together the *kukwa* (pay or dowry) for the occasion. He has been buying hoes, from ten to twenty of them, for these are always a necessary part of the pay, probably because they are all farmers and the native-made hoes always command a good price. In addition to these, he procures a lot of cloth, beads, money, and some assegais. He freely calls on his relatives and friends to assist him in procuring the needed pay, for they have had some choice in the affair. The day is appointed for the wedding, but before this arrives the girl is informed who is to be her husband. She may or may not be pleased; her choice in the matter is wholly ignored. She has been trained all her life to obey, to keep herself hid, and has very little freedom until after marriage. Should she even be pleased with the choice, she is expected for modesty's sake to protest and cry out and struggle and declare she will not submit.

The mother of the bridegroom takes the pay and goes to the house of the bride, the groom and his best man following. They put up a booth near the kraal of the bride for the groom to occupy. We enter the village and find the relatives of the bride, from far and near, assembled for the wedding, for all these expect to receive some of the pay. The women and the girls gather and begin to sing the marriage song, the tune of which is always the same, but the words are improvised for the occasion. One of the older ones will lead off and say, "This girl is going to be married," and the rest will assent by singing in unison, again, "We shall receive some hoes, so that we may dig our gardens," and again the response. All this is done in a monotonous but not altogether unmusical manner. Another will take up the lead, and a day or two will be consumed in this way until everything that can be thought of in reference to marriage, good, bad, and indifferent, is repeated in song. The bride, however, is not among the singers. We pass through the village and a young woman beckons us to enter a hut. The other women greet us, but our guide with a smile mysteriously leads us into an inner chamber. Here is a young woman, greased from head to foot, so much so that the grease drips from her body. A blanket is thrown around her and over her head, and she keeps her eyes down in a miserable-looking fashion, as if she were crying or pouting, and never by the least sign acknowledges our presence. We are new to the situation, but it suddenly dawns upon us that this is the bride. We inquire, "What is the trouble? Does she not wish to be married?" "Oh, yes," is the answer, "but she must be sad because she is a bride."

Native Women—Widows.

In the afternoon the relatives gather around the hut of the groom to receive their presents, and each makes a choice. Of course they are expected to be reasonable in their demands, because sometimes there are forty persons to receive presents. The father or men nearly related to the bride may take more liberty; one or two sometimes demand ten shillings. While the best man is trying to satisfy all these demands, the groom is often berated soundly by some, and even at times suffers bodily violence. If his supply of goods is reasonable in amount, so that nearly all are satisfied, the bride is given to him at once. If very few presents are on hand the proceedings may stop and he or his best man be obliged to go among his relatives and secure more money or goods. If he is slow in this, difficulties may arise between him and the girl's relatives until it come to blows. Not long ago a groom, about four miles from Macha, was so violently attacked that he died from the blows given. This is unusual at the present day, but it may have been more common formerly. Even if the wedding has passed off all right the girl does not at once go to cook for her husband; it may be several months or a year before they fit her out with earthen pots, baskets, and the like and she goes to housekeeping. In the meantime she is supposed to be so modest that she will not speak to her husband or lift her eyes in his presence. The modesty of the Batonga girls is in striking contrast with the behavior of many other African girls, and immorality does not seem as prevalent among the unmarried as in some other places. Even the Baila girls are much bolder, both in looks and actions. If a girl is bold, and goes about alone, she may generally be conceded to be of an immoral character. When the bride is finally taken to the house of her husband, the father may demand a cow or two as additional pay. If the girl refuses to go, she often is carried by force. Sometimes the mother may refuse to have the girl leave home, and then the husband is obliged to live at the kraal of his parents-in-law. If he has two wives he often thus has two homes.

The groom must always show great respect for the wife's parents, and especially for her mother. When she appears on the scene, he must leave, if escape is possible; otherwise he must sit quietly, not lifting his eyes in the august presence of her who gave birth to his wife, so that the life of the native who lives in the same kraal with his mother-in-law is not a very pleasant one. When he meets his father-in-law he salutes him by clapping his hands, and the salutation is returned by the father-in-law tapping his chest with his right hand. The husband may never call his wife by her maiden name, but he gives her a new one of his own.

Kabanzi Chief with His First Wife.

The fact that the marriage is the concern of so many, and is so rigidly controlled by the elders, places many obstacles in the way of the missionaries. It is difficult for Christian boys many times to gain the hand of Christian girls, and for Christian girls to be given to Christian boys, as many of the older people object to their daughters entering the Christian clan. At present the missionary is not allowed to interfere in these native customs, and the girl has no recourse. Custom says she must obey her parents and relatives, and the law upholds custom. Being under such close supervision all her life, she has no opportunity of developing independence of thought and action like her brother. The missionaries are looking for better times, however, and ask that all who read these lines pray that the day may speedily come when the girls and boys may have more right of choice. We have reason to think that the day is dawning when this form of slavery will also be in the past.

Giving the Gospel in Macha Village.

Again, the fact that kinship has such a hold upon the people, and each one is in a measure responsible for or dependent upon the rest, renders freedom of thought and action difficult among all. It tends to retard development of character and makes evangelization difficult among them. It does not interfere to the extent that caste does in India, but it is by no means a negligible quantity. This and blind custom form pretty strong bands, for the native does not like to stand alone or be odd from his fellows. When the Gospel is given to the people they may appear to listen attentively and outwardly accept what is said, but try to press home the question to individual hearts and the leader will answer for all, "Yes, we are all Christians. We accept what you say. Our hearts are white toward God." One who understands the native character cannot avoid being skeptical when he hears of entire tribes turning to the Lord. They may in outward form, for what is popular with the leaders is popular with the crowd. It is easy for them to put on the form of Christianity and go through all the ceremonies of it, but with how many there is a change of heart remains to be seen by the lives they lead.

The Batonga do not build as good huts as the Matabele, nor do they put in a polished floor; perhaps, because the ants are so numerous in this part of the country, the hut soon falls to pieces and must be rebuilt, even though they may have built it carefully at first. Their presence also may account for the

Batonga making bedsteads and chairs, whereas the Matabele do not. Their huts too are not only the home of the people, but at night, goats, a calf or two, dogs, and sometimes chickens are housed in the same hut, so that it would not be easy to keep a respectable-looking place. As their flocks increase they build separate huts for them, as everything must be well housed on account of wild animals.

In many other ways they differ from the Matabele. They do not have digging-bees like the Matabele; in fact, they do not call their neighbors together for any kind of work, except that the men assist one another in building. If they have a beer-drink it is a sociable gathering or a wailing. The beer is brought and always tasted first by the giver, to show that there is no poison in the cup. Each woman digs her own little garden alone, or with her children. When we entered the country the Matabele would not touch fish, the dislike being so great that it almost amounted to a taboo. Among these people fish is the staple article of diet. The only reason that seems plausible is that here there are many large rivers and fish are abundant, while in the other country there are none. These people do not kill twins, but they do the children that cut the upper teeth first. Eggs are tabooed to unmarried boys and girls, and a superstitious reason is given and strongly believed in by them; but back of it the object of the elders in enforcing the taboo seems to have been to prevent young Africans from robbing the nests and lessening the supply of chicks. There are many other taboos among the tribes which are strictly adhered to, the origin of which could easily be traced to expediency.

The Batonga will tell you that the assegai is the weapon of the man and the hoe of the woman. As one sees the men always armed with assegais, so the women generally carry a hoe; nor is it always just an ordinary hoe for digging. Her husband sometimes procures for her a dainty little hoe, having the handle beautifully ornamented with fine woven wire. This has no other use than to be carried with her as she goes on a journey or to a wailing, and she is very proud of it and nothing will induce her to part with it.

They have many forms of salutation, more than any other tribe of natives that I have met, some general and others special, for morning, noon, or night, and they are very punctilious about saluting, but never in a hurry. They greet not only the one they meet, but also inquire about his wife and children, especially the baby, and about what he eats, as well as other questions in general. If a number of persons are sitting down and another group approach, they too will be seated and perhaps a few general remarks may be made; then the salutation begins. Every one in the first group must individually greet everyone in the second group and ask about his health and receive an answer to the same. There is no confusion, no hurry. The native does not shake hands except as he has learned it from the white man; he greets only by word of mouth, or on special occasion by embracing.

A very pleasing incident in reference to one of the salutations, *lumela* (rejoice), is given by Rev. Chapman, one of the pioneers of the Primitive Methodist Mission, and I give it in detail:

"One of these old men could still remember Dr. Livingstone's visit to Sekeletu, about 1855. The doctor was known among the Makololo as Monare. When I showed the old man a photo of Dr. Livingstone he was greatly excited.

"'Yes,' said he, 'really and truly that is Monare's likeness. He wore a moustache just like that; it is indeed Monare.'

"'Can you really remember Monare?' I asked.

"'Of course I can,' said he. 'Why, it was Monare who brought us the salutation we generally use. Before Monare came we used to say, when we met a friend on the path, "*Utshohile*" ["You have got up"]. But when Monare came he said, "*Lumela*" ["Rejoice"], and we replied, "*E Lumela ntate*" ["Yes, rejoice, my father"]. Why, it was he who told the Makololo to live in peace, and rule their people well. See how white my beard is? Of course I can remember Monare.'"

CHAPTER THIRTEEN

Later Years

The work at Macha continued to develop slowly but steadily. There are many daily duties which always fall to the lot of the missionary and which might be classed under the head of drudgery, which do not seem to count, and yet they are as necessary for the advancement of the work as the more noticeable ones, and the year 1912 was no exception to this rule.

During the rainy season there was also a very anxious time, as Baby Ruth became very sick with infantile remittent fever. For over a month she was very ill and we were afraid that we might lose her. Day after day she lay with her face almost as white as the pillow, except for a bright spot on either cheek. The nearest doctor was one hundred and fifty miles away, and the station through which two trains weekly ran was thirty-six miles distant, so that medical aid seemed impossible, save that given by her parents, who anxiously and tenderly ministered unto her; but many prayers ascended in her behalf and the Lord had compassion on us and restored her to health. This climate is treacherous for grown people, but especially so for children.

Macha Mission, 1913.

We have as yet mentioned nothing in reference to the medical part of the work. This was not a prominent feature, yet from the first all who came for help received attention and many were cured or permanently helped. All kinds of diseases are to be met with in this climate, in addition to fever. Skin diseases seem especially prevalent in many forms, some of them the most loathsome imaginable; and nearly every village also has its quota of from two to four lepers. These lepers freely mingle with the rest of the people, no effort whatever being made to segregate them. The native will affirm that leprosy is not contagious, it is hereditary, and there is reason for this view of the case. It makes the heart ache to see women without toes and sometimes without fingers, and full of sores, nursing beautiful, innocent babies, when we think what a life is before these little ones.

These people also have their own remedies. When one is suffering with pain in any part of the body, a very common remedy is to resort to cupping. For this purpose they use the horns of animals, usually of goats. I once watched one woman cupping another. With a knife or piece of sharp tin, she made two incisions in the flesh where the pain was. She then placed the large end of the horn on this, and with her mouth on the small end she removed all the air from the horn, which soon became filled, or nearly so, with blood. Leaving this horn on the place, she in a similar manner applied another horn, until three or four had been applied at various places. She then carefully removed them, one at a time. Since the object had been to extract the blood, it had certainly been successful, and in some respects the natives are only half a century behind—that is all.

In some diseases they very readily come to us, and sometimes fifteen or twenty are present at once, awaiting their turn. At other times we are called to the villages to minister to them. Once some natives came from the nearest village to say that a woman was dying. Her husband at the time was one of the carriers for the brethren on their trip north. We hastened over and found her in a little dark hut, where we could see nothing, so they were told to carry her out into the light, that we might see her. The livid spots, spongy gums, and extreme debility all helped to indicate a bad case of scurvy. She was seemingly in the last stages, and we were fearful that the call for help had come too late. It was a year of great scarcity of food among the natives, and from the report she must have been living chiefly on a sort of greens, with no salt even to season it. It was now about dark, and they said that if something was not done at once she could scarcely live until morning. We looked to the Lord for direction and then hastened home to procure the needed food, which in this instance was quite simple, salt water, and boiled-down grape juice, with a little vinegar. These were used carefully during the night, and in the morning she had improved sufficiently to eat other food. In a few days she was able to be up, and her husband, on the way home, was informed that she had been raised from the dead.

As the work advanced, we arranged to use one of the huts for a hospital, where those who desired might remain and be treated, and a number availed themselves of the opportunity. Both Mr. and Mrs. Taylor were quite successful in medical work, and some difficult cases came for treatment. In this year Brother Taylor treated some very severe wounds, ulcers, cancer, a boy with his hands blown to pieces by gunpowder, a native badly lacerated by a leopard, and an European who had accidentally shot himself, in addition to other cases. We have also had opportunity at other times of ministering to white people.

Whether or not the missionaries have had training in such work in civilized countries, the exigencies of their surroundings, far from doctors and medical help, necessitate their devoting time and study to the cases continually brought before them. Many of them become quite proficient in treating diseases; and perhaps some, in time, become by practice more skilled in treating diseases of tropical climates than some physicians of temperate zones would be, who were unused to tropical diseases, even though they might display their sheep-skin to show a theoretical knowledge of the science. The safest and best course, however, would be to acquire some of the theoretical knowledge before coming to Africa, and then be ready for the practice.

It is needless to state that the missionary's practice among the natives is not a lucrative one. Medicines are very expensive, and a physician must have a diploma from an English medical college before he may charge for his professional services in an English colony. Even then his heathen patients are not prepared to pay much should he feel to charge—which he generally does not. The missionary's labor is one of love, and he rejoices that he has the privilege, in a small degree, of being a follower of the Great Physician. Aid for the body of the natives is one of the best ways of reaching their hearts and souls.

Ruth Taylor.

During the two weeks' vacation in July some of us concluded to spend the time in evangelistic work among the villages. We knew the change to outdoor life also would be beneficial to ourselves. There was one village, Kabwe, composed chiefly of Baila people, where an interest was being manifested, and several there had been attending school. This was distant about fourteen miles by wagon road, and we decided to go there, David and his wife and the dear little baby, who had come to bless their home, accompanying. Word was sent ahead that the people should erect a temporary straw hut for them, while I occupied the tent wagon. When we reached the place we found everything prepared and in readiness for us, and the people also. We received a royal welcome from all and were soon comfortably situated. There were fifty huts in this village, and every evening after the people had finished their day's work and had eaten their suppers, about fifty or sixty of them would come to us, sit around our bright log fire, and listen most attentively, while the Word was being expounded, and then quietly kneel in prayer, and mingle their voices with ours in song. In the morning again, before they went to their gardens to dig, they would assemble for services. On Sunday we gathered on the side of an ant hill, in the shade of some trees, and here a much larger number came for services. Generally during the day David would go to the surrounding villages and proclaim Christ.

There were several in this village who occasionally came to Macha on Saturday and stayed for Sunday services. One Saturday evening at Macha, after the rest of the natives had passed out of the evening worship, two women from this place remained for inquiry and prayer. They very humbly confessed their past life and said they wished to be Christians. We knelt in prayer, and I think I never before heard raw natives pour out their hearts in such intelligent and heartfelt petitions as they did, and their prayers for pardon were heard. We were pleased to learn, while we were at Kabwe, that these women were standing true and being a light to the rest.

First Christian Marriages at Macha.

One evening during the meetings at this place an unusual number of natives were gathered around the fire, and the Word was preached by our native evangelist with unusual power. A hymn had been sung and prayer offered, and the people were told that they could go home. Still they sat there without a word being spoken, and they were evidently in deep thought. Finally a girl arose, and coming forward weeping said, "I want to be a Christian. Will you pray for me?" Before we knelt, a general invitation was given to others who desired to accept Christ to come forward. This evidently was what they wanted, and at once men, women, and girls began to press forward and kneel, and we had a most blessed season with them as one after another began to open their hearts to the Lord in prayer. It was a melting and breaking-up time. Among the number who came was the chief of the village and several other elderly men and women. The next morning they again came together. David had gone to other villages for the day, but his wife and I held the service. This time, as soon as opportunity offered the people began to confess their sins and say that they wished to leave their past lives and follow Christ. Nor do we have any reason to doubt their sincerity. The world about them, peopled with malevolent spirits, seeking to do them harm, and their own accusing conscience would naturally drive them to a Savior Who can give them rest and peace. Praise God! He can give even these older ones freedom from the chains of darkness.

Since we find the younger ones more easily persuaded, I believe we too soon become discouraged with the older ones and expect too much of them, or too sudden a transformation in their lives. I was pleased by a few sentences in Brother Frey's letter under date of April 4, 1914. He says:

"Last Sunday there was a goodly number of the old men present. We have sent out word that Brother Steigerwald will have a special message for the old on next Sunday, and we are giving a special invitation to all the old men to come.... A number of these old men have been coming more or less regularly for some time. Will you not join with us that they might be saved?"

That is the right spirit, and what Brother Frey is seeking to do at Mtyabezi we can all do. The old want to feel that we have a special interest in their salvation, and that we are not going to leave them to themselves in the struggle; but let us help them to know that there is One Who can and will set them free if they will only come. In this little meeting at Kabwe even some of the older ones who started are still striving to get on the Rock. One middle-aged man and his wife, who came forward that night, have finally moved near the mission and built them a hut there, so that they might learn more about Jesus. The chief very strongly urged our starting a school at that place, which we did not long afterwards.

David Moyo and His Wife and Child.

We remained at this place nine days and then moved to Simeoba's village. Although some of the other missionaries had visited this village, I had never had the privilege previous to this. It is larger than the rest and is made up of three different tribes of people, Batonga, Barotse, and Baila, but the language of all is more or less similar. They were stranger and more shy than those at Kabwe, and as soon as we reached the place, Mankunku and I went through the village to meet and learn to know the people. Everywhere we were kindly received. They were greatly surprised to see a white woman who could speak their language; and as the word was passed along, one after another would come and join the number who were conversing. About all were in ordinary native garb, but there were two or three who evidently had been down to Bulawayo to work, and they prided themselves on their European clothes; especially did one of these step about as if lord of the place. Some of the sick asked for help and were ministered unto, and we were pleased to learn that some were helped. All were invited to assemble around our fire in the evening for services, and as soon as their suppers were over they began to gather, about one hundred in number, around the bright, blazing fire, the shy ones keeping in the background where they could not be seen. Many of them no doubt had never been at a service before, while a few who had been at school at Macha could help sing. One or two of those more pretentiously dressed than the rest evidently had attended meeting elsewhere, and were at this meeting self-appointed law-and-order men. With such a raw crowd as most of these were, we always try to sing easy hymns in which there is a great deal of repetition; we also line the hymns before singing and have them repeat after us, so that it was not long before nearly all joined in the singing. Kneeling in prayer is so new an experience that some of the uninitiated sometimes consider it amusing and begin to laugh. In this instance two or three girls caused some disturbance while we were in prayer; and we were scarcely on our feet when one of the self-constituted policemen jumped over some of the others and soundly berated the offenders. Order was then restored and the service proceeded without any further interruption, after which the meeting closed.

The next morning I was awakened by a woman outside my tent clapping her hands and thanking me, saying, "You are my healer." She had been afflicted with neuralgia the day before; and on asking for medicine, she had been given a cup of very strong hot lemonade, which had cured her.

This day was Sunday, and as the people were again invited to assemble, about one hundred and twenty came, and we had an interesting service, to an attentive congregation. We then turned our faces homeward, stopping on the way at Kabanzi, one of our regular preaching places, and holding a service. We reached home that night, ready for school, which was to open the next day, and feeling greatly benefited by our outing.

Rev. and Mrs. Kerswell with Native Carriers on a Visit to Macha.

We were all at this time well housed, but there still was need of a good store building, as the old ones which had been used for this purpose were about all tumbling down. David had already made some brick, so after our return he began on the building, with the assistance of some of the boys. He erected a very good building 33 x 16 feet, containing two small rooms and one large one, with a veranda around it. It was a good piece of work and was finished in about two months. The large room was for his wife and child.

David had never been satisfied with his education and was still anxious to attend school, especially an English school. He had some opportunity for private instruction at Macha, and also taught part of the time, but generally there were so many duties and responsibilities, both temporal and spiritual, resting upon him that he had very little time for study, and he felt that he must get away where school work would be his first work. We greatly preferred that he remain and continue his labors at Macha, but he no doubt realized that the pupils too were progressing, and he needed more knowledge if he was to continue as teacher. The latter part of September he started for Natal to attend school. We receive a good report of him from his teachers. He is said to exert a good influence over the other boys in the school, and he is also frequently called upon to do evangelistic work among them. Will you not join with us that he may be kept humble and not get away from his call to give the Gospel beyond the Zambezi?

His wife remains with us to help in the capacity of Bible woman. Their little girl is a dear, bright, intelligent child as she grows up amid civilized surroundings, and is a good example of what a better environment will do for these people.

Sister Taylor had now been away from America nearly eight years and had not been to the seashore for a change of climate since coming to Interior Africa. She had enjoyed good health nearly all that time and had been diligent in season and out of season in the Master's business. She was a most useful and resourceful missionary always, but the time had come when she was in sore need of a furlough to the homeland. Brother Taylor too had not been to the seashore, and it was necessary for both of them to leave. They were greatly needed in the work at Macha, and we could not see how we could get along without them, but too many missionaries on the field have, under the pressure of work and the needs about them, remained longer than was expedient, and paid the penalty with their lives. In February, 1913, they left Macha for their homeward journey.

About two months previous to this Mr. and Mrs. Jesse Wenger had returned to Africa, and came to Macha to take the place of the Taylors. Unfortunately, however, both of them were stricken down with fever about two weeks after reaching the mission station. They remained seven months, and during that time there was almost one continual combat with fever, especially on the part of Brother Wenger. United with this was great nervous disorder and prostration, so that it seemed impossible for him to stand the climate. They greatly desired to remain and continue the work, but since it seemed impossible for him to endure the climate, he wrote to Elder Steigerwald, who finally arranged for them to try Johannesburg. We felt sorry, both on Brother Wenger's account and for the sake of the work, that they were unable to remain on the field.

During the time of these seemingly necessary changes among the missionaries at Macha, the work continued to grow and develop. There was no increase in the number of boys, but some of those who had been with us were proving helpful as teachers and evangelists among the people. The work had been branching out and six schools were started; in some of which men, women, boys, and girls were attending. In the early years the converts were of those staying at the mission; but since the opening of the out-schools the work was spreading much more rapidly, and some of the married people, as well as the girls, had accepted Christ and were living exemplary lives in their homes. These also attended the Inquirers' Class and church services at Macha on Sunday.

Batonga Chiefs, Near Macha Mission.

There are several services held each week at the mission. Besides the daily worship, there is on Sunday morning an Inquirers' Class and a Members' Class, both held at the same hour but in different rooms. These are held on this day because so many have far to come. Then comes the general church service, followed by Sunday-school, for which all remain. In the evening there is a song and Scripture service for those staying at the mission. Thursday morning early is a midweek service and testimony meeting; and on Friday night the Christian natives have their prayer meeting, presided over by one of their number, while the missionaries have a prayer meeting in English. In addition to these there is a monthly prayer day, the first Friday of each month, on which day all our out-schools are closed and teachers and many of the pupils meet with us.

These were often times of great blessing to all of us, one of which especially might be mentioned, the first Friday in May, 1913. On this day there were nearly one hundred natives present, consisting of members and class members; and eight of our boys who had been south to work for a year had just returned home and were present. On such days many of the Christians were accustomed to spend the early morning hours out alone in secret prayer, before the opening of the meeting. On the above date, as we stepped into the church in the morning, we realized that there was unusual manifestation of the Spirit's presence among us. Several of the boys took part in the opening seasons of prayer in a very impressive manner. We read a Scripture lesson and for a short time spoke on cleansing and consecration and the infilling of the Spirit, and they were unusually attentive, which always helps the speaker. Expectation of some kind seemed in the air. The testimony meeting opened with heartfelt testimonies. Then one's testimony became a prayer for greater outpouring of the Spirit. Again we knelt and he continued in prayer. Suddenly the very house seemed shaken, and with one accord all were prostrate before the Lord. Some were smitten with a spirit of conviction; others began a service of praise, and still others lay low, letting the Lord talk to them and fill them with His own Holy Spirit. The united prayers continued for two or more hours, and while there was noise of prayer and praise there could not be said to be any disorder, as all but one or two remained at their places. Many received a deeper understanding and experience of Divine things that day. Once Brother and Sister Wenger and myself began to sing, but they continued in prayer and we stopped singing. There were some present who probably received no benefit. In Africa, as in America, there are some at such times who follow the rest outwardly at least, but do not seem to be benefited in heart.

The latter part of June Elder Steigerwald came to see about the work at Macha. It had been one and one-half years since his last visit, and we were glad for the privilege of again welcoming him. With him was Miss Elizabeth Engle, who had for six years been a most valued worker at Mtyabezi Mission; also Mr. L. B. Steckley, who had two years ago come out from Canada as a missionary and was helping in the work at Matopo. These two were to take up the work at Macha, while Mr. and Mrs. Wenger proceeded to the Transvaal, to occupy the station at Boxburg, thus enabling Mr. and Mrs. Jesse Eyster to return home on furlough.

While Elder Steigerwald was with us at this time, eighteen native Christians were baptized and received into the Church. Among them were several married men, three women, and four girls. Some of these were the first fruits of the out-schools. We rejoiced that at last we enjoyed the privilege of partaking of the Lord's supper with some dark-skinned sisters of the Batonga tribe. It was now nearly seven years since the mission had opened in this place, and these were the first native women to join with us. The women had also been slow to desire civilized clothing, for our desire had been to impress upon them more the inner than the outer adornment. They were, however, becoming anxious to be clothed, and as many of the boys who had now grown to manhood had adopted European clothing, our congregations were quite different in appearance from the old days. At this time also two couples were united in Christian marriage. These were the first native Christian marriages at Macha. Since natives are so often inclined to extremes on the dress question, in marriage, we made it a special point to say nothing about new clothing for the occasion.

A number of others made application for baptism, but it was thought best for some to wait awhile, so six months later Elder Steigerwald came to Macha again. This time he was accompanied by his wife and Sister Doner. Ten more natives were baptized and there were several candidates who could not meet with us at this time. There were also three more couples united in Christian marriage. There have been fifty-nine baptized at this place, but three or four were not as true as we could have desired. One of those who had backslidden was the first boy brought to the mission, the son of Macha. He had never been very zealous in the Master's service, and yet his life had seemed consistent. The Lord may find a way into his heart again.

It frequently happens on the mission field that young boys will come to the station, learn, and then leave without any special manifestation that the Gospel has entered their hearts, yet an impression has been made on their plastic minds, and it often follows and convicts them later in life. So the missionary need not be discouraged if the first or second invitation fails to bring the native to the foot of the Cross.

We greatly enjoyed the visit of Brother and Sister Steigerwald, and were eager for them to see some of the out-schools. We started out for this purpose, but were all taken with fever, one after another, and the visits had to be abandoned. Sister Doner had come to assist in the work at Macha and take charge of the school. She and Brother Freys had just returned from a furlough to America, and as I had now been in the work nearly nine years and needed a change, she, together, with Sister Engle and Brother Steckley, was to take charge here during my furlough. The latter two had been at the place some months and were beginning to know and understand the people and surroundings. Sister Engle in her capacity as nurse was having ample opportunity to care for the sick, who were always glad for help. She is always a most capable and willing worker wherever needed. Brother Steckley too is a consecrated soldier of the Cross and ready for whatever comes to him.

CHAPTER FOURTEEN

The Out-Stations

Every place that the sole of your foot shall tread upon, that I have given unto you.—Joshua 1: 3.

Just as the Lord told Joshua to rise up and take possession of the land of Canaan for God and His people, so we believe He is saying to all missionaries whom He sends out into the midst of the enemy's country, that He has given the people unto them and they should rise and take possession in God's name. We often live beneath our privileges in this, and our faith so soon becomes weak and wavering. God also says to us, "Be strong and of good courage."

There are two objects which seem paramount on the mission field, and about which everything else revolves. These are, (1) the salvation of souls, and (2) the preparation of natives to become teachers and evangelists of their people. Dispense with these fundamental objects and one might as well remain at home. Missionaries may differ in regard to the best methods of carrying out these purposes, and some may even object to the statement just made. With some missionaries, education and civilization hold a very prominent place, and with a few missionary work spells education and civilization, and we are sorry to say that the number who take this view is increasing. The great body of missionaries, however, of whatever name, are such from love of souls. The aim should be to get the native really saved and on the Rock, Christ Jesus, so that he may become a light in his home. At the same time we should seek to train him to become a soul-winner among his people, so that a knowledge of God may be spread over the country. In this way only can the Great Commission be successfully carried out.

In Africa, especially, are teachers needed on the mission field, for before the missionary comes there is no written language, much less any who can read. To teach the people to read the Word is not only desirable, but it is an absolute necessity if it is to be a Light unto their feet in that dark land. We do not claim that a native cannot be a Christian unless he can read, for some of the older ones live exemplary Christian lives, although unable to read the Word; but among the younger generation they very seldom become established Christians if they are not willing to apply themselves sufficiently to study so that they are at least able to read the Word of God understandingly. Then too the spread of the Gospel cannot continue unless some are able to read.

I call to mind two able and Spirit-filled missionaries who spent two years in self-sacrificing labors among the natives of Africa. They went about from place to place, giving the Gospel to the people, and they were liked by the people and frequently had many attentive listeners. Several years after they returned home one of them wrote, "We spent two years in giving the Gospel to the Africans, and yet we cannot point to one soul whom we definitely helped." We believe they underestimated the value of their work, for they always aimed to labor in harmony with other missionaries on the field and would advise natives to go to the nearest mission station. Yet the fact remains that unless the younger Christian natives attend school and learn to read the Word, and have it instilled into their minds from day to day, they are apt to forget and wander away.

I have dwelt thus at length on the educational feature of the work, because there are many good Christians who fail to understand why so much of a missionary's time is occupied in teaching the natives. It is simply for the reason that that is the only means they have of learning to read the Word of God. Among the natives of Africa there are no schools but the mission schools, and the chief purpose of these is to teach the natives to read the Word understandingly, so that they may "be able to teach others also." On the other hand, since schools are such an essential part of the work, there are not wanting those who confuse the education thus obtained with religion itself, and think all who become able to read are Christians. That is a consummation devoutly to be wished by every missionary, but it is no more true in Africa than it is in England or America. The fact that it is not true in those civilized countries may have much to do with the fact that it is not true in Africa.

Since the day-school at Macha never assumed large proportions, and there were many children all around us, especially girls, who were not in school, it had been the aim from the beginning to train teachers who might be placed in the various villages to teach and give the Gospel to the people in their homes, and thus multiply the work done by the missionaries manyfold. A number of schools had been started in this way. In this work it is always necessary to use great care in the selection of teachers, that they may be teachers of righteousness as well as teachers of books. A boy may be quite apt as a scholar, and so far as is known be a moral person, but if he has not yielded himself to Christ as his Savior and has not a love for souls in his heart, he often does more harm than good as a teacher. In other words, he must be a missionary as well as a teacher, and lift up Christ among them. We often send a boy, who is prepared, back to his own village as teacher, if we have such a one. Mr. Worthington, Secretary for Native Affairs, when informed of this said, "I greatly approve of your custom of sending natives back to their own home to teach their people. I think it will obviate many difficulties in the way of native teachers."

The out-schools are superintended by the missionaries, who if possible visit them once a month and advise the teachers in reference to the work. If the schools are too far away for the pupils to attend church services at the mission, arrangements are made for services to be held more or less frequently at the schools. The native teachers also hold daily worship and Scripture reading with their schools, and all others who desire to attend.

In order that my readers may gain some information in reference to the out-schools connected with Macha Mission, you are invited to accompany me on a visit to them, such as I made shortly before returning to America. Miss E. Engle will accompany me, as she has charge of them during my absence. Two of the boys are also going as leader and driver. While we are absent on this trip, Apuleni will have charge of the school at Macha. He was the second boy to come to the mission, nearly seven years before, and has been with us ever since, except for nearly eighteen months, when he, with other boys, went away to Salisbury to work. He has made good in school, and has accepted Christ as his Savior. He says his chief desire is to know the will of God and do it. He is well versed in the Scriptures, is a good teacher and helper in Sunday-school, and reads, not only his own Tonga language, but also Zulu quite readily, and English, and acts as an interpreter from these two languages into his own. He is also prepared in the other branches taught. As he is our assistant teacher all the time, we know the school will not suffer in his hands.

We are going in the large two-seated spring wagon with a white canvas top, sent out by the Board two years ago. One of the seats is removed, and in the back part of the wagon is placed a box containing food, dishes, and the like equipments for our meals. There is also put in a large five-gallon can of good drinking water, two folding canvas bedsteads, a bundle containing bedding, and a mosquito net, and underneath the wagon in a framework is a tent which we have lately acquired. There is also a small bag of cornmeal, a tin of ground peanuts, some dried greens for the boys, and some whole peanuts for all of us. Where the dashboard was originally is now a long box in which are placed kettles and cooking utensils. And we do not forget to stow away in the box of the seat a quantity of bananas and lemons, of which the mission has an abundance; also some fresh vegetables. A small canvas bag, in which the drinking water is cooled, hangs on the side of the wagon. Four oxen are inspanned and one boy takes hold of the strap in front to lead the oxen, and another, with a long, slender pole, to which is tied a long, slender leathern lash, drives. He sometimes sits on the box in front and sometimes runs along the side.

We remember the times, not so very long ago, when we were not so comfortably equipped for traveling as we are at present. We walked many weary miles to see the people, and thoroughly enjoyed it too, even though the hard earth at times was our bed and the open canopy of heaven our tent, and native food in part supplied our needs. Then it was not possible to visit as many places in a day as now, and frequently when we arrived we were too tired to do justice to the Word. Then also we failed to reach many villages, because of the distance. Now it seems almost too good to be true that we are so well supplied, for the Lord has again wonderfully verified His precious promise, "to do exceeding abundantly above all that we ask or think." Praise His Holy Name! Yet we would not, if we could, do away with those early days and the blessings attending them, and we are better able to appreciate present favors by contrast.

School at Kabanzi Village.

Usually we endeavor to start not later than sunrise, so that we may travel in the cool of the morning; for the sun becomes quite hot in the middle of the day, and it is advisable then to be under shelter. At this time, November, however, the morning is cloudy, so that we may have rain; but the clouds make traveling pleasant and we start. We go north and a little east. Where the roads are good the oxen trot off briskly; but in many places there are deep ruts, caused by the heavy rains of previous years, which make progress slow. In some places the ruts are a foot or two in depth, and it is necessary to make a new road along the side, for there are no government-built roads in the country.

The grass of the previous year's growth was burnt off in June or July; and ever since, as far as the eye could reach, nothing could be seen except the great stretch of undulating reddish-brown earth, destitute of everything, save here and there little patches of dried grass, which had escaped the scorching fires, and scattered trees, almost destitute of leaves. There has been no rain for six or seven months; yet spring is approaching, and already in the rich valleys may be seen tender blades of grass springing up. On the bare brown hills here and there are flowers of various kinds, which gladden the eye and relieve the monotony of the scene. Where the moisture comes from at this season of the year to produce such delicate blossoms is a cause of conjecture. Then too, already many of the trees and shrubs are putting forth their tender, beautiful green leaves, some of which look as delicate and shining as wax; and occasionally one sees a tree or shrub with white, yellow, or red blossoms preparatory to putting forth leaves. All these changes we note with pleasure as we ride along in the cool, bracing air of the early morning.

At one place is to be seen Chikuni stump, which seems almost like a stone, and has been a landmark within the memory of the oldest inhabitant. The majority of trees which are to be seen on this road are hardwood, but very crooked and scrubby looking, no doubt owing to the yearly fierce onslaught of fire and also the nature of the soil. Along the road is one solitary mahogany; a large, spreading tree this is, but not a very good sample of its kind. There is also a large tree known as the sausage tree; its immense bean pods, one to two feet in length and a foot and over in circumference, reminding one of a great piece of sausage. Numerous acacia are to be seen, and as we approach the river, five miles from home, we see six large, fine-looking fig trees, their rich, dark-green foliage furnishing beautiful shade. Although this is the Myeki River, there is no water where we cross, yet the deep, bridgeless ravine makes crossing for heavily-laden wagons difficult at all seasons, and almost impassable during the rainy seasons. Here is a large village, but we proceed two miles further and come to Mianda School, where Charlie Sichamba teaches.

This is not a large village, but it is the home of a number of some of our best boys; those who have been of greatest assistance in teaching and in industrial work. The village has been lately moved, and huts are not yet all completed, nor is the schoolhouse finished. We drive near and are met by a number of the pupils, for we are always certain of a welcome at this place. The rain, which has been threatening, begins to come down, and one of the new huts is given to us. Wood is brought and a fire is kindled in the center, that we may have breakfast. A mat is placed on the nicely-swept floor, and on this the tablecloth is spread and the breakfast placed after it is cooked. This consists of corn porridge, with milk, bread, butter, eggs, fruit, and coffee if we desire it. Muguwe sends us milk, for he always sees that we are furnished with fresh milk when we come here. The boys are given another hut in which to cook their food. The meal being over, we hand the dishes to one of the boys to be washed, while we turn our attention to the school and work for which we came.

By this time the rain is beginning to abate, and the pupils, about twenty in number, assemble in another hut for school. Today there are not quite as many as usual, because there is a wedding in progress. Here is Muguwe, a tall, odd-looking native, over thirty years of age, and a Christian, and so far as we can learn he is consistent in his life. Learning is difficult for him, but he is making progress and is quite persevering. His wife for a long time was opposed to his serving the Lord, but she is changing, and we trust that she too may accept Christ as her Savior. The stepdaughter is also in school and is making progress in Divine life. There are several other women and some girls and boys. Some of them seem very slow in accepting Christ, but there has manifestly been a change in the lives of some, and a number of the old women are believers. During the last year of drought, when the people of nearly every village were so zealous in their heathen worship for rain, this was one of the two who stood true. After school is over, the older ones are summoned to join with us in worship, and we take the occasion once more to give them a Gospel message, to which they listen attentively. Here are Tom's mother, Jim's mother, and Chikaile's mother, all of whom seem to believe as far as they have grasped the Truth.

We are especially grieved today, however, because of the wedding which is progressing, for we knew nothing about it until we were on the journey. The bride is a Christian girl and has had a good experience, although she is not yet baptized. She is only about fifteen years old, or perhaps a little older, and has been given to an unsaved boy, who, however, has no other wife. We inquired of one of the boys if she wished to marry him. He looked at us in sort of a pitying manner, as if to say, "You should know better than to ask such a question," and replied, "They did not ask her." After the service we go up to the hut of the bride, and find her not feigning to cry, as some of the brides do, but in reality weeping most bitterly. At the sight of us her sobs break forth afresh. We try to comfort her, but what can or what dare we say? We speak to the mother, who also has confessed Christ, but she is the first wife in a line of five. She frankly acknowledges that she preferred to give her daughter to a Christian, but was overruled. The brothers too, who are Christians, could do nothing, the older relatives having arranged the affair. Her father is chief of the village and an influential man. He has always been a friend of the mission, but he feels that he can manage his own affairs best, and his children are taught implicit obedience. We know that remonstrance is useless, and from his conversation it is evident that he thinks he has provided wisely for his child, because the groom is son of the chief at Kabanzi, where one of our schools is located, and the young fellow had even attended school for a few days. The affair might be more serious, and we hope and pray that in time both may be Christians.

The next school is four miles farther on this road, at Impongo, and the teacher there is Singuzu, whose home is at Mianda. He is not so far advanced in learning, so he recites to Charlie. He is, however, a conscientious and Spirit-filled Christian. He accompanies us to his place of teaching. This is a new school, has been in session only about three months, and is held out in the open air in the shade of a tree; but they are gathering poles to build a hut. The people had asked several times for a school, and we finally concluded to give them one. The teacher is doing his work faithfully, and progress is being made by the pupils in learning to read; but there are some things in connection with this school which are making the work very unsatisfactory, and both the teacher and ourselves think best to discontinue it. After the recitations are finished a service is held with them and they seem interested. When the late dinner is over it is decided to go about six miles west, to Kabanzi, the next school.

By this time it is somewhat late in the day, but it is hoped that our destination may be reached before dark. Singuzu, who is a better driver than the one accompanying us, is asked to go along and drive. This road is very little traveled and a white man might not be able to find it; but the natives accustomed to these trackless wilds do not soon become lost. Nearly the entire distance is through the brush, consisting of both large trees and short underbrush, so that the journey is more or less impeded. We travel along at a fair speed for oxen, as the driver is accustomed to dodging trees and shrubs; but darkness overtakes us before the village is reached. Progress is now slow, since the veldt from this to the village is full of the stumps of trees cut off, native fashion, two or three feet above ground, and we are fearful of running into these and breaking the wagon. Finally the wagon does become fast and the oxen must be unhitched until it is extricated. We again enter the wagon and move on. The welcome sight of the village fires shining out amid the darkness indicates that the end of the journey is near at hand. As we approach, a pack of dogs greet us with their loud barking, and light after light shines out through the open doors of the huts, or from the courtyard where the men, in the shelter of a semicircle of reeds, sit and palaver. There is no more pleasing sight to travelers through African wilds than the bright and cheerful blaze of the indispensable campfire, which answers for light and heat, for preparing the evening meal and warding off the wild animals.

As we reach the village, a number of natives emerge from their huts in order to ascertain who these intruders are, coming along the back of the village. On seeing their missionaries they gladly offer their services to conduct the wagon through the trees and stumps to the schoolhouse and teacher's hut. Sister Engle and I conclude not to have the tent pitched for the night, but to have our beds placed in the large, roomy schoolhouse, which boasts of a good plank door. We have had a busy day, for we have visited two schools, held two services, prepared our food, and traveled seventeen miles, so we are soon resting on our comfortable stretchers.

In the morning breakfast is prepared early, for the school is to begin earlier than usual so that we may continue our journey. We, however, take time to go over to the village and have a chat with some of the older people. This is Kabanzi village, and it has our oldest and best school. Before the opening of school services were held here frequently, and some were interested, but no one gave indications of wanting to follow the Lord until after school opened.

Several boys from this place were converted while attending school at Macha. The teacher is Jamu, a careful, painstaking and faithful Christian. He is greatly interested in the spiritual as well as the intellectual advancement of his pupils. He carefully reads and explains the Word to them day by day, and he is a good evangelist. While in school at Macha he was always one of our best workmen in laying brick, sawing and thatching. There are generally about fifty pupils enrolled in this school and about thirty-five in daily attendance. Twelve have been baptized and nearly all the rest are in the Inquirers' Class.

We enter the schoolroom and the pupils march around the building, then enter and take their places on the logs extending across the room. All kneel and repeat the Lord's prayer, and then teaching begins. A few are reading the charts, some are in the first book, a number in the "Bible Stories," while a few are reading the Gospels of St. Mark and St. Matthew. A number of pupils are married men and women. The women bring their babies, and yet with the interruption caused by these, they have learned to read well and are in the "Bible Stories." They exhibit remarkable perseverance, for they not only attend school, but dig in their gardens, carry wood and water, grind their meal, and prepare their food. On Sunday they walk nine miles to Macha to church, for they, together with their husbands, are Christians, or seeking to be such. The teacher says that they started to school first; then their husbands followed. The husbands also work in the gardens, build huts, hunt game for food, and part of the time work for the white man in order to obtain money for taxes and clothes. They have also lately been buying cloth to make dresses for their wives, and one day I came upon one of the men carefully washing his wife's dress. The Gospel is making them better husbands and more careful and considerate of their wives. The heathen worship, with its attendant evils, together with vice, beer, tobacco, and kindred habits, is being banished from these few homes at least. When other villages were worshiping their rainmakers, these too were daily worshiping, but it was the Lord of lords Whom they worshiped. When the older ones desired to resort to their heathen worship, the Christians said, "No; if you do we shall build a kraal of our own." This means that there are many in the village who are not Christians, and some of them stoutly oppose the school; but the chief is favorable, as some of his children are Christians. There are also several old women in addition to the pupils who are breaking away from their old worship and accepting Christ. There is one *old* woman here who has come out very bright in her Christian experience. She meets with much opposition, but she does not waver.

Sikaluwa.

After we have remained one session of school, some of the older people are called and we have a service for very interested listeners. The boys then inspan the oxen and we proceed west to Kabwe School, about five or six miles distant. These are the people with whom we held a week's service over a year before. At this place our tent is pitched and we prepare to spend the night. This is a Baila village, and at first Sikaluwa had charge of the school, as he was brought up among that tribe and is a good Christian boy. He did good work for nearly a year, but he did not wish to continue. We were in doubt as to whom we should send to teach them; and after praying over the matter we concluded to consult the Christians in Members' Meeting, and inquire if anyone felt led of the Lord to take up the work there. At the close of the meeting we were surprised to have Chikaile come and say that he was willing to undertake the work, the Lord helping. He had been at the mission for some years and was quite capable of teaching. He is also one of the most cheerful and willing workers, but he is so young, perhaps only seventeen years of age. Because he is such an earnest and conscientious Christian, however, he was given the privilege, and has succeeded beyond our highest expectations. The kraal had just been moved and divided, so that he was obliged to build a new hut for himself. This he speedily did, and then began a schoolhouse which, with a little assistance from the villagers, was soon under roof. There is nothing lazy about the boy, and the school, as well as the work of the Lord, is progressing in his hands. He soon learned to know the people and the kind of lives they are leading, and is fearless in exposing sin, although he is always mild and humble in his demeanor. With him, as well as with other teachers who do not teach in their homes, a boy is sent, so that he need not be alone.

In this school we find twenty-four pupils in attendance, among them two elderly women. One of these, the mother of another Christian woman, has made a good confession. She entered school and we smiled somewhat incredulously, thinking that she was too old to learn; but our next visit to the school revealed the fact that she was making decided progress, and it seemed evident that she would soon be able to read the Gospel. After school was over, services were held and the people invited back for night meeting. We then prepared our food. During these visits to the villages the people sometimes bring a present of a chicken, a dish of peanuts, some milk, or whatever they think we might relish. Occasionally, on a hot day, it is a cup of ibwantu. This is a gruel made of the meal of native grain into which has been placed crushed root with an acid flavor. It is usually made in the evening and consumed the next day. It is not alcoholic, and has a very cooling and refreshing taste. It will be brought in a large cup, and as is their custom, the donor usually takes a sip first to show there is no poison in it.

When this village was moved and divided into three parts, we about gave up the thought of opening school again, but the chief was not satisfied, and promised that if school was reopened he would see that the children came together to learn; so we agreed to send a teacher. Six very nice young girls came from Kabwe to stay at Macha and attend school; but others entered to fill up the ranks and the work continues.

Early the next morning we start on our homeward way. The road takes us back past Kabanzi, and there we turn south toward Macha. On the way we come to a place which at first sight might be taken for an old deserted native village; but a closer inspection reveals the fact that the huts were never finished. Here is the framework of twelve large, nice-looking huts. Some have just been rightly started; of some the walls are finished, and on others the builders had begun to put on the roof. Poles are scattered all around, and some poles are at a distance from the huts, but near the road, and look as if those who were carrying them had dropped them hastily. The whole has the appearance as if a number of people were busily engaged in building a village and were surprised by an enemy in the midst of their labors and slain, their work unfinished. What does it mean? This question we asked ourselves on first seeing it. The answer was this: They were indeed surprised by an enemy, but that enemy was death. The headman sickened and died; his son followed. Concluding that the place was bewitched, the rest at once abandoned it and went elsewhere, leaving all those fine, straight poles to rot.

On the journey homeward we again come to Myeki River, for this is a very winding stream, and this crossing is several miles farther west. At this place there is another school. We stop near the village, where Mafuta the teacher lives, and he, with some of the rest, comes out to meet us. We have driven about ten miles this morning and now hastily prepare breakfast and eat. Some tall, beautiful bottle palms grow in this vicinity, and while we are eating, the teacher brings us the fruit of one, a part of which is eaten with relish. We then start off on foot for the school, which is about two miles distant, near another village. We leave the lead boy to herd the oxen, while the little herdboys of this village drive their cattle ahead, so that they may learn in school and at the same time watch the cattle.

As we walk along the path, through this somewhat dense forest, let me tell you something of this teacher, Mafuta. He is older than the most of our boys and was already grown when we reached Macha, seven years ago. He at that time worked for us a few months. For over three years, however, he showed no inclination to want to learn or be a Christian, and seldom came to Church. He was just like the other natives in the village and indulged in their sinful and lazy ways. Finally he informed one of the boys that he was coming to school until he had sufficient money to take a wife. We were quite skeptical when we heard it; for we did not expect that he would remain long, and then too school was not a money-making place. He came and applied himself to school work. He was slow and dull, but he was diligent and made progress.

He entered the Inquirers' Class and the Lord found a way into his heart. One day in the class, when a number came forward for special prayer, he became in earnest and found what he sought—pardon for his dark past, and peace in his soul. As he took his seat his face wore a look of new-found joy, and he arose and testified as to what the Lord had done for him. In work also he was faithful, and he soon learned to handle the oxen in plowing and in the wagon, and thus he received higher wages. By close economy he gradually was able to get a little money ahead. In time he was baptized. He gained one of the nicest girls in the neighborhood as his wife, is married by Christian marriage, and is now teaching this school. He is not as quick at learning as some, but he is faithful and painstaking and is a living Christian among them. When we look at him and think how little faith we had in the early days, we are reminded of the words, "The Lord seeth not as man seeth; for man looketh on the outward appearance, but God looketh on the heart."

We visit the school and find twenty-four scholars assembled, the teacher's wife among the number. It is a new school, but the pupils are making advancement. After services we retrace our steps to the waiting wagon, and then return to the mission, which is only about four and one-half miles distant. We have spent three days out, have visited five schools and have traveled thirty-six miles in somewhat of a circle. We have enjoyed the trip and the change from the routine of the mission station, but a person is glad to reach home, after a few days spent on the veldt.

Again we desire to visit Chilumbwe School, which is about seven miles northeast. Here the natives were asking for some time for a school. We had come to the conclusion, however, that no more schools would be opened until the people of the village erect some sort of a schoolhouse. They are always ready to promise that they will build, but if a teacher is provided before the house is built they generally are slow in carrying out their promise. Then too it is not best to make the work too easy for them. They appreciate most that which has cost them something. The work among them is new, and as the schools are especially for children, and money is always scarce, we dare not expect too much at present. If they are eager for a teacher they can at least build a schoolhut, feed their teacher, buy their own books, and these they are expected to do. Even the poorest buy their books, and if they cannot bring money they often bring a chicken or grain in pay. The people at Chilumbwe finally managed to build their hut and school began a month ago.

We again take the wagon and go north as before, but soon turn off toward the east. We pass through Chikuni, where formerly there was a large village, and over under that large, spreading fig tree Sikaluwa taught school. But sickness entered the village; the chiefs wife died, a child followed, and then a young man, all in the same village. All these died in a similar manner which, from the description given afterwards, must have been *spinal meningitis*. They thought it was witchcraft and became afraid of one another. So they separated, some going one way, some the other. We pass several kraals on the way and finally reach Chilumbwe.

The chief of this village is rich in cattle and is an unusually intelligent and well-bred native. Jim is the teacher. Yes, he is that short, well-dressed native with the colored glasses on. He is the one who lost his eye and is very sensitive on account of the defect; but he is a splendid fellow, faithful, humble, and an excellent workman. He is moreover a sincere Christian, anxious to know and do the will of his Heavenly Father.

As the wagon approaches the schoolhouse we are greeted by the chief and a number of the pupils, for they are expecting the visit. It is decided to have services first so that the older ones need not remain. The pupils, together with some men and women from the village, gather around a large shade tree, the chief taking a prominent position. All the pupils join lustily in the singing, seemingly anxious to impress upon their missionaries that they are progressing in that at least. A service is then held, after which the pupils gather in the little schoolhouse for school. There are about fifty pupils already enrolled in this school, some being from neighboring kraals, and there are over thirty in attendance today. They are starting out well, but how many will continue remains to be seen. The pupils are all young men and boys, and the teacher informs us that they will not allow the women and girls to attend school. We cannot force them to let the girls come, nor is it wise to attempt it, so we just look to the Lord and wait until He can find a way into their hearts. At all the other out-schools the girls generally outnumber the boys. This being a new school, nearly all read on the charts; only two or three have passed that stage, but we have two beginning books along and they are bought. There are no Christians at this place, and the one that seems most interested in the Gospel is the chief's son. He was badly mauled by a leopard a few months ago, and the chief brought him to the mission to be treated. Sister Engle very successfully treated his wounds; and while he was with us he came under the influence of the Gospel, and we believe he is reaching out for more knowledge of his Savior.

All the schools have now been visited. There is a call for a school southwest about six miles, and there is a teacher for it; but the people have not yet erected a schoolhouse. The villages near have asked for schools and have had them; but many have opposed the Gospel and the work has not proved a success among them. There are a few in each village who are Christians, and some of them are with us and others coming to day-school. We are not yet discouraged with these at our doors who have been hardening their hearts against the truth. God has yet among them some who will come out strong for Him, for we know that His Spirit is striving with them and with some it will not strive in vain. It can be seen that a knowledge of God is slowly spreading over the country and real miracles are being performed in the hearts of some of these erstwhile heathen; miracles greater than the raising of Lazarus from the dead. Souls are being raised to walk in newness of life and are living witnesses to those around them of Christ's power to save to the uttermost. *God's love* has bridged the immense chasm in the lives of some between the densest, darkest paganism and the glorious Light of the children of men. But we must be patient with the slow ones, for it is not always those who are the most ready to accept who are the most stable. Some delay long years and finally come out strong and vigorous for Christ. Where only rude, coarse heathen songs were heard, anthems of praise to God now arise, and daily prayer ascends.

It may be seen that the natives are governed by a number of petty chiefs, and that they frequently change the location of their villages. This makes the work among the out-schools more difficult; but others are calling for schools, and already the past year over 200 children were enrolled in the out-schools, in addition to those at Macha; and this where only a few years ago the names *school* and *God* were not known. We are touching only a small spot thus far and see a great wall of darkness just beyond; a darkness which we occasionally seek to penetrate. Other bodies of missionaries also are laboring in some sections of the country, but there is much land ahead yet to be possessed, and many natives still in darkness who can say, "No man careth for my soul."

The salvation of Africa rests largely upon the native converts, and we rejoice for the manner in which some are coming to the help of the Lord's cause, and we trust they may ever have the prayers of all who are interested in the evangelization of this vast continent. Natives, however, cannot do the work alone. There always is need of white workers to oversee and direct the work, or it will not advance satisfactorily. We believe the Lord desires us to ask largely these latter days, but in this instance we shall be modest in our request, and that is, that the way be open to start at least one more station of white workers in Northern Rhodesia. We believe the Lord is speaking to some hearts to open such a work. Is He not speaking to others to give of their prayers and money for the work? Many of God's children could pay $200 or $300 a year toward the support of a white worker, and others $40 to $50 for a native evangelist, and not need to deny themselves any of the comforts of life in the doing of it. May God help us to see and appreciate our privileges in Christ Jesus.

CHAPTER FIFTEEN

Conclusion

I desire to protest against the unholy thirst for statistics; it is perfectly impossible to put into statistics the results of mission work.—Lord Selborne, Late High Commissioner for South Africa.

In the preceding pages it has been the aim to present some of the work done, as it has been our privilege to see it. Much more might be written about the progress of the work at Matopo, Mapani, and Mtyabezi Stations, for they have a number of excellent out-stations, manned by experienced and Spirit-filled natives, and are doing encouraging work; but that would be beyond the scope of this little volume. We must leave that for the able and efficient missionaries at those places and content ourselves with a summary of the work.

But first we desire to refer to the work at Johannesburg, for during the last few years some of our missionaries there have been laboring in connection with our Mission Board. Over four years ago Mr. and Mrs. Isaac Lehman severed their connection with the other missionary bodies and began building up a separate work, and a little later began laboring under the auspices of the Church. They began the new work under difficulties, but they are persevering and hard workers, both in temporal and spiritual lines, and the work shows excellent results from their consecrated labors. Brother Lehman has worked hard to put up suitable buildings, and their station is now equipped with a good house and church. As I have not had the privilege of visiting that place since the opening of their new work, they were asked to give a statement of what is being done. This they did under date of August, 1914, as follows:

> Our main or central station is at the City Deep Mine, where we reside. The Compound only a short distance from the mission at this place has over 4,000 native laborers in it at one time. This is a very promising mine, and has just lately been opened, and has an apparently long life before it under normal conditions. It will in time employ many more men as it keeps enlarging. We have open doors to this vast multitude of men coming from all parts of South Africa. There are many tribes represented and we can preach the Gospel to them; and we praise the Lord that some have been saved and are seeking to know more of the Lord Jesus Christ.
>
> We have four other mission stations besides this central station. One is Florida Mission, where there is a nice number of baptized members and

we believe a good work is being done. At the Goch Station the Lord has given some blessings and some souls have been added to the Church. At that place the mine has given us permission to apply to the government for a mission site, and the native brethren have already contributed a nice sum of money to put up a suitable church building. Praise the Lord! At the consolidated Langlaagte there is a good work going on; a number have been saved and united with the Church. We have had some blessed seasons at this place owned of God. The Bantjes has had its share of tests, but we praise God that souls have also, at this place, been added to the Church, and the work is progressing.

From all the stations, one main and four out-stations, fifty-seven souls have been baptized. We praise God for all these, and for a number who have heard God's call to them to give themselves to Jesus to work for Him and labor for the salvation of their own people through Jesus' precious blood. Thank God there is power in the blood to save any and all who will come. There are a goodly number who are soon ready for baptism, and we are trying to do all we can to get them fully established in the deep truth of the Bible, a full and complete salvation, pardon cleansing, and the filling of the Holy Ghost. Some have taken a very bold stand for God, and are now preparing themselves for the Lord's work. Our desire and prayer is that we get a band of really consecrated, sanctified, Spirit-filled ones, who are willing to suffer the loss of all things for Jesus, and be made a living power to go out among their own people and help win them for Jesus.

Dear reader, will you pray with us for all these who are yet without the True Light, that they will soon have the privilege of hearing the glad news which is to all and for all? We have very good meetings in the large hospitals, where are many afflicted and dying. This is a good opportunity to give them the Word of God.

Isaac and Alice Lehman.

Brethren in Christ Cottage and Chapel at Johannesburg.

Mr. and Mrs. Jesse Eyster have also been laboring in Johannesburg and have been valiant and consecrated messengers of the Cross. For several years they had charge of the Training School for Native Evangelists near Johannesburg, in connection with the Compound's Mission under Mr. A. W. Baker. They have always been members of the Brethren's Church and several years ago concluded to sever their connection with the other mission and also labor in connection with our Mission Board. They secured a good opening at Boxburg, and with much self-sacrificing labor built house and church and opened an encouraging work. Souls were saved and some added to the Church. Then the labor troubles in Johannesburg caused the mines in the vicinity to close down and the work was checked. We trust, however, that it is only a temporary check and that the work may move on under the blessing of God.

Nothing has yet been written about the last station opened, and this would be incomplete without reference being made to it. I refer to the one at Mandamabge, near Selukwe, Southern Rhodesia. Mr. and Mrs. Levi Doner had been stationed for several years at Mapani Mission and had done most excellent work there in the Master's cause. They, however, thought that that station was near enough to Matopo and Mtyabezi Missions and it could be left in charge of the native teacher, Nyamazana, so that they might be free to open another work in new territory. For this purpose Brother Doner, accompanied by Brother Frey, made an extensive tour among the natives, and he finally decided to locate at the above-named place, over 200 miles by wagon road from Matopo Mission.

In the latter part of August, 1911, Brother and Sister Doner, together with Brother Steckley and Sister Book, started for this place, and opened a work with every prospect of success. There were many natives surrounding them, who at once showed an interest in the work. They were there only about two months, however, before Brother Doner became sick and was called to lay down his life in the undertaking. From the time he had set foot on African soil, over ten years before, he had entered heart and soul into the work of the Lord and had labored continually with the exception of over a year's furlough in America. No labor was too arduous, no distance too great, no hardship feared, if thereby he might carry the Gospel to the people. Many long journeys he made by foot, by bicycle, by wagon, in exploring the country and in preaching the Gospel. Perhaps he was overzealous in the work at times, and if he had spared his strength more he might be still with us. Who knows? He gave the Gospel to many natives and helped many into the light. He certainly laid down his life in behalf of the Africans. While his body rests out in the wilds, far from other white people, we believe he is already enjoying some of the fruit of his labors.

Sister Sallie Doner, his wife, was obliged at that time to return to America on furlough. On account of some difficulty arising in reference to the location of the mission, it was finally decided to abandon the place. Sister Doner and Brother Steckley are now ably laboring in the interests of the work at Macha, and Sister Book at Mtyabezi.

There are now in connection with the African work twenty-one white missionaries, including those who are home on furlough, and thirty native teachers and evangelists. There have been over 300 natives baptized, and there are more than that number in the Inquirers' Classes. As the various out-schools are just being properly launched, the work may be expected to bear fruitage in geometrical ratio. Take for instance last year, 1913; there were 109 additions to the Church at the various missions. These figures are not large, and they indicate only a small proportion of the work really accomplished by the missionaries. As Brother Steigerwald says: "Now that the leaven has been put into the meal no one can stop it from expanding." Praise God for that!

We desire to express our appreciation of the English Government in aiding mission work and in making it possible for missionaries to labor unmolested in their colonies; also in suppressing many customs harmful to the natives, and which hinder the progress of the work. We rejoice also to know that the government, as well as the better class of the general public, as they become more familiar with the work and aims of the missionary are realizing the benefit to the country and are showing their appreciation of the same.

The Church has come up nobly to the help of the Lord's work, both by their prayers and means, so that all have been generously supported and all the stations of white workers have good, substantial brick houses and churches, and the workers have been well cared for. May the Lord abundantly reward the donors and the Foreign Mission Board, who have given the work their undivided support.

We rejoice that a beginning has been made, but it is only a beginning. Only a very small portion of the great continent of Africa is covered by these pages, and that only imperfectly covered. The Lord has condescended to bless the work ever since its inception. It has never gone by leaps and bounds, but what was done has been solid and we hope lasting. We rejoice that we have been permitted to see natives emerge from the dense darkness of heathendom—how dark that is none but those who have lived among them can realize—and become beacon lights in their neighborhood, living witnesses of the truth that the Gospel of Christ "is the power of God unto salvation to every one that believeth," to the pagan African as well as to the enlightened European or American.

Many a time people have said to me, "The people in Africa are more eager to become Christians than those in America, are they not?" It seems to me that there is little difference in the people; if there is any difference in the results it is because of the difference in the methods employed. The missionary, as he goes to his field of labor, is after souls. That is his business; it is not a side issue. It is his business and he makes a business of it and uses business methods. He must begin at the bottom and learn to know his people and enter as far as he is able into their surroundings and their lives. He makes a study of them. He knows from experience that the salvation of these precious ones has meant much travail of soul and deaths oft. He knows that some one has "filled up that which is behind of the afflictions of Christ," in behalf of this part of the body of Christ. He knows they have been followed with anxious, solicitous eyes from the very first when they were infants in Christ, puny perhaps, and his heart was made glad, but with exceeding trembling lest the many pitfalls should entrap them before their eyes were really open to see or understand the danger. He knows some one has shed many bitter tears over the stumbling of some of these babies. He may now rejoice to see some grown to manhood, as it were, in Christ and being divinely used of Him in saving others.

Mr. and Mrs. Isaac O. Lehman and Family and Some of Our Workers, Members and Enquirers. Nos. 1, 2, 3, 4, 5 and 6 Are Satisfactorily Engaged in Work and in Preparation for the Work as Evangelists.

The true missionary keeps at it. It is his central thought day after day as he teaches these dirty, careless ones about him to become cleanly and do their work properly, how he can lead them on to desire a clean life and seek for it. His last thought and prayer at night, as he lays his head on the pillow, is for guidance as to how to win these precious souls, and sometimes he is led, like his Master, to spend much of the night in prayer.

Some people, looking on from a distance, think there is a great deal of romance connected with mission work; that it is full of striking incidents and delightful adventures, and that it is a grand opportunity to see something of the world. On my first furlough home, ten years ago, a little niece gave a glowing account of a friend of her mother, and of the countries that friend had visited. In conclusion the child naively added, "She has traveled almost as much as a missionary." This child unwittingly voiced the opinion of many a grownup; for to some would-be missionaries the prospect of foreign travel occupies a large space in their field of vision, but to the genuine missionary foreign travel is but incidental to mission life; it is the bridge over which he passes to some obscure corner of the earth where he is hid away from the world's gaze and surrounded by an entirely different class of people, of strange language and uncouth ways, often repulsive to the natural eye and to refined tastes. For months he may never see a white face, save those of his colleagues. He does not go with the expectation of finding a house already made to order and everything else he needs, but he is ready to go into the wilds, if needs be, and make a home for himself. He does not go just because he is willing to do certain things in the mission field; but he is willing and ready to do whatever he finds to do, and to go wherever the Lord tells him to go, and to stay as long as the Lord bids him stay.

There is, however, a fascination about mission work, as every one who is in the field will testify. Furloughs are taken because it is an absolute necessity for the missionary to go away for a time from the unhealthy climate and from the absorbing labors which sap the very vitality. But, when he is in his native land, the missionary feels that he is out of his element. He is out of touch with the business and interests which seem to engross the heart and soul of every one about him; and he is homesick to be back again to his field of labor and to see those dear dark faces. He feels that there is only one thing worth living for, and that is to lift up Christ among the heathen so that He may draw all men unto Himself. He feels that the time is short and that the "King's business requires haste," and that our Lord's return is imminent.

Again, as long as a person thinks he is making a *great sacrifice* in leaving home, friends, and his business, and going as the Lord's messenger among the benighted of earth, he would better remain at home. If he is really God-called, the day will come when he will realize something of the inestimable privilege of being His ambassador to nations in darkness without any knowledge of the Light of Life. All earthly things will be lost sight of and his heart will burn within him to lift up Christ among the heathen. He will gladly go through anything, that the blessed Gospel may be proclaimed to the ends of the earth.

Some one may inquire, "What should I study to prepare me for the mission field?" A careful study of these pages will, we think, answer that question. But to sum it up we would say, anything, everything you can, both in school and out; one never knows until he reaches the field what he may meet with. The Bible of course, first, last, and always, and all the knowledge with it one can acquire; then too temporal work of various kinds, medicine, nursing, hygiene, farming, building, teaching, housekeeping, and mission methods. If one has acquired a fair knowledge of these and thinks he is well prepared, then let him be humble enough to acknowledge that he knows only the A B C's of mission work; and that when he has reached his field of labor, the Lord, and perhaps some of His messengers already in the field, will help him to put together into words the letters he has learned, and he may add to it day by day as the occasion may require. If one has this humility and willingness to adapt himself to the work, after reaching the field, it will supply much of his lack of knowledge along some lines.

My object in writing thus plainly is not to frighten any one of God's children from the work of the Lord; but rather to help each one carefully to count the cost, and to disabuse anyone's mind of false notions of mission work. Judging from the stability and perseverance of those already connected with the work, we have reasons to believe that all did count the cost; but the work is only begun, and we trust many more will come to swell the ranks and push on the work into the darker regions.

It has been a little over a century since the first missionaries began their work along the coast of South Africa; but it is only within the last half century that there has been much visible fruit of the work done. Even then the missionary labors have been chiefly along the coast of the continent and along the navigable rivers which are the natural highways into the interior. Much of Central Africa is still unpossessed. In the report of the last Great Missionary Conference it was estimated that there are ninety millions of the population of Africa as yet untouched by the Gospel. Stupendous figures, indeed, to say nothing of the many millions whose knowledge of the Gospel is as yet very superficial!

We have already mentioned some of the difficulties in the way of reaching the people; the great expanse of country to be traversed, the deadliness of the climate, and the high cost of living, which in Africa exceeds that of any other country. Again, the many languages and dialects, 823 in number, together with the illiteracy of the people, are a serious handicap; but with God "all things are possible."

The present generation is beholding wonderful strides in opening the vast continent to commerce and civilization, and above all to Christianity. Railroads are rapidly being built all over the country, uniting the interior with the coast. At the present rate it probably will be a matter of only a very few years until Cape Town will be connected to Cairo by steam through the center of the continent. This central railway is soon to be linked with Benguella, on the west coast, which will form a more direct route into the interior. Twenty years ago Rhodesia had no railroads; in fact, it can scarcely be said there was a Rhodesia; for it was only in its formative period. Now it has 1,466 miles of railway owned and operated by the government, with an additional 204 miles extending to the seaport, Beira, on the east coast. These are only a portion of what has been built in the country. North, south, east, and west other lines have been built.

Boxburg Mission Station. Built by Mr. Jesse Eyster.

When one considers the vast amount of labor required, and the all-but insurmountable difficulties to be overcome in railroad building in Africa, the work already accomplished is little less than miraculous. The Lord raised up men of large hearts as well as large means, to finance much of this. All the building material has to be carried long distances, and many of the ties and telegraph poles are of iron on account of the destructive white ants. The traveler can now take the train at Cape Town and travel to the border of Congo State, a distance by rail of 2,140 miles, for $75, second class. He can have a comfortable compartment, furnished with all modern conveniences, and obtain his meals on the train at a very moderate cost. Freight rates are still high on account of the immense distance to be traversed and the small amount of goods required to supply Central Africa.

The railroads are fast changing conditions, helping to solve the question of gaining access to the people, and providing good homes and wholesome food for the missionaries. There are, however, many millions yet outside the railroad belt who are in need of the Gospel; but even these can be reached with much less difficulty than formerly.

The language question too is rapidly being solved, and great praise is due the noble army of men and women who have labored long and hard to reduce to writing the seemingly meaningless jargon which first greets their ears in going among the natives. Many languages have been reduced to writing by the missionaries, and the Scriptures have been translated into them. Grammars, dictionaries, and textbooks of various kinds have been written. This work, together with the various schools and the united labors of the missionaries, is aiding in reducing the number of languages. There are, however, many tribes which are yet without missionaries and without the Gospel in their language, and they are waiting for some one to say, "Here am I, send me." This is a task worthy of the greatest minds of the age; to reduce to writing an African language and to translate into it the Gospel which tells of GOD'S LOVE THROUGH JESUS CHRIST, to those downtrodden, hag-ridden, demon-worshiping souls.

The time is opportune for spreading the Gospel in Africa; and if every child of God were willing to do his part or her part in the work, the present generation could see it carried to all tribes.

None of the difficulties in the way are insurmountable. When, the "Great Commission" was given it was backed up by the indisputable assertion, "ALL POWER IS GIVEN UNTO ME IN HEAVEN AND IN EARTH. GO YE THEREFORE, ... LO, I AM WITH YOU ALWAY, EVEN UNTO THE END OF THE WORLD. AMEN."

ANGOLA
Portuguese Territory
NORTHERN RHODESIA
PORTUGUESE EAST AFRICA
GERMAN
SOUTH WEST
AFRICA
ATLANTIC OCEAN
BECHUANALAND
PROTECTORATE
TRANSVAAL
INDIAN OCEAN
CAPE OF GOOD HOPE
NATAL
Durban
East London
Delagoa Bay

Lightning Source UK Ltd.
Milton Keynes UK
UKHW042316030123
414627UK00018B/381